WINNERS

A.J.Morris

Authorbynature

To all racehorses, everywhere, and those who ride, love and care for them.

*Where in this wide world can
man find nobility without pride,
friendship without envy or beauty
without vanity? Here, where
grace is laced with muscle, and
strength by gentleness confined.*

RONALD DUNCAN

PREFACE

I first fell in love with racehorses when I was child, when I drew horses, and imagined names and pedigrees for them. My obsession with jump racing came later in life, in 1973 to be exact when my father took my small bet into the local bookmakers to place on a horse called Red Rum.

Since then, for the last forty plus years every winter has been taken over the by the "Winter Game". I have seen my equine heroes come and go; Desert Orchid, Best Mate and of course Red Rum himself. I have cried tears of joy and tears of sadness despite having no connection with the horses themselves.

On a personal level I have thrived on the sport of Point to Point Racing which has allowed me to become more involved and hands on. I have (albeit with modest success) trained my own and (with more success) been involved with the care and race day attention of others.

Racing and the care of its competitors is a complex area. It is not something you can pick up and put down. Racehorses are twenty four hours a day animals, Christmas, a time when most people are tucking into a roast dinner and enjoying a glass of wine sees stable staff mucking out, riding out and spending time away from ther families. It sees jockeys spending the afternoon in the sauna or running in layers if clothing to lose that few extra pounds. There is no "day off" for those in the sport as Boxing Day is one of the biggest in the winter calendar.

It is this dedication, this love of the game that inspired me to write this book. I hope, that although fictional it will allow its readers to see behind the closed doors of a training yard and experience some of the highs and lows of being involved with these creatures.

All the characters on the book are the creation of my own

imagination and any resemblance to any person living or dead is purely coincidental. The horses are also fictional although I have drawn appearance and characteristics from horses I have known when writing them.

I have enjoyed writing this tale, it started many years ago and has needing bringing into the modern era to make it "fit".

For any technical errors I apologise, this after all a work of fiction but it is also a work of passion also and has been written with love.

A.J.Morris

CHAPTER ONE

He knew that death was a part of it. Always had been, and always would. So why did it not become easier to bear?

Turning away from the scene that was hurting both his eyes and his heart Tom Chichester walked off the sodden grass, ducked under the rails, and onto the firmer footing of the car park. A dull crack echoed through the evening air behind him. It made him shudder. Away to his right there were sounds of revelry coming from the member's bar. Its lights glowed, golden and beckoning in the twilight. Tom swallowed hard, hesitating. He could feel the cold glass in his hand, taste the whisky as it burned over his throat. He shook his head and, with regret, walked to his car. He still had a job to do.

Pulling his keys from the pocket of his dripping Barbour coat he stood, a tall, lonely, figure and clicked the car door open. The BMW was warm and dry, and he settled into its welcome comfort, looking into his rear-view mirror as he did so. Dragging his hands through his thick dark hair he squinted at his reflection. There were shadows beneath his heavy eyes and an inch of stubble on his chin. He looked and felt like a man in dire need of a holiday. But there was little chance of that; and turning on the heaters in an attempt at removing the chill that seemed to reach into his very bones he pulled out of the car park and joined the metallic snake of vehicles that blocked the road.

Home seemed very far away.

The clock in the red brick arch that marked the entrance to the stable yard showed seven o'clock. Kitty Campbell took one last look around her and locked the feed room door. Everything was quiet; the only sound to penetrate the still night was the contented chewing of horse teeth on hay. She had left the two loose boxes ready for their inmates return, everything was where Martin could easily find it. A twinge in her stomach reminded her that she was hungry. Grateful to have completed her duties, but aware of the increasing knot of nerves inside her that his impending return always caused, she headed for the cottage that she shared with her work mates. Lights shone from every tiny leaded window of this home from home, and as she opened the door, she was greeted by a blast of music and a tempting smell of curry. She smiled to herself as she kicked off her boots. Only Poppy could occupy the whole building place single handed.

"Bathrooms free if you want it." Her friend was hovering over a giant saucepan full of rice.

"That's no surprise." Kitty tasted the bubbling curry. "Mm. We are the only ones here after all."

"Well, If I was you." Poppy Lawrence had wet hair and a glass of chardonnay in her hand. "I'd hurry before the boys and Sarah get home."

Kitty needed no second bidding and taking the stairs two at a time she collected towels and bath salts powder from the attic bedroom she shared with Poppy and locked herself in the bathroom. Running herself a hot, scented bath, she peeled off her work breeches and sighed with pleasure as the soothing warm water wrapped itself around her. She was a pretty girl, with fine blonde hair that fell below her shoulders, and wary, kitten blue eyes. Slender, pale, almost waiflike in her appearance she was tiny in comparison to the powerful steeplechasers that were her life. There was no greater passion in Kitty's heart than horses and she was devoted to her job. A devotion that was being aided by her ever-increasing infatuation with her employer. Letting her mind roam into unchartered pastures she slid down into the water, hair fanning out amongst the bubbles. Chin touching her chest she began to doze until a loud bang at the door woke her with a start.

"Kit!" It was Poppy. "Are you asleep?"

"I would have been." Kitty grumbled. "What is it?"

"Open the door." Poppy's voice was hoarse and had a catch in it. "Quick!"

Reluctant to leave her cosy spot but alarmed by the tone of Poppy's voice Kitty jumped out of the water and opened the door, snatching a towel around herself. Poppy, still wearing the ridiculous apron with a pink pig on the front had tears slipping down her cheeks.

"What's the matter?" Kitty's heart quickened, and she caught her friends' arm.

"It's Crop." Poppy sobbed. "He broke his leg at the last and they put him down. He's dead Kit."

"Oh my God!" Kitty stared at the carpet, horrible images rushing through her brain. "Where's Sarah?"

"She went straight to bed." Poppy wiped her streaming eyes on the corner of Kitty's towel. "Shall I go to her?"

Kitty didn't reply, continuing to stare bleakly at the floor. This was any stable lads' worst nightmare; the one hurdle they all dreaded having to face. She clearly remembered the awful day when her very first charge had died of colic. But she also remembered that words hadn't helped. It may seem heartless, but Sarah would have to come to terms with this herself, and in her own time.

"Just leave her for now Pop." She shook her head. "Let her calm down. Is the food ready?"

"If you're still hungry." Poppy shrugged.

"Too right I am." She hesitated, taking in what she had just said. Was she becoming hardened? Immune to the darker side of the job she loved? No, she didn't think so; it was just survival, her weary body needed fuel. She bent to pick up her clothes. "Crop's owners are on holiday, aren't they? What a welcome home they are going to have. And poor Tom having to tell them."

Highford House had nestled of the South facing side of the Chaseley valley for centuries. Sprawling, golden, surrounded by a wood of ancient oaks and beeches it had been the ancestral home of the Chichester family for centuries. It was their pride and joy; but it was also an increasingly heavy cross to bear as rising taxes and a dwindling fortune made its upkeep harder and harder. But nothing, no pile of bills, no irate accountants could diminish the pleasure that Tom always felt at the sight of his home. Every time he rounded the corner of the two-mile-long drive his heart would lift at the sight of Highford's beloved face. Tonight, was no exception. The ache in his tired muscles easing as he pulled into the courtyard, he failed to notice the low form of a white sports car tucked away in the corner. But as soon as he opened the kitchen door an all too familiar voice reached his ears and his glow of contentment lifted. A frown marred his handsome features as he entered the kitchen and found his mother.

"I see he's here again." Tom threw his coat onto one chair and sat on another. His little tan terrier, Spock, came running to greet him, tail wagging furiously.

Eleanor Chichester, small, neat, and genteel watched her eldest son and saw the lines around his eyes.   He looked exhausted.

"How was your day dear?" She spooned out roast potatoes.

"Bloody terrible. I lost Top of the Crop."

"Oh no!" Eleanor put down her spoon and rubbed her forehead. "He was your best horse, wasn't he?"

"Was." Tom got to his feet. "I need a drink."

Watching him leave the room Eleanor shook her head. She knew how heavily the burden of running the stables lay on her sons' shoulders. The 'old man' as he affectionately had been known had passed the reins of his beloved training establishment to his son shortly before he died, and it was his, William's, regime that was still adhered to. Eleanor doted on her son and wanted him desperately to succeed, but she could see all too clearly that running the yard and coping with his father's death was taking its toll. Although William had been dead three years Tom had still not come to terms with it and had lately been becoming more and more melancholy. As he returned and sat at the table, she ruffled his air like a child, noting how quickly he emptied the contents of his glass. He drank too much. But tonight, was not the right time to tell him. She could feel the tension in him, fingers drumming on the table, and knew that this strange, preoccupied mood was not brought on solely by the death of a racehorse. As if aware of her thoughts Tom looked up at her.

"So" He paused. "What does he want this time.?"

"Dominic?" His mother automatically picked up the empty glass and put it on the draining board. "I don't really know. He just arrived this afternoon."

"Wants money I suppose." Tom's frown deepened." How long is he staying?"

"As long as he cares to thank you!" Never one to miss his cue Dominic appeared in the doorway. "He does live here remember?"

Custom made to play the lead role in Dracula, Dominic Chichester had coal black eyes set in deep, shadowed sockets. Fringed by long, dark, lashes they were exaggerated by his high, angular cheekbones. The skin of his gaunt, fleshless face was pale and framed by the same dark hair as his brothers; but his was long and straight and tied back from his face in a ponytail. Wearing black leather, the smell of his aftershave filled the room as he entered. Bad tempered, volatile, driven by violent excesses Dominic roamed the world like a high-class gypsy, drinking and gambling away his allowance until he was forced to return home to beg for more. He owed a fortune, ten times the worth of Highford at Casinos all over the world, but such was his magnetism that he was welcomed wherever he went,

Except by his brother when he came home.

Tom's hate of Dominic was almost irrational. He could not pinpoint its origin; perhaps it was Dominic's complete disregard for anyone but himself, perhaps it was the simple fact that they were complete opposites; or perhaps it had its beginnings in some distant memory that he had shut away in his mind. Whatever its reason his loathing of his brother was complete, and he could not stand his presence for more than a day.

"So, to what do we owe the honour this time?" Tom made no attempt to keep his feelings of disgust from his voice.

"Bored." Dominic swung on a Chippendale chair that had only recently been restored. "And I was worried that you might be missing me."

"Don't push it". Tom didn't even turn his head in his direction. "Just make sure you give me a wide berth."

Dominic stared at his perfect nails; the long white fingers spread across his lap. He gave his brother a martyred sigh that went unnoticed and smiled sweetly up at his mother who was placing two plates on the table.

"I'm going to take a shower." Tom pushed his plate away. "Then I'm going out. You can give mine to Spock."

Some minutes later he stood in his study, clad in a towel and dripping water all over the block floor. With a wet hand he searched the pages of his telephone book for the number he wanted. The line rang for a long time before it was answered. He cleared his throat before he spoke.

"Hello Flick. Look I know it's short notice but how do you fancy dinner? Yes? Good. I'll pick you up at nine."

Replacing the receiver, he stood in the French windows, and stared moodily out across the fields into the gathering dark. A group of horses, his father's old hunters, mooched below the trees. It was October, they should be in and working by now, but he didn't have time to take days off anymore. So, they lounged in the fields, fat, hairy, muddy, sniffing the chill mornings that carried the scent of fox and wondered at their inactivity. Beneath the largest Oak

Tree Micky Mouse, so named by Tom's mother because of the size of his overgrown ears, was dozing, a small bird resting in the dip of his back. Micky had been acting as a grandstand for Tom and his father before him for the past ten years. Worn out by his daily trek to the gallops he was sleeping soundly, oblivious to the shower of leaves that fell over his hogged mane.

As if aware of Tom's scrutiny a big, heavy bodied bay mare lifted her head and cocked her ears towards the house.

"You miss him as well don't you girl?" Tom muttered. "It's just not the same, is it?"

Finding himself alone Dominic paced his room like a caged animal. Damned if he was going to spend a night in this mouldering dump. If Tom didn't know how to have a good time, he knew plenty of people who did. Emptying his case, he picked up a brown paper parcel and unwrapped it. With a smirk he lay back on his pillows and began to plan his evening's entertainment.

The small, intimate, restaurant was tucked away in a shadowy Cheltenham side street; dimly lit, it was far enough away from Highford to afford Tom the anonymity he craved. His local pub was hung with photographs of past winners, and the bar lined with punters all eager to hear the latest 'hot' tip. Here he could relax without fear of being pounced on, and it also offered the best Italian cuisine he had tasted outside Italy itself. Sipping the champagne, he had ordered because he knew of Flick's liking for it, he watched his companion picking at her food. She was a smartly dressed attractive looking woman in her early thirties; and everything about her from the neatly bobbed glossy hair, to the designer label clothes hinted at good breeding. When she spoke, she had the clear, commanding air of someone who expects to, and is used to being, obeyed. A complete extrovert Flick lived for the night, using her considerable salary from an exclusive advertising agency to clothe and fuel her headlong flights from party to party. Her weekends were wild shopping sprees; when she wasn't supporting one of her many male friends at Polo matches, and her diary was permanently full. The only person she went out of her way to accommodate, totally unbeknown to him, was Tom Chichester. In her weaker moments, of which there were few, she allowed herself the fantasy of being his wife, the envy of all those fresh-faced young girls who worked for him.

Raising her deep hazel eyes from her plate she was amused, as she always was, to see that Tom had no idea of the depth of her feelings for him. Reaching for her glass she wondered if she would ever get used to the startling contrast that his blue eyes made against his dark skin and black hair. The hair was touched by silver at the temples now, but in her eyes it did nothing to distract from his beauty but merely added to it. Giving him her sweetest smile, she sipped her champagne slowly. Tom leaned back in his chair and held her gaze. This was the only woman he knew who didn't quail under his insolent stare. Felicity, he reflected, would have made one hell of a racehorse: bold, high spirited and not easy to intimidate. The thought made him smile.

Flick raised her eyebrows.

"A smile? I am honoured. "Or do you have indigestion?"

His smile broadened and his eyes roved, restless, over her body. Taking in the pale shoulders that rose like milk from the clinging black dress and vanished into the dark hair, he began to feel waves of lust washing over him. He raised a hand to the waiter.

"Are we going already?" Flick shook her hair, eyes flashing.

"Yes. Come on." Getting to his feet Tom watched her as

she rose, catlike in her elegance and stood beside him, the dress clinging to every taught inch of her lovely body.

"Coffee?" Flick recognised the gleam in his eyes and smiled.

"No." He put his arm around her waist.

"Good." Reaching up she brushed his face with her lips.

Tightening his grip, Tom saw the eagerness in her eyes and frowned.

"Don't I have to ask? Not once?"

"Not at all." She broke away and glided out of the restaurant.

Flick's flat was very modern. Stark white walls contrasted sharply with a black leather sofa and a dark, smoked glass table. A great white rug lit up the black tiled floor and black and white prints hung sparsely on the walls. The only splash of colour was provided by red roses in a black lacquered vase.

"It's like living in a negative." Tom sprawled on the sofa and hung his feet off the edge. Looking up at the print above his head he curled his lip. Born with an inherent love of Gainsborough and an almost God like admiration for Stubbs he despised anything modern. He found it impossible to imagine any home more perfect than Highford with its lofty rooms and antique furniture. He pictured his mother's blue Wedgewood on Flick'fs black dining furniture and shuddered at the thought.

"It suits me." Flick was standing in the window, her head silhouetted against the white curtains. He studied her profile and remembered why he was there.

"Bedroom changed at all?" He asked, a smile dancing across his lips.

"Go and see for yourself."

He needed no guiding across the hall and into the familiar room. The king size bed wore midnight blue sheets that matched to perfection the drapes that hung over the windows. Was there anything in Flick's life that didn't co-ordinate? Pulling off his tie he threw it onto the dressing table and looked out of the leaded pane. Strange, he mused, how something so elegant and traditional from the outside, could harbour a minimalist designer dream on the interior. Except that to him it was not a dream but a nightmare. Perhaps there was something in Flick's life that didn't co-ordinate after all. Himself.

Flick had been watching him, admiring the strong muscles moving beneath his shirt. Now she padded barefoot across to him and ran her fingers down his back, and as he turned to face her, he found that she was completely naked. Smiling, she reached up and pulled his mouth down onto hers. Her tongue tasted of champagne. A heady rush of excitement swept through him, and he crushed her tightly in his arms. Laughing, breathless, she pulled away and only when he too was naked did, she let him kiss her again.

The shaft of sunlight filtered through the gap in the curtains and fell on the face of the heavily sleeping woman. beside her, the man stirred and untangled himself from her arms. Slipping out of the silky warmth he shivered and reached for his watch. Seven o'clock. Tom groaned and frantically began to dress. Tie in pocket, shirt outside his trousers, he briefly stroked the shining head and left.

There was an air of depression hanging over the normally cheerful yard that morning. Heavy faces went about their tasks in silence, a silence broken only by the impatient snorts of the horses, who, although aware that all was not right, had no real idea what was wrong. Sara, having avoided contact with anyone all night, had dissolved into tears at the sight of the empty stable. The others, fighting off their own emotions had left her alone, knowing that they could say nothing to console her. It was with relief that they heard the booming tones of Mrs Benson calling them in for breakfast. The smell of freshly cooked bacon did wonders to lift drooping spirits, as did the sight of Gareth, the swarthy Welsh lad whose hangover was so bad, and face so pale, that he made everyone else feel ridiculously healthy. Ryan Emerson, Tom's assistant trainer wandered into the stone floored room looking gloomy coat collar turned up against the cold.

"Can't find the morning lists." He grumbled, lifting a piece of toast to his mouth. "Don't tell me he forgot to do them"

"He went out last night" Martin spluttered through his bacon sandwich, "Dressed to kill, heading for town."

"Chérché la fémme no doubt" Ryan scraped a chair across the floor and sat down.

"He doesn't have to 'chérché'" Laughed Poppy. "Quite the reverse!"

"Now do you hear that Kitten?" Ryan wagged a finger in Kitty's direction. "You have competition."

"Up yours Ginger" Kitty frowned.

"Hey, hey." Martin scolded "That's no way to speak to your almost boss.!

"The little brothers more my style" Poppy had hazy eyes. "There's something wicked and depraved and downright sexy about that one."

"Plenty of notches on his headboard as well," Muttered Gareth, unable to keep the note of jealousy from his voice "So you'd better join the queue."

"So, had you." Martin looked at his watch. "For the wheelbarrow. Come on, this shit won't shovel itself."

The previous days' rain had died away leaving in its place a clear blue sky dotted with cotton wool clouds that perched on top of the hill. It was difficult to remain miserable on such a day and Kitty found herself singing softly as she hoisted her rapidly filling sack onto her shoulders. Kicking Prince's door closed with her heel she stopped short at the sight of the man entering the yard.

"Shit!" She muttered. Placing the sack against the box door she hurried into the office where Ryan was conducting a work list of his own.

"Panic stations." She shut the door behind her and went to the calendar that hung on the wall.

"Why?" Ryan didn't look up. "Not drunk himself to death, has he? Bugger, I was hoping for a pay rise."

"Not quite" Kitty placed the calendar in front of him. "Look."

"Nice." Ryan looked at the photograph of Desert Orchid in full flight over an open ditch "Wish we had one"

"Not the horse!" Kitty pointed at the date. "That"

"Dave." Ryan looked up at her. "What's Dave?" His colour fell as he remembered.

"That's right" Kitty nodded. "Dave Holloway's outside."

"Hell." Ryan rubbed his face. "What do we do?"

"You're the assistant trainer" Kitty smiled, "So go and train!"

Dave Holloway was a small, stocky, arrogant man in his early thirties with skin the texture of a well-worn riding boot. Never patient, he was aggressive both on and off the track, and never liked to be kept waiting. He had once been one of the most popular bookings in the sport, but a string of injuries and some dubious moments inside the depths of Portman Square had seen his career take a downward turn. He hated schooling, especially on the morning of a meeting at which he had rides, so he was not happy at the prospect of a delay.

"Where the fuck is Chichester?" He snapped at Ryan as he snubbed the offered hand. "This is the second time he's done this to me.'

"Mr Chichester is in town" Ryan smiled. "We shan't keep

you; he'll meet us on the schooling ground."

"Will he?" Dave smirked, looking over Ryan's shoulder. "Business, was it?"

Ryan turned around and caught a deep breath. Tom was entering the yard, heavy eyed, unshaven, and hastily dressed. Hardly the image he had been trying to present of his absent employer.

"Looks like he found his fémme'" Poppy giggled, "And didn't spend the night improving his French!"

Tom greeted Dave shortly and barked hasty instructions at his staff. After seeing them safely onto their mounts, he followed them onto the gallops in the Land Rover. Kitty could hear Dave talking to Gareth as they rode.

"This is the part of the bloody job I hate. Every bugger in the country reckons their horse is a good jumper and nine out of ten are shit. Absolute shit. And" He lowered his voice so that Kitty had to strain to hear the words. "It doesn't help when the trainer's a bloody alcoholic."

Watching Dave skilfully steering the headstrong Mardi Gras over the schooling hurdles Tom felt the usual thrill that he got from watching his horse's work. Mardi Gras was a bad-tempered bay gelding, who despite his lack of inches had proved his worth the previous season by winning four of his six starts over hurdles. Tom quite fancied his chances as a champion hurdler of the future, but there was a long way to go before such ambitious plans could be realised. Dave was trotting back to him.

"Well?" Tom tried to read the impassive face.

"He's improved, definitely, but he still won't settle. Still rushes around everywhere thinking he's the boss."

"Hmm." Tom looked at Mardi's wide eyes. "Have another spin. Let's try something."

Turning to the bunch of horses that were circling behind him he ran his eyes over the group until he found what he was looking for.

"Katriona?"

"Yes?"

"Take Romeo and work with Dave. Hold back, let Mardi have a neck or so on you all the time. Let Dave dictate the pace and don't overtake. Understand?"

Kitty may have understood but Dave was looking at Tom as though he had lost his mind. Put another horse upside this runaway? Lunacy. Especially when the horse was ridden by a slim, if very pretty, blonde who was probably dumb as well as weak. But his job was to obey his orders, so murmuring to Kitty under his breath to 'just humour him darling,' he joined her and hacked back to the foot of the gallops. The two horses, bay and dark brown set off at a leisurely pace, which increased as they headed towards the first flight of hurdles. Tom found his eyes being drawn towards Kitty and not the horse she was riding. As usual her stirrups were too short for her own safety, but she had beautiful balance and gentle hands; even the hardest puller in the yard relaxed under her quiet touch. Old Romeo was being lazy, letting the other horse tow him along, dropping the bit so that Kitty had to keep gathering up her reins and sending him on. In contrast Dave was having a wrestling match with Mardi and was only just winning the fight. The horses head swung from side to side as he tugged against the reins which were much too short for his liking. Every couple of strides he would put in a lunge, and accelerate, and as they skimmed over the second hurdle he began to gallop in earnest.

As both horses began to sprint into the final flight Tom realised something was wrong.

"Whoa you two!!" He yelled. "Steady, you should be cantering!"

A cold thread of panic was starting to knit itself around Kitty's stomach. Her hands were starting to lose grip on the reins as they grew wet with sweat, and she could feel her already tentative control over her mount disappearing. Something had found the racehorse hidden deep in Romeo's soul and he was determined to beat this young upstart beside him to the top of the hill. With the wind whipping her face, bringing tears stinging salty into her eyes, Kitty's heart went into overdrive as she realised, she was out of control.

"Pull up you stupid girl!" Dave was standing in his stirrups, using his weight as a brake. "Pull up! Can't you see I've lost him."

"I can't" Kitty screamed in reply. "I can't! Whoa Romeo, steady!"

Shaking his head as if in reply, Romeo put in a burst of acceleration unlike anything she had ever felt before. Oh God, she thought, I'm going to fall off and be trampled to death. To her right, the ground rose steeply to the top of the hill, ahead was the end of the gallops. If she didn't stop, and quickly, she would be running over rough ground towards the stone wall that marked the boundary of Tom's land. Praying, for the first time in years, she stood in her stirrups, putting all her weight into her right rein. Eyes half shut, lips pressed tight together to stop the scream from escaping, she pulled steadily. With a rush of relief, she felt Romeo veer right and slacken speed as his hooves sunk into the banking. Weak and tearful with fear she slid from his back as he slowed to a trot. Pulling him back to a walk she hastily dried her eyes.

"You ever do that again." She sobbed, "And I'll take you to the knacker's yard myself!"

A shout reminded her that she was not alone in her ordeal. Turning back to the gallop she saw Dave sitting on the grass and a rider less bay horse heading towards the wall. As she watched, horrified, Mardi, his reins flying, gathered himself together to jump the obstacle in his path. His muscles tensed, then with a mighty push he launched himself into the air. There was a terrifying moment when he disappeared, then his head bobbed up and he lobbed rather awkwardly away down the road.

"At least he's heading for home." Said Gareth's voice.

"Which, by the way is what we are supposed to be doing."

Looking around Kitty saw Enigma's friendly grey face in front of her. Gareth saw the colour draining from Kitty's cheeks and slipped off the filly's back.

"Come on" He took her hand. "We'll walk.

The yard was in chaos when they reached it. Mardi had been found limping along the drive, blood pouring from a hole in his knee. Sara was trying desperately to keep him still for Martin to clean it while he waited for the vet. As Kitty arrived, they turned and looked at her with sympathy.

"Oh, poor Mardi." Kitty felt sick.

"Poor you." Poppy was removing Romeo's saddle. "I think you're about to get the sack."

Pacing the office, slapping his crop against the table leg, Tom looked like a tiger about to pounce on its prey. The prey, in this case, was a small nervous blonde, who was sitting in silence staring at her boots and biting her lip. Trying to compose himself, Tom caught sight of the vet leaving Mardi's box with a grim face and failed. This was just another failure to add to the record, another loss that he could ill afford. Trembling with barely contained anger he turned to face her.

"Well?" His voice was so cold that it cut her like a knife. "Let's hear them."

"Hear what?" Kitty looked up from beneath the safety curtain of her hair.

"The excuses." Tom snarled. "I expect there are plenty?"

"I haven't got any." She said quietly. "I couldn't stop"

"What are you girl?" Tom roared so loud that she shot backwards in her chair. "A total incompetent? These are valuable racehorses not donkeys. If you can't ride you shouldn't be here!"

"I can ride!" She wiped her nose on her sleeve "Everyone gets run away with sometime."

"Not in my yard. Not on my horses. I can't afford to carry flotsam."

Kitty forced herself to look at him. It was amazing, really, how someone so handsome could be distorted to ugliness by anger. A nerve was twitching in his cheek. As she waited for his next attack, she began to feel resentment building up inside her. She tried very hard to be good at her job, and now he was using her as a scapegoat, a whipping boy for his frustrations. Angry, embarrassed, hurt, she wanted to slap his face, to pound on his broad chest with her fists and scream at him for being unfair. Instead, she wiped her eyes with the back of her hand and left a dirty streak across her flushed cheek.

The movement dispersed Toms anger in an instant. He should be shot. Taking out his temper on a child. For that was all she was, a child. What was she, nineteen, twenty, older? Or barely out of school, He really had no idea. She was watching him, reading his emotions with her cornflower blue eyes. He looked away quickly, startled by the thoughts that rushed unbidden into his head.

"Get out." He snapped. "Now."

Kitty hesitated, then slowly got to her feet

"Go on girl." He hissed. "Before I change my mind. Get on with your work."

Arching her back to the wall she slid past him and out of the door. Watching her as she hurried across the yard, incredibly slim in her tight dark breeches, the thought flashed through Tom's mind that her fair head would look far more lovely against the midnight blue sheets that Flick's dark one.

"For God's sake!" He spoke aloud. "What the hell is wrong with you man?"

Turning to the filing cabinet he pulled out a manila folder with Mardi Gras' name on it. With an unsteady hand he found the owners 'phone number. He really did not want to do this. At this moment in time, the only foreseeable outcome of this fiasco was a very unwanted loss of income.

CHAPTER TWO

Two days later a large, silver grey Jaguar glided to a silent halt in the stable yard of Highford House. From its luxurious depths emerged a man of equally large proportions wearing a heavy fur coat. He strode up to the office where Claire, Tom's secretary was eating a hasty lunch and filling in spreadsheets. She looked up as the door opened.

"Hello? Can I help you?"

"Is Chichester around?" The man puffed pungent cigar smoke into the office.

"Mr. Chichester is at the house having lunch. Can I call him for you?" Claire couldn't remember the man's name but didn't like his attitude.

"Just tell him that Grant Gardner is on his way."

Martin, hovering in the feed shed door on the opposite side of the yard, gave a groan and shook his head.

"Who is it?" Poppy pushed him out of the way to give herself a better view.

"That my dear girl, is the main shareholder in Mardi Gras."

Tom waited in his study. A log fire crackled in the open hearth; a decanter of whisky sat on his desk. With jangling nerves, he paced the room and jumped as the door opened. Grant Gardner was so big that he filled the doorway and made Tom feel very insignificant.

"Grant." Tom held out his hand.

"Don't mind if I do." Grant ignored him and nodded to the whisky.

"Please take a seat Grant." Tom sloshed whisky into a tumbler with shaking fingers.

Grant watched the twitching nerve in Toms cheek and saw the rigid muscles in his shoulders. Deliberately taking

19

a long time to reply he sipped his drink and stared into the fireplace.

"It's about our horse."

"Mardi Gras?" Tom stammered.

"I believe that's the only one we have with you isn't it?" Grant sneered.

Tom didn't reply.

"How bad is the damage?" Grant lit a cigar.

"Quite severe I'm afraid. It will be quite some time before he'll be ready to come back into work."

"Race?" Grant drew deeply on his cigar.

"Not until January at the earliest." Tom refilled his own glass. Oh well he thought, here we go.

The silence was painful. Grant was looking out of the window. Tom searched desperately for emotion in his eyes and found none.

"January?" Grant swung in his chair.

"That's right." Oh, for God's sake man, he thought, just get on with it. Fighting the urge to grab the man's massive shoulders and shake them Tom bent to poke the fire.

"Well that's not good enough is it? Not really?"

"Pardon?" Tom's throat was dry, and he coughed awkwardly.

"All last season I listened to you. Don't run him here it's too wet, don't run him there he's not ready. We mustn't run him too often. So, we didn't. And now you tell me he won't run at all until January. What are we paying your training fees for? Really? To keep you in the manner to which you are accustomed." Grant ran his eyes around the room. "It certainly doesn't seem to be because we have a racehorse."

"He ran well last year Grant you know he did. Any more work would have finished him. This was just bad luck, an accident. An accident for which I'm truly sorry. But I'm sure we'll make up for it. He'll win races this season, you wait and see."

"I expect he will. But not from this yard." Grant sat quite still as watched his words sinking in.

"Sorry?" Tom's heart was skipping about in his chest.

"I had a word with Dave last night. he seems to think that your staff are incompetent. He said the stable girl couldn't control her horse and caused his to run away. He says she should take the blame for this little 'episode'."

"That's ridiculous!" Tom was getting annoyed. It was one thing for him to take his staff apart, but what right did Dave Holloway have to criticise them?

"My stable girl had nothing to do with it." He spoke slowly. "As I said it was an accident."

"That isn't Dave's opinion." Grant held his hand up." And before you argue the point, I'm afraid that my mind is up. I'm moving Mardi Gras to Peter Stroud at Lambourn. His box will be here at ten in the morning."

Not waiting for a reply Grant got up, replaced his whisky glass with a nod, and went to the doorway.

"One last thing." He didn't turn around. "Dave says that you weren't here when he arrived, and that you turned up with a hangover. I don't like paying my fees to a drunk."

With his parting arrow nestled deep in its wound Grant Gardner left the room, leaving the space empty without his huge presence. Tom waited until he heard the front door slam and hurled his glass viciously into the hearth. hearing the crash his mother came running in.

"What on Earth is the matter?"

"Grant wants to take his bloody horse away."

"Oh dear. Oh, I am sorry."

"Not as sorry as I am Mother, not as sorry as I am."

Losing Mardi Gras was the final straw for Sara. With both

her horses gone she felt that she had no place in the yard, and shortly after Peter Stroud's horse box had left the yard, she went to the house to find Tom who had been lying low. He met her in the hallway, where she was running her fingers along the mahogany hall stand.

"What can I do for you Sara?"

Rummaging in her pocket she produced a white envelope.

"It's my notice." She handed it to him.

"Whatever for?" Tom raised his eyebrows in surprise.

"I'm not cut out for this work Sir. I get too attached to the horses."

"We all do Sara it's part of the job. We'd be no good at it if we didn't."

"I'm sorry Sir. My minds made up."

"Quite sure?" Tom studied her closely.

"Quite sure Sir. Sorry"

"No, I'm sorry." Tom spoke softly. "Sorry to see you go. Thank you for everything you've done for me Sara."

She nodded, a hint of a tear glistening in her eyes and backed away.

As he closed the door Tom felt as though the walls of the house were crashing down around his ears. In just four days he had lost two horses, a member of staff and a very wealthy owner. What the hell else could possibly go wrong?

A week later Sara left. Kitty and Poppy waved her off at the bus station, tears streaming down their faces. Martin, red eyed and sniffling himself, put an arm around each of them and hugged.

"Come on you two. Not the first to go and not the last I'm sure. Shame, she was one of the better ones." He said cheerfully. "I've been cooking. Double chocolate cake waiting at home."

"We don't need a suicide mission thanks." Poppy blew her nose noisily. "I will miss her."

"Not as much as Ryan." Chuckled Martin." Let's get that cake before Taff finds it!"

As part of his mission to make everyone less gloomy, Martin decided to drive them all into Cheltenham for the evening. This kind of joint venture always ended in chaos as four people fought over the bathroom, hairdryer and iron. But by eight thirty, although a little later than planned, they were all ready; smelling, for once, of perfume and aftershave instead of sweating, both human and horse. Martin, fighting to keep his unruly locks in place wolf whistled as Kitty walked in wearing a cropped blue t-shirt that accentuated her eyes, and low-slung black jeans. She had twisted her hair up at the back of her head, a few strands left to spiral down her face and neck. Poppy, wearing her beloved red, hair hanging loose to her waist nodded in approval at her friend's appearance.

"I have to admit it. The boss doesn't know what he's missing."

"Never mind him" Martin was in the hall gathering coats. "We're wasting valuable drinking time."

A fine veil of frost lay over Tom's land as Martin's battered little Fiat bounced down the drive; its headlights glinted on the shining surface and set sparkling lights dancing on the icy tree trunks. A fox, slinking light footed to wherever his business lay was caught in the beam; he froze for a second then bolted over the wall. Passing Gareth and the local boys on their nightly trek to the pub, Ryan blared the horn, shouting and waving as they sped into the lane. Anxious to get into town, Martin drove at a breakneck rate and in no time, they were seated in a plush new wine bar hiding behind Cheltenham's high street. Tense and uncomfortable, Kitty fidgeted, looking nervously around.

"I feel really awkward." She muttered. "I'm sure I've got hay in my hair."

Determined that they should all be having a good time Martin blew most of his wages on beer, although he only drank a weak lager shandy himself. He was a compact, wiry man in his thirties, with wavy brown hair that refused to stay in place whatever he did to it. The typical 'boy next door'; homely, plain, good natured, Martin had been a resident of Highford for the same length of time as Micky and could not imagine being anywhere else. Watching his friends getting steadily worse for wear he sat back and got great amusement from seeing their eyes becoming unfocussed and their speech beginning to slur. Ryan's jokes, always near the mark, got progressively worse as the night wore on, until they were all shrieking with laughter and embarrassment. Poppy stopped short in the middle of one outburst and stared with burning eyes at something across the room.

"Oh." She sighed dreamily. "This *is* good stuff. I suddenly feel like I'm in heaven!"

Turning to follow her stare Martin saw a tall angular figure causing a commotion at the bar. it wore a long black leather coat and dark glasses, that, although they would have looked ridiculous on anyone else, simply added to his striking appearance. As he flicked a strand of black hair from his face Martin recognised him.

"Wrong place." He said shortly "If he's there it must be hell."

"Isn't that the Boss's baby brother?" Ryan squinted through the smoky air.

"Dominic" Crooned Poppy. "Perfect!"

"Perfectly awful." Ryan sneered. "His hair is almost longer than yours."

"Don't bitch" Replied Poppy shortly. "You're only jealous."

Dominic was in fine form. Having partially outstayed his welcome at home he had gone back to the continent on 'business'. Well pleased with the results of his trip and financially much healthier he had come back to annoy

Tom for a little while before passing on his merchandise. Despite the numerous opportunities that he had to brown himself in the sun he preferred to leave his skin deathly pale, deliberately cultivating his vampire look as it contrasted so dramatically with the blackness of his stark eyes. His companions for the evening were a pair of young blondes, barely out of school, as pink and warm as he was pale and cold. Clinging to his arms, they were totally in awe of his glamour and his wealth. If all went well, they would all go to bed soon, hopefully together. Turning to whisper obscenities in their clean ears he noticed a group of people at the back of the room staring at him and stopped.

The boys he didn't recognise, but the girl with the dark hair was familiar and that little blonde in the blue shirt was unmistakable. prying himself free of his companions he headed for them. Poppy stared open mouthed in admiration.

"Well hello." He looked straight past her at Kitty. "I had no idea there were such good-looking fillies in my brother's stable"

Snatching a chair, he pulled it up beside her, lifting his glasses and training his hawk like gaze directly onto her face. Kitty felt a chill travel down her spine; not a thrill of pleasure, but the cold touch of warning.

"I don't even know your name." He whispered, low enough for only her to hear. "But then, I don't think names matter."

Lifting a finger, he stroked it across her cheek. Opening her mouth to speak she stopped short as his eyes met hers with their hypnotic black stare. The finger travelled to her throat and stopped. He could feel her pulse racing. he smiled, his slow, strange, leering smile and Kitty felt as if he had peeled off her clothes with his eyes and left her sitting naked before him.

"You are quite beautiful." He said simply. "Why my brother hasn't screwed you I don't know. Or has he?"

Kitty gasped, flushing scarlet and turned away.

"Oi! Martin leaned forward and sent several glasses crashing to the floor. "You can't talk to her like that!".

"Why not??" Dominic barely glanced at him. His eyes hovered on Poppy for a second and he saw the look in her eyes. Now that would be a lot easier, but he felt like a challenge.

"Do me a favour." He turned to Martin. "Piss off. All of you. Except this one. Or I'll make sure you all have the sack."

"I'm not leaving her with you." Martin snarled, grabbing Kitty's arm. "Why don't you piss off instead? We were here first, so sod off.".

An effeminate waiter had shimmied his way across the room and was smiling coyly at Dominic.

"Trouble Dommie?"

"Nothing we can't fix. Could you show these people out please? But not this one, she's staying with me."

The man pouted and eyed Kitty with envy.

"Come on you lot." He put his hand on Martins shoulder. "Out you go."

"I'm not going anywhere!" Martin was growing red. "And certainly not on the say so of a bloody faggot like you!"

"Now now sonny." A massive hairy hand came to rest on his other shoulder. "that's no way to talk to your betters."

The bouncer who had crept up behind them was enormous. Steering Martin away from the table he nodded to the waiter who caught hold of Poppy's arm

"Hey!" She shouted. "Let go! Come on Kit, let's get out of here!"

Kitty tried to rise but found a slim but surprisingly strong arm holding her back.

"No, you don't." Dominic spoke softly. "You stay with me."

At the door the bouncer gave Martin a shove that sent him face first onto the pavement.

"Bully!" Poppy swung to face him and found the door slamming in her face. Cursing, she banged her fists on the wood.

"Leave it Pop." Ryan dusted Martin down. "There's no way we're going back in there."

"But what about Kitty?" Poppy wailed. "We can't just leave her!"

"She'll be alright." Martin was still smouldering. " We'll go next door then we can grab her when they leave."

"Good idea." Ryan put his hand on Poppy's waist. "Maybe she doesn't want to leave him to come with us. After all, would you?"

Inside the bar kitty wanted nothing less than to stay with Dominic. His quiet refusal to let her leave had frightened her, and every time she tried to rise, he pulled her back.

"What's the hurry?" He insisted. "Have a drink with me at least. I'm not a monster, I'm not going to eat you!"

"I've got to go." She pleaded. "I need my lift!"

"In case you had forgotten you and I live in the same place. I'll take you home, although I can't promise to take such a direct route as your friends would have."

Lifting his long legs onto the table in front of he ran an insolent finger down her thigh.

"I'll get you home eventually." He murmured. "It just might take some time."

A dark gleam had entered his eyes that she didn't like. Pushing his hand off her leg she got to her feet, trying to move his legs. She could feel him laughing, his eyes mocking her. there was a wall behind her. He had blocked her in. Her only escape was past him.

"Sit down you silly girl" Dominic was finding it very amusing. "What's the hurry? Relax for God's sake! Look, your friends are long gone, okay? You don't really think that they'll be hanging around outside waiting for you, do you? And you can believe me that there's no way they are coming back in. If they are still outside when we leave, then I promise you can ride home with them. Okay?"

Kitty looked at him, warily, lower lip trembling. She trusted him no more that she would a snake in long grass, but, like a snake, there was something soothing and hypnotic in his intense, piercing stare. Sitting back in her chair she took a sip of her drink. He was really quite stunning to look at, and she could not get away from the fact that she was flattered by his attention. Why then the voice nagging at the back of her mind that she could get herself as far away from him as possible?

In half an hour Dominic was finding conversation with her extremely difficult. He was beginning, through his ego, to realise that she was afraid of him, something that irked him considerably. She was drinking slowly, one half glass to his two. Really, she was far too innocent and naive for his tastes, but he enjoyed the thrill of the chase, and there was something else that made her so attractive to him. He had seen, from afar, the way his brother watched her. No one else would know, but Dominic knew Tom well enough to read the signs. Oh, he would deny it of course, but he knew; and that made the temptation to have her totally irresistible. He looked at his watch. Hopefully those pratts would be long gone by now.

"Come on then Cinderella, " He drained his glass. "Let's go and get you home before you turn into a pumpkin. I can't go upsetting big brother, now can I?"

Deeply relieved to be going, Kitty was dismayed to find the street outside totally empty.

"Looks like they've gone." Dominic, however, was delighted. "Shame. Never mind, I'll give you a ride home."

There was a tone in his voice, an insinuation that made her shudder, and she backed away. Dominic laughed, a cold, heartless sound devoid of humour, and took her arm.

"This way."

He led her down the road and around the corner into one of the back streets. As he turned again into a dimly lit alley his pace slowed. Kitty hung back, always one step behind him. Feeling her skin beneath his finger's adrenalin started to course through Dominic's veins. He could see her face, pale in the shadows, hear her breath. He loved it, this tingling anticipation. Tightening his grip, he pulled her closer.

"This is a strange place to leave a car." Kitty peered ahead into the darkness.

"A very strange place" He murmured, then in a louder tone. "I prefer to hide it away. I'm always terrified it'll get stolen"

She was standing close to him, he could smell the perfume on her warm skin, and her fear. Lust was beginning to take him over, sending blood pumping hot into his loins. Catching her hand, he swung her around to face him.

"What?" She stepped back. "Dominic, what are you doing?"

"Oh, come on sweetheart." He crooned. "Don't be difficult. All I want is one kiss."

Kitty's reply was muffled by his mouth as he pressed it over hers. Shaking her head, she pulled away. His arms closed on her in a vice like grip, and, laughing, he lifted her off her feet and backed her into an empty doorway.

"Now." He held her arms down by her sides. "Why won't you kiss me? Don't I deserve it? I've bought you drinks, offered you a ride home"

"I'm grateful honestly. I just want to go home now." Kitty was trembling. He seemed immensely powerful, standing over her in the dark. There was a black look on his shadowed face that frightened her. "Please Dominic? Just take me home. It's late and I have to be up so early in the morning"

"Certainly not." He moved closer. "Not yet."

Giving him a shove that took all her strength, she managed to dislodge him, just for a second, and ducked under his arm, darting for freedom. Too quick for her, Dominic caught her and swung her around, sending her sliding to her knees as he did. As he knelt besides her he was laughing all over his malicious, taunting face.

"Okay. Caught you that time. Round one to me. What other little games would you like to play?"

Wriggling, Kitty clambered to her feet, only to find herself thumping back against a wall before she could take even one step. She could feel tears spilling down her cheeks. Why was he doing this to her? He was leaning on her know, pushing her arms tight against her back, his knee nudging at her thighs.

"Dominic!" She gasped "No!"

"Why?" His voice was low and hoarse. "Play time's over."

Pushing his weight against her he crushed his mouth tightly over hers, forcing his tongue through her clenched teeth. She bit his lip, tasting blood, and flinched as a powerful hand slapped her hard across the face.

"Don't be so fucking stupid!" He snarled. "Why can't you just relax and enjoy it?"

She felt his fingers catch her hair, pulling her head backwards until she thought that her neck would break. She was too terrified to fight any longer, it was easier to shut her eyes and hope it would be over quickly. He was so strong, and his malevolent, staring eyes were cutting right through her. She felt his hand slide into her t-shirt and cringed in horror as his fingers closed around her left breast. Horrified, she was shaken into action, and sunk her teeth into the smooth, cool skin of his cheek. Cursing, he pinned her tightly against the wall with his elbow, arching his body away as she kicked at his legs. His hand forced its way back upwards and she closed her eyes, unable to bear the contortions of his face. She clawed at him, desperate to be free, and felt the pressure of his elbow on her chest her throat increase until she was struggling to breathe. Coughing, almost choking, she felt the material of her t-shirt rip away from her body and sobbed as the night air fell cold against her skin. His hands were roaming all over her; tugging at her bra, nails scratching her naked flesh. His teeth were cutting her mouth. She tasted bile in her throat and heaved. Grunting like a wild animal, his breath was heavy in her ear as he began to pull at the waistband of her jeans.

She was afraid now, feeling his insistent fingers travelling downwards, wrenching at her zip. Her head started to spin and for a moment she thought she would faint; then, as he moved his head, she saw the stars framed by the walls around her and remembered that there was a world outside this nightmare. The scream that had been welling up inside her and choked back broke free and echoed through the alley again and again.

"Shut up!" He hissed, clamping his hand over her mouth. "What the fuck is wrong with you? Just relax and make it easy for yourself"

He lifted her head until her eyes were level with his own. For a second, he was still, motionless, breath hot on her neck. She could feel his heart beating heavily, feel him moving his body against hers as he tugged her jeans off her hips.

A roar broke the silence that surrounded them.

The body that was pulsing against hers was wrenched away and sent hurtling backwards, crashing to the floor. Then there was more noise, and a figure crouching over it, striking it with terrifying force. Collapsing onto all fours she retched, giving way to her terror. Through the tangled mass of hair that fell over her eyes she saw the twisted and bloodied form in front of her. Another wave of nausea hit her, and she closed her eyes. Hands touched her back; soft gentle hands, wrapping something warm around her. It smelt of aftershave and was somehow familiar.

"Kitty?" The voice was also familiar.

Wiping her mouth with her hand she warily turned her head. Although his features were hidden by the darkness, she saw the glint of his eyes and recognised the outline of his hair. The second she realised who it was she felt ashamed of her exposed body. Tears spilled off her cheeks onto the warm, soft coat.

"Alright." Tom laid is arm carefully on her shoulders. "It's alright now. Can you stand?" Nodding weakly, she let him help her to her feet, staggering against him. Turning her face away she fumbled with the buttons of his coat, averting her eyes from the groaning figure on the floor beside them.

"Come on." Tom was steering her. "Let's get you home."

Bright lights dazzled her eyes as they emerged onto the main road. A group of people hovered ahead, turning, Poppy saw her friend's battered face and gave a scream of horror.

"Clear off you lot." Tom hissed as they passed. "I'll take care of this!"

When they were out of sight Tom turned her to face him.

"Here." He said softly, "Let's tidy you up."

With kind hands he wiped her eyes and mouth, coaxed the tangles from her hair.

"That's better."

Kitty didn't feel better. Her mouth tasted of blood and vomit, every muscle in her body ached. But far, far, worse was the churning pit of revulsion in her stomach; the feeling that even if she scrubbed her skin raw, she would never be clean again. Holding her close, aware of her tension, Tom guided her to his car, head bowed, so that passers by would take them for a couple helping each other home after too much to drink. Helping her into the car he pulled his coat tightly around her.

"I'll be two minutes." He said firmly. "I'll lock the door, so you'll be quite safe."

Watching him run back down the street and disappear around the corner Kitty felt anything but safe. Slipping down into her seat she shivered. Aware of people walking past, she lowered her face and shut her eyes, feigning sleep. After what seemed an age to her tortured brain but was in reality only minutes, she heard the car door click. Starting upright she looked up and saw Tom getting quickly into the car. Grim faced, he started the engine and drove off without a word. Only when the car was climbing steadily up Cleeve Hill did he break the silence.

"I think we have to talk about this Katriona."

Biting her lip Kitty stared out of the window. Tom glanced at her and saw that he was going to get no response. Sighing heavily, he pulled into the nearest lay by and turned on the interior light. Rubbing his face wearily he saw the drying blood on her lip, the bruises already darkening her fair skin. Impulsively he reached out to touch her and comfort her and as his fingers met her skin she sprang into life. Leaping away from him she scrabbled at door handle, whimpering. Tom was horrified. Withdrawing his hand, he sat as far away from her as he could.

"It's alright!" He said loudly. "Kitty it's me, I won't hurt you!"

Shuddering she turned to face him with such an expression of mistrust in her eyes that it stung him. Anger welled up inside him and he thumped his fist onto the steering wheel.

"The bastard!" He snarled. "The fucking bastard. I should have killed him. Well God help me if I ever see him again I will!"

Kitty recoiled as he turned his blazing eyes onto her.

"How could he do it?" He demanded. "How?"

"I don't know." She stammered. "I didn't" She hesitated, "I didn't want to."

"I know you didn't" Tom was rubbing his eyes again "I Know. I know. I just never thought he would be so stupid. Not again."

Kitty stopped wiping her eyes and stared at him.

"What do you mean *again*?" She whispered.

"Please don't cry any more Kitty." He went to put his hand on her knee and stopped. "Listen. If you want to leave the yard, to be away from any likely contact with him I understand."

She looked at him, confusion written all over her pale tear stained face.

"Leave?" She shook her head. "I don't want to leave. Why should I leave, I've done nothing wrong!"

"Good." Tom's heart was steadying now. "Good."

"But." She paused, and rubbed her tender chest, "I do want to know what you mean by 'again'?"

Tom studied her long and hard as he searched for the right words.

"My brother." He almost gagged on the word. "Has a problem, for want of a better description. Once, years ago, when he was only fourteen. a local girl accused him of raping her. As it turned out it was a lie, partly. He had, he admitted, been trying to convince her to have sex with him and she kept refusing. Dominic, as you unfortunately have just found out doesn't handle rejection very well. He got more and more insistent until he became quite aggressive. As you can imagine."

He paused and judged her reaction. She was sitting quite still, string at her bloodied fingernails. He wasn't sure to continue until she looked up at him.

"Go on " She whispered.

"He gave up." He looked away, unable to stand the haunted expression that he saw in her soft blue eyes. "He ran away leaving her where she was. When she got home, already in trouble for being late, she got scared and added onto the truth considerably when her father tried to drum out of her what had happened. So, she accused Dominic of rape; and after a long very unpleasant time, for all of us, the truth came out and the charges were dropped. Especially when her father's lawyer found out that she was eighteen and my brother only fourteen. They would have been in a very grey area, legally, regarding relationships. She could well have been accused of taking advantage of him as he was still a minor. So, it all got swept under the carpet. No harm done. Except to Dominic.

He turned from being a naughty teenager with overactive hormones into a complete rebel. He tried everything, stealing cars, running away, even drugs, it was as if he wanted to punish us for believing her. Then he found the ultimate cure for all his wounds and insecurities. Sex. With as many different women as he could, all of them older and far more experienced than him. Instead of just punishing us, it was as if he was trying to pay back the whole female race for what they had done to him. He's turned the one-night stand into an art form; and there was never any shortage of women ready to oblige. So, when you said no, it wasn't what he expected, and he couldn't handle it. Despite his sexual activities my brother doesn't like women, at all, he despises them as they have the power to give him the ultimate put down. What would have made it worse, is that in his mind you are way below him and should be flattered."

"Because I'm female?" She was still looking at her nails.

"Because you work for me." He sighed. "Dominic hates me, and everything associated with me."

She looked at him.

"But it is no excuse." He shook his head. "I can only

35

promise you that if you chose to stay, he will never come near you again. Ever. I'll see to that"

She nodded slowly, lifting her eyes warily to his.

"Do you still want to stay?"

"Yes." She lowered her eyes again.

"One thing." He hated asking her this, but he had to. "Not a word of this, please? Not to anyone. Not for my sake, and certainly not his, but for my mother's and for yours. It's all too easy to become labelled as the girl who "asked "for it"

"Okay." She bit her lip. "I won't say anything. All I want to do is forget about tonight."

"Good girl" He rested his hand lightly on her shoulder. "Don't worry about the rest of the staff. I'll tell them you've been fighting"

The ghost of a smile passed across her face.

"Come on. Let's get you home. "Very gently he lifted her face to his. "Remember, you have my word that I'll never let him near you again."

Martin was furious. He simply could not believe that Dominic was going to be allowed to get away with what in his opinion was a simple case of assault. Watching Tom's departing back as he walked away from the cottage door he wanted to run after him and slap his aristocratic head. Poppy was more sympathetic, if not understanding; she could share Kitty's horror of reliving her ordeal to anyone, but it took her until the early hours of the morning to calm Martin down and get him off to bed. Tiptoeing into her own room she found Kitty was still awake, gazing listlessly out of the window. The moon was lighting up the sweep of lawn that led up to the house. There was a light on in Tom's study. They both knew what he was waiting for.

"I want to hit someone." Poppy sat on her bed with a thump. "Are you sure you're okay Kit? I mean he didn't actually."

"No." Kitty interrupted her. "I'm okay. Just leave it."

"We can't just let him get away with this." Poppy sighed heavily.

"I thought you understood." There was a catch in Kitty's voice.

"Oh, I do. really." Poppy tried to smile. "I'm just so angry and I have no one to take it out on."

"Here." Kitty flung her battered teddy bear across the room. "Have Winston. He always works for me."

"Don't you want him?" Poppy pulled the little toy's ears.

"Not tonight." Kitty got into her bed. "I just want my own space tonight. Even Winston would be too close."

Pulling her duvet up under her chin, Kitty took a deep breath. Closing her eyes, she willed herself, with much difficulty, into a fitful and tormented sleep.

CHAPTER THREE

"Big news, big news!" Gareth burst into the coach house and pounced on the toast

"Well don't keep it to yourself." Martin moved the plate out of his reach.

"The Guv has taken up boxing! I was talking to Mr B. up at the house early this morning. He walked straight into him beating the shit out of his little brother! Told him if he ever came near this place again, he'd break his effing neck. Good God Kit!" His voice changed as he caught sight of Kitty, sitting red faced in the farthest corner of the room. "You weren't there as, well, were you?"

Poppy caught Martin's eye as Kitty turned away.

"Oh, that was last night." She gibbered, reaching for Kitty's hand under the table. "Some drunks were fighting, and Kit got in the way."

Gareth studied Kitty's black lip in amazement.

"You look like you've gone five rounds in the ring with Ali!"

"You leave her be." Mrs. Benson, listening from her place at the cooker didn't believe the story about fighting drunks for a second. Her husband had overheard things that he had wisely not repeated to Gareth.

The door swung open, and the room fell silent as Tom entered. The usually immaculate man sported a glowing black eye; his swollen eyelid glowing red and purple, a bloody lip was swelling above his jaw, and the collar of his jumper was ripped to the shoulder. His chin was grazed and an angry shade of red.

"What are you all staring at?" He snapped.

"Christ Guv!" Gareth couldn't help laughing. "You and our Kit look like a pair of bookends!"

Tom frowned at him, but his eyes twinkled. Trying to

look stern he made disapproving noises and looked at his watch.

"These horses will think it's Christmas. Get a move on!"

"Right Guv, sorry." Ryan got to his feet.

"Ryan, I have to go out this morning, don't let Kitty ride today. Martin you're in charge, and Kitty, I don't want any horses beaten up when I'm away."

"No Sir." Kitty blushed unable to meet his eyes.

"Go onto the gallops with Ryan in the Land Rover, don't hang around here on your own."

Kitty looked at him, searching for hidden meaning in his words but he turned away, eyes blank. Poppy caught her arm as she left the room.

"Come on Kitty Kat. That's the worst bit over."

The fresh air cleared Kitty's muddled brain. Watching the sleek, beautiful thoroughbreds streaming across the turf, she felt her shattered confidence start to rise. She wished she could ride and let the wind whip away her emotions, make her numb to anything except the powerful, surging muscles beneath her.

"Need the all-weather soon." Ryan was digging his heel into the ground. "It's getting hard."

"It'll rain again soon." Replied Kitty without conviction, "We didn't need the all-weather until Christmas last year."

Ryan frowned as the horses cantered past them.

"Enigma's running tomorrow, isn't she?" Where's Marty? Who else have we got tomorrow?"

"Martin's up the top." Kitty pointed to a small figure at the head of the gallops. "We've got Bold Brass and Sparkling Wine at Hereford as well. Moroccan Prince and Romeo got to Market Rasen"

"Good job you're here." Ryan smiled. "What a good assistant trainer I am!"

"You'll do I suppose" Kitty laughed as she watched

Enigma trotting towards them, Gareth's face lit up with the thrill of the filly's speed. He grinned broadly as Ryan waved him back up the gallop.

"Ascot sales next week." Ryan sat on the bonnet of the Land Rover. Perhaps the Guv will buy in some new blood. We're a bit short in the class department since we lost Crop."

"What about Lady Ainsley's new horse? The one that came for a few weeks in the summer. I went on my holidays and when I came back, he'd gone."

"The little bay?" Ryan was squinting into the sun. "She took him home, doing all the prep work herself, he should be back any day now."

"Cutting it a bit fine if she wants to run before Christmas!"

"Oh, you know old Margie." Ryan chuckled. "Got her heart set on the Grand National, with a Gold Cup or two along the way."

"She'll be lucky." Kitty watched the next pair of horses cantering past. "From what I remember he can only just see over the fences!"

"He's a good horse if he is small, don't knock him." Ryan frowned. "He won a few hunters chases last season, beat Belle Maison by ten lengths no less."

"Long way from a hunter chase at Newton Abbot to Aintree." Kitty shook her head. "I still think he's too small."

The horses were filing back towards them, Martin at their head, talking nonstop. Whistling happily, he winked at Kitty as he passed.

"Manes dirty. Have to teach you how to use a body brush!"

Pulling a face at him Kitty climbed back into the Land Rover. Ryan studied the cloudless sky as he steered the vehicle onto the track.

"Hope your rain holds off until tomorrow. Brassy loves

this ground. Shit!" he grappled with the steering wheel. "That was ice! It's bleeding October for Christs sake!"

"It hasn't been the best of starts, has it?" Kitty held onto her seat as the Land Rover slipped sideways on the road.

"No, I should say not. I think it's about time Highford had a change of luck."

"Yes." Kitty gingerly prodded her cheek. "Me too."

Many miles away Tom was growing hot under the collar. His lunch was dragging on and his hosts, a syndicate of butchers, showed no signs of bringing it to an end. Having pooled their resources to buy a couple of horses, they suffered from the delusion, like too many of his owners, that theirs were the only charges on his hands. He had fought off the queries about his bruised face and managed to convince them that he had been at the wrong end of a horse that wouldn't load. If they believed him, he couldn't tell, and he cared even less.

"Now have I got this right?" The younger of the two Bowles' brothers somehow managed to look older than the other, and still wasn't a day under sixty. "Sparkling Wine runs tomorrow, but Major Investment won't run for another month?"

"That's right." Tom stared moodily out of the window into the busy city street. He hadn't enjoyed the drive into Birmingham, it had left him with too much time to dwell on the previous night's event, which he had been trying to put out of his head. The bar was noisy and crowded, full of businessmen illicitly lunching with glossy secretaries. The scene made him even more convinced that the life he had chosen was right for himself. This was the only part he hated and would avoid if possible; he would rather be faced with a yard full of unbroken three-year olds than one table full of owners. He found it difficult to make them understand that he had the horse's interests uppermost in his heart, even if it did mean that they sometimes had to wait for their day at the races. He could never understand why some people expected their horses to race week in week out as if they were machines. Fortunately, the Bowles' brothers were more practical.

"I understand," This was the older one speaking now, "That Grant Gardner has moved his horse to Lambourn?"

"That's right." Tom out stared the little man, ready for the inevitable attack.

"He wasn't happy?"

Grant and I haven't seen eye to eye for some time over many things. We had an unfortunate accident with a horse on the gallops. That gave Grant the excuse I suspect he had long been looking for."

Mike Peterson, the youngest and most aggressive of the group, was eager to have his say.

"Grant told me that you refused to run his horse until January."

"That really is between me and Grant." Tom made no attempt to disguise the fact that he didn't really like the man. "I will say that I didn't think the horse's injury would have been healed in time for him to run before January."

"He's running before then." Mike raised a sarcastic eyebrow.

"Well, that's not in my hands anymore. But I will say I think it very unlikely."

"Hmm." Mike Peterson narrowed his eyes. "We shall see. I suppose you know best. But it's common knowledge that you are, shall I say, 'soft', no I suppose 'kind' is a better word, when it comes to your horses."

"That's because I treat them as the sensitive animals that they are and not as pieces of machinery." Tom replied shortly.

Four pairs of eyes watched him. Like a pack of vultures, he thought, waiting to pick my bones.

" Sales next week." Rowley Harris, the smallest and most likeable member of the group, was also the major shareholder. Leaning forward he lowered his voice. "We'd like to buy another horse."

"Good God!" The words slipped out before Tom could stop himself. "I thought you weren't happy!"

"Naturally we'd like to see more of our horses Tom. But what we'd really like is one good horse, something that can represent us in the best races; that wouldn't be outclassed in a race like the King George for example."

Tom drained his glass quickly. He could feel the pulse throbbing in his neck.

"Well, it's a nice thought gentleman, but I doubt that you'll find a horse of that class in this sale."

Rowley Harris smiled again and refilled Tom's glass.

"I have the catalogue, and as you say most of the entries are fairly nondescript. But there is one that caught my eye."

Heaven forbid, thought Tom, the man thinks he's a bloody bloodstock expert now. Running his eyes down the page he followed the excitedly jabbing finger.

"There. This one!"

Tom raised a hand, silencing him. As he read, he felt his heartbeat quicken; prickles of excitement racing each other down his spine. Here, unbelievably was the break he so badly needed.

'To dissolve a partnership', ran the heading, 'Olympic Run, by Greek God, out of Fina's Athlete.' Amazed, Tom read the blurb beneath. 'Winner of six steeplechases, two hurdle races and £55,000, all of his eight races. An exceptionally tough, strong gelding thought to have a top-class future.'

Tom took his time before he looked up at the waiting group, careful not to show the excitement that was gripping him.

"Well?" Rowley looked pleased with himself.

"What the hell is he doing at the sales!" Tom shook his

head. "I thought some agent would have snapped him up!"

The little man shrugged.

"Apparently his owners have been declared bankrupt. He's being sold to the highest bidder to liquidise their assets. Bad luck for them, but I can't say I'm sorry about it!"

"Are you quite sure about this gentleman?" Tom looked at them carefully. "This horse will cost you ten times what you paid for the other two."

"And the rest." Mike Peterson was flushed. "There's a 50,000 reserve on him."

"That's an awful lot of money."

"We know." Rowley Harris was beaming. "But we want to have him, and of we do we want him to be trained with one race in mind."

"Which is?"

"The Cheltenham Gold Cup."

Tom puffed out his lips. The horse was one of the most exciting youngsters on the scene, and Gold Cup class, but this year may be a year too soon. He didn't want to raise the hopes of these men too high.

"Okay then." He ran his eyes from one to another. "We'll try and get him. But he won't be running here there and everywhere in races that are below him, you understand?"

"Fine." The younger Bowles' brother was rather drunk. "Just make sure the other two do their share, and on that note." He raised his glass. "Here's to Sparkling Wine."

Of Which, Tom thought dryly, you have had too much.

Not allowing himself any time to daydream Tom made a detour into Cheltenham on his way home. Flick was rather surprised to find him sitting on the bonnet of her yellow Golf when she left the office.

"Oh my God!" She wailed on seeing his face. "What happened to you?"

"Oh, that's nothing. Sorry I had to dash off last night.

Fancy a drink to make up for it?" He gave her a quick hug.

"I'd rather go to bed." She whispered.

He laughed. On this high of anticipation, he was in exactly the right mood for sex.

"I was hoping you'd say that. I'll meet you there."

Normally a predictable, rather unadventurous lover, Flick was delighted to find her man full of unusual fire and ferocity. Arching her back in delight she ran her fingers through his hair and gave a groan of pleasure.

"What has come over you?" She murmured. "You've never been so, uninhibited!"

Tom raised himself on one arm and kissed her shoulder.

"If I told you, it would spoil the surprise for next time."

He was too much the gentleman to tell her that at times, his thoughts had been on another woman. He had been as shocked as Flick would be hurt to find himself imagining Kitty in his arms. The result had frightened him slightly, as it had made him painfully aware of where his fancy was leading him. Looking down at the beauty he currently held in his arms he saw her smiling up at him, perfect white teeth in a perfect face. Too perfect. Not enough flaws like any other human being. Tom rolled off her and lay on his back staring up at the ceiling.

"What did I say?" She sat up.

"Nothing." He watched her breasts swinging as she moved and caught one erect nipple between his fingers. "I've got to go. Lots to do at home."

"Oh." Pouting she collapsed back onto the bed. After a moment silence she began to laugh.

"What's funny?" Tom was pulling on his trousers.

"Why didn't you ever become a jockey?"

"Too tall and heavy. Why?"

"Pity." She chuckled. "You ride one hell of a finish."

The dawn broke cold and frosty. Martin, loading the horseboxes, blew on his fingers and wished that he'd chosen a career in flat racing. Poppy, grooming Brassy's already slick mane heard Gareth cursing in the next box.

" Problems Taff?" She called.

"I'm trying to plait a tail." Gareth replied. "I've nearly cut off the circulation in my fingers with these bands and the top keeps coming out!"

Kitty's blonde head appeared.

"Can I help? Why don't you do her at the track?"

"Oh please." Gareth waved a bag of plaiting bands at her. "Do her at the track? I'll end up looking like you! Here, have a bucket to stand on."

He watched, fascinated as Kitty's nimble fingers wound Enigma's long white tail into a neat plait.

"How do you do that?" Gareth shook his head.

"Plenty of practise." Kitty smiled. "I had show ponies when I was a child."

"Lucky you." Gareth grinned. "All I had were the donkeys on Barry Island beach."

"Are you all ready?" Martin was travelling with the Market Rasen runners so Ryan, suited and tied was going with them to Hereford. Red hair slicked back he looked self-conscious and flustered. A magpie, dramatically black and white against the red stable roof, was watching them from above. Kitty saluted it hastily.

"What the hell?" Ryan was amazed.

"Superstition." Gareth wound a bandage onto Enigma's tail. "One for sorrow and all that."

"Anymore sorrow in this yard and I'll be permanently in black. Come on for God's sake or we'll be late."

Sparkling Wine stared out of his box with excited eyes as Kitty approached. Smelling the air, he gave a squeal and kicked the wall behind him. A plain, unsociable horse, his only redeeming feature was his brave heart. Sparky never made 'friends' with any of the lads; moody and unpredictable he just did his job, and he did it well. Sparky loved racing; most of all he loved being in the front. Normally he raced over the minimum trip of two miles, but as a concession to the ageing process he was attempting to go half a mile further that afternoon. To date he was the yards only winner that season, having scored way back in August. Showing Kitty his teeth as she slipped the headcollar on over his ears, a tremor of anticipation ran down his short brown neck. Seeing Brassy being led towards the ramp of the horsebox he gave an agitated snort and pushed forwards, crushing Kitty against the door.

"Hey!" She squealed. "Remember me?"

For answer Sparky reared high, narrowly missing her head with his front shoes.

"Give him to me." Ryan appeared at the door and took Sparky's lead rope. " For God's sake be careful Kit, you know what the old sods like."

"Wagons roll!" Shouted Martin as the horse pranced towards him. "Ready Ry?"

"No." Ryan was being towed around by an over excited Sparky. "Come on you old pig!"

"Trouble lads?" Tom stepped out of the office. A heavy woollen coat hung from his shoulders; newly washed hair still damp. As he walked up to them the smell of Ralph Lauren aftershave hung on the air behind him. Kitty, completely in awe of him took a step backwards, feeling her pulse beginning to race. Standing beside Sparky, who didn't look such a giant beside him, Tom laid a hand on the horse's neck.

"Enough of this nonsense you old bugger." He said calmly. "On you go."

Looking as though butter wouldn't melt in his mouth, Sparky walked calmly up the ramp.

"Why does he always make me feel like an idiot?" Ryan muttered.

"That's why he's the boss!" Martin laughed. "I'm off. Good luck you lot."

Tom raised a hand and walked down the ramp. As he descended, he caught Kitty's eye. For a second his eyes lingered, taking in the heavily applied make up which failed to cover her bruised face. His heart went out to her, this girl who had somehow worked her way into his mind. She was carrying this all off so well. Why she was still here he had no idea. Then he saw the expression in her eyes and thought that perhaps he did. Giving her a fleeting smile, he turned away. Raising a hand to his own swollen lip he suppressed a laugh at the thought of what he would have to face at the track. He would have to tell them that Flick had resorted to violence.

In the comparative warmth of the lorry, Gareth rested his feet on the heater and tried to calm his butterfly filled stomach. So desperate to be a jockey, he had not yet given up on the idea of riding for Tom as an amateur, but now was having to tread water and be content with his lot. The yard was not exactly moving upwards, in fact it seemed to be treading water with him. He loved going to the track, but always wished that he could be on the back of his horses, not watching helplessly at the rails.

Kitty was trying to find a music station on the radio.

"Who fiddled with this?" She moaned. "All this news will drive me nuts."

"I did." Ryan was trying to scratch his foot, unwrap a mint and drive at the same time. "I was listening to the boxing last might."

"Ugh." Kitty shuddered. "Violence."

"Ha!" Gareth laughed, prodding her in the ribs. "You can talk! Looked in the mirror this morning?"

"Shut it Taff" Ryan shot him a warning look. "That's not funny."

"No." Kitty spoke quietly. "It's not funny at all."

The journey into Hereford took them longer than expected. Saturday shoppers queued over the river bridge, mingling with the hordes coming into the city from all directions heading for the racetrack. Together they formed a bottleneck and brought the road to a standstill. Ryan was reading the names of the lorries that were queuing with them.

"Look." He pointed to a pale blue vehicle ahead of them. "Peter Stroud. Wonder who he's got on?"

"Whoever it is." Gareth was listening to the horses in the back. "They can't be making as much racket as these three. Listen to them!"

"That's Sparky." Ryan laughed. "I'd know that kick anywhere!"

Kitty stretched up to check her face in the mirror.

"You look fine Kit." Gareth smiled at her and squeezed her leg. "I'll have to teach you how to duck!"

When they came to a halt in the small, slightly chaotic car park they all stayed where they were, watching horses as they were led into the stables. Smart in their travelling rugs their coats bloomed even in the grey afternoon light. Fit, healthy, strong they all looked formidable opponents. One very eye-catching animal jogged past, tugging irritably at his lead rope, nostrils flaring, black coat reflecting light like a mirror. Ryan watched him closely.

"Silent Running." He nodded. "In Sparky's race. Good horse. Sparky will have to pull out the stops to beat him."

"Sparky's favourite." Gareth was lowering himself out of the cab. "In the papers anyway."

"Mm." Ryan still hadn't moved. "My money's going on the black horse. The jungle drums say he's the one to watch this season"

"Traitor." Gareth's nerves were climbing back to the surface. " Now will you stop gawping and give us a hand?"

Sparky, knowing exactly where he was and why he was there, was about to explode. A bath of nervous sweat from head to toe he kicked the sides of the box until it shook, terrifying poor Enigma who quivered beside him eyes huge.

"It's alright girlie." Gareth crooned. "Get this' monster off Kit!"

"This horse is a menace!" Ryan jumped out of Sparky's reach as his teeth swung through the air. "Get a hold of him Taff so I can undo this partition, he's buckled the catch."

As soon as his exit was clear Sparky shot down the ramp, almost flattening Kitty in the process as soon as he reached the ground he reared once more.

"Get a grip Kit!" Ryan hissed. "Tom's coming!"

Tom was watching the scene outside his lorry with some amusement; his horse's characters always fascinated him. As individual as humans their moods were as vital to their performance as their diets. That old rogue Sparky was up to his usual tricks, terrifying the hell out of the staff. Little Enigma was taking in her surroundings with terrified eyes, while Brassy, as calm as ever, stood beside her, ears pricked towards the track.

"Come on Ryan." He called. "Get these horses into their boxes."

Recognising the livery of the box next to his he watched with interest as a groom led a brown horse down the ramp. The jagged white blaze was unmistakable, as was the scar on his knee, the new skin glistening pink. He had been convinced that wound would not heal quickly. But whatever Peter Stroud had done he had been busy, because that brown horse was Mardi Gras.

Not only was Mardi Gras back in action but so was his loud, overweight owner. Holding forth in the owners and trainers bar his main conversation was the reason he had moved his horse. Not content with his little anecdote, he ripped into Tom and his staff with obvious enthusiasm at every opportunity. Even when the object of his derision entered the room, he made no attempt to lower his voice. Peter Stroud had more tact, moving from Grant's side to join Tom at the bar where he was waiting to meet Rowley Harris.

"What can I get you Tom?"

"Something to jam up the old windbag's mouth?"

"I don't know how you stuck him for so long." Peter smiled. "He's very tiring."

"The one and only reason just came off your lorry."

Peter Stroud grinned; nearly twenty years Tom's senior he had spent many hours with his father. Old William had taught his boy well, and he took everything that obnoxious man Gardner had said with more than a pinch of salt. A member of the 'nouveau rich' Gardner thought that money could buy him anything; but it didn't buy respect, or loyalty.

As the younger man took a sip of his scotch Peter noted the strain around his eyes. Tom had taken his father's death hard; the years had passed quickly and hadn't yet removed all the scars.

"So, what has your brother been up to?" He asked.

"What?" Tom spun to face him, shutters dropping quickly over his eyes, hiding all emotion.

"Well, I know you're not a fighter Tom. So, I calculate that the black eye must have something to do with him?"

Tom's eyes remained blank. He shrugged his shoulders dismissively.

"Family tiff. I'm telling everyone that it was Flick Harries."

Peter grinned. He knew that if there was more to this tale then he would never hear it from Tom.

"What have you got with you today?" He changed the subject.

"Three. Little filly in the novice hurdle, Bold Brass in the novice 'chase and the old horse in the handicap."

"Sparkling Wine? Learned any manners yet?"

"Not likely. He'll leave this planet as the pig-headed bastard he's always been."

"Probably!" Peter laughed.

"What about you?" Tom was bursting with curiosity about Mardi.

"One in the handicap and your old horse in the novice 'chase."

"Really?" Tom couldn't keep the surprise out of his voice. "A 'chase? Is he really up to that Peter?"

"Owner's insistence." Peter's voice left Tom in no doubt that he wasn't prepared to discuss it. "I'll see you later Tom. Goodbye."

"Bye." Tom frowned as he watched him leave. Although he had no more interest in the horse, he hated the thought of Mardi Gras being ruined because of an owner's greed. Even more upsetting was the thought that his father's old friend was dropping his standards in order to survive. He glanced at the television screen; the runners were at the start for the first race. He couldn't wait for Rowley any longer, he had to saddle the filly. He checked his watch. Ten minutes. He had time for just one more drink, and then it was down to business.

Much to Gareth's delight Enigma was a close second in her race, beaten only a neck by the favourite. The rapt expression on his face as he led the horse in made Ryan laugh as he passed him.

"You next." Kitty told Brassy. "Mustn't let the side down!"

Ryan was securing the horses protective boots. A tall

figure cast a shadow in the doorway.

"Everything alright Ryan?"

"Fine sir. The filly ran a good race."

"A very good race." A smile crept across Tom's face. "Her owners are already drunk!"

Kitty stroked Brassy's dark chestnut nose as Tom saddled him. Little quivers rippled the horses coat as he stared out of the box over her shoulder. Tom glanced at her under his arm. Her blue eyes were lit up with excitement, but the way she chewed her lip gave away her nerves. She had tied her hair back and clipped it up onto her head. Neatly dressed as ever she looked tiny and very vulnerable beside the big horse

"Off you go then Kit." Ryan slapped the horse's rump as he passed. The two men, side by side watched her go in silence their minds following the same line of thought. Ryan, glancing sideways, studied his employers' profile; Tom had many things that Ryan would love to possess but his brother was not one of them. Then he saw the expression on Tom's face and was surprised. There was more there than concern for a member of his staff. Feeling himself growing red he hastily walked after the horse and into the paddock.

It was a strange sensation watching someone else's groom leading Mardi Gras around the paddock. To Tom's critical eye the horse looked weakened by his time off, lean and light behind the saddle. In comparison Brassy was an equine mountain, with his gleaming hide sleek and supple over his powerful frame. Tom had always had high hopes for this handsome young horse, but so far had precious little to show for his faith. The jockeys were filing into the paddock. A colourful group, yet straight faced and serious. Novice 'chasers were not always the safest of conveyances, and were a test of nerves, especially on Hereford's flat, fast, track and many of them would be making their mounts acquaintance for the first time. '

Rick Cowdrey, the talented young New Zealander, was weaving his way through the group of people in Tom's direction. A new face on the scene of British racing Tom had been impressed enough to offer him a retainer the very first time he had seen him on a horse. It was not a fortune, but when Rick had arrived at Heathrow all he possessed he carried with him, a rucksack, a guitar, and a couple of saddles. So desperate was he to make his name as a jump jockey that he had almost bitten Tom's hand off as soon as it was offered. Despite criticism from owners and established jockeys alike Tom had stuck to his word, and Rick was his first jockey. He had yet to convince all his owners but had succeeded with most. Sadly, his faith in his new disciple was not yet fully vindicated and all he had to show so far for his outlay was a couple of placed rides, and Sparky's one win. But he knew that the slow start to the season reflected the quality of the horses in the yard that Rick had to ride, and not the ability of their pilot.

Rick's shaggy blonde hair was escaping from underneath his skull cap. His skin looked sallow and unhealthy, a legacy of his fading tan which was being dwindled further by mounting nerves. He sported a layer of stubble. every other jockey in the weighing room managed to look neat and well presented; in comparison Rick looked like the poor relation.

"Hi." He drawled. "Mare ran a good race."

"She did." Tom nodded agreement. "I'm still working on that ride for you."

"No worries." Rick grinned. "Without you I'd be busking on Paddington station!"

"The way things are going at the moment." Tom retorted, "You may have been better off!"

Touching Rick lightly on the shoulder he led him over to the horse who was still walking quietly around the outer edge of the paddock with Kitty. Rick's eyes ran over her slim frame with undisguised interest. He hadn't seen this one before. Passing her to mount he gave her a quick smile.

Aware of his stare Kitty put Brassy's big neck between them, catching Tom's eye as she stepped back. He frowned for a second and then looked up at Rick, who was settling himself on the horses back; and found himself fighting a pang of jealousy as he saw the young man's eyes following the curve of Kitty's hips.

Ryan, as he swept the paddock sheet off with a flourish, also noticed the looks and puffed out his lips. Kitty was getting more than her fair share of attention lately, and not always from the most welcome of sources. He was undecided about Rick, could not fathom out his laid-back character. Watching him on the horse he saw a lock of blonde hair straggling to the jockey's shoulders.

Bloody fairy.

The bloody fairy waved the flag of things to come by steering the horse to victory in the novice 'chase. Brassy won by ten lengths, reducing both Kitty and the bookmakers to tears. For Tom, the pleasure of his young horse's victory was marred by the sight of Mardi Gras limping painfully off the course, blood pumping from his reopened wound. Even worse was the look of depression on Peter Stroud's face and the knowledge that it was caused by the loss of a training fee and not the loss of a good horse. But he was not allowed time to brood, as he had to rush to the saddling boxes where Sparky was waiting. He had stopped performing and was standing like a rock as he was made ready. Kitty, still glowing with the thrill of seeing Brassy win gave Tom an animated smile as he approached.

"Ready?" He smiled.

Nodding, and unaware that she dazzled him with her flashing eyes, she led the horse out into the crowd.

Milling around at the start Rick tried to settle the fractious horse. Once in the paddock Sparky had exploded once more and it had taken all Rick's considerable strength to contain him on the way to the start. Even now, he ran the risk of being carted off at any moment.

"Come on man." He muttered as the starter walked towards his rostrum. "Shift your ass for God's sake!"

After what seemed an eternity the Trilby hatted figure climbed his steps and surveyed the ragged line of horses. Aware of Sparky bunching his muscles beneath him, Rick tightened his grip on the reins.

With a snap the tapes rose, and they were off.

For a mile and a half Sparky winged his way along at the head of the field. Having had his arms pulled out of their proverbial sockets to that point Rick was relieved to find the horse beginning to settle at long last. Behind the shadowy figure of Silent Running stalked them, nose level with Sparky's tail, awaiting the right moment to strike. Within the final half mile, the black horse took the lead. Content to have the pressure lifted for a short while, Rick tucked Sparky in behind, letting him get some air into his lungs.

Two fences from home and Silent Running was increasing his pace, trying to stretch the gap between himself and his rival. Skimming over the second last Rick saw the horse drawing away and began to kick Sparky on. They seemed to be travelling at an incredible speed as the last fence loomed black and menacing in front of them. Sparky gathered himself together and put in an enormous leap that carried him alongside the other horse. Their iron shod hooves crashed on the firm turf as they landed and side by side sprinted for the line; locked in battle, neck and neck. The grass blurred beneath their feet as, tired as they were, they raced for the finish.

Sparky hated to be beaten. Ears flat against his head, neck stretched he dragged every last ounce of speed out of his body. Rick swung his whip, urging him on. Sparky's breath roared hot and painful in his lungs, his muscles ached, but he would not give in. Head down, with gritted teeth, Rick drove the horse home with all his strength. With an audible grunt of effort Sparky conjured up one final burst and stretched his nose out in front of the horse beside him and into the lead. Rick glanced sideways and saw that the black horse had no more to give; one final crack of the whip on Sparky's steaming hide and they were home. Dropping his hand's, he took a deep breath and bent to pat the hot, wet neck. As he did so Sparky came to an abrupt, staggering halt. Ricky ran his hand down the plaited mane, puzzled, and saw to his horror bright, red, blood spurting from the horse nostrils.

"Shit." He leaned forward, turning the horses head slightly towards him for a closer look. Sparky staggered again and for a horrible, heart stopping moment Rick though he was going to collapse. Then he snorted hard, gulped some air into his lungs, and steadied himself. Heart pumping with effort and relief Rick started to walk the horse to the paddock, the little blonde and the red-haired man were rushing over to him.

"Sparky!" The girl gasped and began wiping ineffectually at the horse's nostrils with her coat sleeve. Irritated Sparky shook his head and sent a spray of blood all over them. Tom was at the exit waiting.

"It won't stop!" Kitty panted; pale faced.

"It'll stop when he cools down." Tom wasn't as confident as he sounded. "Blood vessel. I'll get the vet."

Tom didn't hang about in the winners' enclosure; all that blood was bad publicity. As he had predicted, by the time Sparky was seen in the veterinary box and had been cooled off at the stable the bleeding had stopped. All the same, he couldn't help feeling that it didn't bode to well for the horse's future. Telling Kitty to keep the horse moving, Tom surveyed the exhausted animal with despondency. Rowley Harris ran up, on the point of breaking a blood vessel himself. Not in the mood for overwrought owners Tom greeted him with stony silence. Relieved to find that Rowley had no more interest in idle chatter than himself he stood beside him and waited.

The vet was flustered. It had been a hectic day. The firm ground was playing havoc with the horse's legs, and he had strapped up more sprained tendons than he like to think about. Listening to Sparky's heart he shook his head and reached for his hypodermic.

"Well Tom, I'd get him checked out at home of course, but I wouldn't be over optimistic."

"What's the matter with him?" Rowley had a quake in his voice.

"His heart's doing the Salsa." The vet's half-hearted attempt at lightening the mood failed. "Nothing life threatening but he'll need a fair bit of rest. That bleeding wasn't a normal blood vessel. Something's gone wrong down inside. Hence the staggering gait"

"Oh." Rowley looked at Tom.

"Don't blame the trainer!" The vet said hastily. "Horses are like us, they can have all sorts of things wrong with them and we don't know until something triggers if off."

He straightened and shook Tom's hand.

"Bloody shame Tom. That was a good race."

Tom escorted him away and when he returned found a glum Rowley sitting on an upturned bucket.

"So that's it." His voice was flat. "No more races for Sparky."

"Now don't be hasty." Tom looked into the stable at the horse. "Let Mike have a look at him first."

"No need. "Rowley got to his feet. "You know as well as I do that was a bad one. His racing days are over."

"Well, we'll have Mike look at him anyway." Tom rubbed his eyes. "What will you do with him if he can't race? I don't know if the insurance company would agree to paying out to destroy him."

"Oh, I'd never do that!" Rowley looked horrified. "No, he can come home with me. I'll have him."

"Really?" Tom looked surprised. "That's very kind of you Rowley. What will you do with him?"

"Let him mow the grass. I don't know if he calms down enough when he's not in training he might make someone a riding horse. I've enough space to try."

"Very good." Tom shook the man's outstretched hand.

"I'll call you in the morning then." He said. "Oh, and Tom, do one thing for me, will you?"

"What's that Rowley?"

"Make bloody sure you buy that horse for us on Tuesday."

As Kitty and Ryan were loading the trunks into the horsebox sometime later, a figure came running across the lorry park towards them, long blonde hair flying out behind him.

"Jesus." Ryan opened his eyes wide. "He looks more like a girl than you Kit!"

"Shut up Ryan and finish what you're doing." Tom snapped.

"How's the horse?" Rick was out of breath.

"Retired." Said Tom shortly. "Permanently. As least it looks that way."

"Hell. What a shame." Rick was watching Kitty bending over to pick up a bucket. She really was a good-looking girl.

"Time for a drink?" Tom looked at the same thing.

"Yeah sure." Rick nodded. "A quick one."

"A quick one it is then." Tom turned to Ryan. "I'll see you back at the yard Ryan. Take care."

As the two men walked away Ryan took another look at the long hair and shook his head in disbelief

"Amazing." He said. "Still, he'll be handy to have around at Christmas."

"Why?" Gareth popped his head out of the horsebox.

"To put on top of the Christmas tree."

CHAPTER FOUR

The wind howled through the trees whistling around the sale ring like a tornado. Pulling his heavy fleece jacket tightly around his shoulders, Tom cursed the racing institution that was Ascot sales. In the summer he enjoyed the activity, the excitement of looking for new stock. But on a cold, windy, October day, when he had thirty horses at home and a million and one things to do, he wished himself miles away. Having wandered without interest around the stables, all he could do now was wait for the appearance of lot number thirty-five. The number board glowed green in the gloom; sixteen. What a way to spend a Tuesday morning. Martin appeared with a coffee in each hand.

"What a rip off!" He winced as the hot liquid spilled onto his fingers. "I've never seen such prices!"

"Ridiculous." Tom eyed his change dismally. "Well, they won't make their fortunes out of the entries that's for sure. The last lot didn't make eight hundred."

Martin narrowed his eyes at the leggy grey that was being led into the ring. Already past its peak fitness it wandered, tired and listless, behind its handler, eyes full of dejection and misery.

"What's this?" Martin peered at Tom's catalogue. "Looks like a riding school reject."

"It's a Jack Coltrane reject. Six runs already, tailed off every time. Lucky if it makes the minimum bid, it's got legs like coat hangers."

Everyone else around the ring had the same opinion and as Tom had predicted the horse struggled to make five hundred guineas. Tom bored and tired wondered if it was possible to sleep on the plastic seats. He had made the mistake of spending the previous night with Flick, with the inevitable results. A blonde, long-haired man was heading towards them. He looked very familiar.

"It's Rick Cowdrey." Martin moved over to make room.

"Is it?" Tom blinked and tried to focus his tired eyes.

"Hi." Rick bounced onto the seat beside him. "Your British weather is sure living up to its reputation."

Tom studied the young man out of the corner of his eye, watching the confident way he lounged in his seat. A red baseball cap was pulled down over Rick's eyes, there were rips in his faded blue denim jeans and his leather jacket had certainly seen better days. Amongst the tweed coats and waxed jackets, he looked completely out of place.

"So" With great effort Tom sat upright in his chair. "What brings you here?"

"Oh, that guy Harris called. Said you were buying a horse for them. So, I thought I might look"

"Well, I think he's being a little hopeful when he says buying." Tom said wryly. "Most of the people here today are here because of that one horse. Let's face it there's not a lot else to look at."

"Oh, I don't know." Rick popped a chewing gum into his mouth. "Some of the stable girls deserve a second viewing."

Tom shook his head at the offered packet and studied the pretty brunette leading the current lot around the ring. Rick might be right.

"There is one nice little horse." Rick was also watching the brunette. "Right out the back."

"Really." Tom closed his eyes. "Which one was that?"

"Here." Rick gave him a prod with his catalogue. "This one. Lot ninety-eight."

Tom opened one bloodshot eye and glanced at the page. It described a seven-year-old chestnut mare who had won three point to point races the previous spring.

"Hmm." Tom was non-committal. "Plenty of people here looking for Hunter Chasers and point to pointers. She'll be snapped up."

"I see you didn't notice who the dam was?" Rick grinned. "Try opening both eyes this time."

Sighing heavily Tom looked again. The mare's dam was a horse called Out of Time, and a list of her offspring ran down the page, all of whom had very decent form. He stopped reading when he came to the name 'First Venture', who had won, amongst others, the Hennessey and Whitbread gold cups. passing the catalogue back to Rick, he gave him a nod,

"Well spotted. It says this horse, the one that's for sale, is homebred. Wonder how they got hold of that broodmare. She wouldn't have been cheap. Or do they look filthy rich?"

"No." Rick laughed. "They don't look a bit like you! They got her dirt cheap because the stud couldn't get her in foal, thought she was too old. These guys knew someone who'd just imported a young colt from New Zealand. They thought they'd try their luck, and, of course, like any true blooded Kiwi male he was rampantly fertile and one year later out pops one chestnut filly."

"You're very well informed," Commented Tom sarcastically

"Very pretty little stable girl, offered her a gum and she was putty in my hands. Fancy a look?"

"At the girl?"

"At the horse!"

"I suppose it will help pass the time." Tom got stiffly to his feet. "Lead on."

The horse was a dark chestnut, small, pretty, and highly strung. Despite her diminutive size she had a chest like a Hereford bull. As Tom entered the box, she swung her teeth at him with a mean glare.

"Chestnut mares!" He laughed. "My father told me to avoid them like the plague!"

Rick grinned.

"Look at the depth of that girth. She'll stay forever."

"Have you got shares in this horse? Why are you so keen?"

"I thought you could do with a horse to replace the one you lost. Another talented youngster."

"Crop's owners don't want another horse."

"They might not but what about you?"

Tom shook his head.

"I'm no owner, and I'm not in the market for random investments at the moment."

"She'll be cheap." Rick persisted "And you'll sell her at a good profit."

"What's the catch." Tom was beginning to smell a rat.

"Me." Rick grinned. "My father wants to buy a horse, I'd be your sort of partner, on his behalf."

Tom frowned at the young man lounging casually in the doorway, kicking straw with his sneakered foot. He looked more like a rock star than a jockey. He turned his eyes back to the mare. He could always sell his half to the Bowles' brothers if he failed to get them Olympic Run. He thought of the talent he had lost that season already and knew he needed to improve his string.

"Only if she makes less than fifteen grand." He nodded.

Rick grinned, flashing perfect white teeth.

"Deal!"

By the time Olympic Run swaggered into the sale ring with his long, swinging stride, Tom and Rick were completely absorbed in a game on Rick's phone. With the sound turned off they were trying to manoeuvre a monkey and pick bananas off a tree. Martin, who found it all unbelievably childish, was conscientiously marking off the prices in the catalogue; the one time he left them to go and have a pee, they had become distracted by the appearance of a coconut and missed two horses. But once the big bay horse was in the ring the monkey was swiftly forgotten. Feeling his heart beginning to pump faster Tom's stomach tied itself up in knots as the auctioneer rambled through the description.

"Oh, get on with it!" Tom shifted in his seat.

As he had predicted most of the now packed ring were here because of the horse in front of them. Cagey at first, they started the bidding at an incredibly low ten thousand. Slowly the bidding warmed up. Feeling sweat breaking out on the palms of his hands Tom played his waiting game until the last minute.

"Seventeen thousand?" The auctioneer was incredulous. "We can't be all done at seven thousand?"

Up went Tom's catalogue.

"Eighteen." The auctioneer sighed with relief. "I have a new bidder at eighteen thousand."

Numerous eyes scanned the rows of seats to see who this new person was. Tom sat back in his seat and waited. Each time he felt sure he would have the horse someone topped his bid. The price started to escalate quickly. Beside him Rick had stopped chewing gum and was sitting with his mouth open. When the bidding reached eighty-five thousand Martin began to feel sick. When it reached eighty-seven it began to slow. The auctioneer looked at Tom.

"Bids against you Sir. eighty-eight if you're bidding"

Tom hesitated.

"Don't lose him for a thousand Sir." The auctioneer's voice was calm and persuasive. It was as though he were discussing pennies not thousands of guineas.

"I know you want this horse Sir. One more bid and he could be yours."

Or he could not, thought Tom. He had reached the Bowles' brother's limit. If this last bid didn't buy him then the best chance, he would have of getting into top class races that season would be gone. Inside his coat pocket he crossed his fingers, the pulse in his throat was threatening to choke him.

He nodded.

"Eighty-eight." the auctioneer smiled, then paused, eyes searching the crowd for more bids. After a long, tortuous minute he raised his hammer. "Going once. Twice." A pause, and the hammer fell.

"Sold." The auctioneer was elated. "Mr. Chichester."

"I need a drink." Tom got to his feet.

"Hey what about our horse?" Rick caught his arm.

"You bid." No more than fifteen, remember. On second thoughts make it twelve, I might not be able to squeeze the extra three grand out of Rowley."

He left the now applauding crowd and went out into the fresh air.

Martin stood at the foot of the ramp, a lead rope in each hand. Tom reached out to him.

"Give one to me." He took the chestnut mare and led her into the horsebox. Then jumping off the ramp he patted Martin's shoulders.

"Take care on the way home Martin. I'll see you at the yard, I'm going into town with Rick for dinner."

"Okay Guv." Martin climbed wearily into the cab and started the engine. He was tired, and it was going to be a long journey. Rubbing his eyes, he thought of his precious cargo in the back. He liked this big horse; he was the sort of animal old William would have loved, a true-blue steeplechaser. Already daydreaming, shaping his own ambitions for his latest charge, he began the lonely drive home.

By eight thirty Tom was regretting his decision. Too much Whisky was affecting his brain. There was no possible way he could drive home in this state. He would have to try and sober up, quickly. Rick on the other hand was drinking like the proverbial fish.

"One advantage of being a skinny little runt." He grinned. "I don't have to be so careful of my weight."

"Not even when you're eating like this?" Tom eyed the mountain of Chinese food in front of him.

"No problem. I'm not riding until Thursday. I'll work of a bit by then. Once my career takes off properly, I'll have to be a bit more careful, but right now it's no problem."

"How do you get it off?" Tom had never been able to keep his weight down.

"Sex." Rick piled his Chop Suey into his bowl and crammed some into his mouth. "Lots of it."

"Oh." Tom speared a King Prawn with his fork and studied it. "Is it any good?"

"Depends on who you do it with!" Rick laughed. "But yes, it does get the pounds off."

"I'll have to try it." Tom fingered his waistband. "Too much food and not enough exercise."

"Not the sociable kind, are you? At least that's what I've been told" Rick gnawed on a spare rib and watched his companion's reaction.

"Who told you that?" Tom's brow creased into a frown.

"Your brother." Rick picked up another rib. "I was at a party with him last night. What a guy! He is the original party animal."

Tom said nothing, stirring his noodles in morose silence.

"He doesn't like you much." Rick couldn't help prying. "At least, that's the impression he gives."

"The feeling is completely mutual." No longer interested in his food, Tom pushed his plate to one side.

Rick saw the raw nerve he had exposed and wondered whether it would be wise to change his topic of conversation. Unfortunately, he had drunk just enough beer to blunt his sense of discretion.

"I gather, that Dominic is the black sheep of the family?"

"No. Not exactly." Tom eyed him coldly.

Rick shifted uneasily under the steely gaze.

"Not a black sheep. That's an insult to the animals. A slug, maybe? A worm. Or maybe he is just a perverted mindless arrogant fucking bastard."

Rick whistled.

"What did he do to earn such high praise?"

"Nothing that you need to know about!" Tom didn't intend to snap as did. Taking a deep breath, he looked around the room. it was beginning to fill rapidly. He was rather alarmed to find his vision blurring. Feeling very far away from home he rubbed his hand through his hair and yawned. Rick raised his glass.

"All right I give in. Subject closed. I'm sorry, okay?"

Tom drained his glass and gave a wry smile. He couldn't help liking the younger man. A case of total opposites attracting.

"Rick! Darling!" A girlish shriek pierced the air and Rick disappeared into a mass of black suede. The girl into whose arms he vanished was a tall, elfin face creature with cropped black hair. She had an androgynous figure clad in a black strapless trouser suit that fitted her like a second skin. Behind her was a girl of equally striking appearance; far more curvaceous than her companion she had a mass of chestnut hair that curled across one eye and emerald green eyes that twinkled in her pale face. She wore a dark, ivy coloured dress, golden shoulders rising from the dropped neckline, cleavage plunging deep. Tom got hastily to his feet and pulled up a chair.

"I can see we aren't going to be introduced." He smiled. "I'm Tom Chichester."

"Megan." The girl had a lilting Irish brogue, husky; it sent shivers down Tom's spine. As she sat, a silken arm brushed his for a second and it was like an electric current against his skin.

"Would you like a drink, Megan?"

"Thank you." Her eyes lingered on his face. "A brandy would be very nice."

Trying not to stagger, Tom made his way to the bar. Staring at his reflection in the mirror, he hardly recognised himself. Tugging at his unruly hair he squinted at his bloodshot eyes and scowled in disgust. It was hardly an attractive picture. Weaving his way back to the table he found, to his surprise, that the others were already getting ready to leave.

"Come on T.C.," Shouted Rick. "Back to my place. Well hotel anyway."

It seemed a shame to waste two full glasses of brandy, so Tom sank them both. Much to his immediate regret when he stepped outside, and the fresh air hit him like a wall. Hailing a cab Rick pushed the two girls in and pulled a dazed Tom after them.

Watery November sun filtered weakly through the curtains and woke him. Reluctant to open his eyes Tom pulled the quilt back over his head, vaguely aware of a figure standing beside the bed. Opening one eye he peered out of his cocoon and stared without recognition at the girl beside him. Reaching out a hand he touched her stomach to make sure that her golden skinned beauty was real.

"Good morning." Megan bent over him. "And how do you feel this morning?"

Tom rubbed his eyes and took in her glorious, stark-naked body.

"I'm not sure." He was trying to retrace his movements of the night before without much luck. Who was she? Worse, where was he?

"Can I get you anything?" Megan sat before him and slid her hand under the duvet. Tom stared at her, and then politely pushed her hand away. Any animal magnetism she had held over him the night before had gone, washed away by the light of morning.

"I'm sorry. I have to get going."

She looked disappointed.

"Are you sure?" She pouted.

If Megan's intention had been to entice him to stay in bed with her, then the look that she gave him was the worst possible thing she could have done. Eyes wide, hair across her face, lower lip full and petulant she reminded him of Kitty. He took a deep breath and closed his eyes.

"I'm sure." He mumbled. "I should never have come here."

Megan stayed where she was, watching him dress. Even in his hungover state he was a handsome man and she tried desperately to think of something, anything that would make him stay. Tom opened the bedroom door and gave a little smile.

"Well goodbye." He said, trying to be casual. "It was nice meeting you."

Ignoring her pleading eyes, he closed the door and walked out of the room. Even then, he still could not remember her name.

"This is absolutely bloody ridiculous!"

Martin stood in the middle of the yard staring intermittently at the drive and his watch.

"It's bloody lunchtime! We've got two new horses, three

runners tomorrow and the useless sod has disappeared!"

"Calm down Marty." Poppy patted his shoulder. "He'll be here soon."

"Yeah." Ryan came out of the office. "As long as he keeps paying the wages."

"But it isn't like him, lately." Gareth paused in his sweeping. "He's always been so fussy about everything."

"I think." Ryan pointed to a small pile of shavings that Gareth had missed. "That he's afraid he's losing his touch."

"No bloody excuse." Martin fumed. "Going off and getting pissed up never changed anyone's luck!"

"Oh, come on!" Poppy pulled his arm. "Let's have lunch."

Bowls of steaming soup lined the table which was centred with a huge mound of ham sandwiches.

"Good old Mrs B." Gareth didn't know which to eat first. "She's the only reliable one here."

"Thanks very much Taff." Poppy sat beside him. "It's so nice to be appreciated."

A small brown horsebox was pulling into the yard.

"Who the hell is this?" Martin stuck his head out of the window. "Oh shit. It's Lady Ainsley."

"On parade troops!" Kitty's head appeared in the doorway. "The lunatic lady is here."

Lady Margaret Florence Elizabeth Ainsley was a small, neat, extremely efficient woman in her late sixties. She wore tweeds and drove a battered Morris Minor; a fully paid-up member of the twin set and pearls brigade she had been prematurely widowed some ten years ago. Her late husband, an ex-major in the household cavalry had been a pillar of the local community whose all abiding passion was horse racing. After his death Margaret had taken charge of maintaining his string of racehorses. She soon found herself completely and utterly hooked.

"Good afternoon you lot!" She boomed. "Chichester

around?"

"Hello Lady Ainsley." Martin shook her hand. "I'm afraid that Mr Chichester is out on business. Was he expecting you?"

"Hell no.!" The grey eyes twinkled in the weather-beaten face. "Keep them on their toes lad! What kind of business would that be?"

"Wouldn't know." Martin grinned. "What have you brought us? A Lama?"

"Cheeky boy." Margaret watched her groom lowering the ramp. "I bred this one myself."

Martin watched with interest as the groom led a small bay horse out of the horsebox. Barely sixteen hands his Arab ancestry was plain to see. A tiny, dished face stood on the end of a long, crested neck. Pricking his little half-moon ears, he surveyed his new surroundings with almost superior interest.

"Little Raver." Margaret was glowing with pride. "Bluest blood of the turf in that little horse. He's the reason they invented that saying about quality being in small packages."

Martin ran an expert hand down the solid neck and felt the sturdy legs. Cold as iron and twice as strong. Patting the horses neck he smiled at the little woman beside him.

"He's in good nick."

"Fit for anything." Margaret beamed up at him. "I don't know why I bother with trainers."

"Neither do I." Martin took her arm. "Believe me neither do I."

Sending Poppy as escort he despatched Margaret to the house and her groom to Mrs. Benson for tea. This gave him a chance to find a suitable home for the new arrival.

"Put Micky Mouse out in the field Kit." He shouted. "Little Bugger or whatever his name is can have his box until we bed down another one."

Strolling to the field with the little cob jogging beside her Kitty saw a familiar blue car coming slowly down the drive. It halted beside her as she struggled with the catch on the field gate.

"Morning Kitty. What are you doing with my horse?"

For a moment she was speechless. Even her biased mind had to admit that her idol looked awful. Bloodshot eyes, no bigger than a pigs, peered out at her from a shadowed face. His stubble made his skin look dark, almost dirty. Even from this distance she could smell the stale alcohol on his breath. Curling up her nose she looked away.

"Lady Ainsley is in the yard." She spoke over her shoulder. " Well actually she's on her way to the house with Poppy. Her horse has arrived, so we've had to put Micky out while we get a box ready for him."

"Oh Lord." Tom studied his reflection in his rear-view mirror and reacted in the same way as Kitty. "Gone to the house you say?"

"I'm afraid so Sir." Kitty could sense his embarrassment.

"Hell. Oh well I suppose I'll just have to face her like this."

"You could always use the cottage." Kitty paused, she couldn't blatantly tell him to go and wash.

"And what?" He grinned meekly. "Wash, shave? Thank you, Kitty, I'll do just that."

Ten minutes later he emerged out of the small front door looking more human and smelling of soap and toothpaste instead of whisky and sex. Striding across the yard, he gave the newcomer the once over and then headed for the house.

"Will you look at that!" Martin seethed. "Off to chat up the Lunatic Lady as if nothing's wrong. Acting like the Lord of the bloody Manor!"

"You're forgetting something Mart." Poppy chuckled. "He is!"

Eleanor, who had given up on excusing her son's absence was making lunch and catching up on the gossip. Margaret was helping herself to Tom's whisky.

"Aha!" She beamed as Tom edged through the door. "Lady friend let you go at last has she?"

"I've no idea what you mean Margaret." Tom helped himself to a fresh scone. "That horse of yours is looking well."

"As well as any of yours I'll wager." The grey eyes sparkled merrily. "Probably better."

Tom ate another scone

"So" He wiped a blob of cream off his lip. "What's the plan Margie?"

"The Welsh Grand National first. Then I fancy a crack at the real thing."

"Are we talking all in one season? Or shall we give the opposition a chance?"

"No way! " A smile spread across the ruddy face. "Life's too short for that!"

Tom smiled.

"We'll see."

"That's a nice horse you bought yesterday dear." His mother passed him another scone. "That little mare."

"What little mare?" Tom raised his eyebrows.

"The one you bought with Rick. For his father."

Good God, thought Tom, I'd forgotten all about her! Not taking too long a farewell of Margaret he hurried back to the yard. It was time to take a firmer grip on the reins.

Rowley Harris and Mike Peterson chatted with eager anticipation as the long, red, Jaguar purred through the lanes. The terrible wind had abated slightly, but the clouds that sat on top of the hills were dark and menacing. The yellow stone houses were made dark and gloomy by the recent rain, their normally picturesque gardens tattered and beaten by the storms.

"I hope to God this horse holds out okay." Rowley had butterflies in his stomach. "My bank manager wasn't over impressed."

"My wife's my problem." Mike swung the car around a tight bend. "Is that Cowdrey fellow coming out to ride him?"

"I think so. But Tom did say that he had a bad fall at Worcester yesterday."

"From one of Tom's?" Mike slowed down as they passed through a puddle that covered the entire road.

"No, Some Lambourn yard. Not a lot of form this year."

"Well, I hate to say this." Mike winced as muddy water sprayed over his windows, "But Tom isn't exactly running away with the trainer's championship, is he?"

From the foot of the valley, they could see the string winding their way up the hill onto the gallops. On the south facing slope, to the right of them, was the sprawling beauty of Highford House. The stone horses that proudly guarded the gateposts were strewn with leaves, their grey manes chestnut with the lingering colours of Autumn. Knowing the way well, Mike took the short cut that bypassed the yard and followed the private road to the gallops. At the bottom of the long, steadily climbing all weather strip the horses were circling. Parallel to the all-weather were the schooling fences, alongside which the familiar cob was waiting. Mike's car scrunched to a halt behind it.

"Good Morning gentlemen." Micky's nose almost came through the window. "Hold onto your hats, this wind hasn't finished with us yet!"

"Cowdrey on top?" Mike pulled his cloth cap down tightly over his eyes.

"He is. He's going to come over the schooling fences and

then give him a little blow on the grass gallop. I just want Rick to get the feel of him."

Waving to Martin, who stood in the middle of the circling horses, Tom called Rick out of the group. Jogging to the foot of the fences, the big bay horse cocked his ears forward and sprang into action. Steadying him, Rick crouched low over the horse's withers and waited. With an effortless thrust of his quarters Olympic Run cruised over the three flights and powered his way on up the gallop. At its head, Rick pulled up and began to canter quietly back down. Gritting his teeth against the pain in his left shoulder he managed a smile of greeting.

"Blow away the cobwebs?" Tom was itching to cheer and acclaim his new charges brilliance.

"Sure did." Rick nodded to his audience. "How did you like him?"

Rowley was speechless with admiration, but Mike was more cynical.

"I'll tell you how much I like him when he wins his first race for us."

Rick pulled a face and took up his reins. He turned to Tom.

"Shall I bring the little mare up?"

"Go ahead." Tom smiled, "As long as you feel up to it."

Two minutes later the chestnut mare, like a coiled spring about to release, bounced away from the string. Leaping through the air like a gazelle she bounded towards the first fence. Too fast, head held too high, she carted Rick into the bottom of the jump; then, at the very last moment she checked herself and soared through the air. Without breaking stride in her runaway gallop, she negotiated the next two obstacles in a similar fashion and accelerated away up the gallop.

"Jesus!" Martin's jaw dropped." What's she sired by? Concorde?"

Not wanting a downward charge at the same speed, Rick dismounted and walked back.

"Who does that belong to?" Mike was impressed by that performance.

"Mine." Tom was grinning like a Cheshire cat.

"I'll pay you twice what you gave for her!"

"Don't be so keen Mike!" Tom laughed. "She also belongs to Rick's father. I can't see Rick wanting him to part with his investment after that little display!"

It was debatable who was the hotter, Rick or the mare.

"What's she called?" Rowley patted the steaming neck as Rick halted beside them.

"Swingtime. The girls have nicknamed her Streak."

"No need to ask why! Who's that?" Rowley pointed to a small bay horse who was mechanically popping over the fences with the precision of a clockwork toy.

"That's Lady Ainsley's horse. Goes well. A real gent."

"Bit slow." Mike got back into the Jag as Gareth and Raver cantered past them. "I take it I get a drink for freezing my balls off?"

"Of course." Tom smiled courteously. "I'll meet you at the house."

"Well." Rick watched the car glide slowly away. "Stunning auto. Shame about the prick at the wheel!"

"You said it." Tom kicked Micky into a walk.

"I don't know how you do it." Rick was waiting for Martin to leg him up. "Thank Christ I'm not a trainer!"

"I thought wining and dining was what you did best?" Tom held the little cob back to wait for him.

"Riding's what I do best!" Rick laughed. "And you can interpret that anyway you like!"

Tom laughed

"How is, what's her name? Emmie?"

"She's good." Rick steered the mare closer to Micky and lowered his voice. "A certain stunning young Irish lady has been asking after you. Why didn't you call her?"

"Who? Oh! Her." Tom could feel his colour rising. "Too busy."

"Well, she been getting really frustrated over you. You really hooked that one. Christ she's pretty."

"If you're that interested then take her out yourself. Now don't try and tell me that you're a one-woman man!" Tom chuckled.

" Not Meg! Her!" Rick pointed to a swinging blonde ponytail ahead of them. "I don't know how you get any work done with her around!"

"Kitty!" Tom raised his eyebrows. "She's only a child."

He looked away from Rick and stared at the road, terrified that his eyes would give him away.

"I guess that she's the same age as Meg. I mean she's no more than nineteen surely?"

"What?" Tom raised his voice against the rising wind.

"I said," Rick shouted back, "That Meg is only nineteen."

"Jesus!" Tom was horrified. "I'm old enough to be her father!"

"But not to act like it!" Rick laughed at the look on Tom's face. "Pull yourself together man, you aren't that old."

"Nineteen." Moaned Tom. "God, I thought she was lot older than that. Well," He corrected, "I think I thought that she was older than that. If I'm honest I can't really remember."

Rick was thoroughly enjoying himself.

"Don't give yourself any grey hairs about it. Meg's a woman of the world. You grow up fast with five brothers and an alcoholic father who beats the crap out of you. Meg got sick of it and took off to make a life for herself. Ended up penniless in London. In that situation you get your money where you can."

"She's a prostitute!" Tom was beginning to feel sick.

"No!" Rick laughed. "To be honest Meg was working as a pole dancer when Em met her, got in with the wrong crowd. But Em got her work as a model. She'll make it big; you wait and see."

Tim scowled.

"Don't look so sour." Rick was surprised at his reaction. "A lot of men would love to have been in your shoes."

"They're welcome to them." Tom shook his head. "If I want to be a dirty old man there's always Kitty!"

"Now there's a thought." Rick grinned broadly. "That one would be worth doing time for!"

Tom didn't reply but rode on in grim silence. Finding no more conversation forthcoming Rick manoeuvred himself alongside Kitty and turned his attention to her instead.

"You lucky sod!" Poppy's voice rang across the tack shed. "He's gorgeous! A party! What are you going to wear?"

"I'm not going." Kitty hadn't been anywhere since that dreadful night she was still trying hard to forget. The thought of being alone with a man still terrified her.

"But you must! I mean he's stunning, you must go!"

"Is he?" Kitty was turning red. "The last man you were this keen on didn't turn out that pleasant to be with, did he?"

Poppy blushed.

"Rick's different Kit. He's lovely. And it'll get you out again. Anyway, it's your Sunday off so there's no excuse. I'll even drop you off in Marty's car. Hey." She called. "Marty. Can I borrow the banger on Saturday night?"

"What for?"

"To drop Kitty off. She's going on a date with Mr

Cowdrey."

"No way." Martin shook his head. "If she goes out with him, I'll never speak to her again. He's a bloody weirdo!"

In the office next door Tom heard the conversation. Staring at the kettle, which was sending steam all over the place, he felt his stomach twisting. He thought briefly of warning Rick off, hating the thought of him having Kitty all to himself. Sitting weakly down in his chair he shook his head. This was becoming an obsession. He had to get this girl out of his head before she took over his life.

CHAPTER FIVE

Poppy turned off the engine and eyed her silent, pensive companion with satisfaction.

"Well Kitty Kat. You look great."

"Huh." Kitty tugged ineffectually at the hem line of Poppy's red dress which was clinging to her thighs. Her nails, painted the same scarlet as the dress, were catching in her tights, threatening to ladder them. Her blonde hair, after an hour of attention from Poppy and her tongs, was a snaking, spiralling mass falling over one eye.

"I feel like a tart." She pouted her red lips.

"Good." Poppy leaned across and opened the door. "Just make sure you behave like one. I've worked hard turning you out tonight, and would I love to be in your shoes!"

"They are your shoes." Standing upright Kitty winced and pulled at the dress again. "And, just like your dress, they feel too tight!"

"Stop moaning." Poppy looked around the car park. "Where is he then?"

A look of relief spread across Kitty's face.

"He's not here."

"He must be!" Poppy wailed. "I burnt three fingers doing that hair!"

A throaty roar disturbed the evening quiet, and a low sporty silver car sped into the car park.

"Porsche." Said Poppy happily. "Guess who!"

Rick was out of the car almost before it stopped. With a bold grin on his face, he walked towards them. Head to toe in black; dinner suit, silk shirt, Gucci shoes, he wore his hear tied back to show off his strong jaw and a diamond glinted in his left ear.

"I'm gone." Poppy sighed. "See you, you lucky bitch!"

Blaring the horn at Rick she started the little car and drove away, looking wistfully in the mirror at the broad-shouldered figure behind her. Knees trembling, Kitty pulled her black scarf over her shoulders and moved warily forward.

"Hi you." Rick brushed her cheek with his lips. "You look good."

Wary eyes stared into his bold ones. A smile touched the corners of his wide, sensual mouth.

"Come on Cinderella," he said quietly. "This way to the ball."

Rick drove his Porsche with the same confident attack that he employed on the racecourse. Transferring his love of speed from turf to tarmac he headed for the motorway, engine screaming in delight as he pressed the throttle flat to the floor. Kitty sank into the cool leather and stared out of the window. Tense, unsure of herself, she was too afraid to speak. Being alone with him terrified her.

"Speak to me babe!" Rick pleaded. "Long way to go yet."

"Where," Kitty's voice came out as a barely audible croak, "Where are we going?"

"Chelsea." Rick overtook an articulated lorry with the speedometer of the Porsche touching a hundred and ten. "You'll love it."

"Will I?" Kitty wasn't so sure.

"Trust me." Rick turned on the stereo and reaching into the glove compartment pulled out a half bottle of Vodka.

"Here." He passed the bottle to Kitty. "Get some party spirit down you."

When Rick finally pulled into the small, cobbled mews the bottle was half empty. The courtyard was in darkness, except for the farthest house of all which poured light and music from every window. The volume became almost deafening as the door opened and an extremely glamorous woman in her mid-thirties greeted them.

"Hello darling." She had a mass of sleek black hair that she threw back as she emerged from Rick's embrace. She eyed Kitty over his shoulder.

"You are a dark horse, where have you been hiding this little beauty?"

"This is Kitty." Rick laid his hand lightly on Kitty's waist "Kit. Meet our hostess, Camille."

"Hello." Kitty stared with trepidation into the seething mass of people that filled the house. They milled to and fro across the hall, glasses in hand, leaving scent and smoke on the air as they passed.

"Go and get yourselves drinks. Oh!" Camille was quickly diverted by more arrivals. "Hello!"

As soon as they stepped past her into the hallway they were enveloped by a wave of hot bodies. Catching Kitty's arm to keep her close to him Rick felt her tighten at his touch. He smiled to himself; she was nervous, a good sign. But when they were jostled by the crowd, and he shifted his grip to her shoulders she darted away and crashed into an ornamental table.

"What's wrong with you?" He frowned at her.

"Nothing." Her voice was high, tight, "I'm just a bit out of my depth."

"Here." Rick snatched two glasses of champagne from a passing tray. "Calm those nerves."

Kitty took a large gulp and desperately hoped that the sweet bubbling liquid would untie the knot in her stomach. Despite all the Vodka she had drunk she was still tense. It wasn't the place, or the crowded rooms full of strangers, it was the strong, warm contact of Rick's hand on her back. It shot a current through her, an electric charge, setting her nerves on edge, twitching, and jumping at every move. Draining her glass, she switched it for another as the tray was passed through the room again. Rick smiled, nodded to the young boy with the ever-full tray and took two more. As the third dose hit her stomach Kitty at last felt herself begin to relax. The alcohol was kicking in now, and unconsciously she stepped closer to Rick. Feeling her brush against him he cautiously took a firmer hold of her waist. To his relief she smiled at him.

"More?" He offered another glass.

"Thanks." Kitty drank this one more slowly, looking about her and taking in her surroundings. Everyone was very well dressed, and very drunk, and from the pungent aroma on the air some were more than just drunk. There seemed to be a focus of activity at the opposite side of the room where a group of people were gathered around something. Howls of laughter kept erupting from this corner. Standing on tip toe she craned her neck to see what the cause of all the hilarity was. She made out a tall figure, dark haired, with its back to her and as she peered through the mass of people it turned. She saw the profile, the familiar shape of his head, and felt bile rise from her stomach into her mouth.

Across the room, eyes hidden from her by his dark glasses, was Dominic Chichester.

The shock of seeing him again cut her like a knife. Trying to suppress her instinct to run and hide she stepped back and hid behind Rick. It was impossible that he could have seen her in this crowd, but the knowledge of his presence was enough. It sickened her, and she looked to the door, thinking, for a second, that she would be able to escape without being noticed. She was about to creep away when Rick's voice made her jump.

"Kitty?" Rick could feel this new tension in her, his palm detecting the tremors that were running across her skin. "Kitty?"

Getting no response, he caught hold of her chin and turned her to face to him. Her wide, terrified eyes stared over his shoulder.

"What the hell is wrong with you?" He gave her a little shake.

She looked at him, cornered, afraid, a hunted animal with nowhere to hide. He could barely hear her reply.

"I'm so sorry Rick. I must go. I can't stay here."

"Why? Are you ill?" Rick looked back over his shoulder and followed the direction of her stare. He saw the group of people at the fireplace and recognised the unmistakable figure of his friend.

"Come on." He took hold of her hand. "There's someone you have to meet."

Shaking her head Kitty pulled away. Then, with a stab of horror she saw Dominic looking in their direction.

"No." She stopped dead. "I can't. I need some air, I feel sick."

Turning away, snatching her hand from Rick's, she darted through the crowd towards the door. Unnerved by the panic in her voice Rick pushed his way after her. Catching her arm, he pulled her to a walk.

"Okay. let's go get some air. Just slow down, okay?"

Taking her cold, damp hand in his he led her outside.

The icy air hit Kitty's reeling head and helped to calm her racing brain. But she still didn't stop walking until she and Rick were completely hidden from the house by shadows. Leaning against the stem of a cast iron lamp post that had probably stood over millions of couples before them Rick looked at her, and gently brushed her hair from her face. Tears spilled silently down her cheeks; her skin was icy to his touch. Pulling off his jacket he laid it across her shoulders, noticing once again how she shrank from his touch. The stark look of fear had gone from her eyes now, but she was still rigid with nerves, staring constantly at the house. He was just about to speak when a loud, drawling voice echoed across the courtyard.

"Hey! Cowdrey! What are you up to?"

The voice caused a reaction in Kitty unlike anything Rick had witnessed before. Clutching her stomach, she turned her face to the lamppost and heaved. Face pressed against the cold iron she retched, shoulders heaving. Puzzled, but directed by an instinct he didn't fully understand Rick turned and stood in front of her, putting himself between her and the tall, angular figure that walked up to him. Dominic smiled his slow, lecherous smile and shook his head.

"Tut tut Rick boy. Bit cold for this isn't it?"

"Shut it Dom." Rick grinned back. "Nothing clears an alcoholic head like fresh air. My little friend feels a bit off."

"Oh, yes?" Dominic twisted his head around so that he could see. "And do I know this little friend?"

"Maybe." Rick wasn't moving.

"Oh, come on Rick." Dominic pulled him aside. "You always introduce me to your latest conquests. Oh."

A strange expression flickered across Dominic's face as he saw the blonde hair.

"If that's who I think it is Rick boy I wish you luck. I hope you get more out of the icy little bitch than I did."

Striding away to the house, Dominic couldn't resist one last parting shot over his shoulder.

"If you do thaw her out Rick, use a bed, will you? Can't lower the tone of the neighbourhood by doing it under a streetlight."

Shaking his head, unable to resist a smile, Rick turned back to Kitty. She was sliding down the lamppost, eyes half shut.

"Whoa!" Rick lunged forward. "Don't do this to me Kit. Come on!"

Relief was flooding through Kitty's veins, making her feel weak and breathless. Filling her lungs with air she slowly stood upright, gripping the lamp post to steady herself. Her mascara had run in long black streaks across her face, the red lipstick smudged around her mouth. The beautiful spiral curls were now a tangled mess. Rick smiled. She looked like a classy tramp, or a whore. Cupping her chin in his hand he raised her face to his.

"Now are you going to tell me what this is all about?" His fingers gently wiped the smudged lipstick from her skin.

"No." She but her lip, lowering he eyes.

"I just can't figure out what Dom could have done to make you feel this bad around him. I mean did you two have something going. Did he dump you? Has he hurt you? I know he's got one hell of a temper, but I didn't think hitting women was his style."

"It's nothing. I overreacted." Kitty stammered, desperate to change the subject. "Too much to drink."

Rick raised an eyebrow, not convinced. Kitty rubbed her eyes and looked up at him.

"I just want to go home. Please?"

"Home?" Rick paused and looked back at the house. Then, he looked at his red eyed companion. Going back into the party was not an option. "Well okay. If it's what you want."

"Thank you." Kitty sighed. "So much."

"One thing." Rick caught her hand as she went to move off.

"What?" Kitty eyed him warily.

"Do one little thing for me first?"

"What?"

Rick smiled into the moonlight.

"Kiss me."

"No!" Kitty's eyes widened. "I can't!"

"Well." Rick leaned back against the lamp post. "You're in a for a long wait if you don't."

Kitty looked at him sideways from beneath her knotted hair. His green, tiger's eyes sparkled in the half dark; there was no malice in them, no intention, just sympathy and kindness. He smiled again and his teeth were pearly white against his shadowed face.

"Come on." The face was getting closer. "Just one."

He laid his hand, surprisingly smooth, against her cheek.

"Close your eyes." He murmured. "Close your eyes and make a wish."

Shaking, but hypnotised, Kitty lowered her eyelids and braced herself. The first touch of his lips made her tense; then, as he gently brushed his mouth over hers, she began to relax. There was none of the terrifying urgency, no brute force, none of the raw animal lust she dreaded.

Rick moved away and instinctively she followed him.

Smiling to himself Rick felt her beginning to respond, slowly, to his gentle touch. Then laying a finger over her mouth he backed away. Enough was enough. He was over the first hurdle. He dismissed from his mind the image of his flat, the red roses on the table, the champagne cooling. It would keep.

"Come on then." He took her hand. "Let's go home."

"I'm sorry." Her eyes were hazy. "I've ruined your evening."

"Not at all. It isn't over yet. Could we at least stop somewhere and eat? I'm starving."

"Okay." She gave a timid nod. "But somewhere quiet, please?"

"I know just the place."

The warmth of the Porsche surrounded Kitty like a security blanket. Totally drained she drifted in and out of sleep. Beside her Rick drummed his fingers on the steering wheel, stealing glances at her as he drove. He had not intended to make this journey again and felt slightly piqued. Changing gear with aggression, he pushed in a CD and let the thumping rock music fill his head. Pushing the Porsche to its limits, he flew up the empty road. Stirring at the increased noise, Kitty opened her eyes and saw his strong, beautiful profile in the dashboard light. His lips were moving as he sang to himself.

"Rick?" She ventured.

"I thought you were asleep." He laid his hand on her knee.

"Not quite. Look I'm sorry. Really, I am."

"Forget it." The hand squeezed. "What went down with you and Dom is not my affair. My problem right now is getting something to eat before I faint at the wheel."

Kitty smiled.

"Don't do that."

"No." Rick glanced at the dashboard clock. "With a bit of luck, we'll just catch this little pizza house I know in Gloucester. We're a little over dressed for a service station."

"Aren't we." Kitty sat more upright. "I hate this dress."

"I don't." Rick's eyes ran quickly over her body. "I like it."

Kitty felt her cheeks growing hot. Rick smiled and ran his hand over his hair. With a bit of luck, he could salvage something from this evening. But not without food.

There were only two other couples at the pizza house when they arrived. The waiters, hoping to have finished for the night, were clearing tables, removing checked tablecloths and terracotta tableware. Smiling at Rick, whom they obviously knew well, they shrugged and regaled him in Italian as they set two new places. Sitting at the most secluded table, Rick leaned back in his chair and studied his companion with undisguised interest. Despite a visit to the ladies, she had made no attempt to replace her washed off make up. He liked that. Emmie was a walking advert for Estee Lauder

"Sorry." He grinned. "It's rude to stare."

"That's okay." Kitty's eyes widened at the sight of the huge Pizza placed in front of her. "I'll never eat all that!"

"I will, and yours too." Rick topped up her wine. "So, Kit, tell me all about yourself."

"Nothing much to tell." Kitty began a little hesitantly.

"My parents live in Scotland, where I was born; but I was brought up in Monmouth, not far from here. We moved back up to the west coast when I was fifteen, but I couldn't settle. When I had just left school, I saw an advert for a job with racehorses. I came here for the summer on trial, and I stayed."

"Long way from home then." Rick was pouring wine again.

"Not as far as you." She shook her head, laying her hand over her glass.

"Home is where the heart is." Rick scratched the nape of his neck and pulled the band from his hair, letting his wavy locks hang over his shoulders. "My heart is here now, I guess. With racing. But I'm a born and bred Kiwi. Hamilton, North Island. I grew up in the Waikato valley, it's like the Newmarket of New Zealand where they breed all the horses. They've always been my life. When I quit school, I bummed around a bit, Australia, the States, did a stint in Ireland. Then I came here to ride point to pointers. I was so hooked on the jumping game that it seemed my only way in. I mean, you don't get too many Kiwi's comings over here to ride do you?"

"Don't know." Kitty had stopped eating. "How old are you?"

"Twenty-four" Rick fought with the mozzarella cheese on his fork. "A bit old to get started really. I was just bloody lucky Tom made me the offer of a job when he did. I was flat broke, couldn't eat like this."

"Poor you." Kitty said thoughtfully. "How come the Porsche then?"

"Things have changed. Got in with the right people. My money works for me now, not the other was around."

"It's strange. You haven't really got an accent, you just sound, well like everyone else!"

"Mm. Must be my nomadic lifestyle."

A shadow fell across the table.

"Good evening." Said a familiar voice. "Do you mind if we join you?"

Kitty froze as she looked up into the very amused eyes of her employer.

"Not at all." Rick, ever cool, looked at the dark-haired beauty on Tom's arm. "But only if you introduce us."

"Felicity Harries, Rick Cowdrey and Kitty Campbell. Will that do? Good. Now can I sit down?"

Kitty was mortified with embarrassment. Pushing her plate away she fiddled with the stem of her glass and sank into a miserable silence. Tom sat opposite, a bemused expression on his face.

"So" He queried. "Where have you two been tonight?"

"Oh, we've been around." Rick narrowed his eyes. "Bumped into your brother."

"What?" Tom glanced at Kitty then quickly composed himself. "How unpleasant for you."

Rick watched him carefully. Not by a flicker, after that first unguarded moment, did Tom betray anything. But Rick felt convinced that there was some big secret here that he was not aware of.

"I think Dominic's an absolute stunner." Flick was feeling left out. "Am I getting a drink Tom?"

"How are the horses?" Rick tactfully changed the subject and looking into the older man's eyes saw the fire of obsession light in them.

"Good." Tom leaned forward, suddenly animated. "All working well. Sent two out today, couple of places, sorry you didn't have the rides, but the connections and the jockey go back a long way.

"Oh, for God's sake!" Flick wailed. "Please don't talk horse!"

"I am sorry." Rick turned his considerable charm onto

her. "Let me get you that drink."

For Kitty the evening began to go rapidly downhill. Rick was soon completely absorbed in Flick, leaving her to face Tom in awkward silence. Desperate to break the ice between them Tom wracked his brain for something to say.

"That's a nice dress." It wasn't the best conversation starter in the world, but the atmosphere was terrible, he had to do something.

"It's Poppy's." Kitty blushed. "Too short. I feel as if I should bend my knees all the time to make it look longer."

He laughed, eyes sparkling, reminding her afresh how handsome he was. He was dressed casually, jeans and a sweater, and his hair was running wild. It suited him. He gave a wry grin and tugged at his wayward locks as he noticed her stare.

"Oh, it's way past my bedtime." He smiled. Looking across to Flick he paused taking in the scene before him. Flick was leaning close to her new companion, looking into his eyes with intensity. Rick was running his finger up and down the inside of her wrist, talking in a low, earnest tone. Tom had seen that look on Flick's face before. Bored, no longer interested in the evening he turned back to Kitty who was watching the same scene with sad eyes.

"I'm going home Katriona, can I offer you a lift?"

"Yes, please." Getting to her feet she fumbled for her bag. "I'll just get my scarf."

As she walked away from the table Rick looked up in surprise.

"Hey, Kit! What's going on?"

"Kitty and I are going home." Tom said dryly. "I'm sure that Felicity can entertain you for the rest of the night." His voice was heavy with sarcasm.

"Good night."

"Kitty!" Rick sprang to his feet. "Kit, wait!"

But she had already left.

"What's the fuss?" Flick ran her hand up his thigh, feeling his strong, well-defined muscles. "So, they've gone. We can still have a good time."

Rick sat back down and squinted at her.

"So, what now.?"

She smiled, the pupils of her eyes dilating as she studied his face.

"What did you most want to do when you left home this evening Rick?"

"Get laid."

He stared at her. Unflinching she met his eyes.

"Then let's get laid."

Outside the fog that had fallen was so thick Tom could barely see the road. Peering through the windscreen he was forced to crawl home at an infuriatingly slow pace. Becoming irrational he thumped at the steering wheel, cursing loudly. Climbing up onto the Cotswolds he nearly ran over a badger shuffling along the verge.

"Oh, this is ridiculous." He pulled onto the grass. "I can't see a bloody thing. My eyes are too tired. I'll have to wait for this thing to lift, or for me to calm down."

Kitty suppressed a giggle.

"What's so funny?" He snapped.

"It's me." She chuckled. "Every time I go out, I have a disastrous evening and you come and rescue me!"

"I don't think that's funny."

"Neither do I." She wiped her eyes. "But if I don't laugh, I might cry. I'm so miserable."

"Don't cry." He begged. "I might join you." He placed his wide, powerful hand on her shoulder.

With an impulse she could never afterwards explain, she leaned over and kissed his cheek. The smell of her warm, scented body reached his nose and stirred his senses. Staring at her, he ran his finger over her flushed cheek, traced the line of her jaw and throat and let his hand fall back to her shoulder. her lips gleamed in the dip light, moist and tempting; he could see the trusting, adoring expression in her eyes. Oh God, he thought, this could be so easy. She was so sweet, and he was so aroused by the proximity of her slender body.

"No." He murmured. "This is wrong."

"Pardon?" She smiled.

It was strange, but with him she felt safe. No trace of the fear that had assailed her with Rick. Only desire. A deep, long hidden desire bred of months of watching and wanting and knowing that only he would really satisfy the feelings that milled inside her. This feeling of safety made her brave, and she laid her hand on his leg, lightly, warily. Tom looked into her eyes and knew that he had lost the battle with his morals. Moving closer he felt her breath on his cheek. It charged his already leaping hormones; and, before he fully realised what he was doing, he had her in his arms, crushing his mouth over hers. His hands ran frantically across her back, her neck, her breasts, and stomach.

"Jesus! What am I doing?" He muttered; his face buried in her hair.

"Don't stop." She was breathing hard, sides rising and falling. "Please don't stop."

More slowly, he kissed her again. It was the single, most exhilarating thing he had ever done in his life. Totally out of control, he began to push her backward into the seat; as he did, the headlights of another car glared into his face. Jerking upright he sat rigid until it passed out of sight; then without speaking he restarted the engine.

"What is it?" Kitty's lip was trembling.

"Me. I'm a disgusting old bastard." He pulled off. "I'm no better than my bloody brother."

"But this is different." Suddenly ashamed Kitty looked away.

"Too bloody right it is. It's bloody impossible, and I should be shot for even thinking about it."

Poppy was stretched out on the sofa reading Horse and Hound and eating chocolate biscuits. A log fire was dying in the hearth and the little room was growing cold. Hearing a car pulling up outside she smiled to herself a peered out through the curtains. To her amazement she saw Kitty getting out of Tom's BMW. Turning hastily back to her magazine, she heard the front door slam.

"Oh, Hi Kit." She tried to sound surprised. "I didn't expect you back so early."

"I didn't expect you to be waiting up for me." Replied Kitty shortly. "And you needn't act so surprised. I saw you looking through the curtains."

"Okay so I'm guilty." Poppy grinned. "So now can I ask?"

"No." Kitty shook her head desperately close to tears.

"But what happened to Rick?" Poppy was bursting with curiosity.

Kitty dropped her bag on the floor and kicked off her shoes. She couldn't remember feeling this low before.

"Oh, come on Kit!" Poppy pleaded. "Please tell me?"

"Thanks for the dress." Kitty went to the door. "I'm going to bed. Good night."

CHAPTER SIX

Gareth leaned against the corn bin and gingerly nursed his throbbing head. Despite spending the whole of Sunday in bed, he still had the most appalling hangover. This, he told himself, was definitely the last time that he got drunk when a horse won. His only memory of Saturday night was lying face down in a ditch at the crossroads. He had never been so ill.

"Morning Taff!" Ryan slapped him on the back. "How are you feeling today?"

"Like death." Gareth turned his face, decidedly green, to Ryan. "Just let me die in peace."

"No chance." Ryan grinned wickedly. "You've got Timepiece in the first lot!"

"Oh my God." Gareth sat on a chair, head in hands. "Please not Timepiece!"

Watching his friend tottering away in search of black coffee and courage, Ryan felt a strong sense of sympathy. Timepiece was a monster of a horse to ride when you felt fit; with a hangover he was a very unpleasant prospect. Turning his attention to the feed bins he began to measure out 'breakfast'. He always did this job on auto pilot, scooping nuts, alfalfa and oats into the feed bowls and adding vitamins and garlic as he went along. Then he stacked three bowls, called out the names of the horses and passed them back to the waiting lads. It was one of Tom's idiosyncrasies that he refused to move into the more widely accepted feeding methods used by most yards. He could never understand how wheeling a barrow full of feed and scooping it into a manger allowed for individual attention. He understood that feeds were designed to be complete, but he could not shift from the method his father had used before him. Each horse was different and was fed according to its needs. So, feed time was a lengthy process at Highford, and it usually fell to Ryans hands to carry out the task. Ryan came back to reality from his daydreams with a jerk as he found himself trying to force Little Raver's feed onto his boss.

"Don't I get milk?" Tom shook his head.

"Oh, sorry Guv." Ryan's face was as red as his hair. "I thought you were one of the lads."

"I'll take that as a compliment!" Tom laughed.

"Morning Mr. Chichester." Poppy breezed through the door with a brilliant smile.

"Good morning Poppy. Does Ryan try and feed you racehorse cubes as well?"

"No Sir." Another beaming smile. "But he does do terrible burned toast!"

Embarrassed, Ryan put two feeds into Poppy's hands and gave her a shove.

"Martin checking the horse?" Tom was watching a small blonde figure struggling with a wheelbarrow full of wood shavings.

"Yes, he's down at the bottom end."

Nodding absentmindedly, Tom wandered across the yard. He had tried very hard to avoid any personal contact with Kitty, to diffuse this potentially embarrassing situation. But even now, after a week, she blushed scarlet at the sight of him. She had spotted him now and was making a show of doing up a bolt. The situation was absurd. One moment of weakness and he had to pussyfoot around his staff for fear of arousing suspicion. It just wouldn't do. But he hadn't a clue what to do about it. Seeing Martin entering Olympic Run's box, Tom changed tack and went to join him.

From the second Martin swept the rugs off the big bay horse and patted the rock-hard neck, Tom forgot that the female species existed. This was all that mattered. This superb equine athlete; this mass of perfectly honed muscle. Tom ran his hand down the horses, cold, strong limbs and smiled. Perfect.

"He's looking good Martin." He straightened. "Do you think he'll be ready for the twenty ninth?"

"You're the boss!" Martin looked surprised. "Aren't you supposed to be telling me?"

"A trainer is only as good as his head lad."

"Your father always said that." Martin smiled.

"I know." Tom patted the horse's rump. "And, as with all things, he was right."

Martin picked up the horse's rugs and began to replace them, watching Tom leaving the box with a melancholy face. His boss was in a very nostalgic mood this morning.

In the privacy of the office Tom stood and watched his staff going through their daily routine. It was still only just beginning to get light. He felt very low this morning. Rick was due to ride work and school, but he had started to turn in late recently. Perhaps a 'phone call would shake him up. Dialling the number Tom got no reply. Puzzled, he tried Rick's mobile but with the same result. About to try Rick at home again he had a flash of insight. Feeling almost nervous he rang the familiar number. A sleepy voice answered.

"Hello? Who on Earth is this?"

"Tom Chichester. Good morning Felicity. How are you?"

"Tom? Good God! What the hell time do you call this?"

"About six thirty I believe."

"It's still dark!" Flick hissed.

"Correct. You are an observant woman when you want to be. You wouldn't happen to know where I can find Rick Cowdrey would you?"

"Very clever of you Tom." Flick's voice was heavy with sarcasm. "I'll get him for you."

So, his hunch had been right. The smile that spread across Tom's face as he listened to the sound of the receiver being passed over was born of triumph; but it was also born of a jealousy that made him snap when he heard Rick's voice.

"Tom. What can I do for you?"

"The same as any other professional worth his salary. You do remember that you're due here to ride out his morning?"

"Sure, I do." Rick's voice was hoarse.

"Eight o'clock sharp. Don't be late again Rick, you're starting to slack."

Without waiting for an answer Tom hung up. The staff were heading to the coach house for breakfast. The smell of cooking bacon caught his nostrils and his appetite. Heading for the Land Rover he thought bleakly about the empty kitchen that awaited him at the house. He refused to let his mother get up and cook at this ungodly hour, although she constantly defied him. Perhaps they needed another housekeeper. Pulling into the courtyard he realised that he had let the MOT expire on the BMW. He'd have to call the garage straight away, or at least as soon as the rest of the civilised world was awake. The smell of toast hung in the air as he opened the kitchen door; bacon sizzled in the frying pan. Eleanor dressed in a flowery nightgown was making coffee.

"Mother!" Tom tried to sound stern. "I've told you about this before."

"Oh, shut up." His mother pushed a mug of coffee into his hand. "Eat that toast, the bacons nearly ready."

Tom stretched his feet toward the Aga, which was just beginning to pump heat into the room. Eleanor watched him with concerned eyes.

"You look tired son; you need a break."

"Stop fussing mother, I'm fine."

"You don't look fine." Eleanor laid her hand on his. "You look ill."

"I've never been better. Where's this bacon you keep promising me?"

"Tom." Eleanor paused, sounding uncertain. "Dominic rang me last night."

Tom didn't reply, chewing on a large mouthful of toast.

"He's coming home for Christmas."

Eleanor watched the emotions chasing each other across her some face. She could read him like a book.

"Tom?"

"No." He stood up. "I don't want him here."

"Thomas!" her use of his full name made him smile. "You and your brother may not always see eye to eye, but he is still your brother and my son. I want to have him here for Christmas, at home, where he belongs."

He looked at her; small, neat, still attractive, and elegant even in that ridiculous nightgown. He remembered how hard his father's death had been for her, how she had struggled to control Dominic as he went further and further off the rails. Tom knew that he was not an easy man to live with; that he could be moody and difficult, that he had been described as arrogant, and was so often preoccupied and self-absorbed. But she never disputed his authority, never questioned his behaviour, merely cared, and listened. He decided to swallow his pride, for her sake.

"Okay. If it will make you happy."

"Thank you, Tom." She smiled the gracious smile that he had grown up with. "I wish you two could be friends, but I realise how different you are."

Crossing the room, she stood on tip toe and kissed him on the cheek. Eleanor thought her eldest son very handsome, and wished, not for the first time, that he would settle down and get married.

"I love you mother." He muttered. "Remember that."

"Go on with you." She gave him a little hug. "You'll make

me cry."

Tom glanced at the clock, and then at the frying pan.

"Can I have another sandwich?"

Eleanor squeezed his hand and reached for the butter. Tom watched, adoring her, but already feeling the spasms of hate and resentment that he knew another encounter with Dominic would bring. Life he decided, was never easy.

At eight o'clock, with the grey winter dawn lightening the hills, the first lot prepared to pull out of the yard. Filing around the immaculate circle of turf at the centre of the yard, they jogged and caught at their bits, eager to be away. Ryan, checking girths and legging up, told each rider where to slot into the ever-increasing line. Martin led out Olympic Run, thrills of excitement tickling his skin. He loved this horse. Getting onto Runny was akin to driving a Jaguar after years of owning a Mini. Martin had never known such power, or such speed; the horse was incredible, and he worshipped his every move. Landing lightly in the saddle as Ryan legged him up, he felt the horse shift into his long, smooth stride and smiled. Running his hand up and down the sleek neck he felt like shouting with joy. What a job! He loved getting on the back of this horse every morning, from the moment he woke he couldn't wait to renew the partnership. There couldn't be a better way to earn a living, and he wouldn't change places for anything, with anyone. Feeling infinitely superior, he took his place at the head of the string.

As Ryan was putting Poppy up onto Brassy, the last horse to be mounted, a silver car shot into the yard and screeched to a halt. Rick took a long time to get out; he was in no mood for riding. he had spent the last thirty-six hours in bed, and precious little of it had been spent asleep. Noticing that Tom was not approaching him with his usual warm greeting, Rick crossed the yard and tried to sound casual.

"Hi. Got something to blow away my cobwebs?"

"You'll be on Swingtime. She needs a good workout this morning." Tom didn't make eye contact with him. "She's very fresh. I hope that you're feeling fit,"

"Great." Rick's bloodshot eyes scanned the yard. Kitty rode past staring straight ahead, followed by an equally stone-faced Poppy. Ryan legged him onto the mare in silence. Oh well, Rick thought, it's going to be a quiet morning at least, I am obviously not the flavour of the moment. The little mare, feeling his weight on her back began to skip and dance.

"Whoa now little lady." He crooned. "You go easy on me know, I've had enough temperamental women to last me a lifetime!"

It's no good, thought Poppy as the mare pranced past her, I don't care who he hangs round with or ends up in bed with I still think he's gorgeous. Watching him settling the mare down, she admired the casual way he almost lounged in the saddle, talking to the horse all the time. Glancing at Kitty she saw her staring at her reins with a fixed expression on her face.

"Poppy!" Ryan was talking to her. "Wake up! Go behind the bloody fairy, and watch that chestnut bitch, she's got quick hindlegs."

The string filed out of the yard in its usual orderly fashion. Tom, opting for the Land Rover as transport instead of Micky, overtook them on route. The sight of Gareth, still an unhealthy shade of avocado, struggling with that murderous old mule Timepiece brought a smile to his face. Ahead of him was Kitty, whose slim frame held his eyes for longer than the others as she gazed across the hills with a faraway expression on her face. Poppy was twisting around in her saddle and trying to talk to her, but her words were landing on deaf ears. Martin and Rick rode one behind the other in silence, each one concentrating on their mounts and their own deep, personal thoughts.

The fresh November air did a lot to clear the head, and by the time the horses were wheeling at the foot of the all-weather gallop, Tom felt he had his life back under control. Watching his horses, he mentally paired them off for work. Olympic Run was really too good to work with anything else, but the little mare enjoyed a challenge and would stick to the big horse for as far as she could. Romeo and Brassy could work together, that left Timepiece and Major Investment. Timepiece was a lunatic, and the Major was a lazy old sod. Perhaps one would rub off on the other.

He sent them up the gallops one pair at a time, cantering at first, until he was left with Martin and Rick, both trying to control their mounts and praying that the others would hurry up and get moving.

"Watch your brakes, Marty." Tom shouted. "Keep a hold on him."

As the big bay horse launched into his easy, ground covering stride, the little mare plunged and dived beside him. Struggling to pull up at the top of the gallop Ricky cursed and shook his hands. The little bitch was pulling his arms out. Martin gave him a patronising smile.

"Hard work, isn't she?"

Rick chose not to answer; he could hear the sarcasm in Martin's voice and decided to let it pass him by. No need to provoke further animosity. Back at the foot of the hill, Tom came across.

"Rick. I'd like you to take Olympic Run this time."

Grudgingly, smile gone, Martin dismounted and handed the reins to Rick. Tom was looking for another horse for Rick to work with. His eyes fell on Timepiece, who was spinning in circles at the back of the group.

"Gareth."

"Yes?"

"Work alongside Rick. Try not to overtake, we're working, not racing. Let's see if a bit of pace will get that idiot to settle."

Oh Lord, though Gareth as he struggled to get his mount

to foot of the gallop, I hope I don't fall off. Please don't let me fall off. Timepiece gave a snort and a little hop with his hindlegs; just to remind these pathetic human beings who was boss around here.

"Ready?" Rick looked completely cool and calm.

"Yes." Said Gareth's mouth, although his mind was thinking otherwise.

Side by side, black and bay, the two sped up the hill. Timepiece, who thought travelling at this speed was tremendous fun, began to pull harder and harder as he tried to pass the bigger horse beside him. As they broke the crest of the hill Gareth was finding it very difficult to comply with Tom's instructions.

"Steady up mate!" he shouted across to Rick. "Or I'm going to lose him!"

"Too late!" Rick was laughing. "Mine's gone already!"

"What the fuck are those two playing at!" The words were out of Tom's mouth before he realised it. "I told them not to overtake!"

Poppy, who was in earshot, giggled. Not like the boss to let slip when they were around. Looking across the field she saw the two horses racing each other. Poor Gareth. This was probably doing his hangover the world of good.

"Poppy!" Tom could feel his temper rising. "Stop smirking and get that horse moving. Kitty, stop bloody daydreaming for God's sake and go with her!"

Kitty started and looked at him in surprise. The eye contact made her blush.

"Sorry." She muttered as she rode past him.

Damn her, Tom thought, as he watched her red face. Why is she always so bloody apologetic? If she was sullen, or moody, or looked like the back end of a bus, this would be so much easier. A mile further on, Rick and Gareth had at last got control of their mounts. As he pulled up, Rick blew out his lips and gave his mount a slap on the neck. That had blown away the cobwebs. Gareth, who was feeling sick, collapsed on Timepiece's neck with a groan, trying to catch his breath. The two girls approached them at a more leisurely pace and halted alongside.

"Look out." Poppy warned as the rode back down the hill. "Mr Charming is out to lunch and Mr Moody is in the office instead!"

Kitty, pink with exertion and embarrassment put as much distance as possible between her and Rick. Undeterred, he manoeuvred his way around the others until he was beside her.

"Hi babe." He said casually. "How are you doing?"

Silence. He tried again.

"Pretty cold up here today."

Nothing.

Bending forward he looked at her downturned face and saw her biting her lip.

"Ah, listen honey, I'm sorry about the other night. I guess I had too much of that champagne."

Kitty looked at him, shaking her head in disbelief. Did he really think she was naive enough to fall for that? Her embarrassment turned to indignation.

"Pardon?" She hissed "That, is the biggest load of crap I have ever heard. You just wanted to get your leg over, and when I wasn't going to oblige you looked elsewhere. Felicity." She spat the name out with contempt. "Was more than willing. It had nothing to do with drink. Just your ego."

Rick took a deep breath and considered his reply.

"So, is that wrong?" He asked. "I'm a normal healthy guy. I've got needs like any other man. What do you think your boss was doing with Flick in the first place? Comparing share prices?"

"What Mr Chichester does is up to him. I'm talking about

me, and you. He didn't dump me and go screw someone else. He just kindly brought me home when we both got sick of the sight of you two!"

"Yeah really?" Drawled Rick. "And what did that little journey entail? I wonder?"

Kitty went scarlet, anger fuelled by the dangerous territory that Rick was entering.

"None of your bloody business!" She shouted. "What do you think I am anyway? We aren't all oversexed egotists like you!"

Rick laughed at her.

"You are a self-righteous little bitch, aren't you? If you're so polite and bloody innocent, then how come this big hang-up with Dominic? I know that he's only interested in women for one thing."

"Like you!" She screamed, swinging at him with her whip. "Get away from me you creep!"

Her whip caught Rick's arm. It stung.

"Oh, now we're getting somewhere!" He sneered, an attitude which didn't suit him. "They say that the truth always hurts. Maybe Snow White isn't as pure as she paints herself? Or maybe he turned you away? Is that it? Yeah, that's it, can't handle rejection."

"Rejection!" She gave a sarcastic laugh. "It would be a pleasure to be rejected by a moron like you!"

"Is that right?" Rick stared at her, never taking his eyes off her face. She began to weaken and felt tears tightening her throat. She turned away, trying to think of some cutting remark she could hurt him with. As she did, she saw Tom ahead of them, face like thunder, eyes very pale in their dark sockets.

"Do you really expect me to waste my time up here while you two continue some pathetic lovers tiff?" He roared. "If you both want to stay out of the jobcentre you'll shut up and get those horses back to the yard. I want both of you in the office the second you get off their backs!"

This time two pairs of eyes faced Tom across the desk in his office. The first pair were cool, uncaring, almost insolent. The second so wide and terrified they bordered on panic stricken.

"Okay." Tom took a deep breath and tried to keep his cool. "Which one of you is going to give me an explanation?"

Rick was watching Kitty, who in turn was watching her boots. She was rigid with nerves. How could an intended romance have turned sour so quickly.?

"My fault boss," He ventured. "I'm afraid I was a bit out of line."

Kitty looked up, startled. Tom watched her and considered his answer.

"Thank you. I appreciate the apology. But I'd appreciate more your guarantee that it won't happen again.""

"You have it." Rick sounded very solemn.

"Good. If I were you, I'd go home and get some sleep; then, get your mind off women and back on your job."

Thanking his lucky stars that he still had a job to get his mind back onto, Rick nodded briefly and left. Kitty, alone and intimidated eyed her boss as he sat in front of her.

"I'm sorry too Sir." She said quietly. "Rick was a bit, well let's just say that I let him get to me."

"Obviously." Tom watched her through narrow eyes. Into his head, totally unbidden, and definitely unwanted came a vivid recollection of her lips on his; he could feel them, taste them. He looked away quickly, unnerved by the reactions that the memory evoked.

"You can go Kitty as well. But I want the same promise to from you as from Rick. Mind on your job, nothing else; and If I ever see you strike anything in temper with your whip, horse or human, again you won't be welcome here.

Understand?"

"Yes Sir."

He heard her get to her feet and hurry out of the door but was afraid to look. Mind on the job. Who was he to ask that of anyone when his mind was constantly on her? He had to find a solution to this, couldn't allow it to go on. The easy answer would be to sleep with her, let it all out, satisfy his curiosity and forget about it. Except it wouldn't work like that, with him it never did. The calendar was staring at him from the wall. Claire had written CHEPSTOW in large red letters beside the twenty second of November. There was his solution. No one had time to worry about women and sex when they had such challenges ahead of them as he had.

November the twenty second dawned with such thick impenetrable fog that Martin wondered if Runny would even be able to see the fences on Chepstow's roller coaster of a course. Tom, having rung to make sure that the meeting was still going ahead before he even dressed, was watching the lorry being loaded with mixed emotions. Today was a trial in more ways than one. Swingtime was having her first outing under proper National Hunt rules; Timepiece was going to stretch everyone's nerves but particularly his as Rick rode him before the real acid test of the day, Olympic Run's performance in the feature race, the three-mile chase. The race on the November card had once been the highly rated Rehearsal 'chase, this was a good equivalent but didn't attract the same stars. Which suited him fine. Both staff and horses were already on edge,

"Why me?" Gareth moaned, not for the first time, as he handed the first aid box to Kitty. "Why do I always get the wet ones, the cold ones, they can't see a hand in front of your face ones?"

"If it was only wet, I wouldn't mind." Poppy could feel the damp creeping down the back of her neck. "But I'm bloody freezing as well."

"Oh, stop moaning you two!" Kitty was in the cab of the lorry. "Anyone would think that you didn't want to go!"

"I don't." Gareth pulled a face at her. "But then, I don't fancy the jockey."

"Neither do I." Kitty thumped him as he passed her.

"I do!" Poppy gave a little grin. "And I've got my best bra on, just in case!"

"That's enough." Martin was lowering the ramp. "Stop gassing and get those horses loaded. And if you're going to moan all the way to Wales you can bloody well walk."

Chepstow was not only cold and wet; it was also very windy. Tom, despite his long Barbour coat and two jumpers, shivered as he walked towards the members bar to meet his owners. Timepiece was owned by a Herefordshire publican who seemed to spend half of his life abroad, and today was no exception. Mike Peterson however was in full voice, already red faced and slurring. Christ, thought Tom, I almost hope that the horse doesn't win, I don't want to be around if Mike gets a television interview in that state! Glad of an excuse to absent himself from his present company, he left to saddle Timepiece, jovial well wishes following him into the cold air. He grinned to himself as he walked to the weighing room for Rick's saddle. If Olympic Run lost, Mike Peterson would have enough spare champagne on his hands to sink the Titanic.

Timepiece ran a reasonable race, but not quite good enough, finishing a short head third in a photograph. Still, it seemed an optimistic start to the day. Rick, bearing in mind his recent behaviour and his subsequent balling out, was being very professional calling everyone 'Sir' and minding his P's and Q's. He came to the saddling box to have a peek at Swingtime, a heavy leather coat hanging off his shoulders. Beneath, Tom could make out the dark green and red chevron colours that he had inherited from his father.

"How's she doing?" Rick could see the dark patches of sweat beneath the paddock sheet.

"Getting a bit excited." Tom pulled a face as he tugged at the mare's girth. "But she's okay."

"I'll try and keep her quiet." Rick rubbed Streak's chestnut nose with his gloved hand. "She's not the only one getting excited. My old man rang three times in the middle of the night. I'll see you in the paddock."

By the time Streak had paraded, been saddled, and paraded again, she had reached boiling point. Springing from foot to foot, she tugged at the lead rein so hard that she lifted Poppy off her feet. Cursing her, and clenching her raw fingers, Poppy was very relieved to hear the jockeys being ordered to mount. Removing the paddock sheet and getting Rick into the saddle was a complicated task that took all three of them, herself, Martin, and Tom. Bucking and diving the mare nearly flattened Poppy and cow kicked Martin in the arm as he tried to leg Rick up. Feeling Rick's weight touching down onto her back she reared high, shaking her head, trying to pull away from a desperately clinging Poppy.

"Let her go!" Rick snapped. "Don't hang onto her head, steady you clown!"

Patting her constantly, feet hanging out of his stirrups, Rick jogged around the paddock, quietly creeping his feet back into the irons as he went. Once out on the track Swingtime was away, head shaking from side to side as she fought to go faster. Tom couldn't bear it. Climbing to his vantage point in the owners and trainers stand he peered through the mist towards the start. His binoculars were no help at all in this weather, all he could see were a load of murky grey blobs. He could only take a guess at which blob was his mare from her erratic behaviour.

The starter was thoroughly wet and miserable, and keen to get the race under way so that he could get back under cover. The horses had barely formed a ragged line before the tape snapped up. Spraying water and mud the nine runners set off on their two-and-a-half-mile journey. Streak had soon pulled her way into the lead, ploughing through the mud with incredible ease. At the third last, she had opened up such a gap that it seemed impossible she would get caught. She soared over the fence at bloodcurdling speed and Tom, squinting through his glasses, began to pray that she would stay in front. The second last stood at the top of the rising ground; at the rails Poppy, unable to see, was leaping up and down trying to get a view of the big screen. The mare met the flight in full cry, stood right back and took off outside the wings of the jump.

A groan rose from the crowd.

Tom stared in disbelief, then threw down his glasses in disgust.

"Swingtime has gone at the second last," Roared the commentator. "Leaving Battle Hill in front."

The rest of his words were now meaningless.

Rising off the ground almost as fast as she had hit it, Streak set off after the other horses. Leaping the last fence, she passed several of the runners and careered to a halt beside the exit to the stables where Martin was waiting for her. Hardly blowing, she jogged beside him to meet Tom, who was standing under one of the trees behind the pre parade ring with a glum face.

"Is she okay Martin?"

"Seems to be Boss. How's Rick?"

"Having the once over from the doc. I hope to God he's okay. Silly bugger." He patted the mare's steaming neck. "Nearly gave me a heart attack."

"Me too." Martin pulled the saddle off the mare's back.

"Give that mare to Poppy, Martin, and get the saddle back to the weighing room. I'd better make sure our star is in one piece before his big moment."

Inside the pre parade ring Kitty was wishing that her head was on a swivel. She had been walking around with Runny when she heard the groan and had seen Streak flying past riderless. Now she was trying to hear the conversation between the two men beneath the tree as she passed. Tom was waving her out.

"Is the mare okay Sir?"

"Of course, she is!" Tom snapped. "Silly little cow. I suppose being female she's intent on making my life as difficult as possible."

Kitty raised her eyebrows. She could see from the tension in Tom's face that nerves were getting the better of him. His eyes had become very pale, and his jaw was set. Martin appeared with Rick's saddle.

"He's fine." He puffed. "But he's lucky. She caught him in the thigh as she got up. Any lower and his knee would have gone, any higher and something else might have gone!"

"Which may have been a blessing!" Tom gave a wry grin. "Come on, let's saddle this horse."

Martin's hands were shaking as he fastened the breast girth. This race was so important for the yard. If Olympic Run flunked, it would be an uphill struggle for the rest of the season.

Runny was the opposite of his stablemate. Cool and calm, he hacked quietly to the start and stood like a statue as his girths were checked then walked calmly forward with pricked ears as he waited for the tapes to go up. One touch of Rick's heels and he set off at an easy gallop, tucked in behind the leading group of horses, skimming effortlessly over the first circuit in a canter. Tom noted happily the ease with which the horse was covering the ground, saw the motionless position adopted by Rick, a sure sign that things were going to plan, and began to relax.

Down the back straight Olympic Run tailed the leader, as they took the final ditch, he was ranging up on its outside. Close behind them, also going well, was Sparky's old adversary Silent Running. This time Rick increased the pace as they rounded the bend into the home straight. As they faced the final climb, he and Silent Running had drawn clear of the rest of the field. Tom, holding his breath, had to suffer as the mist made visibility impossible. There was a terrible moment of suspension when he could see nothing; then, out of the murk, came two dark horses.

Olympic Run was still ahead, his great ground eating stride holding the other horse at bay. But as they reached the last fence Silent Running drew alongside and they rose into the air together. Rick smiled to himself. This was the second time he had been challenged by this horse and jockey. Today there would be no head-to-head battle to the line, no duel to the death. Today he had the power to leave them behind. He crouched low over Runny's withers and pushed the button to go. Like a turbo powered car Olympic Run accelerated and began eating the ground with huge strides. Rick wanted to laugh. The speed of this horse was incredible; looking over his shoulder he saw the big black horse floundering in his mount's wake. The post flashed by, and he thumped Runny's neck in delight. Nothing could have been easier.

As he pulled the horse back to a walk, he couldn't stop the jubilant grin that spread across his face. Kitty ran to meet him, throwing her arms around Runny's neck. Instinctively Rick leaned forward and clutched her shoulder. Looking up at him she smiled, all animosity forgotten. Tom was waiting for them at the rails.

"Well done." he slapped the jockey's leg. "That was a brilliant piece of timing."

"This is a brilliant horse." Rick took Martin's

outstretched hand, another olive branch.

"Not brilliant." Martin grinned. "The best!"

As Tom had anticipated Runny's owners were completely legless within half an hour. Prying himself away with great difficulty he went out into the grey afternoon, already growing dusky on this murky day of clouds and mist. The evening was closing in fast. Overhead he heard the rhythmic whirr of helicopter blades. Looking up he saw the craft moving off, carrying Greg Westwood, the champion trainer, back to Lambourn.

As he opened the door of the BMW, he smiled to himself. In a world full of big fish, he had just scored a victory for the minnows.

CHAPTER SEVEN

The room was smoky and airless and made Rick feel claustrophobic. His head throbbed from the loud pulsating music, and the mixture of alcohol and various other substances that he had forced into his body was making him feel sick. Turning, hazy, unfocussed eyes towards his companion he saw him through a haze of pungent smoke.

"Well Rick boy." Dominic was trying very hard to get high and couldn't quite get there "How did you get on with my brother's little mare the other night?"

"Kitty?" Rick was having great trouble forming his words.

"I don't know her name. Never bothered to find out."

"Not past first base." Rick dragged heavily on his joint. "There is something seriously wrong with that girl."

"Needs a good fuck." Dominic laughed. "I did try and show her the error of her ways, but my bloody brother interfered."

"What do you mean, tried?" Rick narrowed his eyes as he attempted to concentrate.

"I was just winning the argument when he came along and cocked it up. Just as he cocks up the rest of my life. Bastard."

"I don't think he's too keen on you." Rick gave up the battle with his spinning vision and closed his eyes.

Dominic paused for a moment and considered his reply.

"I don't fit in Rick boy: I don't work, I don't ride, I hate horses and I can't remember one bloody line of Hamlet!"

"Choose your companions well then." A smile spread across Rick's relaxed face. "I work, I ride, I love horses, but I admit you've got me on the Hamlet."

Dominic poked him with a long, slim, very unsteady finger.

"You watch my big brother Rick boy. He'll use you. Chew you up and spit you out. Tread you into his stinking muck heap then move on without you. He's just like my bloody father."

"I thought your father was a good guy?"

Dominic screwed up his nose, his eyes blank, expressionless.

"Not to me. He hated me. Just like my brother hates me. I don't want to talk about this crap anymore. Any blow left?"

Rick, opening his eyes, turned the tobacco tin upside down and shook his head.

"All gone you greedy bastard."

"What about women then?" The black eyes scanned the room. "Oh, sod that. You can't smoke them. Let's see what I've got in my little pockets."

Standing up and digging deep into the pockets of his faded black Levi's he pulled out a small cellophane bag.

"Here you go Ricardo. This'll get you to thirty thousand feet faster than Concorde. Now where's that girlfriend of yours? She promised me a dance."

"Throwing her guts up I should think." Rick eyed the small white pills with suspicion. "She can't take all this crap. Neither can I. I've had it."

Dominic laughed and pushed the packet closer to him. A tall girl with an angular frame similar to his own was weaving towards him. Lank, lifeless hair straggled over her shoulders; she wore a shapeless grey wool cardigan and black, threadbare leggings. She looked grimy. Rick eyed her without enthusiasm as she halted in front of them. To his surprise, when she spoke, she had the same upper-class drawl as his companion.

"Dommie darling. How are you? Who's your little friend?"

Dominic kicked the chair beside him.

"Sit down." He flicked the bag of pills across to her, and she opened it without question. "Still enjoying life on the other side, I see."

"Yes." The girl's voice was hoarse. " I'm really into tube stations now, they have such a community spirit at night. You should try it."

"The only spirit I'm interested in comes out of a bottle. Caught anything nasty yet?"

"Of course not." The girl pulled her greasy hair from her face and, as her cardigan fell back, Dominic's keen eyes spotted tell-tale red marks and bruises on her arms.

"Really?" He sneered. "Take a tip from me Clara; snort it, smoke it, or swallow it, never," He leaned forward and put his face close to hers. "Never stick it where it shows."

Beside him Rick grinned and took another pull on the joint that was smouldering away in his hand. This was plenty heavy enough for him. He felt as if he was floating on a bed of cotton wool. Everything was distant, unreal, all except the flashing lights which were dazzling him. They triggered off some sudden emotion in his wandering mind and he found himself full of energy. Getting unsteadily to his feet he headed for the dance floor, cannoning off chairs and tables as he went.

"Look out!" Dominic yelled after him. "Too late!"

He burst into laughter as Rick took a table full of glasses onto the floor with him.

"You are so cruel Dommie." Clara couldn't pronounce her r's. "You really are."

"Am I?" Dominic mimicked her. "Am I cwuel?"

"Yes, your poor little friend there can't handle all this junk and I expect you've been secretly force feeding him just to have a laugh."

"Of course." Dominic grinned. "He'll be okay. I always thought that these Aussie's were born ravers."

"Not that one. Anyway, he's a Kiwi."

"Is there a difference.?" Dominic was getting bored. He had failed to reach the point of complete oblivion that satisfied him. Clara was watching him with dark, understanding eyes.

"Can't find the way to Never, Never Land Dommie?"

"Piss off Clara."

"Only trying to help you out," She pouted.

"Shouldn't it be the other way around?" Dominic raised an eyebrow. "It's a long way up from the gutter."

"Who says I'm in the gutter!" Clara scowled.

"You certainly look like it. Where are you sleeping these days, Clara? In one of these wonderful, ethnic, stinking, tube stations?"

Clara got to her feet; she knew Dominic in this mood, unable to find satisfaction he was getting aggressive. She knew first-hand how violent he could be but couldn't resist her parting shot.

"No one knows where you sleep Dominic, do they? Or with whom." She looked across the room at Rick.

Dominic said nothing. Clara smirked, and picked up the cellophane bag. Dominic reached out a hand, but she pushed it away.

"Payment." She said quietly. "For all the stuff I've peddled for you. And all the bruises from last time."

Dominic's eyes narrowed, flashing, but he remained silent. Clara smirked and walked away.

Left alone Dominic searched the room for distraction. Rick had disappeared. His encounter with Clara had psyched him up and his adrenalin was pumping. He needed an outlet. Picking up a bottle of beer he began to wander the room, prowling, looking for prey. As he passed the front door a woman entered. She was well dressed; far too well dressed for her seedy surroundings. She wore a long black cashmere cloak, pulled tight against the cold. her hair was twisted back to show the diamonds that glittered at her ears and throat. She slipped out of the cloak to reveal a clinging black dress. Dominic ran his eyes over the neat figure and shapely legs; let his eyes follow the creamy white skin into the plunging cleavage. The hunter had found his prey.

Lounging in the doorway he blocked her path into the main room.

"Are you looking for anyone in particular?"

"Yes." She hadn't looked at him, her eyes were scanning the room over his shoulder. "Rick Cowdrey. Do you know him?"

"Rick? I should do, he was my guest. Who are you?"

"That's none of your business." She looked at him for the first time, eyes flickering with recognition. "Aren't you Dominic Chichester?"

"Yes." Dominic grinned. "And how do you know that?"

"I know your brother." The woman held out an immaculately manicured hand. "I'm Felicity."

Dominic ignored the outstretched hand and narrowed his eyes. So, this was the famous Flick Harries. Her air of good breeding provoked his rebellious nature. He liked women he could manipulate, women who were in awe of him. This was not his type, but he knew how much Tom saw of her, and that he cared for her. Purely out of spite, for nothing more than sheer one-upmanship he would have this stuck-up bitch if he drew his last breath trying. He saw the pulse in her neck quickening under his gaze.

Perhaps he wouldn't have to try that hard after all.

"Would you like me to find Rick for you?"

"There's no hurry." Flick was feeling hypnotised by his black eyes. "I'd rather have a drink."

Dominic laid his fingers, very lightly, on her bare arm and steered her to the makeshift bar. With an inspired guess he ordered a glass of Archers.

"How clever." Flick took a sip. "How did you know I liked it?"

"Hallmark." Dominic hitched a slim hip onto a bar stool. "I bet you drive a GTI."

"Wrong. And the hallmark would be a G and T, wouldn't it?" Flick smirked, then looked about her with a puzzled expression. "I wouldn't have thought that Rick would be happy in a place like this."

She raised her eyebrows as two young men passed, their arms twined around each other's shoulders, and shuddered.

"These people look rather seedy."

"These people." Dominic snapped. "Probably earn even more than you, they just know how to let their hair down!"

"So do I." Flick was bemused by his reaction. "But there are other ways than this."

Dominic traced the line of her chin with his finger, watching her skin grow taught.

"I hear you have a few pleasures of you own. Don't sell yourself as a little angel to me."

The hazel eyes looked at him, frankly, offended but not angry.

"Who told you? Your brother?"

"Oh no. The only thing he ever tells me is to fuck off. It was Rick."

"Rick!" Now she did look angry.

"Thought you could trust him?" Dominic gave a leering grin. "Rick and I have no secrets from each other. We share everything."

Flick sipped her drink and lowered her eyes. Dominic moved closer.

"And I do mean everything."

Flick blushed. This handsome young man was trying to

put her off her guard. She had come here purely with the intention of embarrassing Rick who had stood her up the night before. She had lied to the greasy bouncer at the door about an invitation. All she really had was a scrap of paper that Rick had left in her car with the address on it. She had given little thought to what she would do when she got here. Now she found herself being chatted up, for she was sure that was what he was doing, by this strange and beautiful creature she had often admired from afar. Tom was far more her type of man; but there was something untamed and predatory about Dominic that made him irresistible. He drew people to him as a magnet draws iron filings. He had stopped looking at her and was ordering another drink. His eyes were surrounded by blue shadows, his pupils so dilated that they took over the iris and made his eyes one expressionless black ring. One slim hand was resting on her shoulder, a finger stroking her neck.

"Would you like to dance?" He asked the question without looking at her.

"No thanks, it all looks too chaotic for me."

"Is there anything you *would* like to do?" He looked straight at her this time.

"What have you got in mind?" Flick's heart was pumping hard, aware that she was about to embark on a one-way journey.

Dominic smiled and let his hand slide down her back until it rested on her buttocks.

"You don't need me to tell you that."

"Aren't you going to wine and dine me first?" Flick whispered.

"Not my style." Taking her hand Dominic led her into the hall, turning towards the stairs. Flick pulled back. She had no intention of being taken in a flea infested room in this hovel full of junkies.

"What's wrong?" A shadow of impatience flitted across Dominic's face.

"Not here surely? Don't you have somewhere more private we can go?"

"What's wrong with here? Come on, then we'll have plenty of time to party."

Flick shook her head.

"So, we nip upstairs for a quick one and then back here? No thank you. Perhaps I should just leave, I shouldn't have come here in the first place."

Dominic raised his hand in a gesture of despair.

"Women. Why do they always have to be so difficult?"

He could see that she was not going to be won over. Perhaps she was worth a little more effort than he would normally apply. Getting this one into bed and trespassing on his brother's property was well worth some leniency on his part.

"Okay you win. My flat is about thirty minutes away. If you drive us, I'll pick up a couple of bottles of wine on the way."

Following her outside he laughed as he folded his long legs into the Golf.

"Wasn't too far from the mark, was I? Don't pull over on the way. It's too cold for me to stick my feet out of the window."

Dominic's flat was large and sparsely furnished, built into a deserted warehouse on the Thames. It had a neglected air, obviously used as a convenience rather than a home. Dirty glasses, dog ends and empty bottles littered every surface. The only piece of luxury was the leather sofa; apart, that is from the four-poster bed, magnificently draped in white silk and lace.

"I thought that black was your colour?" Flick ran her finger over the duvet.

"I like to wear it, not sleep in it."

Dominic went back into the lounge and collapsed on

the sofa, feet dangling over the edge. Something in his pose reminded Flick sharply of Tom and she felt a twinge of regret. What was she doing here? Chasing around the country after Rick, and then allowing herself to succumb to Dominic's persuasion and ending up here. Tom had more in common with her than either of these men. She should have turned to him for comfort. She jumped as a hand touched her back. She moved away, trying to distance herself while she sorted out her thoughts.

"Don't tell me you're getting cold feet?" Dominic whispered.

"No. I just don't want to be rushed."

"Why not?" He was moving closer. "I thought this was what you wanted, just enjoy yourself."

His eyes had taken on a strange expression; something in the gleaming black depths made her nervous. An uncomfortable feeling of entrapment began to creep over her. The eyes were trained, hawk like, on hers, and his hands were holding her face. Tense, she was pleasantly surprised at how gentle his kiss was, his wide mouth soft and caressing. She relaxed, and leaned against him as, with one hand, he began to undress her. His skin was smooth, and pleasant to touch, and feeling all her inhibitions floating away she began to encourage him, whispering into his ear as he lifted her and carried her to the bed. Her hands explored his body: the firm muscles of his stomach, the surprising strength of his slim frame. She gave a gasp of pleasure as her hand explored lower, and fully aroused now, she opened her eyes and looked up at him.

What she saw made her stomach lurch.

There was no tenderness in his eyes, just a chilling, cold, uncaring glow of lust. Driven by the demands of his body he was devoid of emotion.

"Dominic?" She tried to break into his shell.

"What?" He raised himself onto his elbows and looked at her.

122

"You do want this, I mean me, don't you?"

He shook his head, irritation plain on his face.

"What sort of question is that? I thought you were a grown woman not a child!"

"Sorry." She said meekly.

Her head fell to one side as she looked away, exposing the smooth whiteness of her throat. Heat poured through Dominic's body and with a grunt he buried his face in her flesh, plunging desperately inside her. Blind to anything except his own, urgent, needs he ignored her cries as he pushed harder and harder. She heaved beneath him, whimpering, sounds that slowly, but surely turned to cries of pleasure. As she gave one last cry, he held himself above her and watched the emotions on her face.

An intense feeling of triumph swept over him as he saw her writhing with pleasure. Now it was his turn. Fiercely, totally uncaring of anything but his own satisfaction now, he drove himself to his own climax. He was aware of his nails digging into her flesh, drawing blood as he strained. Then, with a ferocity unlike anything she had ever before experienced he seemed to explode. With a heavy groan he fell forward and lay still. For the first time in her life Flick was glad it was over. She was afraid of this man lying motionless on top of her; afraid of his intensity, of the manic ferocity that had taken over him.

Turning her head, she was surprised to see that his eyes were open and watching her. She was even more surprised to see tenderness in them. He smiled and stroked her hair.

"Did I hurt you?"

Taken aback at this sudden display of consideration she nodded, tears springing into her eyes. Dominic kissed her on the cheek and murmured an apology. Rolling onto his back he stared at the ceiling, enjoying the vengeful surge of pride that washed over him. If only his brother could see him now. At last, he had taken something that was Tom's, trespassed on his property. He saw Tom's outraged face in his mind and laughed softly to himself.

The sound of a key turning in the lock made them both startle.

"Who is it?" Flick pulled the sheet over her naked body.

"Rick." Dominic had recognised the voices coming from the hall. He saw the look on Flick's face and laughed.

"I told you we shared everything."

"Don't let him in, please!" She hissed.

"A joke my dear. Relax, we haven't quite got that far. Yet. Anyway, he's seen it all before, hasn't he?"

"Please!" She was sliding down below the covers.

"Oh alright. Rick?" He shouted. "That you?"

"Yes." Rick's voice was very slow and slurring. "I'm going to bed."

"Good night Dommie darling." A girl's high pitched voice echoed through the hall.

"Who was that?" Flick was puzzled.

"Emmie." Dominic's smile was filled with sarcasm. "Rick's girl. Don't tell me you thought you were the only one!"

"No. Of course not." Flick turned away, hiding the hurt that she knew must show in her eyes. She was appalled to find herself feeling jealous of the girl who was sharing Rick's bed, while she herself was falling in and out of the sheets with different men like a cheap whore. Unhappy, disgusted with her own behaviour, she finally fell asleep.

In the middle of the night Rick woke with the beginnings of a terrible hangover. Staggering into the kitchen he was stunned when he saw Flick Harries sitting in the living room. She was wearing a short black dress and a string of what looked like bruises on her neck.

"Flick! What on Earth are you doing here?"

"Oh Rick. Please take me home." Her voice broke into a sob. "I can't stand being in the same house as him. Please take me home."

Rick waited for his spinning head to slow down before he answered.

"I guess you mean Dom. Well, if you and he have had a blue don't ask me to get involved. He's my best mate. I don't know why you're here, and I don't want to, I just know that it's none of my business."

Flick turned soulful eyes to him; they touched him, their look reminding him of a lost dog, bewildered and far from home.

"Please Rick?" She begged. "I need you."

Rick dragged his hands through his tangled hair and shrugged.

"Well, how did you get here? Did you drive?" A vague memory of a yellow Golf parked outside came back to him.

"Yes."

"Then drive yourself home." Although feeling sorry for her Rick was trying hard not to throw up and was in no mood for playing agony aunt.

Flick got miserably to her feet. She had none of her usual bounce and vigour.

"I thought you were my friend." She mumbled. "I thought you cared."

Rick shook his head.

"I do, I guess, in my own way. But I'm no use to anybody right now."

"I can see that." Flick took a deep breath. "I'll just have to drive. It just seems such a long way on my own."

Rick, unable to stand any longer, collapsed on the sofa behind her. He could see almost every inch of her long, shapely legs in that dress. the sight reminded him of how lovely she was, and his heart softened.

"Sit down baby." He caught her hand. "Tell me what's wrong. Why don't you just stay here and drive home in the morning?"

"No" She shuddered. "It's too close to *him.*"

"To Dominic? What happened?"

She shook her head, covered her face with her hands and burst into tears. Rick laid his arm across her shoulders and felt her shaking. Turning her gently to face him he saw, clearly for the first time, the bruises on her neck.

"Where did you get these?" He traced them with his finger.

"Where do you think?" She shrank back from his touch.

"Dominic?" Something in the way she recoiled was familiar, but Rick's muddled memory couldn't place it.

She nodded and gave another sob.

"Why?" Rick could feel his stomach tightening.

"Because I said no."

"To what? Sex?"

"Yes. Oh, it wasn't the first time. He was very." She paused. "Very, vicious? The first time, so I couldn't face it again. So, I said no when he woke me up for more."

Another pause.

"He got nasty. He tried to force me; held me down and.." The rest of her words were lost in tears.

"Did you stop him?" Rick had gone cold. He suddenly felt very sober.

"Yes. If he hadn't been so stoned, or whatever he was I wouldn't have. He's stronger than he looks."

Rick stared at her. His look was misinterpreted.

"You don't believe me!" She gasped. "I knew I shouldn't have told you!"

Rick pulled her back beside him.

"Look I can't drive you home to Cheltenham in this state, can I? And you're in no fit state to drive that far yourself. What if I get a cab to my place? It's not far, no one there, you'll be fine. I'll bring your car around first thing in the morning."

Flick stared at the floor.

"Is that so bad?" He gave her a hug.

"No." She pulled away. "Thank you, Rick. Will you come with me? I mean,"

"I know what you mean." He interrupted. "I'll settle you in, okay?"

"Okay." She got slowly to her feet. "And you will be there in the morning?"

"Promise."

Flick gave a weak smile.

"I do appreciate this, Rick. You won't tell him where I am will you?"

"No. I would say anytime but I hope I won't have to do this again."

"No. Nor do I."

It took Rick some time to settle Flick into his flat. He sat with her until she was asleep and then crept out. By the time he found himself a taxi and made his way back to the warehouse the first streaks of dawn were breaking up the sky. Feeling very weary he let himself into Dominic's building and climbed the stairs. As he did a cold sneaking finger of suspicion began to prod at him. Not liking the thought, he pushed it aside, but it kept creeping back, nagging at his already exhausted brain. Dominic was up and making coffee with all the animation of a zombie.

"There you are. Sir Rick to the rescue, eh?"

"If it hadn't been for you there would have been no

'rescue' as you put it." Rick snapped.

"Oh, what tales are being told of me now!" Dominic laughed. "Tell me Rick, would you bring a girl back for the night and expect to get the big 'E'?"

"I wouldn't try and force her!" Rick could feel his temper rising.

"A little gentle persuasion that's all." Dominic's eyes were blank.

"Gentle! Never stop to survey your handiwork do you, you bastard?" Rick's voice rose until he was shouting, spitting out the words like venom.

Emmie appeared in the doorway.

"What the hell's going on? Why are you two fighting?"

"Get dressed." Rick snapped. "Now!"

"Why, it's early?"

"Just do as I bloody tell you!" Rick yelled at her.

Realising that this was not the best time to pick an argument Emmie retreated hastily into the bedroom. Rick turned his attention back to Dominic who was nonchalantly drinking his coffee with an amused look on his face.

"You see how easily they get to you Ricardo?" He smirked. "Women."

"Did you?" Rick found himself choking on the words. "Did you do the same to Kitty?"

"Who? Oh, my brothers little tart. Well, let's just say I got a bit carried away."

"Bastard!" Ricky picked up a mug and sent it crashing to the floor. "You sick, twisted, sadistic fucking bastard. My God, Tom was right about you!"

"Probably." Dominic was smirking. "But then we can't all be perfect, can we?"

Rick's mind was reeling with terrible mental images

when Emmie reappeared with her bag in her hand.

"You drive." He threw her his car keys. "Go on move."

"Why?"

"I have to take Flick's car to her."

"Oh, so that's where she is!" Dominic grinned. "Maybe you had a crack at her as well?"

"Don't push your luck." Rick waved a threatening finger at the taller man. "One more comment like that and you'll get a taste of your own medicine."

"I'd like to see you try." Dominic towered above him. "I really would like to see you try."

Seething with temper Rick backed out of the room, hearing Dominic's sarcastic laughter following him down the hall. It was the last time he would go anywhere near that worthless bastard. Almost jumping down the stairs, desperate to put distance between himself and the evil he had just discovered, Rick felt much better when he got back out into the fresh air.

Tom stood on the lawn of Highford House and watched Spock tearing about on a fruitless search for rabbits. He had slowly descended from the cloud he had been sitting on since Olympic Run's win and returned to normality. The next big date marked on the calendar was Boxing Day and the King George 'chase at Kempton, closely followed by the Welsh Grand National at Chepstow. Sometime during the next fortnight, he had to fit in Martin's thirtieth birthday celebrations at The Plough, and Christmas. It was Christmas that filled him with trepidation. He dreaded the thought of being in the same house as Dominic; even worse, having him within such a short distance of Kitty. Pushing Dominic firmly to the back of his mind he began to walk, Spock at his heels, to the yard.

The place was sleepy this morning. The last few days had been quiet, with only a handful of runners and no sign of a winner. It was almost as if the season was going on without him while he marked time and waited for something to happen. Olympic Run had provided a much-needed boost of adrenalin, but he mustn't get carried away with just one horse. His charges were all busy with their morning feeds and only Mick came to greet him, always eager for attention. The little horse's coat was growing thick again, he must remind Ryan to clip him. Watching the way, the old horse sorted out his favourite bits of feed, pushing the rest to one side, Tom didn't hear Martin coming up behind him.

"Morning Guv. Looks like another lovely day."

"After all this dry weather a wet day would be best Martin. Got all these legs to think about. Any problems?"

"Well," Martin looked anxious. "I'm not too happy with old Romeo. He's right off his feed and he's normally a greedy beggar."

"Really? Best let's have a look then Martin."

Romeo did indeed look miserable. His feed lay untouched, and he huddled in the back of his box, head low. Tom checked him over quietly but could find no apparent signs of injury.

"Keep an eye on him Martin. Check his temperature regularly and get Kitty to take him for a pick of grass. No work until he perks up and eats something."

As they both left the box a low rasping noise made them both halt abruptly.

"I hope." Tom said quietly. "That wasn't what I think it was."

They paused, hardly daring to breathe. Another noise. This time there was no mistaking the harsh sound of a horse's cough. Tom pushed his cap onto the back of his head and rubbed his eyes.

"Somebody up there Martin has got it in for me. Get Mike out and move Romeo to the isolation yard; you know the score, usual routine."

As he walked gloomily into the office a raking bark followed him. Now that Romeo had started coughing, he couldn't stop. Sitting at his desk, Tom doodled moodily on a piece of paper and waited for the vet.

Before the vet arrived, the yard had become its usual hive of activity. Tom stood at the window and watched his staff go about their business. Martin was taking Romeo to the isolation yard; the ramshackle old stone buildings were a legacy of the days when Highford was a real estate with sheep and cattle. The barns were in a state of disrepair, but the stables were still good. He had hoped he would never need them. Kitty was washing out Romeo's box with disinfectant. He heard a car pull into the yard and craned his neck. Mike had been quicker than he thought he would be. The figure that crossed the yard was not, however, the one he expected.

"Rick. I didn't expect to see you today."

"Just thought I'd drop in and see how things were going." Rick was staring at Kitty with a rare intensity.

Long way to 'drop by' thought Tom dryly, and why is he looking at Kitty like that?

"Well, you can make yourself useful while you're here." Tom turned back into the office. "I'm afraid that Romeo is coughing so I'll have to wait for the vet, but you can ride out with the others if you will. Do you want breakfast?"

"Yes, please." Rick shook himself. "I'm starving. I could do with something hot."

The only person left in the coach house was Poppy, clearing away the remains of bacon and eggs. Smiling at him she turned the kettle back on.

"Bit late I'm afraid. Mrs. B has popped out to the village for a newspaper, but I can do you some toast?"

"Thanks. Black coffee please." Ricky sat as close to the fire as was physically possible.

Poppy watched him as she buttered his toast. His eyes had huge bags beneath them, and he hadn't shaved. He looked as if he needed a good night's sleep.

"Here." She put a mug in one hand and a plate on the other. "Get that down you. You look awful."

"Thanks." Rick was staring at the flames. "I had a pretty rough night."

Poppy pulled up a chair and sat beside him. It was worth facing the rocket she would get for being late just to be alone with him. Rick looked at her through heavy eyes. There was an unusual air of melancholy about him.

"Cheer up." She said heartily. "Can't be that bad, can it?"

Rick drank his coffee.

"Not for me anyway."

"Do you want to talk about it?" Poppy squinted at him.

He shook his head. He didn't feel safe talking about Dominic and his behaviour. Especially not here. He had accompanied a traumatised Flick to her home and had driven here harrowed by the thought of Kitty in Dominic's cruel hands. Now he was here he felt it impossible to raise the subject.

"Poppy!" Gareth's head came around the door. "If you don't shift your arse the boss will go mad. He needs you to hold Streak for the vet."

"Got to go." Poppy jumped up. She patted Rick's shoulder in a motherly fashion. "Chin up!"

Sometime later Rick emerged feeling fed and a little better. Food always lifted his spirits, Tom, however, was crossing the yard with a gloomy look on his face,

"If you don't normally pray, I suggest you start." He looked at Rick with doleful eyes. "If this thing spreads, we could both be out of a job. The last thing this place needs is a bloody virus!"

CHAPTER EIGHT

The Plough was bursting at the seams. Ron, the landlord was starting to worry about his fixtures and fittings as the party kept growing and growing. This was getting far bigger than he had anticipated. A large banner hung above the bar with the words "Happy Birthday Marty." emblazoned on it in foot high letters. The staff of Highford, their friends, and a cross section of locals were all drinking as though the world were about to end. Tucked away in the back room was a cake with thirty candles on it and trays full of food. Poppy was removing foil and trying to keep a ravenous Gareth at bay.

"Can I have one?" He was looking at the chicken legs.

"Wait until Ron is ready Taff." Poppy laughed. "Is the Guv here yet?"

"No. Do you really think he'll show?"

"Of course, he will. This sort of thing is good for morale."

Gareth had another longing look at the chicken.

"So, I can't have one now then?"

"Bugger off Taff! You can wait like the rest of us." Poppy threw the foil into the bin and pushed an objecting Gareth back out into the crowded room. Kitty and Ryan were leaning at the bar doing The Herald crossword.

"What's this?" Poppy was amazed. "Crosswords at parties?"

"Better than cross words which is what normally happens." Ryan grinned at his own wit. "It's a crossword with a difference. I'm having trouble reading it and Kitty can't hold the pen to answer it."

"Hmm." Poppy looked over his shoulder and saw Martin playing darts. Ron bustled over to them.

"Ready for the food?"

"May as well." Ryan made a show of looking at his watch,

and then at the door. "No sign of the boss, can't wait all night, can we?"

"Food!" Roared Ron. "Out the back."

Ryan, not wanting to stand and queue, flicked through the paper. It really was a rag. Full of the sex lives of soap stars, gay footballers, and topless models. He was about to turn to the sports pages when a headline caught his arm. 'Riding for a fall' read the copy that sat above a photograph of Rick getting out of his Porsche. Eyesight clearing rapidly Ryan took a sip of his pint and read on. 'The latest rising star of National Hunt racing, Kiwi Rick Cowdrey, had his first taste of the British legal system yesterday. During the afternoon he was fined by magistrates for driving in excess of 120mph on the M4, and last night was one of a number of people arrested on possession of illegal substances during a London club raid.'

Ryan's was stunned. He read the piece again shaking his head in disbelief. Was Rick mad? How did he expect to get to the top of his profession with his lifestyle? Poppy placed a large plateful of food in front of him.

"Got you some. I knew you'd be too lazy to get your own. What's that?" She snatched the paper from his hand. A grin spread over her face as she read the article and admired the way the photographer had caught Rick's profile.

"The sod! The boss won't approve, will he? Rick will have to do some smooth talking even by his standards to get out of this one! Good photo though. He looks like a rock star!"

"Trust you." Ryan took his paper back. "Did you get pickled onions?"

"Loads. Hey Kit! Look what your ex-lover boy has been up to now!"

Kitty scanned the page and put it down without interest.

"Sounds pretty typical to me. And he was *not* my lover boy."

Poppy began to tear out the photograph.

"I wonder what these parties, or raves, or whatever they call them now are like? I'll never get to one with my tame lifestyle."

"Why don't you ask the expert?" Ryan pointed a sausage towards the door. "The boss obviously doesn't read this trash."

Tom surveyed the packed room with satisfaction. It was good to see everyone enjoying themselves. Turning to his companion he gestured to the bar.

"What will you have?"

"Beer please." Rick took off the same battered leather jacket he had been wearing in the photograph. Aware of eyes fixed on him he found a corner table and tucked himself behind it. He was on edge; he had flunked out of telling Tom about his impending court case, terrified that he may lose the only real security he had. Ahead of him, their backs turned were a group of people that included Kitty and the good-looking dark-haired girl whose name he could never remember. As he watched them Ryan looked across and smirked. Rick looked away, catching sight of the paper, and reddening as he did so. Embarrassed, he stared out of the window.

A whisky and a pint of ale appeared in front of him, and Tom sat down.

"So. Rick. What have you been up to?"

"Pardon?" Rick nearly choked.

"What have you been up to? I haven't seen you for a few days."

"Nothing." Rick lowered his eyes. "Nothing at all."

"Not what I heard, or rather read." Tom leaned back in his chair.

"Ah." Rick put down his glass. "That."

"Of course, that. My dear brother couldn't wait to get on the 'phone and spread the dirt. Not to me of course, but to my mother, who promptly went out and bought a paper.

What I can't understand is why he was so eager to put you down. I thought you and he were friends?"

"Not anymore. Things change."

Tom watched the young man's face with interest. He could see the agitation present in Rick's eyes, but his face remained calm and composed.

"Why?" He asked. "Why drugs Rick? Do you really want to wipe out your career before it starts?"

"No." Rick looked humble. "It was just somewhere to go. Emmie gets bored easily."

"Emmie." Tom sounded like a father scolding his son. "Is going to get you into big trouble."

"Maybe." Rick was watching Kitty dancing with Ryan. "I'll have to tow the line for a while."

"A long while." Tom's voice was heavy with sarcasm. "Mud sticks Rick, people don't forget, and I do not, repeat not, want any cock ups you understand?"

Satisfied that he had said enough Tom turned to study the jostling crowd of people that filled the room. Martin was already three sheets to the wind, standing on a chair with his trousers rolled up he was reciting poetry to a group of hysterical onlookers. Poppy and Gareth were playing darts, making a pattern of holes in the surrounding woodwork.

"So." Rick decided to try and lighten the atmosphere between them. "Do we go for the Welsh National?"

"Definitely. Margie's got her heart set on it. Providing that Raver stays clear of this bloody virus that is."

"Mmm." Rick was only half listening, his eyes on Poppy. Tom followed his gaze to the tight jeans that left very little of Poppy's figure to the imagination. Her t-shirt ended above her stomach, showing a strip of smooth skin, her navel decorated by a jewel. She was taller than Kitty, broader, more athletic; she was very proud of her curves and loved showing them off. Turning around to collect her darts she saw them both watching her, and colour sprang to her cheeks.

"She's a really good-looking girl." Rick drained his glass. "Dramatic."

Tom raised his eyes to heaven. Lord, he thought, not another one.

"Don't worry." Rick read his thoughts. "I'm off women. Particularly stable girls."

"Good." Tom rose to go to the bar. " I really need another lad around the yard to replace Sarah, but until this virus clears, I can't think of anymore expense. With any luck any female applicants I get will be plain, overweight, and downright unpleasant. I've enough glamour girls on my yard."

"You can say that again." Rick was watching Kitty bending over. "That one's enough to break your heart."

You never spoke a truer word, thought Tom as memories of that Saturday night ran through his mind. More than enough to break your heart.

When Ron called time at the bar, the Pub was in full voice. They sang hunting songs, pop songs and some of Gareth's less vulgar rugby songs. Rick, shedding light onto a previously undisclosed talent, borrowed a guitar and treated them to some rock. Listening to his husky voice Poppy's eyes began to glaze over.

"Oh, he's wonderful." She sighed to an unimpressed Ryan. "Perfect."

Rick, smiling at all the cheers, put the guitar down and pushed his way to the bar. He found himself beside Kitty. Mellowed by drink she smiled up at him.

"Did you like it?" He could see the flush of alcohol on her cheeks.

"Brilliant. You're a real star." Her words were slurring, eyes not focusing on his face. Even in this drunken state she was gorgeous.

"I'm really sorry about how I treated you Kit. It was way out of line."

"It was." She agreed. Way out."

"So, can we be friends? I hate arguments."

"Okay." She stepped forward and kissed him on the cheek. The touch set him on fire.

"You." He murmured. "Are so beautiful."

Kitty raised her eyes to his, frowned, and collapsed against the bar with a little sigh.

"My word you must taste nice!" Giggling Poppy caught her friend's arm and shook it. "Can I have some? Kit. Kit can you hear me. Oops. I think she's had a bit too much to drink!"

"Problems?" Tom loomed up beside them.

"It's Kitty." Poppy began. "She's piss... I mean she's drunk. I'll take her outside for some fresh air."

"I'll do better than that." Tom put his arms underneath Kitty's. "I'll take her home. Come on young lady, good night all of you."

Rick watched as he half carried the helpless Kitty out of the door.

"Don't look so disappointed." Poppy hovered in front of him. "I'll look after you."

Rick took in the deep brown eyes and the glorious mane of hair. Her lips were the same cherry red as her t-shirt. He smiled and slipped his arm around her waist.

"Good." He grinned. "I was hoping you'd say that."

Tom has a strong sense of Deja vu as he helped Kitty into the car. This was getting to be a habit. Except that on this occasion the journey only lasted a couple of minutes and his passenger spent most of that time asleep. Helping her up the path he held her up with one arm and fumbled for the key with the other. As he pushed the door open, she stirred and looked up at him.

"I'm sorry boss. I'll be fine now, you go."

"Rubbish. Come on, I'll help you up the stairs. The last thing I want is one of my staff falling and breaking their neck!"

Watching her swaying precariously into the bedroom Tom hesitated in the doorway as his eyes took in the homely clutter of the place: the teddy bear tucked into the bed, the makeup covering the dressing table, the clothes hanging on the wardrobe. The room had a cosy, lived in atmosphere. Kitty was standing beside her bed, watching him as she kicked off her shoes. It could all be so easy. He could close the door, sit beside her and peel off her clothes. He could so easily take advantage of her. As if she had read his thoughts Kitty pulled the lilac shirt off her head. He stood quite still, afraid to move, as she put it into a wicker basket beside the wardrobe, and then slid the tight faded jeans off her hips. For a second, she stood still, clad only in her silky underwear, then began padding barefoot towards him, fingers fumbling with her necklace. She was so relaxed by the alcohol she had drunk; any shyness she would normally have felt had totally disappeared.

"Can you help me? I can't undo it."

With trembling fingers, he reached under her hair and undid the clasp. The chain fell forward, siding down her chest into her bra. Retrieving it she turned and smiled up at him. He caught his breath, and turned his eyes away, not trusting the temptation that her semi-nakedness was placing in front of him. Reaching for the door he tried to get a grip on himself. He had to go, quickly, before his lust got the better of him.

"Good night, Kitty." He didn't dare look back because he knew that her adoring eyes would be watching him.

"Good night."

He heard her moving away. As he closed the door, he couldn't stop himself taking one last, furtive glance. He saw her sprawled on her bed, already asleep, one slender arm thrown across her forehead. Sleeping Beauty. Waiting for the prince to come and hack away the thorns. But that role was not for him, and definitely not tonight. Feeling proud of his self-control he closed the door quietly and left the silent cottage.

Back in his own room he felt his surroundings austere and bare. Slipping into the cool, pressed cotton sheets he stared up at the ceiling. The room felt empty. His bed felt empty. His whole life felt empty. Perhaps it was time he found someone to share them with.

CHAPTER NINE

Dominic was bored. Having chased his tail around the continent for a week he had returned to his vast, empty flat and brooded alone. Nothing entertained him anymore. He was tired of the readily available girls who filled London's nightclubs and would do anything to spend the night on his arm and his bank balance, dwindling fast, didn't allow him to play the Riviera circuit for the immediate future. He needed an injection of capital to boost his lifestyle, Otherwise, he thought, he would drown in this stagnant pool of boredom he was floating in. He guessed that Tom must know, by now, of his encounter with Flick Harries and although he wanted to gloat and rub salt into his brothers' wounds, he knew that he would be entering risky territory going home so soon. The confrontation with Tom didn't worry him, it was the fear that if the arising friction was too great his mother would not be her usual benevolent self. So, he decided to stay away, at least until Christmas, to let his brother's mind dwell on his actions, and feed his funds from other sources.

He would find them, he always did.

He found the next one in the most unlikely place.

Shopping was just not something that Dominic did. He ordered over the internet, or by telephone from exclusive outlets. He never walked into a shop and picked something up from a rail. But even he, the virtual anorexic, had to eat sometimes, and more importantly to him, he had to drink. One, wet, dismal, Saturday night he found himself in the local off licence. He was tipping change onto the counter, leaving an astonished young assistant to count it, when his nose was filled with the scent of Chanel. Looking around, curious but indifferent, he saw a good-looking brunette studying the limited stock of champagne. Turning to look at her properly his interest grew when he saw the Gucci insignia on her bag and the expensive cashmere coat that hung from her shoulders. He waited; his bottle of vodka untouched on the counter for her to approach the till.

"I'll take this please." Good accent. Well bred, well heeled.

The woman who was, he guessed, older than he, was digging in her bag for her purse. As she pulled out her credit card, she became aware of his stare and looked up. Dominic fixed his eyes on her face, taking in every detail. This was no girl. There was maturity on the structured face, the faint hint of crow's feet around the almond eyes. She had high cheekbones, like his own, but less angular, and a broad full lipped mouth. it would be no exaggeration to call her a beauty. Her brow creased into a frown as he watched her, and she turned away.

Dominic's eyes never left the tall figure as it walked out of the store. When she had gone, he turned to the girl, who had watched the encounter with interest and, more than a touch of jealousy.

"Who was that?"

"Lauren West." The girl found this man strange, but very attractive. "She owns a boutique on Kings Road."

"Does she now?" Dominic smiled. "Thank you. Very much."

The night didn't feel as dismal to Dominic as it had before. Loping back to his apartment his mind began to work overtime. A boutique. Well, he needed a new wardrobe. He had just an idea where he may find it.

A week later he was not alone on the Saturday night. He poured wine while Lauren West soaked naked and beautiful in his bathtub. Their first sexual experience had been a mutually satisfying one. He had revelled in her curved, woman's body, and she had taken everything he had done to her with ecstatic pleasure. It was a good match. One that would relieve his boredom, for now, and one that would give him more freedom. For Lauren, he had discovered, was not only beautiful, and wealthy, she was also one of the most powerful women in the city. What Lauren wanted, she got. Just, he thought to himself as he heard her entering the bedroom, the sort of woman I need.

"Drink?" He offered her a glass.

"Thank you." Lauren was wearing his denim shirt, it pulled taught across her bust and barely covered the top of her thighs.

"Well." Dominic sat on the sofa and stretched. "That was very pleasant."

"Wasn't it." Lauren lifted her long, shapely legs and laid them on his. "We must do it again sometime."

"We must." Dominic's fingers crept upwards along her tanned thighs. "Soon."

"Not that soon!" Lauren laughed. "I've just bathed. Besides. I want to talk to you."

"Talk?" Dominic frowned. "That sounds boring."

"Never mind." Lauren leaned forward and put down her glass. "I think you may be able to help me."

"Go on." Dominic watched her, eyes roaming ceaselessly over her body. She was naked underneath that shirt. Already his satisfaction was lifting, and he could feel his body starting to throb.

Lauren saw his eyes changing and smiled. If she kept creating that reaction in him, she would be happy, the day it stopped, she would be lost. In the short space of time that she had known him Dominic had taken over her thoughts. He was in her head, constantly. At first, she had been offended by the young man's persistence, but once she had caved in and accepted his invitations she had never once looked back with regret. The last couple of hours with him had been unlike anything she had experienced in her thirty-nine years. Until then she had only been half alive. He had opened the doors to a part of her she had never known existed. She liked it, and she knew that from now on she would do anything to keep Dominic Chichester in her life.

"I've heard." She rubbed his bare chest with her toes. "That you may be able to help me."

"How?"

"I'm having a party." She slid her foot down to his stomach. "I've been told that you could provide me with something I need. Something to help it go well."

"Have you?" Dominic caught her foot with his hand. "What's that?"

"Oh, you know." Lauren smiled. "I want the best, mind, and I'll pay you well for it."

"Oh, you will." Dominic placed her toe in his mouth and bit gently. "Believe me you will."

Watching her lie back, eyes closed, he saw his future opening again. What a stroke of luck. A stunningly good-looking woman, desirable, with a libido to match his own and a bank balance that would keep both of them happy. Twisting around he lay on top of her, and she opened her eyes. He smiled. She really was the best-looking cash machine he had ever seen.

Miles away, in his study, Tom poured another scotch and turned the pages of his diary. Six of his inmates now showed signs of the virus, but thankfully only Romeo had been badly affected by it. His isolation boxes were now full, which would mean any more suspects would have to stay on the main yard; that could spell the beginning of a disaster. A photograph of his father looked out at him from its silver frame. He was holding a big chestnut horse. Galloway Boy, the first horse Tom clearly remembered, and the nearest thing Highford had ever produced to a winner of the prize of his dreams, the Grand National. Galloway Boy had finished a gallant third on a day of torrential rain and unbelievable mud. That was in nineteen seventy, thirty years ago when Tom had been a six-year-old boy, completely overawed by the occasion. He could still see the pride on his father's face as he unsaddled the horse. Next year, he had promised Tom, they would lead in the winner.

They never had. Galloway Boy had broken down on both front legs in the course of his brave efforts and, by the time they reached home, was hopelessly crippled. Such was the extent of his injuries that one day after running the race of his life, he was put to sleep and buried under the trees in the orchard. Tom had never forgotten the tears, the anguish, and the way that he, at six years of age, could not understand why the big horse was not looking out over the stable door to greet him the next day. He remembered pulling at his mother's sleeve and asking when 'Boy' was going to wake up. The memory brought tears to his eyes as he turned the photograph over and over in his hands. His father had spent the rest of his life looking for the horse to succeed his beloved chestnut but had never found it. Now Tom had in his care such a horse, a horse that would have refuelled his father's ambition. He just had to keep him safe.

"Well Dad." he spoke to the photograph. "If this goes wrong, if I lose Olympic Run, I'll be taking the sign off the gate."

Finishing his drink, he looked at his watch. Two thirty. All would be quiet on the yard. It was less than two weeks now to Christmas; he really should go into Cheltenham and look for gifts. He hadn't seen Flick in over a month. She normally helped him organise the party he held every year for staff and locals alike.

He had a lot to do and not a lot of time left to do it in. He tracked down his mother watching an old black and white film in the living room.

"I'm going into town." He informed her. "Should there, God forbid, be a crisis, I'm taking my mobile with me."

On his way he called into the isolation yard. Martin was lying on a bale of hay, eating crisps, and reading Dick Francis.

"All quiet?" Tom's ears strained for sounds of coughs and wheezes.

"Very." Martin sat up. "Not even a sneeze."

"Thank God." Tom patted Romeo's neck. "So, is it safe for me to absent myself?"

"I should think so." Martin returned to his book.

"Well call if you need me." Tom buttoned up his coat, cast a wary look up at the grey sky, and left.

The BMW had barely disappeared into the lanes before Poppy came flying around the corner, gasping for breath.

"Martin, quick!" She panted. "There's something wrong with Micky!"

"What is it?" Martin frowned.

"He can't breathe." Poppy was panic stricken. "He's really distressed."

Martin followed her to a small group of very worried people outside Micky's box. The little horse was standing with head lowered, his sides heaving as he struggled for air

"Oh Lord." Martin scratched his head. "Ry, go and get Mike Stone. Trust this to happen now with the Guv just gone." He paused. "No point calling him back now, we'll have to wait for Mike. Poor old Micky. Christ if anything happens to him Mrs. C will break her heart."

Cheltenham town was bursting at the seams with festive shoppers, a moving mass of crowd, all searching for that last-minute bargain. Having been elbowed around for an hour Tom decided he'd had enough. His feet began to automatically tread the familiar path that led to the Grey and Greeley advertising agency. A large, gaudy silver tree decorated the reception. Pausing to wrinkle his nose in distaste he nodded to the security guard, signed the book, and took the lift to the top floor. Smiling sweetly at the receptionist he walked straight up to Flick's door. Her secretary's face lit up at the sight of him.

"Why Mr. Chichester! We haven't seen you for a while. I'll

see if Miss Harries is free."

She returned, blushing slightly.

"Go on in. Would you like coffee?"

"Thank you. I would love one, and some of those chocolate biscuits you keep hidden in your drawer."

Laughing at the secretary's face as she got the biscuits from her top drawer he went into Flick's office. Turning, he stopped short at the sight of her. She was thin and pale, her usually luxurious hair pulled back off her face in a plait. A shapeless navy-blue dress replaced her normal, immaculate, designer suits.

"Good God." Tom sounded as alarmed as he felt. "What's happened to you? Are you ill?"

"Not exactly. To what do I owe the honour?"

He sat opposite her and studied the ravaged eyes.

"You're not pleased to see me?"

Flick said nothing. The last thing she wanted to see on at that the moment was a Chichester.

"I'm sorry I haven't been in touch lately." Tom tried again. "I've been busy."

"No doubt." She was staring at the large pile of papers in front of her. She raised her eyes briefly as her secretary brought in the coffees but didn't speak. Tom sipped from his cup and waited. When after some time Flick still hadn't looked at him, he made another attempt.

"What's wrong Flick? You can tell me."

"Can I?" Her face was bitter and twisted, hiding her inner torment. "You jog in and out of my life as and when it pleases you. Don't pretend that you care about me Tom please!"

"But of course, I care!" Tom was stunned by this unexpected hostility. Flick normally greeted him with such warmth and enthusiasm, however long his absence. "Look, let's go out somewhere and talk. Dinner perhaps?"

"No." Flick shook her head. He could see her lips beginning to tremble.

"Just a drink then? We'll go now if you can finish early, and if you don't mind my jeans."

Flick gave him a furtive glance. Reluctant as she was to talk, she needed desperately to pour her heart out to someone. Trying to keep the tremor from her voice she answered him.

"Come to my place in an hour." She lowered her eyes. Tom hesitated, then got to his feet. She didn't look up as he left the room.

The baggy trousers into which Flick had changed made her look even more haggard. Taking the yellow roses, her tortured brain recognising that they were not red, she turned her mouth away as he bent to kiss her. A half-eaten roll lay on the table with a glass of brandy. She hadn't washed her hair or put on makeup, totally out of context with her fastidious character.

"What would you like to do?" Tom felt her flinch as he touched her arm.

"Nothing." She still wouldn't look at him.

"Oh, come on Flick. Please tell me what's wrong." He bent his head to look into her shadowed eyes. "I can't help you if I don't know what you need."

"You can't help me." Flick held her breath against the nausea in her stomach.

"Come on." Tom put his arm around her, ignoring her rigid muscles, taking them only as part of her rejected mood. "We've had our differences in the past, but we've always worked them out. I hate seeing you like this. To be honest I can't ever remember seeing you like this."

That, thought Flick as she tried to wriggle free, is because I have never *been* like this.

"Look. I'm okay. Please let me go." She pushed at him. Something in his hard, muscular proximity reminded her of Dominic. It repulsed her and she felt tears pricking her eyes,

Puzzled, Tom reluctantly let her go. Backing off he reached for the door, completely perplexed by her behaviour.

"Perhaps I should go."

Flick turned and looked at him properly for the first time. It was as if she was looking at a stranger. Then her memory revived, and tears filled her eyes as she saw the confusion on his face. His strong, handsome face that she had seen in so many moods, so many moments of passion. The vivid blue eyes were so gentle. Surely, she could trust him. The only man she had ever really truly cared for. She had to off load this burden onto someone, she could quite simply not carry it alone. Lowering her eyes, she took a deep breath. The words were simple enough, wouldn't take long to say; but in one simple statement lay the certain knowledge that things would never again be the same between her and this man. The finality of it terrified her. When she finally spoke, the words were so quiet he hardly heard her.

"I'm pregnant."

"What!"

She watched the emotions chasing across his face: surprise, shock, even horror as she could see him preparing for the obvious question. She shook her head quickly, tears falling freely now, answering him before he spoke.

"No, it's not you." She was almost choking on her words. "God, I really wish it was."

"Then who is it?" Tom's stomach was lurching, his initial shock was quickly followed by relief, and then guilt. Then jealousy as he thought of her with someone else. Memories came slowly back.

"It's Rick's." It was a statement not a question. Surely there was no one else? "Does he know?"

"No, it's not him." She was shaking miserably. "I need a drink."

He passed her the brandy then hesitated. Should she be drinking this? But his curiosity was stronger than his moral dilemma.

"Then who is it?" He sounded harsher than he intended.

Her chest heaved with emotion as she struggled to speak. watching her, feeling the need for alcohol himself he went to the cabinet and as he closed his fingers around the whisky bottle the words reached his ears. He froze, bile rising to his throat. He spoke without turning.

"Who?" He prayed that he had misheard her.

"Your brother."

It was a long time before she stopped crying and when she did, she went to the bathroom and was violently sick. On her return she seemed a little more composed. Sitting beside him she offered another whisky which he drained in one mouthful. She could almost see the terrible images that were battering his brain; could read the turmoil of his mind in his staring eyes. When he finally looked at her it was with an expression of such sorrow that she thought her heart would burst. He was devastated, it was written all over him. Why, where, it didn't matter to him. Nothing that she said could explain this turn of events away. Tom stared into the depths of his empty glass afraid to look at her. Rick he could have come to terms with, but Dominic? The thought of his hands on the woman beside him made Tom heave. Even worse was the thought, the image, of Dominic's child growing inside her as they spoke. He had ruined her, defiled her, tainted her with the taste of his hideous perversion. Tom had never realised until that moment just how much he felt for Flick, or the true extent of the hatred he had for his brother. Shaking his head, he rubbed his misty eyes and sighed heavily.

"Oh Tom." She touched his hair. "I wish it was different. But it's happened. I can't change the past, I've ruined everything, all my hopes for the future with one stupid action. I know how much you hate him. Now you'll hate me too."

"No." He sat back. "I just hate him even more."

"Oh God." She was crying again. "I love you so much."

Even now, when he knew she needed something from him; more than she ever had before he couldn't confess his feelings.

"This is partly my fault." He laid his hand on her shoulder. "If I'd offered you some sort of commitment this would never have happened."

She put her arms around him and laid her head on his chest. She could feel his heart beating. He placed his lips on her hair, and out of the habit of their long relationship she raised her face to his. Tom knew what he was about to do was wrong; but he had to exorcise the ghost of Dominic's memory, wash away the residue of his touch on her skin. This would not be making love, it was twisted absolution, a way of reclaiming what was his.

Flick, who had only ever wanted to belong to this man, knew it for what it was and was prepared to give herself to him completely. For the sake of feeling his flesh beside hers one last time she would do anything. She had never known Tom to cry, but as she got to her feet, she saw his cheeks wet with tears. At the threshold of the familiar bedroom, she felt him hesitate, saw the confusion in his eyes. Misreading the emotion, she squeezed his hand.

"It's okay." She said quietly. "He never came here."

Tom didn't move. He was looking through her, past her presence into some picture in his mind. His face hardened and he pulled his hand from hers.

Flick stepped back. Back into the safety of her own space. She took one last look at him, at his hard eyes, his brooding expression and with a burst of courage that rose from somewhere deep inside she slammed the door in his face. Damn him too then if she revolted him that much. What a

melancholy brood they were those bloody Chichester's. She
wished she had never heard the name. Never set eyes on
either of these arrogant men with their history and their
insatiable egos. Users. That was all they were. They had
no feelings except for themselves and their own desires.
She began to shake as she had realised what she had been
about to do. How low had she become? They were dragging
her down, these two, leaving her in a pit of despair and
dejection as they swaggered on. Leaving her alone. Very
well then alone she would be. She needed no one, least of
all the man who she knew was still standing outside the
door.

Tom stood, staring at the pale grey wall, for a very long
time. Until he grew cold. Then he moved back into the
living room and turned on the fire. He felt lost. He had
no idea what to do. Flick's situation horrified him, and he
felt he knew what he should do. He had not caused this,
not directly, but he was her only way forward now. But
there was something else, some other presence that kept
creeping into his mind and holding him back. A presence
with long blonde hair and gentle eyes. Whenever he
thought of the future she was always there, and although
it was absurd, he couldn't imagine it without her. If he did
this thing, if he did what he felt to be right by Flick then he
would wipe her out of the picture forever. He wasn't ready
to do that. Not yet. Confused, unhappy, he lay his head on
the arm of the sofa and fell asleep.

She woke him hours later, when the cold December night
was stroking fingers of frost on the windows. He lay on the
sofa and looked at her for a second, then stared out onto
the night with sad eyes.

"What will you do?" He asked. "It's difficult bringing up a
child on your own."

"There isn't going to be a child." She turned away. "It's all
arranged. Monday."

"Oh darling." He caught hold of her hand. "You don't have
to do that. I'll look after you. We can tell everyone that it's

mine."

His own words shocked him and even as he spoke his mind turned to Kitty and what it would mean to her. Flick was watching him. Do you think I don't know that, she thought, don't you realise I've thought a thousand times of using this to bind you to me? She gave a weak smile.

"No Tom." I've made up my mind. I could never love this baby. He revolted me and being pregnant by him revolts me too. There isn't a minute of the day when I don't feel repulsive and dirty. If I had to live through nine months of this, I'd, well, I wouldn't trust myself. What if I felt the same about the baby?"

"But it would be different when it was born. Your own little baby." He stroked her pale face, his moral instincts rejecting what she had just told him, but unable to stop the feelings of relief.

"No." She shook her head. "By the time I had it I would be suicidal. I've thought of it already believe me. It seems like a wonderful idea when I'm alone. I've never disliked myself before. I do now."

"Don't my darling." He brushed her lank hair from her face. "You must do what's right for you, but don't become bitter. I'll be here to help you, always."

"Will you?" She almost laughed. "I very much doubt it."

Tom couldn't answer her. She knew him too well this woman who he had been close to for so long. She knew what made him tick, what drove him to work so tirelessly day after day. But he was changing, there were things about him that Flick didn't know and would never understand. Like his growing infatuation for a twenty-one-year-old girl.

But the least he could do was keep her company tonight. He couldn't leave her when she was so low. Going into the bedroom he undressed, pulled back the quilt and slipped in beside her.

CHAPTER TEN

Martin was beginning to panic. The injections that Mike Stone had given Micky had taken no effect. At a loss the vet had gone back to his surgery to look for another form of medication. Kitty had been sitting with the horse for hours, holding steaming buckets of eucalyptus and menthol crystals in front of his nostrils, trying to relieve the congestion in his lungs. But her efforts had been fruitless; the little cob's eyes were starting to glaze over.

"Oh Jesus." Martin grabbed the headcollar as the horse began to stagger sideways. "Poppy, help me, quick!"

"What?" The shadow of Poppy's curling hair appeared in the doorway.

"Get up to the house and see if Mrs. C knows where the boss is. I've tried the mobile but there's no answer and he hasn't replied to any messages. I think he must have left it in the car."

Eleanor, who was on her way to bed, was worried by the anguish on Poppy's face.

"Come on in dear." She led the way into Tom's study. "I have a feeling I may know where he is."

Feeling very guilty at her intrusions she looked through Tom's 'phone book and found Felicity's number. A little nervous she was more than relieved when her son himself answered her call.

"Mother? What on Earth's the matter?"

"Martin has been trying to reach you all night. One of the horses is terribly ill dear. You'd better come home quickly."

"Oh hell. Okay, I'm leaving now, tell him I'm on my way."

Eleanor turned to the pale faced Poppy.

"He's coming dear. Which horse is it?"

Poppy hesitated, then decided that a white lie was best

considering the circumstances.

"I don't know, Martin didn't tell me. Thank you, Mrs. Chichester. I'd better get back."

Eleanor let her out and made her way up to bed. As she slipped off her dressing gown, she looked at her husband's photograph which was in its usual place on the dressing table. He seemed to be watching her with accusing eyes. It took her less than a minute to change her mind. Going to the utility room she pulled Tom's socks onto her feet and stepped into her wellingtons. Wrapping her old woollen coat around her she called Spock from his basket and picked up the keys to the Land Rover.

When she arrived at the yard it wasn't hard to locate the right stable. Light flooded out of the loose box and a couple of anxious looking people were hovering outside it. Getting closer she saw that it was Martin and the pretty young blonde girl.

"Mrs. C!" Martin's eyes widened. "What are you doing here?"

"I thought perhaps I could help. Which one is it dear? Not Olympic Run I hope!"

Martin swallowed, then reluctantly stepped aside to let her into the box.

"I'm afraid it's Micky." He muttered.

"Oh no!" Eleanor's hands flew to her face as she caught sight of the little horse, who was now lying weakly on his bed. "Is there anything we can do Martin?"

Martin forced himself to sound bright.

"Mike is on his way back."

Eleanor went into the stable, her legs feeling weak beneath her and unsteadily crouched beside the old horse. He was breathing with great rasping sighs, eyes staring blankly into nowhere, ears flopping sideways. She patted his hot, wet neck.

"Take it easy old boy." She said softly. "You'll be fine."

She took hold of the bucket and held it out to Kitty.

"Will you get some more dear? This had gone cold."

Laying her hand on Micky's back, ignoring the flowered flannel nightdress that draped over the floor, she sat on the straw beside him.

Time dragged painfully by as they all watched the animal growing very slowly weaker and weaker. A car pulled into the yard and Mike Stone came running across.

"Thank God." Martin bustled him in. "I thought you'd never get here!"

"Please Michael." Eleanor got unsteadily to her feet and took his arm. "Please help our old Micky. He looks so sick."

Mike stood in the doorway and studied the horse with concern. He didn't like the look of this, he had deteriorated badly since he had left. Checking him over his fears grew; the mucous membranes were deadly pale, and he didn't need a stethoscope to hear the brass band that was playing inside Micky's lungs. Taking his temperature, he shook his head. One hundred and six.

"He doesn't look too good I'm afraid. I can give him another shot to try ease his breathing, then all we can do is wait for the antibiotics to do their job."

He looked up at Eleanor as he sank the needle into Micky's neck.

"It's his age you see." He said softly. "It gets harder as they get older. Keep that door shut, to keep out the frost, and try to keep him cool but not cold. Lots of light rugs are better than heavy ones. But watch him closely. I'm afraid I can't stay, just had an emergency come in."

"Why don't you go back to the house Mrs. Chichester." Martin put his arm around her. "It's too cold for you to hang around here. I'll keep an eye on Mick."

"No, no Martin, thank you. I'd rather stay."

"Then can we get you a drink? Coffee? Hot chocolate?"

"Thank you dear. A coffee would be very nice."

Kitty ran back to the cottage, tucking her chin into her Puffa coat against the icy air. As she was putting mugs onto a tray, she saw headlights on the drive. Pouring milk into another mug she cursed the ancient kettle for being so slow. Despite her best efforts most of the coffee had found its way onto the tray by the time she made her way back to the stable. Tom was standing outside, hands deep in his pockets. She was shocked by his appearance; pale, drawn, his shadowed eyes sunken far back into their sockets. He looked as if he was carrying the weight of the world on his shoulders.

"Here." She held out a mug. "I made you one as well."

"Thanks." Absent-mindedly he took the cup from her, raising it to his lips but not drinking. She had never in her life seen anyone look so low. His arrogant air had completely disappeared leaving his turmoil on show for all the world to see. His mother also read the signs of her son's distress, with no understanding of the cause and slipped her arm through his. He looked down at her and gave her a weak smile. The grandmother, who wasn't to be. He closed his eyes.

A loud groan took them all to the doorway of the stable. Martin was feeling the already thready pulse in the horse's neck.

"Boss, I think he's getting worse."

Tom placed his mug on the window ledge.

"Come on Martin, let's try and get him to his feet. If he lays down flat, he'll just give in."

Together they pulled at the horses headcollar. Kitty and Poppy went behind him and pushed at his rump. The horse gave a weak, half-hearted attempt to rise, then collapsed back into the straw.

"Come on Micky!" Shouted Tom. "On your feet!"

After three more fruitless attempts they gave in, gazing despondently at the horse, who rolled onto his side and lay flat on the straw.

"Right." Tom stood back. "There's absolutely no need for all of us to hang around here. It's all up to him now. Martin, take my mother back to the house, you girls get off to bed, I'll stay with him."

Refusing to listen to any arguments Tom closed the door and sat beside the little cob. He laid his hands on the wet neck, which was starting to grow cold. Eyes closed; Tom listened to the rasping breath with heavy heart. His mind began to wander.

Pictures flashed through his head; confused images that were neither present nor past, but always his mind returned to Dominic. To the tortured expression on Flick's face; to Kitty on her hands and knees in a dark alley. His eyes jerked open abruptly, and he waited for them to focus. Micky was still breathing in great heaving sighs. Leaning back against the wall Tom let his heavy eyelids lower again, and as sleep eventually overtook him, the rambling of his tormented mind turned to dreams.

The sun rose in a scarlet ball, streaking the sky with pink, edging the few clouds with a golden glow. The heavy frost that lay in the fields turned the grass into a glittering sea as the fierce light reflected on its surface. Deep in the valley a veil of mist shrouded the river, skeleton trees rising bare and dark from its depths. Kitty stretched as she looked out of the window and watched the Cotswold stone of Highford House turn orange, the windows glittering darkly then springing to life as the sun moved on. What a beautiful morning. One of those mornings when it was good to be alive and able to see nature at work. Pulling on her sweatshirt she remembered Micky and her mood changed. Dressing as she ran down the stairs, she bolted through the kitchen pausing only briefly to pull boots onto her bare feet and sprinted along the gravel path. The horses, seeing her approach, began to call, banging their doors in anticipation of breakfast. Martin always called the crescendo 'the dawn chorus', and it normally brought a warm smile to her lips. But today it failed to move her. Terrified of what she might find she took a deep breath and walked to the loose box door. Peering in she uttered a silent prayer and blinked, trying to adjust her eyes to the gloom that still filled the stable. A weak ray of light filtered through the window and shone on Micky. What she saw made her heart falter, then race out of control. Deep brown eyes looked into hers, a pair of large mules like ears cocked forward as she approached. He was still very weak, but Micky managed to make a strangled sound that passed for a whicker of greeting. Beside him, stretched out on the straw, was a tall dark figure, a woollen jumper pillowing its head. Kitty gave a laugh of pleasure and tiptoed through the door. Crouching in front of Micky she patted his neck. The sweat had dried in salty streaks on his neck, but the heat had gone. Pulling his wonderfully cool ears through her fingers she planted a kiss on the broad white blaze.

"Hello boy." She crooned. "Are you feeling better?"

The sound of her voice, soft as it was, disturbed Tom in his lightening sleep. Blinking his eyes in the light that fell on his face he saw a vague, distorted, golden haze. Dis-orientated he blinked, shaking his himself. The soft, purring noise became words and the soft, ethereal vision became Kitty's head. Smiling, he lay on his side so he could see her better. She was kneeling in front of Micky, kissing him. His movement caught her attention and she looked at him, her face lit up with happiness,

"I thought I was hearing Angels" His voice was hoarse and un co-operative.

"Just me." Her smile widened. "Isn't it marvellous? He's so much better."

"Marvellous." Tom was entranced by her beauty. "I woke earlier, and he was looking at me with a very amused expression on his face. I'm ashamed to say I was far too comfortable to move."

"Would you like a cup of tea? Or coffee? I can fetch some?"

"Thank you." The sunlight was filtering through the window and the sifting curtain of her hair. As she pulled it back from her face the longing, he had deliberately suppressed for so long became unbearable. It was so strong, his desire, that it physically hurt. Kitty sat back on her heels and looked at the man beside her. There was an unfamiliar, almost disturbing light in his eyes. Tom sat up, brushing straw off his shirt. The buttons had undone, baring his dark chest. Kitty looked quickly away.

"I'll get that tea."

"No. Wait." He caught her arm and pulled her towards him. Losing her balance, she fell against his chest, her hair brushing his skin. The contact was like an electric current, sparking him into action. His lips found her mouth as he pushed her back onto the straw, his arms encircling her waist, holding her so tightly that he almost crushed the breath out of her. Pulling back, holding himself above her he looked down at her golden beauty and had a brief, painful vision of how wonderful it would be to make love to her. As he hesitated, she caught his neck and pulled him back down to her, kissing him passionately. Pleasantly surprised he grew bolder. Carefully cupping her breast in his hand, he buried his face in her neck, tasting her warm, scented skin. He could hear her breath growing heavier, feel her pulse quickening beneath his lips. Sliding his hand inside her jumper he was surprised when she pushed him away.

"No." She gasped. "This isn't fair. Get off me."

"I'm sorry." He held her tight. "I thought"

"I know what you thought." Her own feelings were confusing her, making her angry. "I'm such an easy target for you, aren't I? You know exactly how I feel about you. So, you play along with it, and roll the stable girl in the hay!"

"Oh, my poor girl." Tom stroked her neck. "Don't you realise I spend every day trying not to think about you? Not to want you. I tell myself it's impossible, but the feeling doesn't go away. I just can't stop it. You're so beautiful Kitty, it's not fair on me either."

"Don't do this to me." She pleaded.

"If you really want to go you can." Tom sat back and moved his hand. "But I don't think you do, do you?"

His deep blue eyes were burning straight into her heart, tormenting her. The most desirable man she had ever laid eyes on was telling her what she had always dreamed of hearing; that he wanted her, and she was turning him away. She wondered if she was crazy. She had dreams about this man, lay awake long into the night fantasising the feeling of his hands upon her body. She could have him now, and the dreams would become reality. No more fantasy; only memories. She could feel his breath on her neck as she drew closer. Shaking with nerves she placed an unsteady hand on his chest and slipped her fingers inside his shirt, curling them through the dark hair. Slowly, cautiously, his hand reached out until it moved underneath her jumper and curved over her silken skin. He felt the hardness of her nipples and stroked them gently.

"I want you so much Kitty." His voice was deep and harsh, heavy with lust. "Don't turn me away."

For answer she slipped her hands around his broad back, feeling the hard muscles, and pulled him down on top of her. Minutes later he rose and shut the top door of the stable, slipping home the inside bolt. Kneeling beside her he removed her clothing until she lay, soft and beautiful in her nakedness in front of him. Her eyes looked up at him, wary, nervous, yet adoring. A sacrificial lamb, watching in awe as he undressed himself, reaching out her exploring fingers to touch his body, feeling his skin, his hair, tracing the muscles of his chest. Bending down to kiss her he felt those fingers reach his groin and sighed with pleasure. Kissing every inch of her warm body, feeling her shudder as his fingers slid upwards, he realised how badly she wanted him, and that he had not been alone on the battlefield of desire. Reminding himself to be gentle, he lowered himself on top of her.

"Look at me."

Obediently she opened her eyes and watched him, hazy eyed, eyes which widened as he pushed himself inside her. Staring at him, mesmerised, as she began to move her body with his. With great effort he restrained himself until, at just the right moment, he unleashed the torrent of emotion that had been building up inside him. Driving into her with all his strength he cried out, a rush of relief and satisfaction pouring through him. Her eyes were still fixed, unmoving, on his face. Eyes heavy now with sex and emotion. Her fingers ran lightly up and down his spine, sending shivers jumping across his skin. A warm glow of contentment filled him, and he gently brushed his lips over hers. Laying his head on her breast he was just drifting back into sleep when a noise from outside brought him back to reality with a jolt and sent her hugging tense against him.

Martin's whistle grew louder as he walked along the yard and entered the next loose box. Kitty panicked, pulling away, reaching desperately for her clothes. Shaking his head, cradling her tightly in his arms he kissed her head.

"Don't worry." He whispered. "The doors locked."

"Boss?" Martin was rattling the latch. "Boss? Are you awake in there?"

"Yes." Tom called out, his voice perfectly calm. "Mick's fine, I just woke up."

"He's okay!" The bolt shook again. "That's great. How about I make him a warm mash?"

"Good idea. Make one for me as well, only put some coffee in mine!" Tom bit his lip, containing an adolescent urge to laugh.

"Will do." Martin's footsteps faded back across the yard.

"I've got to get dressed." Kitty was scrambling through the straw looking for her scattered clothing. "Poppy will wonder where the hell I am."

"Come here." Tom pulled her back down beside him. "You don't have to go yet."

"Let go!" She squeaked. "Quick before Marty gets back!"

"Kiss first." He laughed as she struggled feebly against him.

"No!" She was laughing as well. "Let go!"

"Never." Tom stole his kiss. "Not again."

Kitty smiled, grew still in his arms, and lifted her face to his in a long lingering kiss.

"Now can I get dressed. Sir?"

"Certainly Miss Campbell. And don't report for work with all that straw in your hair, you look like a scarecrow."

Kitty blushed, lowering her eyes, and pulled on her breeches. Tom, laughing at her, pulled on his own trousers and went to unlock the door, unable to keep the smile off his face. He felt like a schoolboy after his first date; this gorgeous young girl had given him a pleasure he hadn't dreamed to be possible. Roused by all this activity Micky rose to his feet, a little unsteady at first, but soon making his way to the manger in search of breakfast.

"Oh, you're better." Kitty laughed. "Greedy guts!"

Laying her hand on the horse's neck she placed her cheek on his coat. A strange sight he had just witnessed. Giving him one last pat, she headed for the door. Tom stood in front of her.

"This won't be the last time Kitty." He buried his face in her hair. "I promise."

"I love you." She said simply; and left.

CHAPTER ELEVEN

Poppy licked the seal of her final envelope and pressed it down. Ticking the last name off her list she surveyed the pile of neatly written envelopes with pride. This was the first year since she had left home that she had finished writing all her cards in time for the last posting date. Not that she wrote much. Just 'Poppy', with a curling flourish. But still it was done. Looking into the corner of the room she saw Kitty putting the fairy back onto its perch on the Christmas Tree. Baubles and tinsel clustered in the branches, and presents were already starting to appear at its base. The fairy, cruelly named Rick because of its blonde locks, tended to topple sideways and hang upside down. Poppy said this was caused by too much Christmas spirit, Ryan insisted it was taking after its namesake. Tired of pricking her fingers on the pine needles Kitty was now manacling its legs to the top branch with a plaiting band. The fairy settled at a very peculiar angle but seemed secure.

Poppy watched her friend through narrowed eyes. Kitty had been a very distant companion lately, her mind always somewhere else. For the last week she had been distracted, distant; she was dreamier than ever, gazing endlessly into space. Occasionally some private thought would make her blush. Poppy was convinced that there was man behind it all but couldn't for the life of her think who it could be. She had even read all of Kitty's Christmas cards in search of a clue.

The fairy in place Kitty sat beside the fire and rested her feet on the hearth. Seven days to Christmas, eight to the King George 'Chase and twelve to the Welsh Grand National and Little Raver's big race debut. The horses that had suffered the virus were mending nicely and mercifully the rest had somehow managed to stay clear of it. Life at the yard had settled back into its usual routine. With one exception. Her life would never be the same again. Having made her excuses to her unhappy mother, she had opted to stay at Highford all over Christmas and the New year. The reason, which she had wisely omitted from giving to her mother, was that she couldn't face being away from Tom.

Living with her memories had not proved as easy or as pleasant as she had thought it would be. She could confide in no one, not even Poppy, and had bouts of black depression as a result. At night she tossed on her bed fretting for the touch of his hands on her body; by day she was a walking ball of nerves, terrified that she may give herself away each time she saw him. Despite his promise he had not been anywhere near her. Feeling more and more like the proverbial roll in the hay he had assured her she wasn't, her memories twisted themselves into painful embarrassment. Hope, however, was on the horizon in the shape of the Christmas party, when, all together at the house, and fortified by drink, she may manage to steal a few moments with him alone.

Tomorrow for the first time in months, she and Poppy shared the same afternoon off and were going Christmas shopping. Allowing herself to daydream, she saw herself choosing presents for Tom. Poppy, coming perilously close to her own thoughts, interrupted her reverie.

"I think I'll buy Rick a present. What shall I get? Something personal? Clothes? Aftershave? Rubber doll?"

"Don't waste your money Pop. I'm sure he won't"

"How do you know?" Poppy pouted. "How do you know he isn't festering away with unrequited love for me?"

As I'm festering away for Tom, thought Kitty, but didn't answer.

"Jingle bells, Jingle bells." Martin's tuneless voice boomed out of the kitchen. "Oh, what fun it is to back a winner every day!"

"Shut up!" Poppy shouted. "You tone deaf idiot!"

Martin's friendly face appeared in the doorway. His clothes were covered in a fine dusting of icing sugar, giving him a ghostly appearance.

"What do you think?" He smiled, holding out his hands.

"Marty! It's lovely!" Poppy stared at the perfectly iced cake held in them. "I don't know how you do it!"

" One of my many talents, I guess. Anyone for a cuppa?"

"Please." Poppy stretched. "Coffee please, two sugars and a bit of that brandy that you've got stashed in the back of the cupboard."

"Sneak!" Martin grinned. "I thought it was going down a bit quick. I'll have to mark the bottle! Kit?"

"Mm? What? Oh yes." Kitty pulled herself out of her daydream and got to her feet. "I'll help."

"Good girl." Poppy lay down on the sofa. "I'll keep the seats warm."

Martin chatted to deaf ears as he clattered mugs on the kitchen table.

"Kitty!" He gave her a nudge. "I'm talking to you!"

"Oh. What?" Kitty put three sugars in Poppy's mug, frowned and tipped it out.

"The Christmas presents."

"What Christmas present?"

"The one we always get for the boss. What do you think?"

"I have no idea." Kitty poured brandy into Poppy's mug and then, after a moment's hesitation, into her own.

I, she thought to herself, am the last person you should be asking. When it comes to knowing what Tom Chichester likes and dislikes I'm completely in the dark.

Tom had been helping his mother with the enormous Norway Spruce that dominated the dining room in which the party would take place. They had already trimmed up their own smaller, more personal tree in the living room. He had hung the lights on the ancient fir outside, decorated the ancient fireplace with holly and garlands of Poinsettia and now all that remained was to settle this light-hearted argument over whether to have a star, or a fairy. Both were stating their claims when the door at the top of the room burst open and a tall, black clad figure strode in. Tom stared; first in amazement, then horror, then finally in total, undisguisable hate.

Eleanor dropped the fairy she had been holding with a cry of delight and threw her arms around her younger sons' neck. Gone was Dominic's black mane, his hair had been cropped close to his arrogant, handsome head, spiking upwards and forwards at the top. Dressed in his beloved black he looked paler and gaunter than ever before. His cavernous eyes gleamed like bottomless pits of coal above his angular cheekbones, his skin so pale it was almost translucent, his lips bitten to a bloody shade of red. He reminded Tom of a biblical lost soul. Closing his arms around his mother Dominic looked at his brother.

"Season's greetings Thomas." The use of his full name, which Dominic had always used as a child, did nothing to soften Tom's heart or his expression. "I can tell you are delighted to see me."

"You know my feelings." Tom replied shortly. "Let's just keep the peace for her sake." He nodded at their mother.

"You can rely on me." Dominic collapsed into a chair like an overgrown insect, all arms, and long legs.

"Are you hungry dear?" Eleanor ruffled his spikes. "I do like your hair."

"It's a hair hog." Dominic grinned. "If I put gel on it, it's quite a lethal weapon."

"Barbed like your personality." Commented Tom dryly.

"Tom." His mother's attempt at sounding stern was weakened by her obvious pleasure at having her younger son home. "You stay here Dommie, I'll get you some food."

"So" Dominic kicked a booted foot onto the table. "How's my big brother? Still playing with the gee gees?"

Tom didn't answer but began placing unwanted baubles back in the box.

"As talkative as ever I see!" Dominic laughed. "Just thought you should know; I've invited a guest for Christmas. She'll be here shortly, lovely woman. More your type than mine really, but she has her advantages. I'll let you borrow her for a night if you like."

Tom glowered at him. It's Christmas, he reminded himself, I mustn't kill him at Christmas.

"To be honest." He studied a piece of tinsel on the floor and bent to pick it up. "I don't care what you do, or who you do it with as long as you stay out of my hair and away from my staff."

Dominic saw the tension in Tom's face and grinned. Time to deliver his best shot, to hit the bullseye.

"How's Rick? He doesn't seem to be my biggest fan at the moment. Every time I call, he hangs, up or swears at me in his ridiculous accent for five minutes, and then hangs up.

"I think." Tom was tying the piece of tinsel up in knots. "That he has finally seen the light."

"I think I can guess why." A malevolent smile spread across Dominic's face. "How's Flick Harries?"

He watched the colour draining from his brothers face with intense satisfaction. His arrow had gone straight into the centre of the target.

"I said." He repeated, slowly. "How's Flick Harries? I met her at a party. Didn't she tell you? Lovely body."

Dominic liked to watch his victims squirming as he tortured them; like a cat, he tormented his mouse long before the final death pounce.

"She told me." There was an edge of steel in Tom's voice.

"I'll have to call her." The smile was getting broader. "She was quite good in the sack, once, that is, she shook off her inhibitions."

"I don't think she wants to see you." Tom turned his back to him. "She, like Rick, has learned her lesson."

"Shame. Maybe I can talk her around? What do you think? I suppose you know her best. Although I think I exposed a side of her she hadn't seen before."

"Don't go near her." Tom rose his voice but didn't dare to face him. "I'm warning you."

He didn't dare think of Kitty. Shut it out he told himself, or you really will kill him.

"Are you two at it already?" Their mother entered the room. "If you weren't so tall both of you, I'd knock your heads together."

Dominic smiled up at her.

"Sorry Mother. Just discussing mutual acquaintances."

"As long as that's all your doing." Eleanor placed a tray of sandwiches in front of Dominic. "You eat this dear, while Tom and I finish that tree."

"Let him help you." Tom put down the shredded, tangled tinsel. "I've lost my party spirit."

Martin turned the lock in the tack room door, took a last look around him, and then headed for the cottage. Hearing a car passing the gate he paused, curious, as it halted and reversed back into view. One of its doors swung open and a tall, attractive woman got out. He could tell that she was lost.

"Can I help you?" Martin went across to her. "I'm afraid that the yard has been closed up for the evening."

"I hope you can." The woman had a very haughty air. "I want Highford House."

Don't we all, thought Martin, and everything inside it.

"You're on the right road." He smiled. "Straight ahead, you can't miss it. Mr. Chichester is in, I think."

"He should be." The woman raised an eyebrow. "I just finished speaking to him."

Then why didn't you ask him? Martin thought but forced the affable smile back onto his face.

"Then you're okay then" He nodded. He didn't like this woman. He had a feeling that Kitty would like her even less.

Some things, he thought to himself as the woman got back into her Jaguar and drove off, are best kept to yourself.

The other three inhabitants of the cottage were watching a DVD of Gladiator. Poppy, who watched the film at least once a year and knew almost every word still had tears cascading down her cheeks. Kitty was sitting silently at the back of the room, only half attentive to the images on the screen. She looked up as Martin entered and spotted the secrecy in his eyes immediately.

"Okay Marty." She stood up. "What's happened?"

"Nothing." Martin replied, truthfully.

"Something is." Kitty narrowed her eyes. "I've seen that look before."

"Nothing for you to worry your little head about." Martin sat beside Poppy and studied her red eyes.

"Oh dear." He put an arm around her shoulders. "Anything I can do?"

"Yes." Poppy sniffed. "Bring me Rick Cowdrey. He's the only cure."

"Hmm." Martin grinned. "Unless he's into Scuba Diving you have no chance."

"She's got no chance anyway." Ryan yawned. " Wasting her time dreaming about him. She's far better off making me a cup of tea."

Tom met Flick as he had promised and gently broke

the news to her that Dominic had returned home for Christmas. Thin, pale, tired and depressed after the termination he was prepared for hysteria. However, she said nothing; but when he held out his arm to help her into her coat, he could feel her shaking.

In the white E-type that was the only nonblack thing that Dominic was proud to possess, Lauren West lay naked, gazing with love into the fierce black eyes of the man on top of her. By performing incredible physical contortions, he could just about manage sex in this confined space. Fortunately, Lauren didn't shy away from a bit of pain and discomfort. He knew just how badly she had become besotted with him; and because she was the only woman, he had met who would tolerate, even enjoy, his sexual excesses, he convinced himself that he felt the same way about her. Removing himself to a more comfortable position he looked at her exposed body in the moonlight. She was lovely: long, slim, soft. In her eyes he saw the shadowed reflection of his own restless, dis-satisfied spirit.

Birds of a feather.

"Now then." He touched her stomach. "I want to know everything that's happened to you in the last few days."

Lauren smiled up at him, contented, and began to talk. By the time she had finished he had studied her body for so long that he was aroused again.

"I hope that you're feeling fit my angel." He pulled her onto his lap. "Because it's going to be a long, very hard night."

CHAPTER TWELVE

The Music blared loud, pumping around the cottage, rattling the little windows. Dancing across the landing Martin hammered on the bathroom door.

"Poppy! Come on, hurry up! We're going to be late!"

"I'm ready." The door swung open.

"Wow!" Martin was knocked sideways by the scent of Dior and warm flesh. "Very nice."

Poppy flushed slightly. Clad in a purple dress that clung to her taught figure, she had scrunched and teased her already thick hair into a wild mass of curls. Black eye liner defined her upper lids, and her lips were coloured a deep bronze. She was wildly excited about this party and her nerves were giving her an unusually high colour. Martin was impressed. But, he thought, poor Gareth was going to be heartbroken when he saw this vision of female wantonness and realised that it wasn't for him. Sliding past him Poppy skipped downstairs to pour herself a drink. Kitty was already waiting in the kitchen. Seeing her friend, she smiled broadly.

"If he doesn't fall for that he must be blind!"

"Do I look okay? Really?" Poppy wasn't usually so unsure of herself.

"You look great. Honestly." Kitty was just as tense but for slightly different reasons. She wasn't looking forward to this; it was going to be a big strain on her already fraying nerves. This was going to be crunch time. The test. If there was any hope, at all, for her and Tom, then tonight would tell. She wore a black silk jumpsuit, the strapless top held up precariously by bones. Poppy had twisted her hair up into a French pleat, she looked elegant, and much older than her age. Martin surveyed them both with pride.

"I feel like a father taking his daughters to the ball." He laughed. "You both look stunning."

"Ah." Poppy pouted her glossy lips. "But are we stunning enough?"

"Of course, you are." Martin squeezed her arm. "And I'll floor anyone who disagrees."

Kitty looked at her reflection in the mirror. There were blotchy red patches all over her chest and arms. reaching into her bag she pulled out her compact and dabbed at them with powder.

"I've got some bronzing stuff that'll help." Poppy was watching her. "Hang on I'll go get it."

"Why so worked up Kit?" Martin smiled. "You normally only get those hot spots before big races!"

"I know." Kitty shrugged. "Must be the wine. They just appeared."

"Here." Poppy brandished her brush over Kitty's bare arms. "That's better. Do you want to take it with you?"

"No thanks." Kitty shook her head. "A few more drinks and I'll be red anyway."

"Are you lot ever going to be ready?" Ryan's head came through the door. "We're late. All the punch will be gone by the time we get there."

"We are." Martin bustled them out into the hall. "Have you got coats you two? All this bare flesh is worrying me. I can't have the staff off sick with pneumonia!"

The grand, but normally sombre house had been transformed into a sparkling grotto of lights and decorations. Shining trimmings hung from the lofty ceilings; lights twinkled on the giant Christmas tree in the dining room and outside the entrance fairy lights hung, twinkling against the pale stone. Eleanor greeted them like old friends, chatting as she led them into the panelled hall with its grand chandelier. Through an open door they could see a log fire roaring merrily in the drawing room where people stood, drinks in hand. Gareth came out to meet them.

"I'll take their coats up Mrs. Chichester." He smiled. "You go and enjoy yourself."

Leading the two girls up the wide staircase, past numerous oils, and watercolours, he showed them into a small room already full of coats and wraps of all descriptions.

"In case you can't remember, the bathroom, for our use that is, is at the end of this landing on the right."

Kitty stared along the corridor, wondering which of the many doors led into Tom's bedroom. Poppy was hanging over the balcony looking for Rick.

"He's not here." She moaned. "I can't see him anywhere."

"He's here all right." Gareth failed to keep the jealousy from his voice. "He's holed up in the study with the boss."

The house was packed with people, every room full of jostling bodies, most of whom Kitty and Poppy had never met, owners, friends and rivals all loved the Chichester's Christmas parties, and some turned out for their annual airing and would disappear afterwards for another twelve months. After several gin and tonics Poppy began to unwind and enjoy herself, all thoughts of Rick pushed to the back of her mind. Kitty, greatly relieved that there was no sign of Dominic, danced with Gareth. Already slightly drunk she laughed as they swung around beneath the twinkling lights. She was looking around her at the crowd of happy people, when, as she spun, her eyes met a pair of deep blue ones watching her from the other side of the room. Her heart lurched and she felt the familiar rush of blood through her body. Halting in her step she stared. The eyes held hers for a moment then looked away.

"Oh Kit." Gareth put his arm around her waist. "Don't waste your love on him. He'll only make you sad."

"How do you know?" Kitty snapped, furious with herself for displaying her feelings so plainly.

"Because he will. Do you really, honestly, think that you two could ever get together? Just look at this place Kit!"

Her mood instantly spoiled, Kitty pulled away from him and went to find Poppy. Her friend was sitting at the foot of the stairs with a very large drink in her hand.

"Still haven't seen him Kit." She said heavily. "If it gets any later my makeup will have smudged."

Kitty sat beside her.

"Do you remember last Christmas Pop? We both got absolutely legless and didn't give a toss about men."

"Yes." Poppy smiled at the memory. "And Taff was sick all over Mrs. C's best Chinese rug."

"Good evening girls." The voice that sounded above them was deep and familiar. "Having a good time?"

Kitty's toes curled so hard that she thought they would disappear into the balls of her feet.

"Yes, thank you Mr. Chichester." Poppy smiled up at him. "It's a lovely party. I hope you've got lots for us to eat, I'm starving!"

"Enough for you and Gareth anyway!" Tom laughed. "We're just about to bring it out. And please, no Mr. Chichester, or Guv, or Boss stuff tonight, okay? I'm just Tom."

Kitty braced herself and looked up at him for the first time. He stood in front of her, so distinguished in his dinner suit; clean shaven, his dark hair curling into the back of his neck. She felt a wave of depression washing over her. Gareth was right. She was just wasting her love on him. What could this wonderful, handsome, man possibly want with her? Then he looked down at her and his eyes were so intense, so probing that she felt naked, and cringed with embarrassment. Poppy, glancing from one to the other, read the signs clearly for the first time and got hastily to her feet.

"I'm empty." She smiled. "Time for a refill."

The ensuing silence was painful, each of them awkward, not knowing what to say. Tom stared up at an oil painting of one of his ancestors, who was mocking him from his lofty position. Go on, the eyes said, what are you waiting for?

"You look very nice tonight." Damn, he hadn't intended to sound so superior.

"Thank you." Kitty heard the tone in his voice and her heart sank even further. She lowered her eyes, unable to face him any longer. It almost felt to her self-tormenting mind that he was playing games with her: teasing her, enjoying watching her squirm. He knew how she felt, and was keeping himself this close, but still out of reach, just to torment her.

"Tom." A strange voice made her lift her eyes again. "There you are."

Kitty watched, sick to the stomach, as a handsome woman wearing ivy green taffeta and diamonds planted a kiss on Tom's cheek.

"I have been looking for you everywhere."

"Excuse me." Kitty muttered, getting to her feet

"Kitty." She felt the fingers touch her arm but brushed them away, darting blindly into the kitchen.

"Why hello." The voice that greeted her made her stomach turn over. She froze in her tracks, blood tingling icy in her veins.

"You do look good this evening!"

Dominic was sampling the food, a bottle of wine in one hand. Unable to break her eyes away from his stare Kitty began to shake. He was watching her, enjoying the effect that his presence was having on her.

"Oh look." His fingers picked up a green leaf from the table. "Mistletoe. How sweet. Shall we?"

"NO." Tom's voice sounded behind her shoulder and she felt relief flooding through her. "You shall not. Your guest is looking for you."

"Another time then." Dominic gave Kitty a wink and slipped the mistletoe into his pocket. "But I'm sure I won't have to waste this."

As he left the room Kitty collapsed, her shaking legs unable to hold her any longer, onto a chair.

"I'm sorry." Tom was still in the doorway. "I should have warned you."

She shook her head, unable to trust her voice.

"That woman." Tom paused. "Is Dominic's latest affair. I didn't want you to think that..."

"You don't have to explain yourself to me." She said quickly. "Not at all."

He looked down at her, saw the bronze glittering on her shoulders, the silver chain at her throat moving softly with her pulse.

"Kitty?"

"Yes?" She looked up at him, her eyes wide with her tortured emotions.

"Will you help me? I have to take all this into the dining room." God, he thought to himself, is that the best you can come up with?

She looked at him, uncertain; then she saw the light in his eyes; his own uncertainty echoing her own.

"Okay." She got slowly to her feet and picked up a tray. Heart racing, she followed his broad, black back into the dining room.

The room was empty, except for the huge Christmas tree. Standing spellbound, like a child, in front of it, its branches a myriad of twinkling lights she saw the glow lighting up her own skin and looked down at the patterns dancing on her shoulders. Tom was watching them too. The fire cast a ball of orange at her feet, and shadows across her face, hiding her features until she looked back up at the lights. Tom swallowed hard and turned to the door. Making sure it was tightly closed he placed his tray on the table beside him and went to her. Her eyes were nervous as he turned her to face him, shivers ran across her skin beneath his hands.

"Cold?"

"No." She lowered her eyes. "Afraid."

"So am I." One finger was travelling upwards over her throat. "That you'll say no."

As his lips brushed her cheek Kitty smelt the citrus tang of his aftershave, and the musky warmth of his excited body. She felt the strength of his arms as they circled her, cradling her to his chest. Hesitant, she lifted her face to his. When she tasted his lips, her nerves vanished and she threw her arms around his neck, kissing him passionately. Broad, powerful hands stroked her back, her shoulders, her stomach, pressing, feeling, caressing her bare skin. Growing taught at the contact she pushed herself into his outstretched hand, forcing her body against his. Tom had never thought himself capable of igniting such a fire of passion and the feeling of power overwhelmed him. His hand stroking the smooth skin of her bare back he looked at her.

"Do you want me?" He murmured.

"Yes." He could barely hear her voice.

He could feel her heart beating through his own chest. This girl was like putty in his hands. Turning her away from him he undid the zip fastener of the top of her catsuit. She gasped as it fell away, and she felt the heat of the fire on her skin. Stroking her flat, soft stomach he slipped his hand lower. Trembling with pent up desire Kitty leaned back against him, letting every inch of her body lie against his. Turning her face, she begged him to kiss her. Shaking his head, enjoying this newfound power, he began to slowly pull down her lace panties.

The handle turned in the door.

Tom whipped her around, shielding her with his own body. The door opened briefly, then closed again. Without a word he picked up her jumpsuit and zipped her back into it. Watching her breasts rise and fall he planted a kiss on her neck.

"I'm sorry." He whispered. "This isn't the time or the place. I got carried away."

"When?" She clutched at him, voice breaking, terrified to let him go, to lose this precious contact.

"Later my darling. Somewhere more private."

His skin was rough on her cheek as he held her close, his breath warm and moist on her neck. Frustrated, she pulled away. He could see the irritation on her face.

"Don't." He pulled her back into his arms. "This isn't easy for me either. Now, let's go and finish this food, before people get hungry and the whole of Highford walks in on us."

In the kitchen his mother was filling the last tray of sandwiches while Margaret helped herself to the whisky. Waiting for her friend to move out of the room with Kitty, Eleanor caught her sons' arm.

"I do hope that you're going to be careful Tom."

"What do you mean?" Tom's eyes went blank.

"Kitty's very beautiful Tom, but she's very young. Do be careful."

"I don't know what you're talking about."

"I'm not blind son." Eleanor said softly. "I can see what's happening."

"Don't worry." He patted her shoulder. "I know what I'm doing."

"Well." Eleanor took a gateau out of the fridge. "I hope so son. You could be getting into something very awkward, something that could make your job difficult."

"I'm well aware of that." Tom snapped. "But I'll thank you to stay out of my business."

Poppy looked at her friend's tangled hair and laughed.

"Carrying trays of food never had that effect on me!"

"Seen Rick yet?" Kitty swiftly changed the subject, tugging at the hair clips that had become knotted in her ruined pleat.

"Not a glimpse." The bronze lips pouted. "He hasn't even poked his nose out."

Narrowing her eyes, Poppy lowered her voice.

"And you're a dark horse!"

"What?" Kitty could feel herself blushing.

"Well for weeks I've guessed that there was someone, but I never would have guessed who!"

Kitty looked at her, and Poppy saw the confusion on her friend's face.

"There isn't anyone Pop." She said sadly. "Not in the way you mean."

"It's okay." Poppy rested her chin on her friend's shoulder. "Whatever this thing with you and Tom is, or isn't, your secret's safe with me."

Predictably, after she had taken such pains to look good for him all evening, Poppy finally encountered Rick when she had drunk several Gins and half a bottle red wine and had a mouthful of turkey. Watching him crossing the floor, looking for an empty seat, she saw that the only likely space in the crowded room was beside the chaise longue that she and Kitty were sharing. Tousling her hair so that it fell over one eye she yelped as Gareth got to the chair first.

"No!" She spluttered. "Let him sit there!"

"Piss off." Gareth was trying to prevent his over full plate from spilling onto his lap. "Let him sit on the floor."

"Or on top of the tree." Chuckled Martin.

"Hi you guys." Rick's voice was hoarse. "Any chance of a

seat?"

He nodded to the head rest at the top of the chaise longue.

"Feel free." Martin smiled.

Moving around the chaise longue Rick hitched his slim hip onto the corner next to Poppy. The touch of his body on hers shot through her like an electric current.

"Rick, do you know?" A mischievous twinkle, born of envy, appeared in Gareth's eyes. "That this is the first time Poppy has been quiet all night?"

"She's got her mouth too full to talk the greedy mare. She's only ever quiet when she has a mouthful" Martin grinned wickedly. "Now she's trying to swallow it quickly so that she can make an impression on you"

Poppy went scarlet, and nearly choked. Beside her Rick smiled. He enjoyed the banter that went on between the staff. It was a welcome relief after minding his manners all evening with owners and other trainers and jockeys. Turning a vol-au-vent over in his fingers he began to feel sick. Every mouthful he swallowed felt like razor blades being dragged over his tonsils. I can't eat this, he thought, it stands more chance of coming back up than it does of staying down.

"Don't you want that?" Gareth had quickly spotted the discarded plate.

"No." Rick shook his head. "Not hungry."

"Leave it here." Gareth was a renowned foodaholic. "I'll find a good home for it."

Rick slipped off his uncomfortable perch.

"Anyone for a beer?"

"Me please." Martin raised his hand.

"And me!" Shouted Gareth.

"You." Kitty wagged a sausage roll at him, "Are the greediest person I know."

"I'm a growing boy!"

As soon as Rick disappeared Poppy flew to the bathroom to tidy herself up. Rushing back down the stairs she almost sent him flying as he came out of the kitchen.

"Oops! Sorry!" She rescued a can of beer as it rolled across the hall.

"No problem." Rick was taking in the freshly applied make up and breathing in the wafts of Dior; he knew that it was for his benefit. She looked incredibly sexy in that tight dress, and he already knew how pleasant her firm body was to touch. Hungry to find out more he looked at her boldly.

"I'm sick Pop." He croaked. "I think I've got the 'flu."

"I can tell." Her pulse was racing. "You should be in bed."

"But not on my own." Rick's eyes were holding hers.

"No." Poppy couldn't believe that the words were coming out of her mouth. "You need to keep warm in such a draughty old house."

Rick's eyes twinkled. A cough caught his throat and he spluttered. Poppy caught his hand.

"Bed." She said firmly. "Now. I'll bring you a brandy."

"Please." Rick wiped his watery eyes. "Third room on the right."

Poppy, having heated the brandy with hot water, went cautiously up the stairs, hot glass balanced on a saucer. Rick had left his door open. Breezing in she stopped abruptly when she saw him lying in the bed, damp hair sprawling on the pillows.

"I had a quick shower." Rick's amber shirt lay on the floor in a crumpled heap. Putting the glass down on the dressing table, Poppy picked it up and folded it.

"You should have dried your hair." She muttered.

"Shut the door Pop."

Obediently she quietly closed the door. Turning back to him she nearly shot a foot in the air when Rick threw back his quilt and exposed his lean, completely naked body. There was a heat other than fever in his eyes.

"Take off your clothes." He said softly. "It's lonely in here."

Two bedrooms along the hallway Dominic inhaled deeply on his joint and listened to the music rising from below. Beside him, Lauren propped herself up on one elbow and watched his pupils beginning to lose focus.

"Here." She took the joint from his hand. "Save some for me for God's sake! Haven't you got anything a bit more upmarket?"

"Not an ounce." Dominic stretched.

"What happened to it?" Lauren frowned. "You didn't use it!"

"Don't be ridiculous." Dominic looked at her. "All moved on sweetheart. To a better home."

"Good boy!" Lauren smiled broadly. "There are plenty more customers out there, just waiting."

"Lead me to them." Dominic pulled the sheet away from her body and ran his eyes over her curves. "I've got more coming in next week."

"What a star you are." Lauren laid her head on his boyish chest. "I am so lucky to have found you."

Dominic kissed her head and narrowed his eyes. Not, he thought to himself, as lucky as I am to have found you. My bank balance has never had so many zeros at the end of it.

"This is a lovely old house." Lauren was stroking his hollow stomach, waiting for the usual reaction. "I would be very happy here."

"I wouldn't." Dominic scowled. "Not while he's here."

"He's handsome." Lauren looked up and saw a shadow flit across Dominic's eyes. "But not as handsome as you."

"Sure about that?" Dominic caught her chin with his

hand, eyes intent on hers.

"Very sure." Lauren slid her thigh across his hips and pressed herself against him. "And you are far more exciting."

"Not tonight I'm not." Dominic grinned; at ease again, teasing her.

"We'll see." Lauren sat up, straddling him. "What a pity I have to leave tomorrow."

"Best you do." Dominic began to move slowly beneath her. "I've things to do."

"Of course." She bent forward to kiss him, her breasts swinging. He snapped at them with his teeth, and she pulled back, laughing.

"Naughty. You make sure you do a good job."

"I will." Dominic caught hold of her hips with his hands. "Don't I always?"

"Always." Lauren gasped. "So far."

Dominic propped himself up so that his face was near hers.

"I'm the best you'll ever have." He said quietly. "Don't forget it."

Lauren looked at him, black eyed, pale, and felt her heart twisting. She had to keep him. He was right, she'd never felt like this about anyone before. In an envelope, beneath the Christmas tree was a cheque for ten thousand pounds and the deeds to her Kensington apartment. If she had to buy him, then she would. The thought of never feeling his satin smooth skin against hers again cut her like a knife.

"Let's make this quick." Dominic lay back. "You know I hate to miss a good party."

At midnight Margaret served mulled wine. Hot, laden with spices, it sent the not quite drunk over the edge and the already drunk reeling senseless, looking for somewhere to lie down. Martin had appointed himself DJ and began to play rock music that vibrated off the ancient plaster. Dancing with Gareth, hair hanging loose now, Kitty found herself being thrown around until she nearly passed out. Martin, seeing the chaos on the dance floor, decided that the plaster had been punished enough and announced that it was mistletoe time. Wrapping her arms around Gareth's neck for support Kitty listened to him crooning into her ear.

"Last Christmas I gave you my heart." For a moment the bloodshot eyes filled with tears. "I gave Poppy my heart Kit. The minute I met her. But she threw it back at me. Unwrapped. She'll never want me. I haven't even had a Christmas kiss."

"Poor thing." Kitty planted a kiss on his lips. "Have one from me instead."

Laying her head on his shoulder her thoughts turned to Tom. The soft lights and gentle music made her longing for him deepen. Closing her eyes, she imagined that it was his body she leaned against, his hands stroking her back in time to the music. A wail from Gareth interrupted her dreams.

"What?" She blinked to focus her eyes.

"Look!" Gareth was gazing soulfully across the room. Two figures were dancing very slowly, barely moving, entwined with each other. As they watched Rick slipped his hand inside Poppy's dress and began to kiss her.

"Don't look." Kitty turned Gareth away.

"Merry Christmas, eh?" He said sadly. "I need another drink."

"Not for me." Kitty patted his arm. "I've had too much already. I'm going to sit down."

Collapsing into the nearest easy chair she kicked off her shoes and curled her feet up beneath her. Feeling her eyes almost rolling in her head she took a deep breath, then another. The lights of the tree danced before her eyes, and she quickly fell asleep.

She woke much later to find that the room was empty. A CD spun silently in the deck; the fire had dwindled to embers in the hearth. Voices carried softly from the drawing room. A chill drifted across from an open window and she shivered. Stiff, nauseous, and depressed she got to her feet and shuffled barefooted into the hall. She felt very low. Passing the hall mirror she saw her reflection and studied her blotchy complexion and red eyes. What she saw deepened her mood of depression and showed in her dispirited face.

The front door opened, and a blast of icy air hit her. Looking behind her she saw Tom in the doorway, brushing a fine dusting of snow from his shoulders.

"Hello." He said softly. "You look tired."

"I am." She was far too down hearted to smile. "I'm about to go home to bed I think."

"No." He put his hand on her arm. "Have a drink with me first. He opened the door to his study.

"What would you like?"

"Coffee. Black." Kitty hesitated but looked with longing at the still roaring fire.

"Irish" Tom led her in and pulled a chair across to the hearth. "That'll warm you up. God girl, you're freezing!"

Kitty sank down into soft cushions and stretched her toes to the fire. When Tom re-joined her, he sat alongside staring into the flames. There was stubble darkening his chin and shadows beneath his heavy eyes. Heavy, tired eyes tinged with sadness. The heat was making him sleepy. Rubbing his forehead, he tried to make conversation.

"So Did Poppy get her man in the end?"

"Yes." Kitty grinned. "Poor Gareth is broken hearted."

"Ah. And You've been consoling him?"

"Sort of." She slipped lower in the chair and put her feet beside his. "Ugh. I feel terrible."

"You look wonderful." He laid his hand on her bare arm. "Will you dance with me?"

"Here?" She raised her eyebrows. "There's no music!"

"Who needs music?" He got to his feet.

Slipping so easily into his outstretched arms she began to move her body slowly with his. The room was dark, lit only by the glow of the fire. Her soft hair fell across his shoulder. Placing her face lightly against his neck she breathed deeply and inhaled perfume. With a jerk she pulled away. A picture flashed before her eyes, a memory from earlier that evening; Tom talking to a woman who she now recognised as Flick Harries. She had passed her on the way to the bathroom. She had been wearing that perfume.

"What's wrong?" Tom was still holding her in his arms.

"This is." She hissed. "How can you? No wonder I haven't seen you all night. You crawl out of bed with Flick Harries and bump into me when you get home. Oh, there's Kitty. She'll do to finish off the evening. You're no different to him, really, are you? No different to Dominic. You just go about it a different way."

"I have not." Tom's voice was very low, and had she known him better she would have realised how angry her words had made him. "Been to bed with anyone. Even if I had, it would have been none of your business."

"Gareth was right." She hissed. "All you can ever do is hurt me! What a fool I am; do you enjoy it? Watching me make a fool of myself over you?"

"Kitty please!" Tom tightened his grip on her arms. "I didn't mean to snap at you like that. You're accusing me of something I haven't done, something I have no interest in doing, not anymore. I took Flick home, and yes, I could have slept with her if I wished to, but I didn't. All I wanted was to get back here and find you."

"Liar." She was on the verge of tears. "God, I feel so stupid! A silly, pathetic girl living her life on daydreams. Except that the dreams were better than the reality. How can it ever be the same again? I've ruined it!"

Tom looked over her shoulder out of the window. A blanket of snow was clothing his fields. Heavy, silent. All his life he had erected an emotional barrier between himself and his women but with this girl he found it impossible. He felt every tear, every sobbing breath that came from her as if they were his own. Looking down he saw her gentle eyes staring into the fire. Aware of his eyes on her face she looked up at him.

She never was sure which one of them moved first; but they quickly became a twisted mass of arms and legs, and this time it seemed like hours before they lay, sated, in each other's arms. Heavy with sleep Tom tried to lift his head from her warm breast but couldn't. His legs were like lead and he lay there immobilised until the cold air on his spine stirred his senses and he lifted himself off her sleeping figure. Covering her with his jacket he heard voices outside. Isolated by his passion he had been oblivious to anything, or anyone, other than the beautiful creature beneath him. Getting to his feet he pulled on his trousers. As he moved away, she stirred, and he gently tucked the jacket more tightly around her. Kissing her forehead, he smiled as she drifted back into a deeper sleep. Moving softly, he slipped out of the room.

The boys had formed a circle around the two figures. Rick, eyes red and streaming with his 'flu, looked deathly pale and impossibly small as he faced the tall dark figure in front of him. Shivering with cold, snow soaking his shirt, he knotted his hair behind his head and glanced at Poppy who, with mascara running down her cheeks, was screaming hysterically.

"Stop it! Stop them!" She turned to the group of young men. "One of you stop them!"

The black eyes, deep and emotionless in their dark

sockets ran over the row of faces.

"Anyone care to try?"

Nobody moved.

Like a terrier onto a rabbit Rick pounced. Poppy screamed so loud that inside the house Margaret, who was collecting glasses, dropped them all with a loud crash. Running into the hall she bumped into Tom who was doing up his shirt.

"What was that?" She gasped. "It sounded like someone being murdered!"

Roars and cheers rang through the open doorway.

"Outside!" Margaret gasped. "Quick!"

Bolting across the lawn Tom slid to a treacherous halt beside the group of people. Two figures rolled on the ground; and, as he watched, a familiar dark head raised itself, one arm poised, ready to strike.

"STOP!" Tom's voice echoed around the valley, scattering the clustered group instantly. "Get up NOW!"

Dominic's dilated eyes looked up at him, a hideous grin distorting his angular face.

"What the hell are you doing?" Tom spat. "On your feet man. Now!"

Feigning compliance Dominic started to rise, then, at the last moment, he swung his fist into Rick's face, spraying the snow with blood.

"Bastard!" Poppy leaped forward and sprang on his back. "You bastard!"

Too quick for any of them Tom pulled her away, at the same time blocking a blow from his brother.

"Enough!" He roared. "What the hell is going on?"

"None of your fucking business." Dominic snarled.

"This is my house. This is my business!"

"Our house." Dominic spoke deliberately. "Never forget

189

that brother dear, never."

Tom's eyes grew very pale as he felt anger welling up inside him. Dominic saw the raw nerve that he had touched and turned to Rick who was sitting in the snow with his face in his hands.

"That self-righteous little prick." He sneered. "Tried to stop me giving his latest slut a Christmas kiss. Then he got personal. I think he's been listening to your tall stories."

"Like the one about Flick?" Tom swallowed and lowered his voice. "Or the one about Kitty?"

"Can't stand it can you?" Dominic wiped his bloody mouth. "Can't stand the fact that I nearly had her first, can you?"

Tom's fingers dug deep into the anorexic arm.

"Get inside." He snarled. "Now. Unless you want to have another go at me?"

Dominic hesitated. He remembered the bruises, the battered ribs. He was very drunk now and not at his best. Tom would keep. He would deal with him in his own way. Giving Rick a final kick as he passed him, he pushed through the onlookers and loped back to the house.

"Show's over." Tom snapped. "So is this party. Poppy get him inside; my mother will see to him."

Turning away so that they couldn't see the emotions raging across his face Tom looked up at the sky. A single star was peering down through a break in the cloud. Wish on a star, he thought. I'd wish for a peaceful life and someone to share it with.

A figure was standing on the lawn behind him. Clad in his jacket and very little else she approached him with caution.

"Are you okay?" She whispered.

"I am now." He put his arm around her. "Let's go and have that drink. This time I need a brandy, a large one. But." He smiled as the jacket fell open at her neck. "We'd better put some clothes on you first."

CHAPTER THIRTEEN

Martin surveyed the tiny bronze horse and felt tears pricking his eyes. Neck arched; it was leaping over an imaginary fence. It was the most beautiful thing he had ever seen. Turning it over and over in his hands he looked into the eager faces of his friends and shook his head.

"It's fantastic. I don't know what to say, Thanks!"

"It's Runny." Poppy gave him a big kiss on the cheek. "When he wins tomorrow."

"One more thing." Ryan fished in a carrier bag. "This is from Nigel and all the weekend lads."

Tearing off the wrapping paper Martin burst out laughing at the huge bottle of Jack Daniels he held in his hand.

"Are you saying I like a drink?"

"Am I interrupting anything?" Tom's head appeared in the doorway. "That's nice Martin. The horse, that is."

"Come in boss. Have a drink. Merry Christmas."

"Thank you." Tom put his carrier bags on the table and surveyed the chaotic kitchen. Piles of wrapping paper lay on the floor, a smell of mince pies wafted temptingly out of the oven and the work surface had disappeared underneath bottles of all shapes and sizes.

"Sherry?" Ryan picked up one of the fuller bottles. "We're a bit low on Whisky thanks to Martin."

"Sherry will be fine thank you Ryan. It's very cold out there this morning."

"Don't we know it." Gareth was waiting by the oven door for the mince pies. "My poor bloody hands froze to the wheelbarrow this morning."

Christmas Carols were playing in the little living room where Martin cleared a space for Tom to sit. Poppy was sitting on the floor reading a Good Health and Beauty book, a present from her sister. Kitty was looking in the cupboard for more plaiting bands to secure the still wayward fairy.

"Rick's fallen off again. I hope it's not an omen. Oh. Hello Guv." She straightened, a pink flush on her cheeks. "Merry Christmas."

"Merry Christmas Kitty." His face softened at the sight of her. "I agree. I very much hope that it isn't an omen."

"Here you go boss." Martin placed a large box in his hand. "From all of us."

Tom opened his parcel warily, remembering gifts of the past. Last years had contained a Shetland wool jumper, cunningly concealing a Porn magazine and calendar that his amused, if slightly shocked mother had discovered weeks later when she threw out the box. A pale blue shirt with a dark spotted silk tie lay on top of the tissue paper. Digging deeper he found a gold tie pin with a tiny horseshoe on it. Deeper still he found a paperback book entitled 'Horse keeping for beginners.'

"Thank you." He laughed. "I'll read it in bed tonight. Perhaps I'll learn something!"

"Excuse me Sir." Poppy cleared her throat. "Could you give this to Rick for me please?" She hadn't seen him since that passion filled night and five days had badly waned her confidence.

"I will." Tom took the parcel. "But you could give it to him yourself. He's coming for lunch later."

"No. I'd rather you do it thanks." Poppy blushed. "I'll leave it to you."

"Oh well. I'll send him over anyway. But keep him away from the mince pies." Tom grinned, laughter touching his eyes. "Aren't you going to open your gifts? You're all very restrained this year."

"Me first then." Gareth hoisted a large square box with his name on it from the depths of the carrier bag. "I bet I know what this is. Yum, Belgian chocolates. Thanks boss."

Tom watched with amusement as they pounced on their gifts, handing out chocolates and spraying perfume and aftershave until the air was so full of scent that he could hardly breathe.

"I must go." He got reluctantly to his feet. The chaotic room, the happy atmosphere, reminded him of his childhood. Of the days when he had no pressures, and a brother who loved him. "We'll be leaving for church in half an hour, if anyone wants to join us."

To a chorus of well wishes he went to the door. As he was about to step outside a hand touched his shoulder. Knowing full well who it was he turned with a smile on his face.

"Sorry." Kitty was scarlet. "I couldn't give this to you in front of the others."

Tom took the small box from her trembling hand, and, opening it, found a pair of cufflinks to match his tie pin.

"Thank you, Kitty. I shall be very smart tomorrow don't you think. Here." He pulled a black velvet pouch from his pocket. "This is for you."

With unsteady fingers Kitty plucked at the drawstring and removed a gold chain that held a single blue sapphire.

"Oh, it's beautiful!" She gasped. "Thank you so much!"

"Matches your eyes." He kissed her on the cheek, once, and left.

The tiny village church was packed full of people. It was Highford tradition that the Christmas staff accompanied their boss to sing Carols on Christmas morning. Not that anyone was forced to go; it was something that had become a pattern over the years, and it was now one they all enjoyed. It gave them all a sense of belonging when they were far away from their own homes and family. The smell of perfume and damp wool mingled with the older, muskier odours of age and wood. Outside, the harmonious singing echoed softly across the snow-covered landscape and touched the already heavy heart of Eleanor as she lay a holly wreath on William's grave.

Inside the church both Kitty and Poppy were having very unholy thoughts about the two men standing in the pew in front of them. Kitty, twiddling with her hymn book, was convinced that every well-dressed woman in the place was here to look at Tom.

"Look at them all!" She eyed the furs. "Rich bitches!"

"Shh!" Poppy whispered. "They'll hear you. Don't get paranoid Kit."

Singing her heart out in the next hymn Poppy was knocked off guard by Rick who, hearing her clear voice, turned and gave her a dazzling smile. Stammering, she sang the wrong verse.

"Pop!" Kitty giggled. "Everyone's listening!"

In front of them Rick, who was inside a church for the first time since he was five years old, slipped his hand back and stroked Poppy's knee. She gave a loud squeak.

"Will you two shut up!" Martin leaned across. "You're like a pair of love-struck schoolgirls!"

"Love struck calves more like." Gareth snorted. "Who will one day turn into cows!"

Walking back through the slippery lanes, cold and hungry, the boys had a snowball fight, soaking everyone in their enthusiasm. Turning into the drive they were greeted by a snowman. Wearing a trilby and carrying a hip flask his face had been arranged into a drunken leer.

"Nigel." Explained Martin. "Clown. I didn't think he had it in him."

The smell of turkey was drifting out of the coach house

in appetizing waves. Gareth quickly lost all interest in snowballs and started walking faster.

"Have a nice lunch." Tom halted at the gate. "Business as usual this afternoon. Don't forget, big day tomorrow."

Some hours later Martin lay on the tack room bench and polished Olympic Run's bridle.

"Do you think he'll win?" Kitty was washing bits.

"Streak will." Poppy folded a paddock rug and laid it in the racing box. "So, we've got something to look forward to."

"Don't be so sure." Martin surveyed his handiwork with satisfaction. "She hasn't got around a course yet. The only reason she's got in the race at all is because something with a higher rating than her didn't declare!"

"Cheek." Poppy straightened her aching back. "I'm telling you she'll win. With my boy on top, she's bound to."

Rick wasn't sharing her optimism. Besieged by indigestion and pre-race nerves he walked over to the cottage that evening with Poppy's present tucked under his arm. He was excited about the King George, looking forward to riding in the biggest race of his career, but the expectations of the horse's owners were worrying him. Olympic Run was a class act, he had as good a chance as any other horse in the race, but he was terrified of letting the connections down. At least the white Christmas of the Cotswold's hadn't spread as far south as Kempton Park. Seeing Streaks familiar face with the crooked white blaze, he went in her direction to give her a pat. She'd given him two nasty falls already, and he hoped that the big crowd tomorrow wouldn't unnerve her. Scratching her ear, he was surprised to see a tall figure crossing the yard. The figure was heading for the feed shed, moving quickly. Curious, Rick followed.

Dominic spun around when he heard Rick's footsteps behind him.

"What are you doing here?" He snapped.

"I was going to ask the same of you." Rick halted a little away from him. His ribs still ached when he breathed deeply, and he was in no mood for a repeat performance.

"Believe it or not Ricky boy, I have every right to be here." Dominic's voice was flat.

"True. But that's never tempted you in the past."

"My mother wants something. I said I'd fetch it for her as my brother has locked himself away to brood in his study."

"From the feed shed?" Rick raised his eyebrows.

"Oh hell." Dominic shook his head, a smile, not quite ringing true, on his face. "You're right. I don't come down here very often, do I? I wanted the office."

"Over there." Rick pointed. "But it's locked."

"I've got the key. Thanks." Dominic gave a sarcastic nod.

"I'd say it was my pleasure." Rick began to back away. "But it would be a lie."

"I hate liars." Dominic was staring at him. "Don't you?"

Rick saw the laughter in Dominic's eyes and felt his throat tighten. He wanted nothing more than to throw himself on the arrogant bastard and beat him to the floor. But he couldn't. Not only did he have a big day tomorrow, but he also knew Dominic's deceptive physical strength. So, he ignored the mocking eyes and backed away.

"I'd wish you luck for tomorrow." Dominic laughed. "But I don't."

Biting his lip, taking deep breaths to steady his rising temper Rick walked quickly away from the yard. Opening the cottage gate, he felt suspicion nagging at him. He couldn't shake the feeling that Dominic was up to something, and he had a terrible nagging feeling that he knew what. Dominic would stop at absolutely nothing to get at Tom.

The door swung open, and Kitty greeted him with a smile. So relieved was he to see her safe that all thoughts of Dominic and his mysterious actions vanished. Poppy, fortified by Jack Daniels, untangled herself from the Twister board and pounced on him with a sprig of mistletoe. Accepting the can of beer that was thrust into his hand, he put on a pink paper hat and joined in the fun.

The crowds began to file into Kempton Park at nine a.m. Vehicles packed high with extra layers, turkey sandwiches and champagne picnics carried crowds whose festive spirit pervaded the atmosphere until the track began to buzz with anticipation. At the racecourse stables the tension grew until it was an almost touchable, physical, presence. Polishing Olympic Run's already gleaming coat Martin trying to ease his pounding heart.

"Calm down." Kitty told him. "He'll be fine. Just calm down, you're making him nervous."

Tom popped in on his way to the owners and trainers bar where he was meeting Rowley Harris.

"I don't know who worse Martin, you or Rick!"

"Why should he be nervous." Moaned Martin. "He gets to ride him. I have to hand over the reins and watch!"

"Oh, will you stop twittering!" Poppy hissed from the next box where she was trying to plait an excited Streak's mane. "You're like an old woman! You're upsetting my girl."

Tom chuckled to himself and left them to it. They would probably come to blows before it was all over. Crossing the lawn, he was intercepted by Shane Murphy, ex jump jockey turned TV presenter. Cameraman in tow he waved a microphone in Tom's face.

"Interview Tom?"

"What on Earth for?" Tom was too tense to be sociable.

"You do have a pretty well fancied runner there. Come on it'll only take a few minutes. Think of all the potential owners out there."

"Oh, all right. But make it quick. I'm busy."

Following the small, blonde-haired man to the paddock Tom warily eyed the equipment and tried to sound calm.

"Tom." Shane began smoothly. "How do you see your chances today. Realistically?"

Tom shrugged and gave a smile that later, when the interview was broadcast, broke the hearts of unsettled housewives all over the country.

"We'll have to wait and see I'm afraid. We wouldn't be here if we thought we had no chance, but anything can happen in racing. I'm pleased with the horse, and as long as he has a safe passage, I think he has every chance."

"My God he's photogenic." The producer's assistant whispered to one of the sound engineers. "Can't we have him every week? Why on Earth isn't he married!"

The sound engineer had been thinking along similar lines, but for completely different reasons.

"I heard." He lowered his voice. "That he's got a long-term thing going with some advertising executive. A couple of days ago I had lunch with a friend who works in a Private Clinic in London. The very same woman had an abortion a few weeks ago."

"What!" His companion's eyes came out on stalks. "What a shit! He doesn't look that sort, does he? The type to run out on you. Coward."

Only a few feet away, but mercifully out of earshot, Shane was wrapping up the interview.

"So, you're not giving anything away?"

"I'm afraid not." That smile again.

Shane gave a nod and smiled broadly.

"Thanks Tom. All the best."

As Tom rushed away the sound engineer eyed him with interest.

"You're right, he doesn't look the type to desert you, does

he? Perhaps he's been playing in the wrong half of the court and doesn't realise it."

"You wish." His friend laughed. "Might not have been his anyway. Apparently that jockey of his isn't backward in coming forward so to speak."

"Excuse me." A spotty faced young reporter had been listening to the interview and also to their hushed conversation. "Would you like to tell me a bit more?"

In the saddling boxes Martin was on the verge of having a nervous breakdown. With Rick's saddle on his arm, he looked frantically for Tom.

"Oh, come on!" He muttered. "Where are you?"

"Hi Martin." A freckled face popped out of the next box. "How's it going?"

"Hello Bob. I'll tell you in about forty-five minutes!"

Bob emerged from the box followed by a young red headed lad leading a huge grey gelding.

"I know who that is!" Grinned Martin. "Favourite, isn't he?"

"Yup." Bob watched Arctic Fox walking away with obvious pride. Then his face changed as he lowered his voice. "Keep the lid on this Marty but his legs are on the way out. He's swum more laps this winter than an Australian Gold medallist. I hope it doesn't, but this sticky ground could just about finish him off."

"Hell. What a bummer." Martin pulled a face. Arctic Fox was not only Greg Westwood's star performer he was a huge favourite with the racing public

"So, do you think yours is worth a couple of quid?" Bob could see Runny's noble head protruding from the saddling box.

"I put my Christmas bonus on him." Martin confessed. "I've never sat on anything like him."

"In that case I may join you. Here's your man. Good luck."

Tom nodded to the little man as he hurried after the grey horse into the paddock. Then he stopped in his tracks staring at the animal in front of him.

"Let's saddle up Martin." He drew a deep unsteady breath. "It's judgement day."

The parade ring was twenty deep with spectators, all craning over the rails to get a good look at their personal favourites. Olympic Run's bright eyes and glossy coat caught everyone's attention and in the betting ring his price began to fall rapidly.

"Someone's putting big money on him." Martin whispered to Poppy as they watched Kitty parade the horse. "I'm glad I got on early. Better get in there and do my bit. They'll be coming out soon."

Rick, still sporting a bruised nose that matched, rather unbecomingly, Rowley's red colours, was taking big gulps of air to still his chattering teeth.

"It's no good." He moaned as he bent his leg for Martin to leg him up. "I'll never get used to it. Big races will scare the shit out of me for the rest of my life."

"Glad to hear it." Tom patted his leg as he landed lightly on the horse's back. "The day there's no adrenalin is the day it's time to quit. But for Christ's sake don't hyper ventilate!"

Rick's nerves began to abate as he settled himself in the saddle. The familiar feeling of the horse's long stride as they filed out onto the course for the parade began to fill him instead with confidence. He looked around at the crowd and felt thrills of anticipation tickling his skin. A group of young girls were waving at him.

"Rickmania!" Laughed Martin as he walked by the horse's flank. "Poppy's got competition!"

The circus like atmosphere of the parade soon faded as the runners cantered to the start. Circling like Indians on the prairie the jockeys checked their tack, fiddling with stirrup leathers and breastplates. Wriggling in his saddle, Rick adjusted his gloves, his goggles, anything that would fill the void that felt to him like an eternity, but that was in fact only a few minutes. His mouth had gone dry. The only sound he could hear was that of his own blood rushing through his own head. He stared at the tape as they made a line, hands shifting endlessly on the reins, heels tightening on the horse's sides. The starter raised his flag, and the jockeys took a collective intake of breath.

With a snap the tape flew up, and the muscles of nine magnificent thoroughbreds punched into action.

The pace was fast and furious from the start. Arctic Fox, adopting his usual pace setting style, towed them along at a furious gallop; Rick tailed him, knowing how dangerous it was to let the grey horse get a big lead. Arctic Fox was a relentless galloper, eating up the ground with mammoth strides, flicking over the fences without missing a beat. As they passed the crowded stands, which broke into a roar, for the first time, Rick brought his horse alongside the grey. Pulling fiercely on the reins Runny felt as if he had all the power of a Ferrari in his quarters. Racing back out into the country Rick picked up the pressure, knowing it was early, but also knowing that the best way to beat the grey horse was to crack him, to pressurise him into making a rare error at a fence. It was the only way he could possibly beat him without pushing Runny beyond his limits at the end of the race.

"He's taking him on." Tom's voice was a little shaky. "I hope he hasn't gone too soon."

"So do I." Rowley's voice was worse than Tom's. "They've got a long way to go yet."

Then, only a few furlongs later, Runny began to go backwards through the field. It wasn't that he started to struggle, or falter, he never made a mistake at a fence; it was as if someone had quite simply pulled out the plug and cut the power supply. He was stopping, dramatically. Rick's whip swung on Runny's flank as three horses passed him with ease: a snarl, another swipe at the heaving flank, but to no avail.

His Ferrari had just run out of petrol.

"What's wrong?" Kitty caught Martin's arm so tightly that he winced. "Is he hurt?"

Martin watched his pride and joy struggle over the next few fences and wanted to cry. The leaders were already turning into the home straight. Arctic Fox, showing no sign of the leg trouble that had been plaguing him was being chased by a black horse wearing sinister looking black blinkers. At the rear of the field, a full two fences behind, Runny was staggering to a walk. He looked barely able to stand.

Ignoring the screaming clamour of the crown as they witnessed the black horse overhauling Arctic Fox right on the line, Tom slipped onto the course and ran anxiously to meet his charge. Rick had dismounted and was walking beside the horse, his bitter disappointment plain on his face.

"Well?" Tom halted a few yards away, eyes narrowed.

"Nothing left. Just stopped. He's all in the poor bastard, He can hardly breathe."

A figure, grey coat and binoculars flying, came racing up to them. Rowley looked as distressed as his horse.

"What's wrong?" He panted. "He hasn't broken down or anything?"

"No." Tom gave a rueful smile. "Nothing as bad as that. But I've got no answers for you Rowley I'm afraid. Not yet. We'll have to run some tests. I would have sworn my life on that horse's fitness."

They had reached the green space outside the winners' enclosure. Rick pulled off his saddle and headed for the weighing room, head low. Martin looked at the horse in despair, appalled by the horses' heaving sides and lifeless eyes.

Tom handed the reins to Kitty.

" Get plenty of water on him and keep him moving"

The racecourse vet, who had pulled alongside them as they walked back was baffled. Having checked the horse's pulse and lungs he stood back and watched him with a puzzled look on his face.

"Well?" Tom wanted a dramatic prognosis; one that would explain away without doubt the horse's dreadful performance.

"Nothing." The vet straightened. "He's just exhausted. Heart rate is high but perfectly normal"

"Damn!" Tom shook his head. "Where the hell do I go now? I was sure he was as fit as I could get him!"

"His blood may tell you more." The vet was sympathetic. "These things happen."

A small man wearing a suit and a badge came bustling up.

"Mr. Chichester? The stewards would like a word with you, they have been calling you. Can you take the horse to the testing box please?"

"What?" Tom's eyes blazed. "What the hell for? Are you saying I doped my horse to come last! He wasn't a favourite, what would I possibly have to gain!"

"The stewards decision Sir." The man was unmoved. "They feel it appropriate in the circumstances."

"What circumstances?" Tom snapped. "We lost! I, my jockey, my owners, we lost! That's the circumstances!"

"You don't know?" The vet was packing his bag. "Your brothers horse won."

"My brother?" Tom was stunned. "My brother doesn't have a horse."

"I'm afraid he does." The vet straightened. "Here."

He pulled a race card from his pocket.

"Number seven." He read aloud. "Revelation. J. Coltrane trainer owned by Miss Lauren West and Mr. Dominic Chichester. Your brother."

"What?" Tom had gone very pale.

"So, you understand, Mr. Chichester, that in the circumstances?" The steward was getting impatient.

"Oh, all right, I'll" Tom began, but was interrupted by a large rumbling noise.

"Hey wait a minute!" The vet waved to Martin who was heading back to the stables. "Bring that horse here."

Puzzled, Tom watched the man listened to Runny's stomach, which was suddenly rumbling and gurgling like an erupting volcano.

"Well." The vet was almost smiling. "You can take a test from this horse if you like, but I doubt you'll find anything. This poor old fellow's coming down with colic!

"Colic!" Tom's voice came out in a squeak. "How the hell has he got colic!"

"Impossible." Said Martin firmly. "I always feed this horse myself."

"I'll give him an anti-spasmodic." The vet filled a syringe. "Help him relax, keep an eye and Ill check him before you leave if you don't mind."

Tom watched the needle sinking into the horse's neck and his mind began working overtime. Martin whose train of thought was following a similar track, looked at Tom and saw the familiar set to his jaw. Hovering by the horse's head Kitty thought that she had never seen him look so angry. Eventually his steely eyes turned onto her.

"Go and help Poppy with that mare." His look never changed. "Let's try and save something from this fiasco!"

Kitty nodded and hurried away. There was an emotion on Tom's face that she had never seen before.   An emotion that she was sure would render him capable of anything.

The last person on Earth she would want to be at this moment was Dominic Chichester.

CHAPTER FOURTEEN

Rick's devoted female fans were rewarded for their unfailing loyalty by Streak's victory in the novice 'chase. Slightly mollified by the result Tom managed to smile as he received his trophy as winning trainer, and on behalf of Rick's father, winning owner. The stewards, after a brief discussion, had accepted the vet's explanation that Olympic Run was suffering from colic. Informing Tom that they would await the results of the dope test before considering the matter further, they laid the case to rest for the time being.

Tom himself had no such intentions and on his return to Highford the staff found themselves on the receiving end of an interrogation worthy of the Spanish inquisition. They were all taken aback by the ferocity of Tom's questions; but they all had the same answers. No, they had not seen anyone near the stables. No, they didn't know that Dominic had a horse in the race. No, they had no idea what could have given Runny colic. It wasn't until they had all left Tom's study did Rick emerge from the shadows and relay his experiences of the previous day.

"I'm afraid I suspected him of completely the wrong thing." He said apologetically. "I thought that, well, he'd go after Kitty again."

"Kitty?" Tom looked surprised and then lowered his eyes. "Oh."

"Yeah; I know." Rick nodded "I guess that you and she won't be a secret for too much longer anyway."

"Poppy?" Tom raised an eyebrow.

"Partly. Some of it you've been kind of giving away yourself. But the other thing." Rick hesitated, unsure of the ground he was about to walk on. "He confessed to that incident himself. Bastard. I thought that he might have tried again."

"No." Tom said hastily. "Not that. He has no idea about Kitty and me, that we've, well. Good God. What the hell will he do next?" He shook his head.

He stared out of the study window for a moment then spinning on his heels burst out of the door, slamming it behind him. Rick heard raised voices in the kitchen, and then, just as suddenly, Tom was back, red faced.

"He's gone! Bolted, the bloody coward! Didn't even have the guts to stay and face me!"

"Let it go." Rick said quietly. "He's out of the way now, and I don't think even he will be stupid enough to try it again. As long as he stays away, you're safe."

"I hope so." Tom was shaking. "For his sake, I bloody well hope so."

The press quickly got hold of the story, as did the Jockey Club, who summoned Tom to headquarters, wanting the minutest details from him about himself, his staff, and his family. While their main concern was getting to the truth behind the drama and reprimanding the guilty the daily rags were interested only in the sensational circumstances. The Daily Herald, lacking any other news, promoted it to front page. 'Olympic Disaster.' It announced in bold black type. 'Punters suffer as family feuds.' Anything they printed was purely circumstantial as any callers got very short shrift from Tom. The only words he spoke on the subject were to Lauren herself, who got a 'phone call early on the morning of the Herald's article.

"Give my brother a message." Tom's voice had made her stomach turn cold. "Next time tell him to come to me, and to leave my horses out of it. If he shows his face around my yard again, I'll kill him."

A week later the BHA Integrity Committee, who had drawn a blank in their investigation and found nothing amiss in the drug test, decided that they would never be able to identify the culprit and filed the matter away. Immediately after their call Rowley Harris arrived at the yard.

"How is he?" The little man looked nervous.

"He's fine Rowley. Back to his usual self. I really don't know what to say. I'm just so sorry."

"Well." Rowley hesitated. "Mike was all for moving him, I'll be honest, but we talked him down. Our horses have all done well with you and if all this speculation about your brother is true then it would only be giving him exactly what he wanted. If it isn't true then it would reflect badly on you, even finish you. I don't want to be responsible for that. So, he stays."

"Thank you." Tom's relief was audible.

"Good." Rowley brightened a little. "What I really came to talk about is Cheltenham. The entries don't close for a bit yet, do they?"

"No." Tom raised an eyebrow.

"Well if everything is okay with Runny, we'll go for that as planned, Mike wanted to go to Cheltenham in January as well, but I prefer the Racing Post 'Chase myself."

"Either would have done." Tom looked puzzled. "You may have got a better guide from running him at Cheltenham, possibly."

"The thing is, as we lost the King George Mike has developed another ambition. One that the brothers fell for straight away."

"And what's that?" Tom was as still as a statue.

"The Grand National."

"Whew." Tom blew out his lips. "He doesn't expect to actually win them both I hope. I know Mike is ambitious, but the double is virtually impossible."

"You know Mike." Rowley was rising, about to leave. "I'll be happy with a safe journey and a place! In either race.

Aintree wouldn't be my choice I admit, but in this instance, I was outnumbered."

" He's your horse." Tom offered his hand. "I'll make the entries by all means. Then I suggest we have a look at the weights for the Grand National and make a decision then."

"Fine by me." Rowley put on his hat. "I can't stop I'm afraid. I'll be in touch."

Tom wandered into the yard and scratched his head. He had not intended to run the horse again until February and had put all thoughts of Gold Cups and the like out of his head. The horse still had a hell of a lot to prove if he was to be taken seriously. Martin had been waiting outside Runny's box on tender hooks.

"Well?" he asked anxiously.

"If all goes well Martin, we will two have runners in the Grand National instead of one."

"Oh my God." Martin paled. "My nerves will never stand it."

"Join the club, Martin. Mine have had it already."

The chaos of Boxing Day was firmly put aside when on the last Saturday in December Little Raver was loaded onto the lorry and headed for Chepstow and the Welsh Grand National. It rained for the occasion and Gareth shivered in the chill as he led the little bay horse down the ramp. Kitty waited patiently behind with Romeo, who, fully recovered from his cough was making one of his final racecourse appearances in the stayer's hurdle race. Although not quite as electrifying in atmosphere as the King George, the Welsh Grand National was still a big race and the track was a hive of activity.

Strolling towards the Owner's and Trainer's bar in search of his mother and Margaret Tom recognised a familiar blonde mane in front of him and smiled as Rick's catlike green eyes turned to meet his. The tension was showing on the young man's face; the pressure to get this one right after Boxing Day was enormous.

"Okay?" Tom shrugged his coat around his shoulders as a blast of wind caught him.

"Sure. Damn it's so cold! I've never shivered so much in my life."

"Not nervous?"

"As hell." Rick hugged himself to keep warm "I'm off inside. See you later."

As he entered the weighing room Rick wished that he could also have gone for a drink to calm his nerves. He was young enough to thrive on a normal diet of no sleep and adrenalin, but today he felt double his twenty-four years and almost wished that he could jump straight back into the Porsche and head home. Shaking himself he went and sat in a corner of the crowded weighing room and looked at his surroundings. The jockeys, some changed, most in various stages of undress, were busy chatting away, ribbing each other with the usual banter. Bright coloured silks hung from the rows of pegs, clashing gaudily with each other. The lion's share of the space belonged to Brian Hales the reigning champion. He was sitting quite calmly reading the Racing Post. Like most of his colleagues he was a single-minded man; he ate, drank, slept, and breathed racehorses. It was a necessity if he wanted to maintain his position at the top of the table. If he made one lapse, one slip, there was always someone ready to take his place.

For this reason alone, Rick was the odd man out in this group. His interests, not always wholly legal, were diverse. Riding was his main passion, and he felt privileged to have the ability to make a living from it. But he loved so many other things; music, fast cars, night clubs, long hot days on the beach followed by even hotter, passion filled nights. He drank too much, drove too fast, often in sequence, and liked to relax with a joint in his hand. His counterparts were, on race days at least, well groomed, besuited and neat. Rick's long hair and torn leather jacket made him stand out like a Shire in a field full of Shetlands. The knowledge that he was so different added to the terrible attack of nerves that was besieging him. Pulling off his lucky baseball cap he wrung it in his hands.

Brian Hales watched him over the top of his newspaper. Tension made Rick's high cheekbones dominate his drawn face; the green eyes were dark, shuttered beneath the long, almost feminine black lashes. Watching the younger man suffer Brian felt sympathy. He could remember being a lone nervous figure sitting silent in the corner. Now he was the King of the Castle, and everyone sought his company; but he was convinced that sitting opposite him was the young pretender to his crown. Rick possessed a brilliance in the saddle the like of which Brian had never seen before; and a presence out of it that he himself could never match. Racing needed Rick Cowdrey. It needed his style, his artistry, his quirks, and his charisma. He was talented enough to satisfy the pickiest of critics, and good looking enough to wrench the hearts of every pony mad girl in the country.

"Ready Mr. Hales?" The valet was waiting to tie his silk.

Rick hardly looked up as Brian got to his feet, but when he and the others in the first race had left the room seemed very quiet. Unable to contain his nerves any longer, he bolted to the toilet and was sick.

The only one displaying no nerves at all was Little Raver. Coolly surveying his opposition, he sniffed the air through flared nostrils, little head held high. Not a tremor disturbed his smooth hide. Beside him Kitty wasn't sure if she shivered with cold, nerves or the proximity of a tall figure in a black woollen over coat. The firm set of Tom's jaw was giving away his own tension. Unable to help herself she stared at him as Gareth removed Raver's paddock sheets. Running her eyes over the strong profile; the long, almost aquiline nose, the dark lashes on the now pale cheeks, she felt a pang of longing so strong that it took her breath away. Caught out, she was still staring when he turned his vivid blue eyes onto her. Blushing she lowered head quickly. Tom said nothing, but as she moved aside for Gareth to take the horse, she felt his fingers on her arm for just a second. Shaking herself firmly she went out onto the course behind them. Now was not the time for daydreams. Now was the time for Highford House to redeem its reputation.

"The twenty runners for our feature race of the day, the Coral Welsh Grand National are beginning to make a line." Shane boomed into his microphone. "They are under starters orders, they're off!"

Margaret Ainsley, firmly attached to the bar, didn't want to watch. Her baby was about to undergo his biggest test yet and she couldn't bear to look. Tom, out on the balcony, could see her purple colours clearly through his binoculars. Rick's hair, tied in a ponytail, hung down his back. From here, with his slim figure and narrow hips he looked like a girl. It was only when you looked closer and saw the hard, muscular thighs and powerful forearms that you realised his strength. As the horses drew into a ragged line, Tom's hands began to shake.

"They're on their way" Roared Shane, his usual excitement overtaking him.

Dead on cue, the rain fell so hard that it obliterated all vision. Rick, crouched low over Raver's neck, winced as the ice that started to fall among the rain stung his cheeks. Riding this course always reminded him of being on a rollercoaster; having climbed steadily uphill, they now swept downwards into the bend, gathering speed as they went. Sitting in the middle of the bunch, Rick realised he was unsighted for the next fence and switched Raver to the outside. The little horse changed legs as neatly as a cat and took the fence on a perfect stride. Beside him a horse fell, hooves flailing in the air, bringing the next horse down with him. Rick breathed a sigh of relief, that had been a little too close for comfort.

As the field thudded wetly past the stands Tom was well satisfied with the way his horse was travelling. Beside him a well-groomed woman was training her binocular on the same subject, but for apparently different reasons.

"My God he's handsome." She drawled. "Such lovely style, so balanced."

Tom shot her a sideways glance. He had never thought Raver a particularly striking horse.

"It's his hair." Her companion agreed. "I would love to have his hair; or those beautiful green eyes."

With a chuckle Tom realised that they were talking about Rick. Moving away so that they wouldn't hear him laughing, he watched the little horse leaping the open ditch.

The torrential rain had turned the already soft going into mud. The horses were rapidly tiring of pulling weary muscles out of the glue-like substance beneath their feet. Rick could hear Raver's breath whistling through his dilated nostrils. He steadied the horse behind the three leaders, giving him a 'breather', letting him fill his lungs with air ready for one final effort up the hill. As they approached the third last, on the final climb before the freewheel down the home stretch, Rick spotted a big chestnut horse pulling away from the other two runners, who were visibly slowing with every stride. Giving Raver a smack he drove him past the two weakening horses and went after the leader. Tom was starting to worry. He could see that his horse was almost out on his feet now, barely able to clamber over the second last; Rick was working as hard as he could; kicking and punching with his hands and heels, his whip swinging, not making contact, just keeping the horse in a straight line. Ahead the big chestnut, its white face splattered with mud, was also beginning to wander, legs weaving wearily to and fro. Its jockey, seeing the final flight ahead of him, gathered his reins and almost lifted the horse over. The horse climbed through the birch, rather than over it, and dragged his white nose along the floor before gaining his feet on the other side. Behind him, Raver landed sideways, alongside the fence, almost standing still, and then lurching on.

Knowing that he was beaten Rick sat up, took one look behind him just in case, then dropped his hands and trotted to the line.

Gareth caught one of Raver's mud-covered reins and steered him off the track. Rick was slumped in the saddle, exhausted, unable to speak. Both horse and rider were more than happy to let Gareth take charge and steer them into the unsaddling enclosure.

"Well done." Tom greeted them. "You did your best."

Rick raised his head, face almost completely covered in mud, two white circles around his eyes where his goggles had been.

"He's all in." He gasped. "Nothing left. But he tried his heart out."

"You don't look to good yourself." Tom caught Rick's arm and steadied him as he slid off the horse.

"I'll be fine." Rick was struggling with his saddle, too weak to unbuckle the girths. Gasping for air he leaned weakly against the horse's flanks, sliding the saddle slowly towards him.

Margaret, running into the winner's enclosure was beside herself. She remembered all too clearly the days when every horse she ran either fell or failed to finish the course.

"Well done both!" She hugged Rick and slapped Raver's steaming neck. "Poor little man. He's very tired."

"He'll be right as rain Margie." Tom looked over her shoulder as Rick staggered away to weigh in. "It's the jockey I'm worried about, he looks ready to drop!"

Anthony Morgan, the valet, took one look at Rick and formed the same opinion. Seeing Rick's white face as he sat in his corner, too weak to even get out of his wet colours, Anthony alerted the doctor. Going back to check on Rick he found the corner empty.

"Where's he gone?"

Brian Hales was peeling off soaking colours and struggling to get his wet body into new ones.

"In the toilet. Throwing his heart up."

The doctor stood Rick down for the rest of the day. His temperature was way too high, and he was as weak as the proverbial kitten. Tom came looking for him with an anxious face.

"Sorry." Rick couldn't lift his face from his hands. "I've been throwing up all day. I thought it was just nerves."

"If you do feel up to it later, I dare say you'll find my mother in the bar. She'll look after you, then we'll sort out a lift home for you. Now." His eyes scanned the room. "This means I've got a spare in the last race."

Dave Holloway got nervously from his seat.

"I can ride." He spoke quietly

"You'll do." Tom spoke shortly. "You know old Romeo; he'll go well enough for you."

Having no wish to entertain any further conversation he went back to his horses.

The mud- soaked ground proved too much for Romeo. With the wisdom that comes of age he began to drop himself out of the race on the second circuit. Dave, not wanting to incur Tom's wrath again pulled the horse up in the back straight. He wanted to redeem himself; if there was ever a spare ride on that big bay, he wanted to be on it.

The media, loving a good feud, quickly picked up on the intended rematch of Runny and Revelation in the Cheltenham Gold Cup and went to town on it. Every week they managed to find some new angle, true or otherwise on which to base a new scandal. Both sets of connections were plagued by 'phone calls, day and night. Jack Coltrane, one of the country's most controversial trainers who often fell into the media's spotlight was undisturbed by all the attention. He answered all queries with a rude disdain that did little to enhance his reputation.

Tom, who hated the whole thing, had come out of it all as the good guy, but still insisted on keeping a low profile, letting Claire field all callers. Rick meanwhile was rapidly being promoted from jockey to superstar. Having tried to magnify his 'bad boy' image, the press found that instead of a rebel they were dealing with the biggest racing celebrity since John Francome. People either loathed Rick or loved him, such was his personality that there was no middle road. As a rule, the institution hated him and the public, especially the female public, loved him. His golden good looks had young girls in raptures and Poppy went through heaven and hell as his face appeared in countless magazines. Olympic Run didn't escape the prying lens either; Martin discovered a photographer hidden in the bushes at the top of the gallops poised for a sneak shot.

Revelation, the 'dark horse' in more ways than one, turned out to be inaptly named, as he was kept well out of sight.

As if Tom didn't have enough to contend with, he also received a panic-stricken call from Flick. The spotty faced reporter had wormed a story out of the sound engineer after a few pints and had sold the details of Flick's clinic visit to his paper. Although the clinic was bound not to release details, the lure of money worked on many ex-employees, and in the light of a renewed anti-abortion campaign the paper rang Flick and asked for her side of the story. She had slammed the 'phone down on them and rang Tom in hysterics.

"What am I going to do?" She wailed.

"Tell them to fuck off!"

On a more practical note, Tom rang Ned Benson, the family solicitor, and asked his advice.

"Bit difficult if they've seen the books, but if it's all hearsay I'll tackle the paper with libel and the clinic with breach of confidence anyway. That should hold them off."

With all the furore that was going on it became difficult to maintain any kind of normality. Sick to death of being hounded by press and female admirers alike Rick uprooted himself and rented a tiny cottage in the Gloucestershire countryside to hide himself away. The seclusion was totally alien to his nature, but it was his only escape from the prying eyes of the outside world. Hating being alone at night he got himself a dog from the local rescue kennels for company. Grey and white, with one brown and eye and one blue it looked like a cross between and sheepdog and a hearth rug. It was the ugliest thing he had ever seen clumsy, stupid, and fiercely protective. Delighted with his new companion Rick named him Bozo and took him everywhere. He was soon a familiar sight watching the horses working, big ears flapping in the wind. Poppy, who couldn't get anywhere near Rick when Bozo was around, spent most of her salary on chocolate drops and bones trying to win him over. She soon began to spend all her free time with Rick, being ferried around in the Porsche, with Bozo's ridiculous head poking out of the window.

At the end of January Rick appeared in front of the magistrate's charged with possession of illegal substances. Ned, duly appointed by Tom, pleaded Rick's case with gusto, and he walked away from the courtroom with a hefty, but not crippling fine. Facing the barrage of press outside he firmly refused to open his mouth. From the courthouse he went straight to headquarters where the jockey club stewards imposed their own punishment of fines and a five-day ban.

"Think yourself lucky." Tom said grimly as Rick got into the car, sighing with relief. "That could have been worse. Much worse."

"Phew." Relaxing in the comfort of the BMW Rick felt as if it were safe to breathe again. "Thank God that's over."

"Thank God you got off as lightly as you did you stupid bastard." Tom was grim faced. "I hope you've learned your lesson."

"Sure." Rick was unabashed.

"I mean it!" Tom snapped. "This could have cocked up your career before it started. Mud sticks. Just tow the line from now on. I have enough trouble with Mike Peterson as it is without him wanting you off his horse as well!"

Trying his hardest to act on that advice Rick ignored the dozens of party invitations he received each week. Through Emmie, who still hated the thought of letting him go and messaged and rang him several times a week, he heard of another drugs raid. This time there had been a massive haul for the police, and of a much heavier nature. Thanking his lucky stars that he hadn't been involved, Rick settled into his new, more monogamous, drug free lifestyle.

February was not a good month for the racing world. The weather was so cold during the first week that every meeting was abandoned. The ground, hard as concrete, refused to thaw. In the North it snowed, great blizzards that blocked the roads. Shivering in the sub-zero winds, wearing three and four rugs apiece the horses began to lose form. Desperate not to miss any time with his big race hopefuls Tom drove the miles to Lambourn every day to use Peter Stroud's equine pool. Runny hated it, ears flat to his noble head; Raver thought it a great lark and made a great deal of noise splashing on his way in and out. It was hard graft, but it was worth it. Returning at night Tom would collapse exhausted into bed, only to rise at five and start all over again. Never before had he worked so hard or wanted so badly to win. He would never admit it to anyone, but Dominic was the goad that drove him on.

If Dominic was the goad, then Kitty was the reward for his labours. Despite his weariness he still managed to find the time and energy to make love to her. Fleeting secret meetings became more frequent; if he was using her, he was unaware of it, and if he was, she didn't care. Poppy, with the security of her new relationship with Rick intact, was very scathing.

"It'll end in tears."

"Don't be so bloody patronising! Just because you've got wonder boy dangling on a string for a few minutes!"

It was the closest they had ever come to falling out. Poppy was secretly jealous of the fact that Kitty had been Rick's first choice, something that rankled deep inside her; in turn Kitty fought with her jealousy of Poppy's more normal, public relationship with Rick. Martin watched them niggle at each other night and day and failed to comprehend what could possibly mean more to them than Olympic Run and the Gold Cup.

Valentine's day saw the first rain of the month. It came down in sheets, rushing across the yard in little waves of water, rattling the windows of the cottage, waking its inhabitants long before dawn. Staggering bleary eyed into the kitchen Poppy found Martin staring at a red envelope.

"I've got one!" He muttered. "I've never had one before in my life!"

Poppy smiled and kissed his forehead.

"Well, you deserve one."

Neither of the two girls said anything out loud, but their faces gave away their disappointment when no roses or champagne arrived for them. Immersed in melancholy and self-abuse Kitty rode her horse back from the gallops in a black despair. The landscape was grey and bleak today, the trees hoisting stark naked branches against thunderous skies. It suited her mood.

As they finished evening stables the calm was disturbed by the booming roar of Rick's Porsche. Bozo, wearing a red ribbon around his neck bounced out and began to race around the yard. Horrified, Poppy began to rub her grimy hands on her breeches.

"Hiya gorgeous." Rick stood in the light from Streak's box wearing a dinner suit and a diamond earring. "Fancy dinner?"

Poppy, knocked sideways by his beauty, forgot her earlier despondency, and stammered like an idiot.

"Tell you what I fancy." Rick moved closer. "You."

"I'm filthy!" Poppy squeaked. "You'll get dirty!"

"You can wash me." Rick grinned. "Just be careful with that pitchfork."

Sometime later, completely desolate, Kitty watched them roaring into the night and turned miserably back into the cottage.

"Cheer up." Martin put his arm around her.

"Cup of tea?" She forced a smile.

"Sorry lovey. I'm off down the pub. Coming?"

"No. I'll be fine here." Kitty had a feeling that the sender of Martin's Valentine would be there and was in no mood for playing gooseberry.

When the cottage was empty, she mooched about, tidying up, washing dishes, removing muddy wellingtons from the hall; doing anything that she could think of to take her mind off Tom. Running a bath, she was annoyed to find herself watching the lights of the house. She had just undressed when the doorbell went. Wrapping a towel around herself she went to the top of the stairs.

"Who is it?"

"Me." Said Tom's voice. "Hurry up, it's pouring down."

Holding her towel with one hand she opened the door. A large bouquet of red roses came through it followed by a smiling Tom.

"Oh!" In her excitement she forgot about holding up the towel and reaching out for the roses sent it slipping to the floor.

"Oh!" Said Tom mockingly. "What a greeting!"

Laughing, she bent to retrieve the towel, but he quickly kicked it away with his foot. She stood upright, holding the flowers in front of her.

"You look like Eve." His voice was husky. He took the roses and laid them on the floor. "Now you look perfect."

The tiny bed was barely big enough for them both to fit in but had the benefit of keeping them very close together. Studying Winston, who was starting to look his age, Tom remembered the night of Martin's birthday. So much for his self-control. Tossing the little bear onto Poppy's bed he turned to the girl in his arms.

"Didn't get very far, did we? I came to take you out."

For answer Kitty snuggled closer to him, burying her face in his chest.

"Hungry?" he lifted her hair, letting it fall across his stomach.

"Starving."

"Come on then." He began to untangle himself.

"No." She clung to him. "Let's stay here."

"Kitty." He moved her arm. "I couldn't raise a smile at the moment. If I don't eat something soon, I'll pass out."

Floating home, much later, high on champagne and love, Kitty found her housemates sitting around the living room drinking hot chocolate.

"Hello." She sat beside Martin. "Good evening everyone?"

"Wonderful." Poppy yawned. "You will never guess what was on the news."

"What?"

"Dominic's been arrested."

"What?" Kitty stared at her. "Why? What for?"

"Drugs. Remember Rick told us about that big raid in

London? They've got the dealers as well this time, and our dear friend is one of them."

Kitty, despite her fear and loathing of Dominic, couldn't believe it.

"Rick says." Poppy continued. "That Dominic doesn't use the hard stuff himself, at least not in public anyway, just sells it on. They picked up everything you can think off. Rick thinks we won't be seeing Dominic for quite some time once he's been in court."

"Does a lot of thinking doesn't he?" Sneered Martin. "Still, I suppose he'd know."

"Oh, shut up Marty!" Kitty pushed him. "This is interesting!"

"Anyway." Poppy continued, ignoring Martin. "They picked him and two others up this morning. Found even more stuff stashed away in his flat. They'll be in front of the magistrates tomorrow. "

"Good God." Kitty was thinking of Tom.

"It's Mrs. Chichester I feel sorry for." Martin said sadly. " What could such a lovely woman ever have done to deserve a son like that?"

CHAPTER FIFTEEN

Highford House was in darkness. Closing the front door as quietly as he could Tom's ears picked up a faint noise coming from his study. Puzzled, he moved stealthily across the hall and pushed the door open a couple of inches. Barely distinguishable from the surrounding gloom he could just make out a shadowy figure sitting in his leather chair. The cold hand of fear laid itself on his spine as the figure reached out an arm for the whisky decanter on the desk; the hairs on the back of his neck standing upright as the form poured liquid into a glass. With a thumping heart he forced himself to reach for the light switch. The brilliance of the light after darkness was dazzling. Blinking his eyes, he heard a crash as his decanter smashed to the floor.

"Who is it?" He demanded. "What are you doing in here?"

The figure rose from the chair and took on the familiar homely shape of his mother. Tom slumped against the wall weak with relief.

"Jesus Christ mother! You scared me to death. I thought you were a.." He stopped. A ghost? What a ridiculous thing to say.

"I'm sorry dear." Eleanor sounded strange. "I thought that sitting here in the dark might help. I know it's stupid of me, but I thought that if I sat here, at his desk, in his chair and thought about him hard enough he might come back and talk to me. But we don't do we? Come back I mean. Not really. Only in films and silly stories. The end is the end and that's it. Oh, don't listen to me Tom. I'm just a daft old woman."

Her voice broke slightly and looking closely at her Tom saw that she had been crying. A lump rose into his throat. Her thoughts had come so perilously close to his own. How many times in the past few months had he tried the very same thing, desperate for guidance? Picking up the shards of broken glass he tried not to look at his mother. When he stood upright, he realised that the whisky fumes came not only from the decanter but from her breath.

"Mother?" He narrowed his eyes. "You've been drinking!"

"Yes." His mother was gazing with sad eyes at the photograph of his father. "I'm sorry dear. I've been here rather a long time. I'm afraid I'm a little drunk."

"But why?" Tom was incredulous. "You never drink!"

"I was lonely Tom. I needed someone to talk to so I came in here and talked to the thin air, hoping that someone might hear me. But of course, no one did."

"Mother." Tom crouched before her and took her hands in his. "Has something happened? You're not ill, are you?"

His mother raised her tear-filled eyes to his.

"You mean you don't know?"

"Know what?" He asked patiently.

"About Dominic?"

"Oh, what the hell has he done now!" Tom's voice was so harsh that Eleanor shrank from him.

"He's been arrested. They say he's been selling drugs, what do you call it, dealing."

Tom stared into the empty hearth and wished with all his heart that it was his brother lying in the village cemetery and not his father.

"They are going to charge him in the morning." His mother was continuing. "Ned says he'll get bail, whatever that is. We have to go to the court in the morning. I'll have to pay whatever they want to get him out."

Tom didn't reply. He was wishing that he could turn the clock back to a time when this great weight of responsibility didn't lie so heavily on his shoulders. Oh, to go to sleep then wake to find it had all been a bad dream. Taking a deep, shuddering breath he straightened and helped his mother to her feet.

"Go to bed love." He spoke softly. "We'll talk about this in the morning."

Walking with her to her bedroom he helped her in and sat beside her until she fell asleep.

The magistrates, as Ned had expected, were willing to grant bail. It would possibly be months before the slow turning wheels of the legal system brought the case to court, so Dominic was bailed subject to certain conditions and payment of a hefty bond. Grudgingly handing over the cheque Tom waited with growing impatience as the clerk checked his credibility with the bank. Minutes later Dominic appeared, escorted by a burly, stern faced, policeman.

"Remember." He hissed as he let Dominic go. "One step out of line and your straight back inside. I've got a teenage daughter; personally, I'd like to strap you into the chair and pull the lever myself."

"My my." Dominic raised a sarcastic eyebrow. "Whatever happened to good old English justice, innocent until proven guilty?"

"Take him." The officer looked at Tom. "Before I show him the true meaning of Police brutality."

"And I." Muttered Tom as Dominic passed him. "Want every penny of that money back. Every last penny you understand?"

Despite loud protests from both brothers but for different reasons, Eleanor won her battle to take her younger son home with her. Dominic could not be trusted that much was obvious, and although she could not believe that he was guilty, she could believe that he would jump bail and disappear without trace. Furious, Tom drove at manic speed back to the Cotswold's. Depositing his passengers at the house he went straight to the stables.

The staff carefully avoided their boss as they went about

their tasks; recognising all too well the pale eyed monster of barely controlled temper that appeared before them. Only Streak shrieked an ecstatic welcome, kicking her door with delight as he approached. Letting himself into her box he ran his hands down her strong limbs. Bigger, more powerful in the body than she had been, he was well pleased with her. As usual, the contact with his horses; their warmth, their trust, calmed him. Next door Raver poked his little Arab like head out for a pat, lunchtime feed stuck to his muzzle. On Friday he would make the long trek north to Haydock Park to run in one of the established Grand National trials on the Saturday. It would provide Tom with a guideline, a clue as to whether Raver really did have the scope and stamina to tackle Aintree. One of the horse's quirks was that he would not drink when travelling, so Tom had booked him and Gareth in for the night, wanting to give the horse every opportunity to prove his worth.

More pressing in his mind was Runny's return to Kempton the following week for the Racing Post 'chase. From there on all eyes turned to Cheltenham, and every race was analysed and criticised in terms of its festival form. Anyone who rode, trained, or owned a racehorse wanted a festival winner and Tom was no exception. He dearly wanted Runny to redeem himself after the tragedy of Boxing Day, but more importantly he wanted to see, for himself, the proof of his belief in the horse. Then, and only then, would he allow himself the thrill of preparing for, and dreaming about the greatest jump meeting on Earth.

In the north the torrential rain had washed away the snowdrifts and turned them into floods. Haydock Park, only just managing to hold onto its meeting, had its turf turned into quagmire as leg weary horses returned splattered with mud. It was sods law that Raver should have to face another battle through heavy going. Although his action made it easier for him to deal with wet ground, Tom had prayed that it wouldn't be as bad for him as last time.

Someone on high wasn't listening.

Having borne his night away from home with dignity Raver was totally unaffected by his strange surroundings. Having eaten a good breakfast he sailed through the preliminaries, totally untouched by the nerves that wrecked his human counterparts. Margaret wandered around in a daze, avoiding anyone she knew because she was too nervous to speak. Rick, who had never ridden at Haydock before walked the course three times and then vanished into the sauna to try and lose one stubborn pound in order to do Raver's low weight. There were fifteen other runners, so the parade ring was busy as Gareth walked the little horse around, chattering to him nonstop. Although Enigma was his big love he was devoted to his latest charge and to have them both running on the same day filled him with anxiety. As the jockeys filed into the paddock Tom headed off Rick, who was tucking a stray hair into his skullcap, still pink from his sauna.

"Okay?" Rick was more relaxed today. "Nearly killed myself in that sauna. I'm not used to it!"

"Well if you're thirsty stick your tongue out as you go around. There'll be plenty of water off the rack." Tom quipped.

"Cheers." Rick grinned. "Size of these fences I may end up in a cloud."

"Try and save as much energy as possible." Tom bent to leg him up. "Hold him up."

Nodding Rick took up the reins and patted Raver's neck.

"Good luck." Gareth grinned as he turned out onto the track. "You look after him now."

Collecting Poppy who was waiting in the wings Gareth ran back to the rails to watch the race. Tom and Margaret were high up in the stands, glasses trained on the runners as they came into line.

The mud flew thick and fast as the runners ploughed over the first few fences. Following Tom's instructions and holding Raver at the back of the field, Rick found himself scrabbling for his clean goggles, unable to see. Raver was jumping well, making light work of the stiff fences, but the ground was becoming churned up and as they went out onto the second circuit the take offs were becoming treacherous underfoot. Pushing to clear the fences the little horse began to feel himself slip and slide; his ears flicking to and fro as he tried to steady himself.

"It's okay little man." Rick told him. "It's a long way home. You just take your time."

Swinging into the Open Ditch Rick let Raver run wide, looking for better ground. Ears pricked Raver saw the fence and quickened into it; spotting the ditch yawning in front of him he gathered himself for a bigger leap. As he pushed off the ground Rick felt a second's uncertainty from the animal beneath him; a hesitation, a moments loss of grip, felt the fluent jumping action falter; then there was a noise, a loud crack, and Raver's hindlegs dropped behind him into the ditch as his ears disappeared downwards. The ground came rushing up to meet Rick and he reached out, trying to throw himself clear. As he hit the ground with a thud there was a strange noise, an almost a human scream, and then his whole world became a thrashing mass of flesh and steel-clad hooves that pushed him into the turf until everything went black.

Around Tom and Margaret, the stands had gone quiet.

At the fence, two ground staff stood rooted to the spot.

"Who screamed?" The youngest one whispered. "Him or the horse?"

His words spurred the older man into action. Ducking under the rails he waved frantically at the ambulance which was sliding around the inner ring of the track. Bending beside Rick's motionless body he felt for his pulse. Beside them the horse, who had been laying as motionless as his rider, began to struggle to get up. Sitting on his haunches like a dog he made several attempts to rise, then, with an audible groan of pain, lurched to his feet.

The younger man stared in horror, unable to move. The little horse's hind leg was completely broken in half, the bone protruding from the flesh above his hock. The whole limb stuck out at an angle like some grotesque caricature. Terrified by the pain, desperate to free himself from this horror that clung to him, Raver kicked and kicked, spraying blood over the two men on the floor beside him.

"Oh my God." The younger man caught hold of his reins and tried to keep him still. "You poor sod."

The ambulance reached them first, closely followed by the vet. A figure was running towards them with a silent scream escaping from its open mouth, lead rope trailing in the grass. Darting onto the course, Gareth stopped when he saw the horse. His stomach churned. Assailed by a wave of sickness and horror he turned away, clinging to the rails. A hand grasped his shoulder.

"Go Gareth." Tom's voice was shaking. "No need to stay here."

Grey, stricken, guilty because of his fear, Gareth staggered away. At the rails, below the still quiet stands, Martin was holding a hysterical Poppy.

"Let me go!" She screamed. "Let me go!"

"Calm down." Shouted Martin. "He'll be okay. Just calm down!"

"He's dead!" She shouted back. "He's not moving!"

"He is not dead!" Hissed Martin, aware of Gareth approaching with head down, and hoping to God that it wasn't true. "Now please calm down."

Poppy stared at him, eyes huge in her terrified white face, then with a sob she collapsed into his arms.

The vet was appalled by the horse's injury. One look at the horse's face sent him running back to his truck for the humane killer. The younger of the two ground staff who was still shaking, helped the driver of the horse ambulance with the green canvas screen.

"Doll that fence off." The vet told him. "They'll be here again soon."

Looking over his shoulder he saw coloured hats already approaching.

"Too late to move him. Flag them around the fence and we'll have to try and keep him still."

With great difficulty, cupping their hands over his eyes, they managed to keep the crippled horse beside the rails as the field thundered past them. Through his pain, through his fear, Raver's inborn urge to run rose and he plunged wildly about, trying to get free.

"Right." The vet stepped forward. "Let's put this poor animal out of his pain."

With the screen closed around them, blocking the horse from the view of the sickened crowds they heard a cry piercing the air.

"No!" The wail was ghostly, almost inhuman, and made the vets blood run cold. "No! No! No!"

Margaret had dodged all the officials and run so fast she was near collapse. Ashen faced she gave a scream of horror when she saw the hideous limb.

"Oh, my boy!" She sobbed. "Oh, my poor baby!"

Throwing her arms around her horses neck she buried her face in the steaming skin.

"Margie." Tom laid a gentle hand on her shoulder. "Come away."

"Please?" Margie turned pleading eyes onto the vet. "Don't kill my boy, please save him!"

For the first time, in all the years he had known her, Tom saw Margie as she really was; a lonely, sad, old woman. Swallowing his own tears, he turned away. Raver, through the fog of his pain, recognised the voice he had known since the moment of his birth and pushed his muzzle into the woman's body.

"Oh Lord." The vet was close to tears himself. "If there was any way I could save him I would."

The little woman looked at him, and slowly the familiar facade of the brisk army widow returned.

"Of course." She patted the horse's neck, trying, without effect, to stop her hand shaking. "We can't let him suffer, can we?"

"No." The vet said kindly. "It would be better if you didn't stay."

"I must." Said Margie firmly. "I brought him into the world, and I'll see him out of it."

"Come on baby." She was choking on her words. "Mummy's going to stop the pain."

Tom, his back to the horse, heard the whispered words and felt his heart lurch. Shutting his eyes tightly, he shuddered as the dull crack sounded across the racecourse, and Margaret said goodbye to the pride and joy that had become her whole life.

His staff had gone to pieces. Gareth was locked in the toilets audibly breaking his heart. Poppy, no longer hysterical, was sitting outside Enigma's stable shivering like a whipped dog. Martin was in a daze. Unable to help either of his friends, and wanting to break down himself, he fiddled around, trying not to keep still, afraid of what would happen if he did. Turning away from the filly he saw Tom approaching. Searching the man's face for emotion he found none.

"Get her ready Martin." Tom laid his hand on Poppy's head. He couldn't let them see that he also wanted to sit down and cry. "I'm going to try and find out how he is."

The weighing room was quiet. Its occupants looked up as Tom entered.

"Well?" Brian Hales got to his feet.

AJMORRIS

"No news I'm afraid. Can you ride my filly in the last?"

"Yes of course." Brian looked weary. "I do hope he's alright. It was a horrible looking fall. You will let me know?"

"I will." Tom backed out of the room. He would have one more attempt at finding out about Rick and then he had a very difficult task to perform. Somehow, and he had no idea how when he was struggling himself, he had to give Margaret the strength to pick up the pieces and carry on.

Lights drove bore holes into Rick's brain. Trying to open his mouth he felt hot needles of pain stabbing at his muscles and groaned. Blinking against the searing brilliance of the lights, he tried to lift his arm to block them out and found that he couldn't. Panic stricken, he tried to sit up, and passed out.

When he next opened his eyes again it was dark. Disturbed by the silence he cautiously turned his throbbing head, trying to recognise his surroundings. Remembering his last attempt at movement he nervously wiggled his fingers, flexed his elbow, and finally raised his arm. To his immense relief it came up without too much resistance. After testing each limb in turn, he let out his breath. Focusing his reluctant eyes, which kept blurring like a worn videotape, he made out a shape sitting at the far side of the room.

"Pop?" He had to make several attempts at forming the words. "Is that you?"

"Sorry." A man's voice answered. "Will I do?"

The figure rose and from its height Rick realised it was Tom.

"What happened? Where am I?" Rick's voice was pitifully weak.

"You had a fall." Tom wanted to save him the details of his horrific roller coaster ride through the air, and the subsequent steam rollering of his body. "You're in hospital."

"I'm thirsty." Rick tried to swallow.

"I'll get a nurse."

When the nurse came, she turned on the light as she entered. Shocked by the pain in his head Rick screamed. Hastily putting the room back into darkness, the nurse turned on a very dim wall lamp; even this was uncomfortable at first, but slowly Rick's discomfort eased, and he grew used to it. Sipping his water, he tried to remember what had happened, but his last clear memory was getting onto Raver in the paddock. His mind had mercifully wiped out the rest.

"What happened?" He asked again. Then a shadow flitted across his face, and he barely whispered his next question.

"What happened to Raver?"

Tom sighed. He felt exhausted.

"We had to lose him I'm afraid. Broken hind leg. There was absolutely nothing we could do."

"Oh no." Rick fell silent and Tom could see mist forming on his already hazy eyes. "I'm sorry. He was a great little horse. Damn."

He looked up at Tom.

"You look like hell." He commented.

Tom glanced at the young man, his face as white as the hospital pillows, he lay on and tried to force a smile.

"You don't look so clever yourself."

Rick blinked at him, his eyes rapidly losing focus once more. The long eyelashes were beginning to drop like shutters over the cat's eyes. Eyes that were growing dim.

"Go to sleep." Tom removed the spilling glass from his hand.

There was no answer; slipping back into unconsciousness Rick looked as peaceful as a baby. I wish I could do that, thought Tom, with a twinge of envy, go to sleep and forget it all.

The nurse had come back into the room.

"Is he asleep?"

"Yes. Lucky sod."

The young nurse looked at the tired eyes and wondered what could possibly be bad enough to make this handsome man look so tormented.

"You need some yourself." She said sweetly. "He'll be fine. Don't worry."

"If it was only him, I had to worry about," Tom forced a smile, took one last look at Rick's sleeping form, and wandered, listless, into the wet night air.

The press was emblazoned with horrible photographs of Raver's fall. Some of the tabloids had picked up on their usual thread for the time of year and were questioning the morals of steeplechasing. 'A cruel way to die.' Announced The Herald. 'Can we, as a so-called nation of animal lovers, continue to stand back and watch these noble creatures sacrificed in the name of sport?'

"They write some crap!" Martin threw the paper onto the table in disgust. "A nation of animal lovers my arse! Tell that to that poor dog we saw dumped on the side of the motorway yesterday!"

"Or that skinny pony." Agreed Gareth. "Living on a patch of mud with no shelter."

"They make me sick!" Martin warmed to his subject. "They know sod all about horses, or racing. I mean if I was to come back as a horse, I'd rather be a racehorse and treated like a prince, than some poor swine being kept by an ignorant prat who treated me like a motorbike."

"It is a terrible picture." Kitty studied the angle at which Rick was flying through the air. "Poor Margie. Having to look at that this morning."

"Poor Poppy." Gareth said grimly. "She rang the hospital again this morning, they won't tell her anything."

On cue, Poppy entered the room. Unwashed from the previous day she had patrolled the living room all night, watching the 'phone but to no avail.

"They still won't tell me anything!" She moaned. "I don't know what to do!"

"Eat lunch." Martin was steering her to a chair.

Poppy was turning a sandwich over in her hands when the door opened, and Tom walked in.

"What?" Poppy's hands flew to her face. "What's happened?"

"Calm down Pop." Kitty took her hand.

"Well." Tom ran solemn eyes over them all and then his face crumpled into a smile. "Not a single broken bone! Just severe concussion and some pretty psychedelic bruises. He's being transferred to Cheltenham general this afternoon. I'll find out when so you can go and see for yourself Poppy. He won't be there long, it's just to make sure there are no complications."

"Oh, thank God!" Poppy burst into tears.

"He needs peace and quiet mind you." Tom told her, not unkindly. "So, go easy on him. he's been stood down for the mandatory three weeks as he was unconscious for more than three minutes."

"What!" Martin wailed in protest. "They can't do that! He'll miss the Racing Post 'chase!"

"Not a problem." Tom assured him. "Brian will take the ride."

"I hope he wins." Martin watched the weary man heading to his office. "We can't take any more bad luck. I think the Guv would pack it all in."

Sixty miles away Margaret Ainsley looked across her land and saw the first cautious green buds appearing on the bare branches. Behind her, the cold empty house brooded beneath its shelter of fir trees, dark and silent. A heavy old grey mare nodded by the field gate, dozing in the weak sunshine. With a memory that was almost too painful to bear Margaret saw her eight years ago, proudly showing off her little foal. The same foal that now lay in the newly dug grave in the orchard. She had just planted flowers on the mound of earth; laid a red rose on its summit. She had wanted Raver home, to rest in the field he had grown up in. Looking at her dirty nails she rubbed them irritably on her jumper.

What had she to do now? She tried to remember and couldn't. What time was it? She looked at her watch. It had stopped.

Everything had stopped.

Except her.

She had to carry on, alone. She had to face the world every morning with the knowledge that the things she had loved most had left her behind. She longed to touch Raver's silken coat, to feel the warmth of his skin. But he was gone. He was as cold as the stone wall beside her. The beautiful head would never again raise to greet her in the morning; just as Richard would never again walk up the path and take her in his arms. She had never felt so alone; or so terribly, terribly cold. Lowering her aching limbs onto the step she felt the chill of the ground gnawing at her bones. The same chill that was eating at Raver's body, taking it into the earth forever.

A great cry tore from her, echoing off the walls, fading unheard across the empty fields. The mare lifted her head and Margaret saw her deep brown eyes watching her. Did she know, she wondered? Did she realise what they had lost, both of them?

Giving way to the grief she had carried for so long she dropped her head, and cried her tears into the silent, uncaring grey stone.

CHAPTER SIXTEEN

Rick watched with a mixture of pride and envy as Runny and Brian Hales poleaxed the opposition in the Racing Post 'Chase. Stiff, depressed, irritated by media speculation that Brian Hales would keep the ride on Runny for the Gold Cup, he mooched around his tiny cottage desperate to get back into the saddle. Even Bozo's ridiculous antics failed to cheer him up. He couldn't face going to Highford to watch the horses working, so this in turn put a strain on his relationship with Poppy who hated being apart from him. Three days after Runny's magnificent victory, unable to stand his enforced inactivity any longer, Rick took off. Failing to contact him for two days, Tom was just starting to panic about his welfare when he received a faint 'phone call in the middle of the night.

"Hi." The voice, although crackling, was familiar. "You missing me yet? I'm with my sister. I'll be back to ride out Monday morning. Bye."

It took Tom's sleepy brain a few minutes to realise that the caller had been Rick. A bit more brain wracking made him remember that Rick's older sister lived in Florida. As he returned to bed, it crossed his mind that Poppy would be rather unimpressed at the thought of Rick on a beach full of scantily clad women.

He was absolutely right. Poppy's initial depression was replaced quickly by indignation and anger.

"Not a word!" She stormed. "Not a single bloody word! Well, that's it, it's all over. If he thinks he can treat me like that, he can forget it. Bastard. He can bloody well piss off!"

"Thought he already had." Ryan commented, full of sarcasm.

"You can shut it as well." Came the irate reply. "You're all the bloody same!"

However, when Monday morning arrived, Kitty noticed that Poppy spent ten minutes longer than usual in the bathroom. When she emerged, she was beautifully made up and smelling strongly of the Chanel Rick had given her as a Christmas gift. Ignoring the sarcastic wolf whistles from the boys, Poppy sauntered across the yard with her nose in the air.

"Going anywhere nice?" Tom raised his eyebrows as he made his morning inspection.

The horses were saddled and walking around the neat turf circle in the centre of the yard when a familiar roar disturbed the calm. The Porsche scrunched to a halt on the gravel and Bozo, having suffered the indignity of the local kennels, skulked out. There was a pause as Rick rummaged about in the back and then he sprang out, beaming all over his suntanned, handsome face. The second she laid her eyes on him Poppy's resolutions went out with the rubbish. Glowing, golden, his blonde mane bleached white by sun and surf, Rick shone with health and vigour, a taste of hot summer days on a dull late winter morning. Clad in a thick padded jacket and jeans he jogged across to Tom.

"Hi." He smiled. His teeth looked whiter than ever against his dark tan. "How's it going?"

Tom looked at the bronze face and glowing green eyes with envy. It was a very long time since he had taken a holiday.

"You look well recovered." He took the young man's hand.

"Fit for anything." Laughed Rick. "Nothing like riding the waves to pick your spirits up. How's the boy?" His eyes scanned the yard, looking for the big bay horse.

"Waiting for you." Tom nodded to the stable. "I'd better put dark glasses on him, that hair is a bit dazzling"

Crossing the yard, Rick's eyes searched for Poppy. She was mounting Streak, avoiding his stare. Pale and almost chunky after the thin golden girls that lined the Miami beaches, she still made his hormones race as he looked at her. When she finally turned to face him, he gave her a brilliant smile. Poppy's knees weakened, and she turned her gaze quickly away.

"He can forget it." Taunted Kitty. "He can bloody well piss off!"

"Oh, shut up!" Poppy was scarlet. "I'd forgotten how gorgeous he was."

Rick's break had done him the power of good. Feeling Runny's muscles bunching and releasing beneath him as he sped up the gallop, he wanted to whoop with joy. There wasn't a jockey in the country who wouldn't like to be riding the bay horse in the Gold Cup. But the privilege, the dream job, belonged to him. Circling at the top of the hill he looked out at the panorama of the Cotswold's and was struck afresh by the beauty of the place. After the arid heat of Miami, it was another world. It was his world, and he loved it. A chestnut figure was pulling up beside him.

"Hi." Rick's love of life showed in his sparkling eyes, completely taking Poppy's breath away. Face filled with adoration she stammered nervously in reply.

"G.. G.. good holiday?"

"The best. My sis has been feeding me up, I'll have to watch my weight."

"I know the feeling." Poppy fiddled with Streak's mane, suddenly lost for words.

"You know what the best cure for that is." Rick laughed at her, amused at her embarrassment.

As they began to hack back down the hill Kitty thundered past in the opposite direction on Moroccan Prince, ponytail flying in the wind.

"How about dinner?" Rick watched Kitty's backside as she disappeared up the gallop.

"Thanks." Poppy was still looking at her reins. "Where shall we go?"

"My place." Rick gave her a wicked grin as she looked up at him. "I'm not in the mood for sharing."

Eleanor was cooking roast lamb and trying to avoid Dominic's black mood that seemed to penetrate every corner of the house. Looking up as the kitchen door swung open, she was relieved to see Tom taking off his coat. He was looking permanently exhausted these past weeks, and he was drinking too much. Even now he was heading for his study and the whisky. Suppressing her natural urge to reprimand him she turned instead to her potatoes, which were boiling over. Hearing the clink of glass behind her she spoke without turning.

"Good day dear?" She asked the same question every day.

From the corner of her eyes, she saw Tom drain one glass and fill another.

"Same as usual." He was drinking this one more slowly. "Where is he?"

"In the drawing room. Are you sure that woman can't come out and visit him? He might be less bloody if she did."

"No." Tom replied firmly. "I'm not having her anywhere near the place. God, after what they put me through. They could have finished me. If it hadn't been for Rowley's good nature, they would have. Don't you realise that?"

He had refused Dominic all contact with Lauren, removing all the house telephones except the one in his study, and barring numbers on that one. His study he kept locked, not even his mother had a key. Dominic's car keys were locked inside his bureau along with his mobile phone, and, just in case, he carried the keys to that everywhere with him. He derived some perverse personal pleasure from his role as goaler, and from seeing Dominic confined to the house. The tension, however, was growing unbearable, as the two men prowled around the big house, locked in enmity.

"Felicity rang." His mother was straining cauliflower. "It's such a long time since I spoke to her."

"And I." Tom ignored a pang of guilt. "How is she?"

"Very well. She rang to tell us that she's getting engaged, wondered if I wanted to go to the party."

"Engaged!" Tom's eyebrows shot up. "Bloody hell that was quick!"

"Known him for years apparently. Never thought of him in that way, but when, well." Eleanor hesitated. "Well, she couldn't have what she really wanted I suppose."

An awkward silence followed.

"Who is it?" Tom's jealousy was irritating him.

"Plays Polo for Cirencester. She did tell me his name but I'm afraid I've forgotten it."

Tom stared at the sizzling meat she had pulled from the oven and chased his mixed emotions around in his head. He had abandoned Flick badly after all the hassle from the press. He had become so obsessed with the Gold Cup and wreaking his revenge on Dominic that everything else had ceased to matter. Now, thanks to his neglect, the only woman who he had ever been really close to was marrying someone else. Well, more fool you Tom Chichester, he thought, you're a bloody fool for letting her go, that's the worth of all your bloody obsessions. Then he remembered that there was something else that mattered in all this, something that mattered more than he dared to admit. Getting to his feet he gave his mother a kiss.

"Nothing for me sweetheart. I'm going out."

"Tom!" His mother scowled at him. "You're not going to Felicity, are you? Let the poor girl be happy. Tom!"

"No, I'm not going to Flick." Tom paused. Perhaps it was time that he faced up to the other obsession that had been driving him these past weeks.

"I'm taking Kitty out to dinner."

Stirring her pasta Kitty listened in silence as Tom told her of Flick's engagement. She thought she detected a note of jealousy in his voice.

"Do you mind?" She asked quietly.

"A little I suppose." Tom poured her more wine. "I've been close to her for a very long time. But that's not important. What is important is that she'll be happy. I would never have made her happy."

"Why?" The restaurant was so quiet that she spoke in a whisper.

"She needs attention. I've got too many things that occupy my time. She would never have coped, living with a trainer."

"She didn't like me." Kitty looked at her plush surroundings and wondered if the other silent couples were listening to their conversation.

"That's because she knew how much I fancied you." Tom smiled at the expression on her face.

"How?"

"Saw straight through me I suppose."

It was one of the quirks of their relationship that they never talked about their mutual attraction. She never questioned him on their time spent apart and he offered no information. Theirs was a here and now relationship, built on passion, and broaching this delicate area made her nervous. Watching the candlelight flickering on her creamy skin, Tom wished he could offer her more than this off beat love affair. But he still could not convince himself that this was the right thing to do. He had never let anyone inside his head as he had let her, never been so attracted to anyone; and as a result, had never been so scared of his own feelings.

Kitty watched his eyes as he brooded on his personal

thoughts. The flickering flame cast shadows over his face, illuminating his dark skin, hiding his intense eyes. Taking in every line of his familiar face she felt the hot warmth of lust rushing over her. The sexual tension between them was so strong that she thought she would explode.

"I'm not hungry." Tom pushed his plate away. "Let's go."

"Where?" She was trembling like a frightened mare, meeting her mate for the first time.

"Anywhere." He got to his feet. "Anywhere that I can make love to you."

The sexual tension finally exploded in a frenzied climax in a small hotel outside Stow. Releasing his pent-up emotions Tom was moved to tears by the intensity he felt. Pushing himself away from her he stared at her lovely face and wondered, not for the first time, how he had managed to resist her for so long. Running his hand over the silken warmth of her young body he felt he had never loved another living being as much as this; if only he could push aside his barriers and tell her.

Kitty had no such reservations.

"I love you." She whispered, burying her face in his shoulder.

Stroking the golden head, Tom wished he could give her the answer she wanted. I'm not ready, he thought, better to say nothing than break her heart. Slipping out of his arms Kitty put on his shirt and padded into the bathroom. Following her he caught her by surprise, pinning her up against the wall. She laughed, pushing him away. The mock struggle reminded him of Dominic and the terrible thing that he had tried to do to her. Catching her waist, more violently than he intended, he crushed his mouth over hers, trying to expel the demons that taunted him. Frightened by his ferocity Kitty pushed at him.

"Don't!" She gasped. "You're hurting me!"

"I'm sorry."

Relaxing his hold, he shook his head, running his finger across her flushed cheek. She looked so sexy, half naked, that he felt himself growing hard again. Kitty smiled and pressed her flat stomach against his groin.

"Hussy." He smiled. "What am I going to do with you?"

"I'll give you three guesses." Kitty lifted her thigh and hooked it over his hip.

"Only need one." He muttered. Lifting her face to his, eyes locked with hers, he pushed himself into her.

"Good." She gasped. "I'd be really disappointed if you didn't know by now."

Soaking her aching body in the bath the next morning, Kitty pushed the bubbles around with her toe and felt blissfully happy. She wished she could spend the rest of her life in this bath, with the man she loved moving slowly around behind her. Tom broke her fantasy by rising out of the water.

"Time to go Miss Campbell. We've got work to do."

Climbing out of the car at the cottage gate, Kitty was mortified to see Martin standing in the doorway.

"Good Morning Ma'am." He teased. "I hope you're not going to muck out in that dress?"

"Shut up Marty." She pushed past him, blushing furiously.

Poppy, also still in evening clothes, was making toast.

"Doesn't he feed you then?" Kitty pinched a slice.

"Very funny."

Kitty turned at the catch in her friend's voice.

"Pop? Is something wrong?"

"No." Poppy's tear-stained face and swollen eyes betrayed her.

"What is it?" Kitty put her arms around her shoulders. "Is it Rick?"

"I hate him!" Poppy burst into tears. "Bastard."

"What's he done now?" Kitty asked patiently.

"What hasn't he done? He's a creep, a cheating bastard and I hate him. First, he buggers off to Florida without a word, and then he screws every bitch who'll have him while he's there,"

"Oh, come on Pop." Kitty hugged her. "You're just imagining things."

"No, I'm not." Poppy sobbed. "Some American whore rang him this morning, we were still in bed, but you should, you should have heard it. It was horrible; I could hear her telling him all the disgusting things that she wanted to do to him. And he just sat there and laughed! I never thought he'd do that to me Kit. What am I going to do?"

Burying her head on Kitty's shoulder Poppy sobbed bitterly.

"Are you quite sure about this Pop?" Kitty stroked the tangled curls.

"He didn't even try to deny it. We had a huge row." She raised her streaming eyes. "I can't work today, Kit. Will you tell the boss I'm sick? I can't face him today, I just can't."

"I'll tell him." Kitty fumed. "Then I'm going to break Rick Cowdrey's conceited bloody neck!"

"No!" Poppy clutched at her. "Don't mention it please. I'll look such a fool anyway when everyone finds out what he's been doing."

"Oh alright." Kitty hugged her. She could almost feel Poppy's heart breaking as she sobbed. "Go to bed Pop. Take Winston, he won't let you down, he's the best friend I've ever had."

Ten minutes later she ran into the yard, tying her hair up as she went. Her blissful contentment of earlier had been replaced by a terrible anger. Tom was standing in the office doorway. Shooting Rick, a look of pure venom she ran into the tack room.

"Excused morning stables, were we?" Ryan sneered as he handed her a saddle.

"Don't pick on me." She snapped. "I'm not in the mood!"

Bolting towards Prince's box, she cannoned into Rick.

"Hi babe." He grinned. "You're in a hurry!"

"Get out of my way." She snarled. " You bloody cheat."

"Hey!" Rick snapped. "What the hell have I done to you? Back off!"

"Oh, fuck off!" Shoving him to one side she burst into Prince's box. Tom, bemused by this sudden display of ferocity, looked over the door.

"What's all the fuss?"

"Search me." Rick shrugged. "Bloody women."

Tom leaned on the wall and watched Kitty's rear with appreciation as she saddled the horse. Her face, when she turned, was far less welcoming. Her anger was making her clumsy.

"Oh, fuck it!" She hissed, as the saddle pad slid off Prince's glossy back.

"Tut, tut." Tom laughed. "I'll have to sack you for using bad language in front of a horse."

Letting himself in he laid his hand on the saddle, keeping it steady while she fastened the girth.

"What's the problem?" He asked quietly.

"Him." She hissed. "The peroxide poof out there."

"What's he done? I thought that you two called a truce a long time ago?"

"It's over." Kitty turned her blazing eyes onto him. "He's broken Poppy's heart. I could kill him."

"Ah." Tom raised his eyebrows. "And where is Poppy?"

"She's sick."

"Oh. Is she now? I thought that she, and for that matter

you, would have known by now that no one gets pity in my yard. We all have personal problems; we all have to deal with them. But the work doesn't stop. Go and get her."

"Get her yourself!" Kitty was amazed by his total lack of compassion.

"Do as you're told girl and stop being hysterical!"

"I am not hysterical." She yelled, forgetting, in her anger who she was shouting at. "And as for personal problems, how many times have you shown up two hours late and stinking of whisky?"

As soon as the words had left her mouth, she realised what she had done. Tom's face turned to stone; the softness in his eyes disappeared. Watching the cold, hard expression that replaced it, Kitty knew that she had gone too far.

"Thank you." The steely edge to his voice cut her like a knife. "Let me remind you who is the boss around here. Unless something has happened that I'm unaware of I own this yard. You work for me. What happens between us personally has absolutely no bearing on our working relationship. At least I thought it didn't. Perhaps I was wrong. But I won't be wrong again. Go and get Poppy. Now."

Leaving Prince half saddled Kitty darted out of the stable and raced to the cottage with a lump in her throat. Poppy was lying on her bed, staring at the ceiling with lifeless eyes, tears sliding down her cheeks. She was the epitome of misery.

"Sorry Pop. No go. You've got to get over to the yard."

"Now?" Poppy turned pale.

"Afraid so."

"I can't! If I see him, I'll go to pieces."

"No, you won't." Kitty sat beside her. "Don't let him get to you. Besides, I think that my love life has also come to an abrupt end, so we can be miserable together."

"Oh not because of me?" Poppy wailed. "Oh Kit, I'm

sorry."

Throwing her arms around Kitty's neck she clung to her.

"Very touching." Tom's voice made them both start. "I hate to interrupt but I do have a yard to run. They are all waiting for you Katriona. Go and get on your horse."

Quailing under the icy stare, Kitty bolted down the hall. Tom, staring without emotion at Poppy as she sat red eyed and swollen lipped in front of him, could feel himself shaking. Not with anger, but with disappointment. He had always known that this absurd affair with Kitty was wrong, and now he had the proof. He could not afford to feel this bad whenever he reprimanded her, nor could he have her defying him. Hearing Poppy give a strangled sniff he looked at her again and saw just how hard she must have cried. A tiny worm of sympathy wriggled into his brain.

"Lunchtime." He said sharply. "That should give you time to pull yourself together."

Poppy listened to his footsteps fading down the hall and got to her feet. From the landing window she could see the string moving down the drive, Rick's bleached hair was blowing across his shoulders. A pain, almost unbearable, wrenched at her gut; like a knife her jealousy and sorrow twisted into her heart. Closing her eyes, she felt the heavy, gnawing ache in her stomach and sobbed. The silence of the empty cottage was overwhelming. She ran a bath, desperate to wash away the smell and taste of Rick, but at the same time not wanting to take away the last trace of his presence on her. Watching the steam rising from the water she began to cry again. She had never been so unhappy. It felt as if someone had dropped a piece of lead into her throat and it was silently choking the life out of her. Stepping into the water she closed her stinging eyes. Lunchtime was not that far away; she must, as Tom had said, pull herself together and not let everyone see that she was falling apart.

Rick wisely removed himself to the safety of Tom's

study as soon as he dismounted. Away from the hostile stares and whispers he began to relax. Waiting for Tom to come and discuss their plans he nibbled on one of the sandwiches that Eleanor had brought him. He was just pouring himself tea when Tom came in with a solemn face.

"You bloody love being the centre of attention, don't you?"

Rick raised his eyes warily.

"No more so than anyone else."

"Rubbish. You're a proper little glory boy. But if it's glory you really want then you've got to put everything, and I mean everything, into your work. We've two weeks to go and then you're going to find yourself in the middle of something bigger than you've ever even dreamed of. This meeting could make or break you, and I don't just mean Olympic Run, I mean every ride you'll have. Everything you do will be scrutinised by thousands of racegoers, and millions more on television. You're in demand right now, people are starting to sit up and take notice."

Rick nodded in agreement, his mouth full of sandwich.

"My voicemail was blocked when I got home."

"Exactly." Tom poured more tea. "So, make them take notice for all the right reasons, not the wrong ones. Your talent in the saddle, not your notorious lifestyle out of it."

"Mmm." Rick was watching a sheet of rain moving across the valley.

"Rick!" Tom snapped. "Have you listened to a single bloody word I've said?"

"Sure." Rick grinned. "But it's going to be hard work."

"Bloody hard work. It may help if you give all these women a miss for a while."

"Bollocks!" Rick laughed. "Only if you do the same thing!"

"I'm serious." Tom suppressed a smile.

"So am I. I couldn't ride a mile if I had to give up sex. It keeps me sharp."

Tom shook his head, a smile twitching the corners of his mouth.

"Well try and keep the emotional dramas at bay at least. My female staff have gone to pieces."

"You've contributed to that yourself." Rick got to his feet. "Serves you right for hiring girls that should be in Cosmopolitan not the Cotswold's. Speaking of beautiful women, I've got to meet Emmie."

"Not back to your wild ways I hope?" Tom frowned.

"It's her birthday." Rick paused. "How's the Prisoner of Zenda?"

"Horrific." Tom opened the door for him. "The sooner I get him out of my hair the better."

CHAPTER SEVENTEEN

No hangover could have been worse. Rick lifted his throbbing head off his arm and blinked his swollen eyes. The debris of the party was mostly human, interspersed with cans, bottles, and ashtrays. A pungent aroma still lingered in the air. He had forgotten just how chaotic Emmie's parties could be. Rising to his unsteady feet, he began to make his way to the kitchen, but had to divert quickly to the bathroom, not recognising any of the bodies he stumbled over en route. Having been violently sick, he emerged from the bathroom wiping his mouth and feeling slightly more conscious. A very tall, ashen faced woman was weaving her way towards him.

"Rick?"

The voice was somehow familiar, but he had no idea who she was.

"Yeah?"

"How are you?"

Rubbing his eyes, he tried to focus on her face, but it kept splitting into two. Trying again he spotted a gold locket on her throat, and something triggered off his memory.

"Lauren?"

"Yes." Lauren West looked nothing like the stunner he had been introduced to at Christmas. "How are you? Have you seen him? Dominic?"

"No." Rick shook his head. "Nor do I want to."

His recall of the previous night was vague, to say the least, but he had absolutely no recollection of Lauren being there.

"Look." Lauren seemed to be having problems staying upright. "I'm only telling you this because I like you, and Tom. He doesn't deserve to be hated in the way Dominic hates him. I think Dominic will try and get at the horse again. Tell Tom to be careful."

"Thanks." Rick's expression showed that he wasn't sure whether to believe her or not.

"It's true." She read his thoughts. "He's put every penny he owns on Revelation. He'll stop at nothing."

"Why do you care?" Rick narrowed his eyes. "He's your horse as well, don't you want him to win?"

"Of course." She nodded. "But not like that. I'm happy with what we've got. Of course, I want the Gold Cup, who doesn't. But I have limits, Dominic doesn't."

"Don't try to tell me you had nothing to do with the last little affair." Rick shook his head, almost tempted to laugh. "Dominic had never been near a horse until he met you!"

Lauren hesitated. She was torn between her loyalty to Dominic, the admiration she felt for the man in front of her and her desire to preserve her own self-image.

"I knew nothing about it." The desire to protect herself and win favour with Rick won. "It was all him."

"I doubt it." Rick's eyes were cold. "But thanks for the warning."

"Wanting to win a race is one thing." Lauren sounded near tears. "But this obsession he's got with beating Tom. It's not normal. It's some personal vendetta. It's scary."

"Why do you stay with him?" Rick narrowed his eyes, fighting a fresh wave of nausea.

"Have you ever been in love Rick? Have you ever loved someone so much that you would do anything to keep them close to you?" Lauren's voice was trembling. "Maybe you haven't. In which case I envy you. It's not a pretty place to be."

"I can believe it."

"Don't fall in love, Rick." One elegant hand touched his arm. "Not like this. It hurts."

Tell me about it, he thought as he watched her moving away, I never knew how much.

In the kitchen Emmie was handing out black coffee.

"Big one for me babe." He gave a wry grin. "Then I have to go face the music."

By some miracle Rick managed to avoid being pulled over by the police on his drive to Highford. Arriving in the middle of the afternoon, far too late to be of any use, he found Tom doing the rounds with Mike Stone. Paranoid about coughs and viruses Tom was having the horses checked every week. They were in Streak's box, trying vainly to keep her quiet for Mike to use the endoscope.

"All clear." Mike grinned, as Poppy removed the twitch. "If I were you, I'd stop panicking."

"Thanks Mike but that's easier said than done. Same time next week?"

"Oh, if you insist." Mike laughed. "It's your money. Or your owners anyway. Hello Rick! You look worse than all my patients put together? Want a check-up?"

"Cheers." Rick stopped in the middle of the yard. "How about a bit of 'Bute?"

"No can do." Mike laughed. "Can't afford to fail any drug tests, can we?"

"No." Said Tom dryly. "We can't."

As Mike got into the Range Rover Rick turned warily to Tom.

"You look bloody awful!" Tom roared. "Can't I rely on you at all?"

"I've got some news." Rick ignored the snipe. "I saw our would-be friend Lauren West last night. She sent you a warning. She thinks Dominic will try and get at Runny again."

From the corner of his eyes Rick was watching Poppy hustling into the tack room, head low.

"Did you believe her?" Tom was watching the same thing.

"Not sure. But it couldn't hurt to be more careful, could it?"

"Hmm." Tom considered the possibility. "Maybe I'll have to lock him in the house every day."

Poppy, peering out of the tack room window, saw the two men heading in her direction. Plunging into the rug box, she began to pluck at a tangled muddle of rollers.

"Lost something?" Ryan was checking the bridle work.

"Not yet." Poppy turned pink. "But my sanity is getting a bit misdirected."

Tom hovered in the doorway and surveyed his immaculate tack room. Why he had come in here he had no idea. Rick was staring, hypnotised, at Poppy as she crouched beside the box. She was deathly pale. With a sudden flash of insight Rick realised what he had put her through. She's lovely, he thought miserably, worth ten of any other women I've met, and I've kicked her in the teeth. Wishing that he could turn the clock back, that he could do something to put things right between them, he was disappointed when Tom moved off.

"Riding tomorrow?" The tall man was speaking to him.

"Yes, thank God. Three rides two different meetings. I'll have to be sharp. If my name was Hales, I'd have a helicopter. As it is, I've got to get to Worcester in time for the last."

"Is it worth it for one ride?" Tom frowned.

"I hope so. It's a bumper horse that's heading for Cheltenham. I want to keep the ride."

"Well make the most of your popularity." Tom gave him a scornful look. "And for God's sake sort yourself before you get there."

Returning to his car later that afternoon Rick realised that he had no idea of the route he had to take between the two meetings. He had been leaving that detail of his life to

Poppy of late. It wasn't only at night that he was going to miss her comforting presence. Feeling completely lost, he drove slowly out of the yard.

Kitty stared insolently out of the feed shed window and let Tom's words on tighter security wash over her head. They had not spoken directly for three days. Her outrage at his callous disregard for Poppy's feelings had made it easier for her to handle the downturn in their own relationship. Aware that she was being antagonistic, but beyond caring, she deliberately ignored his orders, making him repeat himself, pushing him to the point where he would snap. She knew that she was walking a very narrow tightrope but couldn't stop herself. To meekly back down would let her feelings rush in and take over. People moving around her made her realise that he had finished. She was following them out of the building when he called her back.

"Katriona." It was never Kitty anymore. "Wait please."

Without turning she halted and kicked at a piece of straw with her booted foot.

"Have you been listening to a word I've said?"

"Yes." She still didn't look at him.

"Repeat it please."

With a heavy sigh, she mumbled about tighter security and Olympic Run.

"So. You were listening. I was beginning to think that your work was suffering, but I'm glad to see that it's not. I like to think that I still have your full attention in that respect at least."

Petulant blue eyes looked up at him, shooting pain into his heart.

"What other respect is there. Sir?"

Seeing his jaw tighten as she spoke, the familiar muscle twitching in his cheek, Kitty knew that her antagonism was getting to him and felt a perverse twinge of pride.

"None." He towered above her. "None at all."

"Is that all?" Despite her pride, despite her sense of injustice, if she had to stand here alone with him any longer, she would weaken and let him see how much she was hurting.

"Yes, that's all." Tom resisted the temptation, strong as it was, to grab hold of her and shake the pout off her lips. He knew that between them their stubbornness would destroy what they once had. Watching her walk away, head held high he swung at the corn bin, irritated. Damn her! She had no right to torture him like this. What did she expect him to do? Feeling his temper rising, he made himself scarce before he lost his already tentative hold over his emotions.

Poppy was waiting for her friend in the coach house.

"Don't do this for me Kit? Please? I can see how much it's hurting you."

"It's his fault." Kitty was shaking. "If he can be this heartless about you, how do I know he'd be any different with me?"

"Because he cares about you. He risked so much getting involved with you. It could have ruined his authority. He must care a lot."

"Well, he knows how to apologise. I am not going to give into him."

Dominic prowled the walls of Highford House like a caged tiger looking for escape. His brooding black presence was everywhere. Never a patient man his tremendous temper was beginning to expand beyond the bounds of his anorexic frame. Watching his brother approaching the house he felt the nerves of his hate tightening his stomach.

If only he could get away. He needed space, to be free from Tom's hawk like gaze. Pacing the drawing room, he heard the front door slam, and his quick, ever alert ears picked up the clatter of keys in the hall stand. Something must have rattled his brother badly to make him so careless. He never left the keys where he, Dominic, could get to them. Moving quietly to the half open door he peered into the hall. He could just see the key fob protruding from behind the silver rose bowl. Hearing Tom climbing the stairs he crept out, inching towards the hall stand. Hardly daring to breathe he slid the keys from behind the rose bowl and moved soundlessly back into the drawing room. His back to the door, alert for any sound, he looked at the keys on his hand. There in front of him was the key to the study. A smile stretching his pale features he flitted back across the hall and held his breath as he turned the key in the lock. With a barely audible click the door opened. Tom's bureau was in front of him. He tried the keys. None of them worked. Damn. Where was it? Then he remembered something. Something he had learned as a child when he had crept in here to nose through his father's things. Something he had never forgotten.

His hand began to fumble with the panel at the back of the bureau. It felt solid. No, it couldn't be, this piece of furniture hadn't moved for thirty years. One more push and it gave, the secret loose panel of wood that the clever furniture maker had built in to amuse himself all those years ago. The panel he had found when he was five years old. Thankful for his long, bony fingers, he pushed his hand inside and began to feel around the little compartments. If his keys were locked in the lower drawer he was lost. Something cold touched his fingers. Closing his eyes, letting his fingers feel the way, he pulled his keys out through the gap. With a smile of triumph on his face Dominic looked around him. If he left through the French windows, he could be across the orchard and into the yard before he was seen.

Like a shadow, silent and evasive, Dominic slipped through the windows and ran swiftly across the grass. Hurdling the orchard gate, he bolted into the yard. Finding his car still safe behind the hay barn he almost cried with delight at the feeling of the steering wheel in his hands. Turning the key, he prayed that it would still start. Whooping with joy as the engine roared into life, he floored the accelerator and drove off with a squeal of burning rubber.

Opening the window to let the cold air rush over him he had reached the main gate when he slowed. He couldn't resist playing his final trump card. Spinning the car around he raced back down the drive, past the yard gate and up to the house. Mounting the lawn, tyres sliding on the wet grass, he raced towards the study. Seeing Tom's horrified face looking out of the window he raised his two fingers.

"Fuck you big brother!" He yelled. "Catch me now!"

Laughing like a hyena he left a trail of destruction behind him as he drove through the flower beds, raced down the drive and out into the narrow lanes. Feeling in his glove compartment he found his spare wallet, which thankfully contained a twenty-pound note, his spare mobile 'phone and a bottle of Vodka. Unscrewing the top of the bottle he took a huge slug. Turning the stereo on full blast, he headed for the motorway.

The roar that came from the study brought Eleanor rushing to the stairs in her bath towel.

"What's wrong?"

Tom was standing in the hall, hands on his head.

"He's gone! I left the fucking keys on the hall stand. What an imbecile. Bloody stupid imbecile!"

"Calm down." Eleanor kept her distance. The anger in Tom's eyes was frightening. "Where are you going?"

"After him, He's not bolting from me."

"Let him go. Tom! Please!" Eleanor's voice rose to a scream.

"No." The hard, iron edge of Tom's voice made her

tremble. "He never listens, never learns his lesson. He just goes on abusing people. This time I'm going to teach him a lesson he'll never forget. Never!"

"NO!" Eleanor's scream fell on an empty space, as the door slammed so hard that every window of the house rattled in their ancient frames.

The engine of the BMW burst into life and shrieked in protest as it was driven with manic ferocity down the drive. Martin, sleeping bag under his arm, was on his way to set up camp in Runny's stable. He stopped and stared in amazement as the car sped past him.

"Whew?" Ryan had also witnessed Tom's Formula One exit. "Who lit his fuse?"

"Guess." Martin pointed to the hay barn. "The E type's gone."

"Who was that?" Kitty emerged from Prince's stable.

"Your would-be fancy man." Ryan said sarcastically. "Late for another date."

Before Kitty could think of a suitable answer the valley echoed with a piercing squeal of brakes, followed by another throaty roar of engine.

"Oh God!" Kitty was white. "He'll kill himself!"

"He'll kill Dominic when he catches him." Ryan said. "I have a feeling that he'll get a hiding for anything, even if it isn't his fault."

"Can't say I feel sorry for him." Martin moved on.

Poppy had watched Dominic's escape from the kitchen window. Seeing Tom race after him she went out to the yard and found her friend standing on the yard gate, staring aimlessly down the road.

"I'm scared Pop." Kitty whispered. "If he catches Dominic, I really think he will kill him."

Poppy pulled her off the gate.

"As you and I have been demoted to being mere stable

girls again, I'm afraid to say that it's none of our business."

Kitty's fears of murder were needless. Having sped through the lanes and driven as far as Cheltenham Tom knew he had lost his quarry. Pulling onto the verge he took deep breaths, trying to calm his adrenalin filled body. Dusk was settling on the hills, cloaking the valleys with darkness. He would never find him now. Pushing the first disc he laid hands on into the stereo Tom sat back and listened. Mozart. Letting the soothing strains wash over him Tom's thoughts turned to Flick. Mozart always made him think of her. Lacrymosa. A requiem. How appropriate. A requiem for his life and the mess he was making of it. He should never have let Flick slip through his fingers. Putting the car into gear he began to drive.

He had no idea why he went there, but as the disc ended, he found himself outside Flick's building. Her car was parked under the streetlight. A light shone in the living room. As he watched, Tom saw a strange young man look out of the bedroom window. Embarrassed, terrified of recognition, Tom bent and searched through his glove compartment. His hand sifted through betting slips, old receipts and business cards and closed around a hair clip. Kitty's. He had untangled it from her hair after one steamy session parked in the edge of the woods. Raising it to his nose he sniffed it, then threw it on the seat, disgusted at his own sentimentality.

Cursing himself for a fool, he straightened up to find that the bedroom curtains had closed and that the light had gone out. Starting his engine, he shook his head. He had no business here. Pulling out of the square he headed back into the hills. As his emotions began to slowly drain away, he felt tired, and by the time he turned into his own drive his eyes were heavy. A figure was standing by the cottage gate, a figure with swirling pale hair.

Shivering with nerves and cold Kitty watched the car coming slowly down the drive. It pulled up beside her and the window slid silently down.

"What on Earth are you doing out here?"

She could hear the weariness in his voice. Her heart crashed against her ribs. She knew that this was the moment in which she could revive their relationship or kill it forever.

"I was afraid." She muttered. "I thought you'd crash."

"Silly girl." Tom gave a half smile. "Go on, get inside before you catch your death. Oh, wait a minute, I think this is yours."

Stepping over the gate Kitty took her hair clip from his outstretched hand. Her fingers touched his and the contact sent shock waves running up her arm.

"My God, you're freezing girl!" Tom caught hold of her icy hand. "Go and have a hot bath."

"I will." She stepped back but left her fingers in his, reluctant to move, to break this moment. It was the only time they had spoken without animosity in days. He was watching her with brooding eyes. He looked exhausted. She wanted to hold him and rock him like baby; let him sleep until all his troubles had left him. He was so beautiful, if she never felt another man's arms around her in her life again, she wouldn't care, because he was all that mattered. One word and her silly, proud resolutions would tumble down around her.

Tom could see her weakening under his gaze, could see the pulse beating in her throat; the glow of desire was lighting up her eyes.

"Better still." He spoke softly. "Why not take a bath with me?"

Shaking her head, trying to maintain her composure, Kitty shook her head.

"No." She said quietly "Not tonight."

"Get in the car!" Tom laughed. "Stop tormenting me woman!"

Blushing furiously, she got into the car.

"So." He looked at her, rigid in the seat beside him. "When is it all going to end?"

"When you say sorry." She looked away.

"For running a business?" Tom grinned. "I won't say sorry for that. But I was a little hard on Poppy, I had no idea how badly hurt she was."

There was a pause.

"Will that do Miss Campbell?" He was laughing.

"I suppose so." She turned to him. "And I suppose I'm sorry for being so insolent."

"I can't forgive you for that." He tried to sound stern. "You should obey my every wish."

"Huh." She laughed too. "No chance!"

"Really?" He bent over her and touched her stomach with his fingers.

"Really." She pushed his hand away.

"Tut." He could see her relaxing. "In that case you'll have to be punished. How about one of Ron's pies and a pint?"

"Ugh." She laughed. "Not that! Can't you punish me with a bag of chips?"

"Chips it is then." He said softly, his hand resting on her knee. "Later."

With his hand still on her knee he began to turn the car around. Tonight, would be like the first time all over again.

Shortly before midnight Lauren West was roused from a deep slumber by someone banging on her door. Warily peering through the one-inch gap afforded by her safety chain, she saw the tall angular figure in the hallway and felt her heart lurch. With a sigh of relief, she opened the door and let him in. Swaying across the hall he went straight into the bedroom.

"Sorry Angel. Too wrecked to speak." Dominic groaned

and collapsed onto the bed.

At around the same time, but many miles away, Rick turned off the recording of the Racing Post 'chase and went to bed. His nerves were preventing him from sleeping. On the chair beside the bed hung Poppy's shirt. Poppy red. It still carried the heady smell of her perfume. Picking it up he threw it onto his pillow and got into bed. If he couldn't have Poppy beside him, then her clothes would be a good substitute.

CHAPTER EIGHTEEN

Mike Peterson handed the glass of brandy to his wife and surveyed the room. People were thronging the ancient hall; scarlet coats clashing with the brilliantly coloured ball gowns. The band, a bunch of paunchy, grey haired jazz lovers, were playing with more enthusiasm than skill; encouraged, someone was trying to blow 'Gone Away' without much success. Every five minutes or so someone would stop and wish him good luck for Thursday's race, and, displaying his pride like a peacock, Mike confidently told them all to put their shirts on Olympic Run.

"Strange." Claudia Peterson was spilling out of her black velvet dress. "Tom isn't here. He's never missed the hunt ball before."

"Working too hard." Mike watched a pink faced blonde in a very revealing dress dancing with her drunken partner. "He's starting to look his age."

"He's still very attractive." Claudia had eaten too much dessert and was secretly glad that Tom wasn't there to see the fabric of her dress straining over her bulging stomach. "Quite a heart throb with the young girls I've heard."

"That brother of his doesn't help." Mike wasn't listening. "He'd put years on anyone."

His wife, who was all too aware that he was more interested in the pink faced blonde than her, and not in the least bit upset by the fact, wondered, not for the first time, what Tom Chichester was like in bed. Made bold by half a bottle of brandy she employed shock tactics.

"I've heard he's quite something in the sack. A real stallion apparently."

"Don't be ridiculous woman." Her husband gave her a scornful glance. "Tom hasn't got any stallions."

Suppressing a giggle Claudia searched the room for distraction. A familiar looking woman, with a glossy dark bob, was smiling at her across the room.

"Flick!" Claudia saw the chance to dump her husband and took it with both hands. "There's Flick. Darling, I must go and talk to her."

Bustling across the room, she bumped into a very dashing young man in officers' uniform.

"Excuse me." He smiled politely.

"Who's he?" Claudia whispered as she halted beside Flick. "I haven't seen him before."

Flick beamed in pleasure and offered her left hand which was adorned by a large diamond.

"He's, my fiancé. Guy. I'll introduce you." She called the young man who turned, displaying a perfect profile. "Guy, this is Claudia Peterson, her husband owns a share of Olympic Run."

"Pleased to meet you." Guy smiled broadly. "I do hope he does well for you."

"Guy plays polo." Flick smiled adoringly into the smooth, tanned face.

"Really?" Claudia was impressed. "I'm afraid I don't know the first thing about polo. Do you know the Prince?"

"Not that well." Guy smiled. "Excuse me."

"To tell you the truth." Flick whispered. "I don't know anything about polo either. I just pretend."

"Oh look!" Claudia was quickly distracted. "There's Tom. He made it after all."

Flick lowered her eyes as Claudia waved enthusiastically at the tall figure hovering on the other side of the dance floor. Watching him approach she felt her pulse racing.

"Good evening." Tom's voice was unusually husky. "I trust you're both enjoying yourselves?"

"Much more now that you're here." Claudia's gushing enthusiasm was embarrassing. "You must dance with me. Come on."

Watching Tom reluctantly taking the chattering woman onto the dance floor, Flick felt a pang of regret that he was no longer in her life. Swallowing her drink in one gulp she signalled to Guy, who was already at the bar, to get her another. Guy was handsome, rich, well-educated, and totally devoted. She couldn't have dreamed herself a more perfect partner. But there would always be something about Tom's brooding beauty that would turn her knees to jelly.

"May I?" The familiar voice sent shudders down her spine.

"Of course." Feeling heat come into her cheeks she followed Tom's broad back into the middle of the room. Wincing as a stiletto heel caught her foot, she pulled a face.

"Why the middle?"

"So, we can't be seen by clinging Claudia." Tom smiled, taking her familiar body in his arms.

Avoiding his eyes, which she knew never left her face, Flick kept him at arm's length. She felt his eyes moving, over her cheeks, her neck, her cleavage. Looking under her lashes she saw him looking down her dress.

"Stop that!" She laughed. "Control yourself!"

"Sorry. Old habits die hard." Pulling her closer Tom breathed in the scent of her perfume. His senses reeled as memories stormed his brain; and without thinking of what he was doing, he laid his cheek on her head, pressing his lips to her hair.

"Tom!" She squeaked, pulling away.

"Sorry. I wasn't thinking." He stepped back, reddening slightly.

"Obviously." Flick frowned, then laughed.

"Where did we go wrong?" Tom was taking in every inch of her face, her glossy lips, her smooth skin. "What happened?"

A shadow crossed her face.

"You know what happened."

He was still holding her, reluctant to let her go.

"I let you down, didn't I?"

"Yes, you did." Flick looked straight into his eyes. "I worshipped the ground you walked on. But you never noticed. You were always too busy."

"That's not true." Tom looked surprised.

"Isn't it?" Flick looked serious then laughed. "Do you honestly think we could have lived together Tom? You don't really know me at all."

"Oh, I think I do." He began to move her in time to the music. "I think I know you pretty well."

"In some ways." Something flickered in her eyes. "How are the horses?"

"Wonderful. Olympic Run is really working well, and Rick's riding like a star at the moment, rode a treble today."

He paused and saw laughter in her eyes.

"What?"

"Don't you see!" Flick giggled. "That's why it would never have worked. Horses' morning, noon, and night. And." She added. "I couldn't have coped with all the jealousy."

"What jealousy?" Tom frowned.

"All those young girls that work for you. Especially the blonde one." Flick couldn't keep the little daggers from her voice.

"Kitty?"

Tom's eyes had softened. There was a familiar expression in them. Flick stared at him, realisation slowly dawning on her.

"My God! You're sleeping with her, aren't you?"

Tom lowered his eyes but said nothing.

"That's very convenient." Flick knew she sounded bitchy but couldn't help herself. "Don't have to go very far at all do you?"

Tom looked surprised by her words.

"There's nothing convenient about it." He said coldly. "I like her. A lot."

There, he had said it. Admitted it to someone other than himself.

"Like?" Flick could read him like a book. "Don't you mean love?"

Tom stared across her head towards a corner of the room where he knew the subject of his discussion was sitting. He should be with her now, not dancing with someone from his past. Someone with a future of her own.

"Yes." He spoke slowly. "Yes, I think I do."

He felt Flick's lips on his cheek and looked down, startled.

"Be happy Tom." She said quietly. "You deserve it."

He watched her walking away, knowing that this was it, the finale of their relationship. Despite himself, he felt sorrow.

Like a hawk on her prey Claudia saw him alone and pounced.

"Come on Tom. Fair is fair after all. I deserve another dance."

Cursing the things, he had to do to keep his owners happy, Tom smiled politely and offered her his arm.

Pulling up outside the light emblazoned hall, Rick looked in his rear-view mirror and prodded the darkening bruise on his cheek. The days three winners had been followed by a fall from a rather manic novice 'chaser. The horse had continued merrily on its way leaving Rick bruised and winded on the floor. Warily prodding his teeth, thankful that none of them were loose, he got reluctantly out of the car. He wasn't at all sure that he wanted to be attending this ball, but Tom had thrust a ticket on him, pleading moral support against Mike and Claudia. He'd already missed the meal, which was all to the good as he was watching his diet, so telling himself that a few glasses of Vodka and Tonic wouldn't do the scales any harm, he pulled his aching limbs up the stone steps and into the hall. He was quickly spotted by Tom, who was moving rather hurriedly away from the dance floor.

"Nice eye makeup." He laughed at the shining bruise. "Been fighting?"

"Only with a hindleg. Christ it's hot in here."

"Even hotter when you've been clawed by Claudia." Tom was leading the way to the bar.

"You are supposed to say, 'You can't drink'." Rick laughed. "But as you're not I'll have Vodka and Tonic please, lots of tonic."

Rick leaned wearily on the glass strewn surface. He didn't recognise any of the people around him. A group of young girls, heavily made up in an attempt to look older than their years, were eyeing him from the other end of the bar. Tom followed Rick's eyes, and grinned as he handed him his glass.

"The fan club's here I see."

"It's not funny." Rick tried to look serious. "They aren't a day over twelve. I mean too young even for you!"

"Slight exaggeration. The ages I mean; you cheeky sod." Tom took him to a quieter part of the room and sat him down. "You look tired."

"That's because I bloody well am. I'll take you up on the offer of a bed tonight. I couldn't drive home."

Letting the alcohol relax his tender muscles Rick listened without much attention to Tom's conversation. A dark-haired girl was spinning around on the dance floor. The sight made him sit up, peering through the crowds for a better look.

"Is that who I think it is?"

"If you mean Poppy, then yes, it is. Martin is good friends with the huntsman. He gave him about eight tickets. Hard to keep a well-run yard when your staff are out getting pissed with you at the Hunt ball!"

"Kitty here?" Rick was watching the dancing figure with soulful eyes.

"Yes. I don't know whether to be pleased or disappointed. She hasn't looked at me all night."

"Getting serious, isn't it?" Rick teased. "What happened to being old enough to be her father? Are your morals slipping in your old age?"

"Watch it." Tom grinned. "The seasons not over yet"

The sight of Poppy in her clinging black dress had disturbed Rick far more that he dared to admit. Drinking more than he had intended to he began to revive. Standing at the side of the dance floor he saw Claudia approaching.

"Hello Rick." Claudia ran her eyes over every inch of his lean frame. "Do you jive?"

"I do everything." Replied Rick wickedly. "Lead on."

At the back of the room Poppy, who had lost count of the Bacardi and Cokes she had poured down her throat, recognised the flying blonde mane and sat down with a thump. The evening had suddenly lost its appeal. Kitty, sprawled across Martin's lap, noticed the dramatic change of mood, and gave her a prod.

"What's up?"

"He's here." Poppy moaned. "The copulating Kiwi."

"Don't let him get to you." Martin kicked her with his foot. "You deserve better than him anyway."

"No." Poppy stood up again. "You're right. I do deserve better. Come on Gareth, I refuse to be outdone. Let's dance."

"Come on Marty." Kitty pulled him to his feet. "Just in case she tries to deck him."

271

Rick was still jiving with Claudia; a small group of people had clustered around them, clapping them on. Rick's fan club were squealing and giggling at every gyrating movement of his slim hips. Determined to steal the limelight, Poppy sprang into action on the opposite side of the floor.

"Oh no." Martin halted, holding Kitty's hand. "This is turning into Strictly Come Dancing."

"I'd call it Dirty Dancing." Kitty pulled him onto the floor. "Come on Mart. Strut your stuff!"

Gareth, full of his usual zest, was ricocheting around like a misguided missile. Weak with laughter, Poppy forgot all about Rick until one particularly vigorous move sent her spinning through the crowd into Claudia. Giggling, she was unable to keep her feet and fell to her knees, taking Claudia with her. Not liking the public humiliation, Claudia was outraged.

"Get off me you stupid girl!" She squawked. "You're drunk, aren't you? Get up before I have you thrown out!"

"I'm no more drunk than anyone else in this place." Poppy was helpless with laughter. "And I can't get up because you're lying on my dress!"

A hand caught Poppy's arm.

"Come on you alcoholic." The voice was also laughing. "Up you get."

Poppy looked up and her smile faded as her eyes met Rick's. Resisting his pull she staggered awkwardly to her feet, snatching her skirt from beneath Claudia's arm. She was about to saunter off but found him blocking her way.

"Pop." His face was suddenly serious. "Wait. I need to talk to you."

Her dark eyes glared at him, full of suspicion and jealousy.

"I've nothing to say to you." She tried to push past him.

"Please Poppy." He held her back. "We need to talk."

Poppy didn't move. He could feel the tension in her, see the aggression in her eyes. Terrified that this may be his last chance he caught her wrist and felt the pulse racing beneath his fingers.

"Let go." She whispered, aware of the eyes that were on them. "I told you I've got nothing to say to you."

Rick shook his head. Standing back, he released her wrist.

"I'm sorry." He said quietly. " I was a real bastard, I know that. But I'm sorry, you have to believe me."

"You broke my heart!" Tears sprang into Poppy's eyes. "Do you think that saying sorry can mend that? I'll never forgive you Rick. You showed me what you were really like. I'm glad you did because I really thought that you cared about me."

With as much dignity as she could muster Poppy strode back to Gareth. Biting his lip, Rick ignored Claudia's pleas and headed for the bar.

Some hours later Kitty sat on the of the steps of Broadwater Hall and took deep breaths of air, trying to clear her fuzzy head. The normally sleepy village of Broadwater was still ablaze with lights, a twinkling little toy town in the valley below. Here on the hill the wind was gathering strength, whistling through the still bare branches of the ancient oaks, creeping through windowpanes. She watched a couple fall into a taxi; arms wrapped tightly around each other. How nice, she thought, to be able to do everything together. Feeling the wind lifting goose bumps on her bare arms she got to her feet and turned back to the hall. A tall figure was standing behind her.

"Hello." The wind was blowing Tom's hair across his eyes.

"It's cold out here." Kitty was concentrating very hard on

getting up the steps.

"I've lost Rick." Tom helped her up, smiling at her fondly. "He seems to have disappeared."

"Found another woman no doubt."

"You're getting cynical." Tom slipped his arm around her waist. "Come and dance with me."

She looked up at him, frowning slightly.

"Here? With all your friends?"

"Why not." Tom kissed her forehead. "I feel like a bit of scandal."

Arm through his, a little nervous, she walked beside him into the hall.

Martin lifted his head off the pillow and groaned. His room was spinning faster than the disco lights of the previous evening.

Moving slowly, so as not to upset his delicate balance, he went to the window and peered out. Sheets of rain obliterated his view of the valley, and a heavy mist lay over the hills. Opening the window to remove the smell of stale beer from the room, he padded barefoot across the hall and peered into Ryan's room. Ryan's chestnut head was almost totally obscured by his quilt. Crossing the bare floorboards Martin gave the sleeping figure a prod.

"Come on lazy. Time to get up."

"Go away." Ryan moaned. "I want to die."

"Five minutes." Martin gave him a little shake. "I'll put the kettle on."

The kitchen was in a state of complete disarray. A mirror, items of makeup and a hair dryer cluttered the table, glasses filled the sink. Poppy's dress, for some reason, was draped across the back of a chair. Moving cans and glasses to find the kettle Martin heard footsteps behind him.

"That was quick. Oh, it's you." Martin was surprised to find Poppy coming gingerly through the door. "Oh dear. How's the head?"

"What head?" Poppy collapsed onto a chair and picked up her dress. "Is this mine?"

"Well, it's not mine. What's it doing in here anyway?"

"How the hell do I know? I don't even remember taking it off. What time is it and where's the paracetamol?"

"About quarter past seven, I think. Thank God Nigel and the lads came in to do breakfasts, I never would have made it. Is Kitty awake?"

"Kitty's not here." Poppy made a face as she forced the paracetamol down her throat. "Last seen heading into the night with the boss."

"Getting a bit serious, isn't it?" Martin stirred the two coffees and sat down.

"No." An indignant voice came from the hall. "If anyone had bothered to look, I've been in the living room."

"Why?" Poppy turned her head slowly to look at her friend and saw she was still wearing her evening dress. "Why haven't you changed?"

"I've been playing nursemaid. I found Rick totally legless in a corner, so I brought him here in a taxi. I've been making sure that he didn't drop dead overnight."

"Noble of you. I suppose he wants coffee?" Martin put the kettle back on.

"No, he's out cold. But will you make me one please Marty? I'd better change."

Martin stirred coffee noisily and watched Poppy as she crept to the living room door. Following her he rested his chin on her shoulder.

"Thought you two were all finished?"

"We are." Poppy put her hot cheek against his. "But my heart keeps forgetting."

"Look at him girl!" Martin couldn't keep the disgust from his voice. "Two days away from the biggest meeting of his life and he can't move. He should be thinking about Cheltenham and the Gold Cup, not getting pissed at the Broadwater Hunt ball."

"Not everyone's as obsessed as you Marty."

"All the best boys are. Do you think Brian Hales is lying comatose in a stable lad's house? I bet he's eating a healthy breakfast before going to ride work somewhere. *He* looks as though he's on his way to the morgue."

Rick, as if he heard them, rolled over in his sleep. Facing them, his black eye and bruised cheek stood out in ghoulish comparison with his grey face.

"Shit!" Ryan poked his head in on his way to the kitchen. "I thought I looked rough! He looks like the Phantom of the bloody Opera! I'm going to call Andrew Lloyd Webber!"

Giggling, Poppy backed quietly away from the door. Martin's disgust was starting to rub off on her. She thought how pathetic Rick looked in his drunken stupor. What was she doing, pining away for that stinking, semi-conscious object on the sofa? What a fool.

At lunch time Ryan made his weekly journey to the village for the Sunday papers. In the supplement was a feature on Runny and the forthcoming Gold Cup. Throwing the paper onto the kitchen table he heard Poppy's breath catch in her throat when she saw Rick's name on the cover. Reaching quickly for the supplement her quick fingers were beaten only by Martin's, hungry for a look at the write up on Olympic Run.

'Olympic Gold." Ran the headline. Below it were three coloured photographs, Runny jumping an open ditch, Revelation winning the King George and Rick, not in his breeches, but in a dinner suit and leaning on the bonnet of his Porsche. Martin admired the 'photo of Runny for a second then began to read.

'When I met Richard Drew Cowdrey,' it began, 'it was Valentine's Day, and I was surprised to find that his tiny cottage was not bursting at the seams with red roses.' Martin paused to look at the author's name and rolled his eyes. Typical. Had to be a woman! ' Because if any man,' it continued, 'from the world of horse racing has captured the hearts of the female population, this must be he. Old ladies put their pensions on him, housewives beat their husbands to the Racing Post and teenagers cover their bedroom walls with his picture. Handsome, charming, witty, and very, very single Rick Cowdrey must be *the* eligible bachelor of the sport. Rick drives fast, defies tradition, and loves a good party. But above all, put him on a racehorse and he's a genius.'

The article rambled on giving a potted history of Rick's youth, a profile of Highford and Tom and narrative by Rick on Runny, and the Gold Cup. Martin finished reading and spun the magazine into the middle of the table.

"What a load of crap! Only one paragraph about Runny. The rest is aimed at those horny teenagers who want to hang the photograph above their beds!"

"Jealous?" Poppy snatched the magazine.

"Not at all." Laughed Martin. "Shame whatever her name is can't see him now!"

Poppy gazed at the picture of Rick and realised that it must have been taken just before he took her out to dinner. A gremlin of suspicion began to work on her already injured pride, and, although she knew it was ridiculous, it kept nagging and nagging until it was the size of a soap opera in her head.

"You okay Pop?" Ryan prodded her. "Not going to be sick, are you?"

"No." Poppy slammed the magazine shut. "I'm going to clean tack."

"At this time of day?" Martin watched her go from his

prime spot beside the fire. "I'm going back to bed!"

At the house Tom was reading the same article. Stretched out on the sofa, he was enjoying a rare moment of relaxation. He shared Martin's view that the article was aimed more at Rick's female fans than at the general racing public. He wondered briefly what had happened to Rick the previous night, then thought more intently about Kitty. Yawning, letting the vision of her slender body dance through his mind, he wished that she could be curled up beside him. His mother, noting the look of contentment on his face, smiled to herself, pleased to see him so at ease. An ease that was avoiding her. Pushing all thoughts of Dominic to the back of her own mind, she concentrated on her book

In Kitty's bed, buried beneath the mound of her quilt, Rick slept off his hangover. Having roused long enough to make it up the stairs he had collapsed thankfully into the cosy warmth. Stirring, he poked his nose out into the cool air and squinted through still bleary eyes at the windows. The light was beginning to fade, making everything look grey and hazy. With a start he realised that he had slept through the entire day. Sitting up, he waited for his head to stop pounding and looked around the room. There was a quiet knock at the door.

"Come in." He croaked.

"Kitty, carrying a tray came backwards into the room.

"Tea and sandwiches." She said shortly. "There's hot water if you want a bath."

"Thanks Kit." Rick was looking sheepish. "You've been really kind to me."

"More than you realise. Poppy was all for tipping the tea over your head."

"Sounds about right. I've been such an idiot Kit. I just wish she would talk to me. I'm scared out of my mind about next week, I need her to hold me together."

Pulling his tangled hair from his face, his hand brushed cheekbone making him wince.

"Ouch. I forgot about that."

"I'll get you some Witch Hazel." Kitty was going out of the room. "And some paracetamol."

Sipping the hot, sweet tea, Rick was beginning to revive when Kitty returned.

"Here." She threw two boxes on his lap. "Bathroom's empty. But don't take too long about it."

Nodding his thanks Rick watched her leave. Running his eyes over the room he took in the clutter of his surroundings and began to feel awkward in this female domain, insecure. Getting out of bed he made his way awkwardly into the bathroom.

Within minutes the tiny room was filled with steam, better than any sauna. The warmth wrapped itself around his heavy limbs and soothed him. Closing his eyes, sighing deeply, he laid his head back on the bath and closed his eyes. Drifting in the sub-tropical haze of steam he dreamed, a tapestry of confusing images; Poppy on hands and knees at the Hunt ball, waves on a hot, sun kissed beach; a racecourse full of people, all waving betting slips and cheering. Then a dreadful image of himself riding Runny in the Gold Cup; taking off at the last only to find that his horse had vanished and that he was left plunging face first into the mud of oblivion. A bang woke him with a start, and with pumping heart he stared at the shadowy figure that formed through the steam.

"Who's that?" He peered through the mist.

"It's me you idiot!" Poppy's familiar voice echoed in the small space. "You've left the taps running! No one else would come in and tell you."

"Oh hell!" Plunging forward Rick stopped the flow of water and looked dismally at the waves of water splashing over the edges of the bath.

"You are useless." Poppy snapped. "Can't you do anything without making a mess of it?"

"Not at the moment." Replied Rick dolefully. "I'm jinxed."

For a second their eyes met; neither one voicing the thoughts that ran through their heads. Poppy, the first to break away, began mopping at the floor with towels.

"I'll do that." Rick was staring at her.

"No need." Poppy straightened. "I'll get these when you've finished."

"Please Pop." Rick couldn't stand it any longer. "Please will you let me talk to you?"

She turned to look at him with her huge dark eyes. The shape of her face told him how much weight she had lost.

"I'll listen." She said quietly. "But I don't say I'll understand. Or forgive."

"Thanks." Rick hesitated, then began in a rush. "I know that it was way out of line, what I did, and I know how much I hurt you, but you've got to believe that I didn't mean to. It's so easy to lose reality over there. I mean everything's so easy. I was waited on hand and foot, treated like some sort of hero, all my sister's friends falling over themselves to meet me. I lost touch with my real life. That's here; in the cold and rain, risking my neck, riding my arse off to win. Part of that life is this place, and most of all you. I never knew how much I needed you until you weren't there. I can't get my act together, can't sleep, can't eat. I'm scared stiff about this meeting and the Gold Cup. Everyone's got such high hopes, and I'm all in pieces. I just can't do it without you. I know I can't change what I've done Pop, I can't turn the clock back, but I can't go through this without you. Will you at least be my friend?"

Rick paused to try and compose himself as he did so Poppy sat on the toilet seat and dried her streaming eyes with the corner of a towel.

"Don't do that." He pulled the towel out of her hands. "You wiped the floor with that one!"

A flicker of a smile touched Poppy' face. She could see him studying her reactions. His cat like eyes looked enormous above his flushed cheeks, the bruising swollen and dark. Reaching out she touched it gently.

"Does it hurt?"

"Mm." Rick's eyes closed. "That feels good. I never thought you'd touch me again."

"Tell me something." Poppy had to ask the question although she dreaded the answer. "That reporter. The one from the Sunday mag. Did you screw her?"

"What!" Rick burst out laughing. "I'm not a complete nympho! She was about sixty!"

Poppy nodded slowly.

"Friends. That's all?"

"If that's all you want, yes."

"No." Poppy got to her feet.

"No?" He couldn't hide his disappointment.

Poppy walked to the door and locked it.

"You should have done that earlier. Anyone could have walked in."

Turning to face him she pulled her woollen jumper off over her head. Her tight black t-shirt emphasised the size of her breasts.

"What are you doing?" Rick tried to gain control of his excited body.

"Getting in." Poppy's jeans slid to the floor. "No room for friends I'm afraid. But plenty of room for lovers."

Rick laughed, half relief, half anticipation.

"Will we both fit?"

"Definitely." Poppy lowered herself on top of him. "But we may need more towels for the floor."

Pulling her down so that he could kiss her, Rick nearly submerged them both in his passion.

"Whew!" He gasped, shaking his wet hair from his eyes. "I missed you like hell."

"Me too." Poppy reached for the soap. "Are you going to win on Thursday?"

"The Gold Cup? I will now; and when I do, I'll be doing it for you."

The yard was in darkness. Sliding deeper into his sleeping bag Martin tried to shut off the unnerving sound of rats scuttling about outside. It didn't matter how much poison he used, they just kept coming back. Reprimanding himself yet again for leaving Runny unsupervised the night before he flicked his torch around the box. Runny blinked at him, nose deep in his hay. It was bitterly cold tonight, so he had wrapped Runny up in an extra rug. Closing his eyes, he willed himself to sleep; but there was so much going on in his head he couldn't relax. He was just starting to drift into troubled dreams when he heard footsteps in the yard. Slipping out of the sleeping bag he closed his hands around the handle of Ryan's baseball bat. Creeping to the door he crouched, ready to strike.

"Martin?" The door opened. "Are you there?"

"Jesus! Guv! I nearly brained you!" Martin got to his feet. "Why didn't you put the lights on?"

"I didn't want to wake the whole string. Everything okay?"

"Quiet as a mouse. Unless you're a rat that is then it's all systems go. What time is it?"

"One thirty. I couldn't sleep."

"Nor me." Martin looked out over the door. "Want a coffee? I've got a flask."

"No thanks." Tom laughed. "You're well prepared!"

"That's Kitty for you. She makes me a hot water bottle as well. She's a real angel. But then." Martin grinned, slightly embarrassed. "You already know that."

"Yes." Tom smiled in the torch light. "I do."

Martin turned his red face back to the horse.

"He's looking good boss."

"He is. I hope that he's feeling as well as he looks. He'll have his final workout in the morning. It's bloody cold Martin, are you sure you want to do this?"

"I'm fine Guv. You get inside. No need for both of us to freeze."

"Goodnight then Martin. I'll let you get back to that hot water bottle." Tom closed the top door.

"Night Guv."

The last thing Martin saw before he finally fell into a fitful sleep, were flakes of white falling silently past the window.

CHAPTER NINETEEN

The wail that echoed around the snow-covered yard brought Martin leaping out of his sleeping bag and to the door.

"Martin!" Gareth's voice was ringing off the walls. "Martin get out here quick!"

"Oh my God!" Martin surveyed the white scene in horror. "Look at it!"

"Oh, never mind that!" Gareth was pulling at his arm. "It's turning to rain. Come with me!"

Following him like a sleepwalker Martin found himself inside Enigma's box. Gareth jabbed an anxious finger at her near foreleg.

"Feel it!" He moaned.

Martin ran his hand down the horse's leg, pressing and probing the rear tendons. At first, to his tired brain, all seemed normal; then, as his senses kicked into action, he detected a patch of heat, and a small, but unmistakable area of swelling.

As he closed his fingers on the area Enigma flinched, pulling her leg from his hand. Letting the leg drop lightly to the floor Martin felt like crying. What terrible luck. Could there possibly be a worse time to get a big leg than on the eve of the Cheltenham festival?

"Sorry Taff." He shook his head as he straightened. "That's definitely a sprain."

"But she was fine yesterday!" Gareth was so agitated that he couldn't keep still.

"Have you led her out?"

"No need. Look." Gareth took the filly's head and led her around the box; even in this confined space she was horribly lame.

"Damn. Damn, damn, damn!" Martin scratched his

unruly hair. "There's some tendon stuff in the freezer. Slap some on and I'll get Mike out to scan her. Then I suppose I'd better break our latest piece of good news to the boss."

Gareth had turned away and hidden his face in the filly's neatly groomed mane, trying hard to hide his feelings. Martin's heart went out to him. This would have been his favourites big day, her first real chance of fame and glory. Time would work its usual healing powers and Enigma would be fine, but there would not be another Triumph Hurdle for her. This would have been her one and only crack of the whip. Next year she would be too old, and her precocious speed may have left her. Leaving the lad to cope with his disappointment Martin went to collect his things.

Tom was as crestfallen as Gareth when he heard the news. Giving the mare a quick once over he agreed with Martin that only a scan would give them the full picture.

"Then we'll see how much damage has been done. Well, that's one less to worry about I suppose." He pulled his Barbour up around his ears. "We can't work the others yet. The gallops are treacherous, we'll have to wait for it to wash clear."

Passing Prince's box Tom paused to give Kitty a furtive smile. Looking up at him, his shadowed features blue and red with cold, she thought that he would collapse if he didn't slow down.

"Good morning Miss Campbell." He grinned. "Where's your partner in crime?"

"Poppy?" Kitty came to the door, only too willing to be able to stand close to him, to feel his strong presence beside her. "She called about an hour ago. Rick can't get his car out."

"Is that what he calls it?" Tom grinned again.

"You can't say that!" Kitty giggled and looked over his shoulder into the yard. "You're the boss!"

"I am." Tom moved a little closer to her, leaning on the door. "And don't you forget it. Can't you pitchfork any faster?"

Kitty smiled and lifted two fingers at him.

"Now that's what I like to see." Tom laughed. "A bit of respect!"

"Shame about Enigma." Not wanting to break this moment of closeness, but aware of Ryan approaching, Kitty moved back to her pile of shavings.

"It is. Here's another long face. It seems that Rick will be the only one smiling this morning. What's up Ryan?"

"Feed merchant just rang. He can't get his lorry up the hill. He hopes to be here after lunch. There's nothing I hate more than moving a ton of oats on a full stomach!"

"Don't eat so much!" Tom patted him on the shoulder. "If anyone wants me, I'll be in the office. I have to tell Enigma's owners that they don't have a runner at the festival after all."

Enigma's owners, a small group of Gloucestershire art dealers, had pinned high hopes on their little horse and were inconsolable. Enigma was their only horse, and in the current climate where art was a very insecure business, seconded only by bloodstock, they struggled to pay the training fees. Hanging up, Tom felt deeply sorry for them. The long rest that the filly would need to recover would incur more expense that in all probability they could not afford.

After several abortive attempts Rick finally managed to slither and slide his way out of his cottage and up to the yard. His nerves, that were beginning to fray badly, were not being helped by the local radio station, which was beginning a preview of Cheltenham and all the fancied runners. Quickly turning it off, Rick tried to put all thoughts of birch fences out of his head and turned his favourite Bon Jovi CD up to full volume to help him. Poppy, cocooned in an afterglow the like of which she had never experienced, was totally oblivious to it all. Munching her way through a bag of crisps she gazed out of the window at the snow-covered fields, unaware of Rick's mounting tension.

"It's so pretty." She said dreamily. "Like a Christmas card."

"It's a nightmare!" Snapped Rick. "It's the last thing that we needed!"

Poppy paused, crisp halfway to her mouth, and looked at him in surprise.

"You're not getting nervous?"

"Of course not!" Rick ground the gears as he slid around a corner. "I'm just sick of you gassing at me!"

"Sorry." Poppy's face fell. "I'll shut up."

As they glided to a precarious halt in the yard, they met an array of gloomy faces. Gareth, his mood blacker than the coal that was mined in his hometown, was working like a dervish, snarling at anyone who got in his way. Kitty had fallen on a patch of snow behind the feed shed and twisted her ankle; wincing with pain, face stained by her tears, she was arguing with Ryan who had just had another heated discussion with the feed merchant and now faced a teatime weightlifting exercise. Only Martin was cheerful as he saddled Olympic Run.

"Just in time!" He shouted. "The all weathers clear at last!"

"Only an all-weather in the right weather, eh?" Rick grinned as he pulled on his gloves.

"Are you intending to do any work at all today?" Gareth opened Poppy's door. "You've lost your half day because of this morning."

"Who cares?" Poppy sat in the car and stared at him. "It was worth it."

"Don't push it Pop!" Kitty hissed as she hopped past. "Today is not a good day!"

They were being legged up onto the cold, fretful horses when Tom arrived, dressed to ride. Pulling his hunting cap into his head he walked over to Rick.

"Has Martin told you?"

"About Enigma?" Rick looked down at him from the superior height provided by Runny. "Yeah. It's a real shame."

"It is." Tom turned to Martin who was holding the little cob. "I hope you have your skates on Mick!"

"He doesn't need them!" Rick laughed. "With feet like that!"

Poppy, rapidly changed, was walking an excited Streak around the yard.

"She does." She muttered grimly. "She's slipped twice already!"

Shivering in the icy wind, Kitty pulled her scarf up over her nose and laid her hands underneath Brassy's warm mane. He was as solid as a rock, totally unperturbed by the arctic weather. Through his ears she could see Timepiece swishing his tail, already threatening to buck as Gareth tightened his girths.

"For God's sake be careful Taff." Martin was helping Nigel onto Major Investment. "He's dangerous enough on a good day."

Tom was already on Micky, about to lead the string out of the yard.

"Follow us up in the Land Rover Martin." He called. "Then if my feet get any colder, I can put you up on Micky and ride back in comfort!"

Laughing, Martin patted Runny's rump as he passed and watched the five horses filing away with pride. Glad of even the tepid warmth that the geriatric Land Rover prescribed as heating, he studied the horses as they worked smoothly up the gallop. Runny stood a hand higher than any of his companions; with his proud arched neck and long elegant head he was pure class and Martin worshipped his every hoofbeat. Seeing his muscles contract and expand as he worked Martin felt chills of excitement running over his skin. What a thrill, to be taking a horse like this to Cheltenham. Micky's head, stubby and plain in comparison appeared beside him.

"This is it, Marty." Tom's thoughts were running on a similar path. "If they aren't right now, we're too late to do anything about it."

On the gallop, fighting with the headstrong Timepiece, Gareth tried to fool himself that the tears in his eyes were caused by the wind. But he couldn't hold his emotions in any longer. He would have cut off an arm to see his beloved filly in the winner's enclosure at Cheltenham. He had lost his sweet Little Raver and now his beautiful grey mare was injured too. There were times, and this was definitely one of them, when all he wanted to do was go back to the valleys and work in a factory. Tactfully averting her eyes Poppy pulled up beside him and patted Streak's neck. Looking at her, Gareth felt another twinge of regret that his feelings for her had come to nothing. Heavy hearted, filled with self-doubt he began to walk back down the gallop towards Tom. As he did so, a big bay horse strode past him, ears pricked forward, taking in his surroundings with calm eyes, walking as if he owned the ground beneath his feet. All thoughts of home, and factories vanished, and Gareth realised just what he had become part of. Look ahead, he told himself, this is a team and you're a member of it, you've got to do your bit, or it won't succeed. Beneath him Timepiece gave a snort and a dart sideways.

"Yes, I know." Gareth said quietly. " And I care about you too, you old bastard."

"Everyone okay?" Tom was blue lipped with cold. "No problems? Right let's get back down before we freeze."

They jogged down the track, single file, to the gate. Martin was holding it open.

"You go." Tom waved him on. "I'll close it."

Rick waited politely as Tom bent to close the heavy gate. Tom spoke to him under his arm.

"Don't hang about Rick, this damn gate needs rehanging, it gets heavier and heavier."

Standing in his stirrups as Rick walked off Tom pushed the gate as hard as he could. Micky fretted, anxious to follow his friends. Tom gave the gate one last shove and heard the click of the latch just as Micky spun around. As the little horse jogged forward there was a sharp, cracking noise; spinning round in the saddle Tom saw the gate swinging back open. Before he could get out of the way it caught Micky firmly on the hocks. The normally placid little horse reared high, startled by the impact, then plunged forward, bolting down the lane.

"Look out!" Tom called. "Whoa Mick you old fool!"

Jumping and snorting the horses pulled to one side as Micky clattered past. Once he had passed the leading horse he slowed down, and Tom gave another determined pull on the reins as they reached the corner. Then, to his horror, he felt the horse losing his legs on the slippery surface. Frightened, Micky braked sharply only to find that his hindlegs shot underneath him and out through his forelegs. With a snort of fear, he went up into the air and flipped backwards, sending Tom crashing to the floor.

For a second, they both lay still, side by side, and then Micky clattered to his feet and, in a hurry to get away from this unpleasant place, took off at a more cautious pace towards home.

The five riders paused, all eyes on the man on the floor. Kitty held her breath, resisting the impulse to leap off and rush to his aid; a sick feeling in her stomach as he got slowly to his feet replacing her initial panic. Gareth, finding himself in difficulties, got off Timepiece, who was all for following Micky.

"Are you alright?" Rick rode over to Tom who was standing still, a very strange expression on his face.

"Not quite." He spoke through gritted teeth. "I think I've broken my arm."

Jumping lightly off Runny's back Rick took hold of Tom's right hand which was already turning blue.

"Looks like it." He agreed. "You look awful."

Tom's face was grey with pain.

"I'd forgotten what falling off felt like!"

Rick couldn't help laughing.

"Your turn, eh?"

"Something like that." Tom winced. "Look, get this lot home for me, will you? And send Martin back up with the Land Rover."

Kitty, not wanting to leave her man in such obvious distress, was arguing with Gareth.

"You can lead them both, I can't just leave him like this!"

"I can't control mine let alone yours as well! Stop being so bloody dramatic, he'll be fine!"

"I'll second that." Tom interrupted. "Now get those horses home."

Boot faced, Kitty jogged after Rick, leaving Gareth trying to vault back onto a panicking Timepiece.

"Bitch!" He yelled after her. "You could have waited for me to get on first!"

"Here." Tom caught hold of the horse's head with his good hand. "I'm not a cripple."

Once Gareth was out of sight Tom sat on the snow-covered verge. The pain in his arm was sickening. He couldn't believe it. How the hell was he going to cope now? After what felt like hours, he heard the ancient vehicle rattling up the hill. Not wanting to be seen as he was, he clutched the wall and climbed to his feet. Martin bounced into view.

"Are you okay Guv?" Martin was frowning.

"Fine, fine. Just get me home Martin."

"Don't be stupid Guv, any fool can see that it's

broken." Martin prodded the purple hand. "I've got strict instructions to take you to hospital. Don't worry, Rick's in charge, I haven't seen Poppy move so fast for days."

Reluctantly, swallowing the sickness in his throat, Tom got into the Land Rover.

The radiographer couldn't believe her luck. She was a keen racing fan and had spent many afternoons admiring Tom's broad back on television. With a bit more luck that handsome jockey of his might come in and visit him. Chattering away as she took x-rays of the offending limb, she soon realised that her small talk wasn't welcome. The sullen expression on Tom's face became worse when he heard the results.

"Compound fracture I'm afraid." The casualty doctor didn't look old enough to be out of school. "A complete break, and the two ends are out of alignment. In my opinion it will need pinning."

"Oh alright." Tom snapped. "Just let me know when it's got to be done. Put something on it and give me some painkillers."

"I don't think you understand. "We have to set the fracture and pin it straight away."

"When will that be?"

"As soon as possible which in this case will probably be the morning. We can keep you comfortable overnight."

"What!" Tom grew even paler. "I can't stay in here! I've got five horses to get ready, I have to go home!"

"There's no other way Mr. Chichester."

"There must be! This is my whole life we're talking about. I might never get another chance like this"

The young doctor sighed. He knew all about Olympic Run and the family feud from the radiographer. He looked at Tom and saw the desperation in his eyes.

"I shouldn't advise this." He paused, unwilling to go on. "But I can set the arm in the normal way. But it must be pinned. Must. Eventually, otherwise if the ends won't meet the break won't heal. Or even if it does, you'll have limited use of the arm because it won't be straight. But the earliest you can be out of here is this evening."

Tom glared at him.

"That's too late. Can't you just stick a bandage on it?"

"It's that or lose the use of your arm altogether."

Tom cursed under his breath.

"Well get on with it then." He snapped.

"Right. Nurse, can you get Mr. Chichester ready please, then take him to the plaster room."

It was still dark when Rick pulled up in front of the house. Helping a still groggy Tom out of the car he paused, lost for words."

"Well. I'll see you tomorrow I guess."

"Yes. Thanks for everything Rick. Are you sure you won't stay?"

"No thanks. I have to get myself together. There is one thing. Can I take Pop with me? I'm a bag of nerves."

"Is that wise?" Tom frowned at him over the roof of the car.

"She'll be here at the crack of dawn I promise. And no sex."

"Try telling her that." Tom blinked to steady his vision. "When I employed these girls, I never thought I'd have to be their guardian as well."

"Thanks." Rick got into the car. "Get some rest."

Tom felt panic clutching at his throat as the sound of the engine faded away. He wasn't ready for this. He needed more time."

"Tom?" Eleanor was in the doorway. "How are you son?

I've been so worried."

"I'm okay." Tom was moving slowly up the steps. "Just a little groggy still."

"The 'phone hasn't stopped ringing. Everyone wants to wish you luck. Rick's been marvellous, some man from the press turned up and he saw him off better than any guard dog!"

"Good for him." Tom put his good arm over her shoulder and rested his chin on her head.

"What's the matter dear?" His mother looked up at him.

"I wish Dad was here."

At three a.m. Poppy pushed a mug of hot chocolate into Rick's hand and tried to persuade him to come to bed. Rick, staring at a video he had stopped taking in hours ago, blinked at her with heavy eyes.

"No point Pop. I can't sleep."

"Listen." She said soothingly. "The Gold Cup is three days away. There's no point stressing about it yet. You've got some cracking rides before then and if you don't sleep, you'll fall off every one of them."

"Oh, the Gold Cup. I'm not worried about that. I've got to ride that bastard Timepiece in the Champion Hurdle tomorrow. I might not even make it to the Gold Cup. He scares the shit out of me Pop!"

Poppy laughed.

"You and everyone else!"

"There's no brakes, there's no steering. Nothing!"

"You'll be fine." Poppy pulled him to his feet. "But only if you get some sleep."

"Okay." Rick took her chin in his hand. "Where would I be without you?"

"In someone else's bed." Poppy said dryly. "Come on

superstar. Time for bye byes."

CHAPTER TWENTY

Martin slammed the door of the lorry. Turning to the row of tense faces below him he gave a wry grin.

"Well. Here we go."

"Good luck." Ryan, suddenly solemn, came and shook his hand.

"You'll have plenty to do. Don't let *him* out of your sight." Martin pointed at Runny. "See you tonight."

As he started the engine cries of 'Good luck' and 'See you on telly!' reached his ears. Beside him Poppy and Kitty wore pale faces. Gareth still sunk in deep depression over Enigma had requested that Kitty come with him to help in the dubious pleasure of taking care of Timepiece at a racecourse. In the back of the lorry the horse was already beating a rhythm against the side of the partition with his hooves.

"Trust us to get landed with him." Moaned Poppy. "I hope that you're feeling strong Taff!"

As the lorry moved slowly through the lanes they were joined by Tom and Rick in the BMW. Tom, grey faced, was biting the nails of his free hand. The pain killers were doing little to numb the throbbing ache of his right arm; but far worse was the ache in his stomach, which grew and grew as they turned down Cleeve Hill. From his seat Martin craned his neck as they descended, trying to catch a glimpse of Prestbury Park and the racecourse. Even at this early hour Cheltenham was bursting at the seams with traffic.

All headed in one direction.

Horseboxes, Range Rovers, Jaguars, mingling with coaches and minibuses: crowds of Irish revellers flocking the pavements and congesting the entrances, blocking the path of two enormous vehicles with the words "Racetech"

296

on the side of them. Overhead, the whirr of helicopters filled the air as they brought trainers, jockeys, and owners from all ends of the country. Looking upward, Rick peered through the windscreen.

"One day I'll have one of those. My own. With a big Kiwi bird on the tail."

"Very pretty." Tom shifted his arm in its sling. "This thing is getting on my nerves."

"Don't fidget." Rick knocked the car out of gear as he came to halt in a traffic queue. "Christ! Is it always this busy?"

"Usually." Tom looked dismally at the stationary line of vehicles. "No one wants to miss anything."

A bang on the window scared them both and Rick turned to find a large camera lens pointing at Tom through the window.

"Shit." He sprang out of the car. "Get lost you limpets! Leave the man alone!"

"Rick." A journalist pounced on him. "What's the latest on this family feud? Are the reports true that someone has tried to dope Olympic Run? What's Tom done to his arm? Have you got a winner for us today?"

"I've got a fist." Snarled Rick. "Which is about to go down your throat. Now back off and leave us alone!"

The traffic began to creep forward. Rick leaped back into the driver's seat and thumped the steering wheel.

"Bastards. Will they be at it all week?"

"I hope not. Dope Olympic Run!" Tom was laughing. "Their spies obviously haven't heard about Martin and the baseball bat!"

The racecourse was already buzzing with anticipation. Anxious trainers, smart in suits and wool coats, darted about greeting owners and guests. The general public, who were already massing through the gates wore an assorted mixture of Tweed, suits, and padded jackets. Owners wore suits and ties, punters waterproof jackets with pockets big enough to take the Racing Post. Farmers, businessmen, professional gamblers, racing clubs and working men's clubs, all drawn together by the magical lure of the festival. Irish accents were everywhere, greeting their English friends some of whom they only saw once a year, renewing the friendly rivalry that made this occasion so special.

Getting stiffly out of the car Tom attempted to rearrange his hair with his good hand, and pulled his long, black coat over his shoulder. Martin was jogging across to them, unusually neat in a dark blue suit. Under his arm was the little leather satchel that contained the colours.

"Hi boss." Martin tugged at his tie, irritated by the feeling of the collar at his throat.

"Everything okay?" Tom's eyes were roving the packed car park. This was the worst part. If only they could start now and not have to wait.

"Almost. We need a new partition. Timepiece decided he didn't like the old one and kicked it to bits. Took all of us to get him to the stables!"

"Hell." Rick was hoisting his bag into his shoulder. "I don't want to hear this bit. I'm off!"

Martin watched the slim figure dodging through the cars and felt a twinge of envy. Despite Martin's numerous reservations he had to admit that Rick had everything going for him: looks, talent, popularity, and a ride in nearly every race. As the figure reached the entrance it was besieged by reporters, all eager to hear the latest chapters of his turbulent life. Rick would never have privacy as long as he remained in this sport; he had too much character.

"Well." Tom's mind was on a similar track. "We'd better make sure the stable is still standing and that Timepiece hasn't killed anyone. Then they really would have something to write about."

The horses for the first race of the meeting, The Supreme Novices Hurdle, were walking around the immaculate parade ring. The jockeys, Rick included, were stood on the centre talking to owners, getting last minute instructions from trainers. Tom, tension building, had worn a trench from stables to weighing room. He wished that he had a runner in the first as it would make the time pass more quickly. He had done his duty with the owners, declared his intention to run with the stewards and was now in a strange state of limbo. Martin, who was thoroughly enjoying himself, appeared beside him.

"Need me for a bit Guv? No? Good, then I'm off to the bookies."

The Champion Hurdle was one of the big feature races of the meeting and drew great attention from press and public alike. Even though Timepiece was one of the real outsiders the nerves of his connections still jangled, and tempers frayed as everything was made ready. Lathered with sweat, unable to contain himself, Timepiece jogged his way around the parade ring, throwing his hindlegs into the air at regular intervals. Poppy and Gareth, a lead rein each, walked one each side of his head. Kitty, who had failed to get boots on the horses' front legs and given up in disgust was watching from the rails. Rick, standing beside Tom was watching the horse without enthusiasm.

"Apparently I'm making the running. No one wants to go on, and, as I won't have any choice I volunteered."

"Might be a good thing." Tom watched Gareth struggling to turn the horse into them. "Maybe he'll settle in front. Look out Rick, watch yourself!"

Dodging the horses hindlegs as they flashed past him, Rick sprang forward to Martin who quickly hoisted him into the saddle. Feeling the quaking mass of horseflesh beneath him Rick looked to Tom for reassurance, but he was deep in conversation with the horse's owner.

"Rather you than me." Poppy was struggling with the horse's head, wishing that the long walk out onto the track would end quickly.

"Rather not me at all." Rick tried, without much success, to settle the horse down. "This is the one I could definitely do without."

Poppy looked at the swarming army of people at the rails and hoped that Timepiece wouldn't start kicking out again. A bunch of girls, obviously members of the 'fan club' were hanging over to wish Rick luck.

"Good luck!" He muttered. "I need more than luck; I need a bloody miracle!"

Martin, following behind at a safe distance as they paraded in front of the stands looked up in awe at the enormous crowds. This was racing at its absolute best. Even the paddock was like a great Roman amphitheatre the crowds gazing down on the Gladiators as they prepared to do battle.

"Ready?" Poppy could see the trepidation on Rick's face and wanted to kiss him.

"It's now or never. Let him go."

With a leap that would have put a Lipizzaner to shame Timepiece bolted, waving his head wildly against Rick's restraining hands down the all-weather strip and out onto the turf towards the start. Unable to watch the dreadful experience of Timepiece in full flight Poppy ran back to the pre-parade ring to find Kitty.

"I can't watch!" She wailed. "Help!"

"Come with me." Kitty was folding the paddock rug. "I'll hold your hand."

Anyone in the crowd who had taken a piece of the 200-1 offered about Timepiece must have thought they were onto a very good thing as the horse bolted into a thirty-length lead and stayed there for the first mile. Even Cheltenham's switchback ride of hills and slopes failed to curb the horse's flight. Clinging onto the reins as they hurtled downhill toward the home turn Rick could not believe that they were still in front. Head still swinging, Timepiece took him at full tilt into the next flight of hurdles.

Before the horses began the long struggle up the final hill, the ground dipped and swept into a hurdle placed just before the corner. Looking over his shoulder Rick could see a cavalry charge of horses waiting to engulf him. Bracing himself he sat tight as the horse raced into the hurdle; three strides off Timepiece took off, way too early; hit out of his rhythm by his rollercoaster run through the dip he had totally misjudged his take-off. Forelegs stretched in front of him like a diver's arms he reached for the flight, but too short he landed not over it, but on it, his hindlegs sending it cracking to the ground. His head flew up and, all momentum gone, he came to a standstill; only briefly, but it was enough. The rest of the field surged around him. Even without the tiring pull up the hill Rick knew that all was lost. Despite brave, heroic efforts from himself and the horse, and a hairy moment when Timepiece hung badly right-handed through the field, he could only finish twelfth of the sixteen runners.

The horse's owner, far from being disheartened was full of gratitude; having backed the eventual winner anyway he had only wanted a day out.

"Maybe next year!" He roared, slapping Tom on the shoulder. "Oh sorry! Did that hurt?"

It was a tired group of horses and people that clambered out of the lorry that night. Brassy, despite Herculean efforts from Rick had only managed a distant fifth in the novice 'chase. Poppy was over the moon with the young horse's performance but Tom, although quite satisfied for himself, was desperately sorry for Rick, who after a full day's riding had not had so much as a sniff of the winning post. Timepiece, quiet for the first time in his life, hobbled down the ramp like an old man. His crash landing had badly jarred him, and he looked very miserable as Gareth rugged him up for the night.

"I actually feel sorry for him." Kitty stroked the horse's soft muzzle. "He's never hurt himself before."

Poppy hung over Streak's door and stared at her beloved horse.

"You tomorrow girlie. You've got to put us on the map."

Tired as he had never been before Tom lay in the bath with a plastic bag over his arm. He wasn't sure if he could cope with another two days of tension. Wriggling uncomfortably, he looked up as his mother peeped through the door.

"Do you mind if I come in? I've made you a coffee."

"Not at all." Tom laid his head on the side of the bath. "Nothing you haven't seen thousands of times before!"

His mother placed the coffee cup on the edge of the bath beside him, carefully averting her eyes. He was so dignified, her son, that it didn't seem right to sit here while he was naked. The days when she felt comfortable like this were long gone.

"I put some whisky in it." She went to the door. "I know I shouldn't have but I thought you might need it. Dinner won't be long."

She looked back.

"I'm sorry you didn't have a winner today."

"I didn't expect one." Tom closed his eyes. "God I'm tired."

Daylight came too soon for the members of Highford. Crawling out of his sleeping bags Martin made his usual check on Runny. Satisfied, he felt a pang of regret that he wasn't going to the meeting today. But to him lay the great responsibility of exercising Runny and making sure that he was tuned up for his big day. Going to the door and stretching he saw Poppy hard at work polishing Streak's golden coat; Nigel was washing Major Investment's socks. Wheeling past with a barrow full of hay nets Kitty grinned at the puzzled look on Martin's face.

"Who forget to set his alarm clock? Sleepy head." She teased. "Runny's even finished his breakfast!"

Martin looked at his watch in horror. He had overslept by an hour. Bolting to the feed shed he cannoned off Ryan who had just finished.

"Oh, shit Ryan. I'm sorry, I was supposed to do that!"

"No problem." Ryan's brown eyes were heavy with sleep. Picking wood shavings out of Martin's tangled hair he gave him a pat on the shoulder. "One more day and you can sleep in a bed like the rest of us!"

Tom, who to his shame, had also overslept, was eating a hasty breakfast, and being watched by Rick, who was sullenly sipping a black coffee and eyeing Tom's bacon with envy. Hungry, but unable to eat because of the light weight that he had in the first race, he was even more nervous today than he had been yesterday. Made irritable by his nerves he had started the morning by rowing with Poppy. The added pressure of representing his father's interests were getting to him. Tom' attention was being diverted by the morning racing programme. Tomorrow would include a preview of the Gold Cup and footage of Runny working at home. Shane had warned him to stay by the 'phone until the broadcast was over. More pressure. But that was tomorrow; he had to concentrate on today. Eleanor collected plates with a lot more noise than usual, and splashed water into the sink.

"When are you leaving?"

"Now. Why?" Tom eyed her suspiciously. "What's wrong? You sound edgy?"

303

"I'm fine darling. Just nervous for you."

Giving her a puzzled glance Tom kissed her on the cheek and followed Rick out of the room.

Once the car had pulled away from the courtyard Eleanor rushed to the drawing room and picked up the 'phone. From here she could see the drive. Dialling the number that she had hastily scribbled on an old recipe she waited for it to be answered.

"Hello. This is Eleanor Chichester. I believe that you have my son staying with you?"

At the other end of the line Lauren rolled over in bed and prodded the angular frame beside her.

"Dommie darling it's your mother."

Dominic opened his red rimmed eyes.

"Thanks, be an angel and make me a coffee?"

"Is that a cue to get lost?"

"You are so clever." Dominic kissed her bare shoulder. "Two sugars please."

"Dominic?" Eleanor's voice was shaking.

"Hello mother. I take it you got the message before the chief whip heard it?"

"I did."

There was an awkward pause.

"Look." Dominic lowered his voice so that there was no chance of being overheard. "I never thought I'd be asking this, but I need your help. Badly this time. I'm back in court on Monday and I really need your support."

"You should have thought of that before." Eleanor's voice was tense. "You know I'll be there for you Dominic, but what do you want me to do? How can I help you?"

"I've put everything I own on this race. I mean everything. What if I lose? Where the hell am I going to go? Even if I get out of the court case in one piece, if I lose that race, I'm ruined. I've got nothing."

"What about your flat?"

"I sold it. I mean it mother. If Revelation loses tomorrow, I've lost everything. Absolutely everything."

Eleanor sighed.

"You know I won't turn you away, not if you have nowhere else to go."

"Oh, thank you!" Dominic snapped.

"You know what I mean Dommie. I love you, but Tom? It won't be easy."

"So, you'll iron out the creases with him for me?"

"No." Eleanor said firmly. "You must do that yourself."

Dominic shivered and pulled the quilt up under his chin.

"I saw him on T.V. yesterday. Not looking good, is he?"

"Is that surprising?"

Lauren was coming back into the room.

"I have to go mother. I'll be in touch; and I'll see you soon. But not too soon, I hope."

Lauren placed the mugs on the bedside table and perched on the edge of the bed.

"Paving the way home?" Her thick hair was swinging around her shoulders.

"Something like that. I must be sure. If I lose, then at least I have somewhere to go."

"Don't be so dramatic darling!" Lauren laughed. "You have here!"

Dominic didn't answer; shutters came down over the dark eyes, blocking out all emotion. Despite her loyalty, despite her unbending faith in him whatever he did, he hadn't told her that to pay Jack Coltrane's extortionate training fees he had handed over the deeds to this flat.

The sun shone on the runners of the Queen Mother Champion 'chase. Coats gleaming in the March light they made a glorious sight as they paraded in front of the packed stands. Rick, relaxed now that he was on his mare, indulged in a display of showmanship, waving to the admiring crowds at the rails.

"Will you stop it!" Poppy hissed up at him. "It's embarrassing!"

"It's good publicity. Don't be so jealous."

"Balls." replied Poppy as she unclipped the lead rein. "Good luck. You just bring her back in one piece."

Streak, coat like molten gold, struck out into her long, easy stride and drew gasps of admiration as she flew past the eager crowd. Tom, training his binoculars on the mare as she went to the start felt a tinge of pride at the sight of the family colours being displayed so magnificently. At the rails Poppy met Nigel and Ryan, who was carrying the paddock sheet.

"She's looking good." He was chewing one end of a leather strap. "What are the odds?"

"About sixteen to one." Poppy was facing away from the course, unable to watch.

"What!" Nigel's eyes came out on stalks. "I'm going to put my shirt on!"

At Highford the remaining staff and helpers had gathered around the television in the cottage. Kitty and Gareth, kneeling at the front, were in danger of being crushed by Martin who was hanging off a chair and leaning on their shoulders.

"Look at Ryan!" Kitty giggled. "The ginger monster!"

"Known to his friends as copper balls." Grinned Martin. "But keep that quiet!"

"Poppy looks glamorous." Said Gareth wistfully. "She

should have been a model."

"Shut up!" yelled Martin. "They're at the start!"

The crowd burst into a deafening roar as the small bunch of runners galloped at tremendous speed into the first fence. Sitting comfortably behind the leading three horses Rick felt the mare settle into her quick, powerful stride. Fence after fence flashed by the mare negotiating each one with ease. Rick held his breath as they raced through the dip and into the 'bogey' fence; but Streak whisked easily over it with a flick of her muscular quarters. Around the home turn and he was alongside the leader, the two horses drawing steadily away from the other runners. The stands erupted into noise as, neck and neck, the two horses battled up the hill, drawing steadily away from the others.

"Come on!" Poppy was screaming. "Come on my darling come on!"

Clutching Ryan's arm so tightly he winced, she closed her eyes as the horses raced into the last. The noise from the crowd was so deafening that she couldn't even hear the commentary.

"Poppy!" Ryan shook her. "Poppy, look!"

Through spread fingers Poppy opened her eyes and saw Streak, ears flat to her beautiful head, straining every muscle in her body as she stretched out and beat her rival to the line by a neck.

"Yes! Yes! Yes!" Ryan leaped into the air, paddock sheet flying, lead rein clattering to the floor.

"She did it!" Nigel was whirling Poppy through the air.

"Let me go!" Poppy shrieked. "I've got to get to my girl!"

As she ducked under the rails she looked up and saw Rick turning the mare towards her. With tear filled eyes, she ran to meet him.

In the stands Tom lowered his glasses with a trembling hand. Below him he could see Poppy, hair flying, throwing herself into Rick's outstretched arm. Eyes like torches, Rick gave the most dazzling smile.

"You beauty." He slapped the horse's steaming neck again and again. "You absolute beauty!"

At Highford the chair had finally collapsed under the strain. Tears pouring down her cheeks Kitty listened to Ricks postrace interview with pride and then sobbed as she watched Tom receiving his awards with bursting heart.

"It's alright Kitty Kat." Gareth hugged her. "This is the hard part."

As the lorry pulled into the village much later the inmates of the pub ran out to greet it. Rick, behind, blared his horn and waved to the cheering group as he drove past.

"Well done you!" yelled Ron. "Keep it up!"

The yard was full of the homely glow of lights. As Ryan got out of the cab he was deafened by the whoops and hollers. Tom smiled as Rick halted at the gate to watch the scene. Scanning his eyes over the group he found who he was looking for, she was staring back at him. Opening the door, he got to his feet and held out his hand. As she ran to him, and he clutched her tight, he breathed in the smell of her newly washed hair.

"I'm so proud of you." She whispered. "But I wish I'd been there."

"I wanted you to be there." He muttered. Over her shoulder he could see Martin tactfully turning away. Rick, on the other hand, having untangled himself from Poppy's embrace, had no such reservations. Laughing, he took them both in his arms.

"When are you going to face up to it? Life's too short to hide in the shadows, you two were made for each other."

CHAPTER TWENTY-ONE

Olympic Run swished his long, perfectly groomed tail and stared out into the night. Behind him Martin crouched, unable to settle. Sounds of riotous laughter came from the cottage. Nigel, having multiplied his 'shirt' by sixteen had placed half of it each way on Major Investment, who to everyone's delight had finished third. His newfound wealth had gone to his head, and he had raided Ron's, buying enough beer to drown himself in and was throwing an impromptu party. Feeling that tonight, of all nights, would be Runny's danger zone Martin had given the revelry a miss and retired to his corner. Looking up he saw someone watching him over the door.

"Hello you two." Kitty planted a kiss on Runny's long nose. "I've brought you goodies."

Slipping past the horse she handed Martin a carrier bag.

"Sandwiches, two cans of lager, a flask of coffee and a hottie."

"Thanks." Grinned Martin. "You cherub you."

Laying her cheek against the horse's neck Kitty closed her eyes.

"Big day tomorrow boy." She ran her fingers down the hard line of muscle. "Your chance for a piece of glory."

"And ours." Martin winced as the lager spat out of the can. "Then there'll be a party!"

"There's enough of a party tonight." Kitty rubbed tired eyes. "There'll be a few sore heads in the morning. But not mine, I'm off to bed."

"Poppy coming with us?" Martin was back inside his sleeping bag, curled up like a large blue slug.

"I think so. Rick would flap if she wasn't there, and the boss is getting soft hearted in his old age."

"I'll tell him you said that." Martin had a mouthful of sandwich. "Been a funny old season; so much has happened."

"Not over yet." Kitty's mind was on Dominic. "Let's keep our fingers crossed. I couldn't cope with another disaster."

"Mm." Martin closed his eyes.

"Good night, Marty." Kitty went out. "See you in the morning."

Martin woke long before the first streaks of dawn painted the sky red. But if he rose early the media were up and at it long before him. As the horsebox pulled out of the gate, it's paint work newly washed and shining in the sunlight, it was besieged by cameras. In eager anticipation of the day's events the press and its photographers were anxious to catch any glimpse they could of the most talked about horse in training. Cursing them Martin revved the engine, scattering reporters as he did.

"I don't believe it!" Short of sleep and already pumping adrenalin he was on a very short fuse. "They must have been here all night!"

His temper was not improved by the crowd that awaited them at the racecourse. Reporters swarmed forward like an army of ants only to draw back, rather disappointed when they saw only Kitty and Martin.

"Good job they don't know about you and the boss." Martin said dryly. "Or they'd be after you as well!"

Another horsebox appeared and caught the pack's attention.

"Coltrane." Martin stared at the vehicle. "I hope we aren't going to have to put up with them all day."

Poppy's head poked through from the horse's quarters.

"What's going on. Oh God, Look!"

Looking ahead Martin saw a camera crew waiting to film Runny's arrival.

"Lord help us." He sighed. "Here we go again."

Kitty was greeted with cheers and best wishes as she led the horse down the ramp. Ears pricked; he surveyed the scene with interest. Patting his neck, the touch comforting her as well as him, Kitty led him to the stables, feeling very proud to be associated with such a noble horse.

Tom was waiting outside the stable manager's office. Somehow, he and Rick had managed to get into the course through the barrage of press with the minimum of fuss. Immaculate, even in his plaster, he had a cavalier air about him, his coat hanging loose over his useless arm. Only the unusual pallor of his face betrayed the inner battle that he was having with his nerves. he was wandering restlessly around in a circle when he looked towards the gate and saw a big bay horse, coat like bronze in the sunshine, jogging to meet him.

His heart missed a beat.

This was it. This was the day he had hoped for, dreamed of, worked so tirelessly to achieve. This was the moment he had driven himself to exhaustion and beyond for. Here, at last, was his finest hour. A strong sense of humility overcame him, and his eyes grew hot. Blinking furiously, he saw Kitty looking at him quizzically as she halted the horse beside him.

"Are you okay?" She could see the mist in his eyes.

"Never better." Tom lied. "My God he's a picture."

"He is, isn't he." Kitty's smile was spoiled by a quiver of nerves. "I hope that he feels as good as he looks; and that he isn't as scared as I am!"

Martin arrived, hauling the trunk, and pulling at his tie.

"Is it hot? Or is it me?" He moaned. "I bloody hate suits, but I hate all these reporters more!"

"Here comes the enemy." Poppy dropped her end of the trunk with a thud. Looking backwards over her shoulder she watched Jack Coltrane's groom leading a lean black horse. In silence they studied the animal as it passed. Superbly fit, he carried not an ounce of surplus fat, but lacked Runny's pride; there was no brilliance, no sparkle, the will to win didn't burn bright in his eyes.

"Poor thing." Martin lowered his voice. "He's just a racing machine. Something to have a gamble on. He hasn't got that, what did the old man call it?"

"The look of eagles." Tom narrowed his eyes.

"That's it." Martin turned to the bay nose beside him and visibly glowed with pride. "Now this one's got enough to fill an eyrie!"

A few hours later Tom wandered around the grounds, waiting for Mike Peterson to arrive, and fighting his growing nerves. The racecourse was rapidly becoming an airfield as people spilled out of helicopters and small aircraft. Coach loads of people were flocking through the turnstiles, people from all walks of life. This was their Mecca. They had come to worship their God. The thoroughbred.

Mike Peterson, with Cynthia in tow, was already half full of champagne when he made his way to meet Tom. The Bowles' brothers and Rowley Harris, pale faced and silent were with him, the contrast in their personalities standing out even more as the all-important hour approached. Mike had booked a box to entertain his guests. He introduced them all to Tom, briefly and then hustled them away. Rowley, always the opposite had declined the invitation to join Mike in the box and had opted to watch the race with Tom and be closer to the action. If he could have, he would have spent the time waiting for the race at the stables gazing in awe at his most prized possession.

Sitting on the wicker trunk outside that stable Kitty was feeling isolated. She could not go with Tom; Poppy had rushed off to be with Rick, who was walking the course for the tenth time, and Martin was simply on another planet. Studying her nails which, no matter how hard she scrubbed them, never looked completely clean, she had the eerie feeling that someone was watching her. Looking around she was shocked to see Lauren standing in the door of Revelation's box. For just a second their eyes met. A faint smile, almost sarcastic, drifted across Lauren's face and she turned away. Poppy was running back to the stable, side-stepping Lauren with a distasteful glance she jogged up to Martin.

"Eyes peeled Marty. The head nobbler's sugar lady is here."

"I know." Martin was starting to turn a strange shade of green. "She's been here three times. God knows how she has a stable pass. Evil bitch."

"Oh, lay off her." Kitty picked at her boot. "What happened wasn't her fault. I feel a bit sorry for her."

Poppy and Martin exchanged glances.

"Want to explain that one Kit?"

"Well." Kitty paused. "Look who she's with. Isn't that enough to make you feel sorry for someone? God only knows what he's doing behind her back and what lies he's told her."

"True. But it's her choice." Poppy swung the blonde ponytail. "Come and watch Rick? They are in the paddock for the first."

"Okay?" Kitty got to her feet. "You coming Marty?"

"No fear!" Martin bolted the bottom door. "I'm not leaving this horse until he's on the track. Tell Cowdrey if he falls off, I'll kill him!"

Time had never passed so slowly. Martin was at steaming point when, at long last, he saw Kitty coming back.

"Okay Martin?"

"No." Martin pulled a face. "But there' no putting it off any longer. Let's go and saddle this horse."

Kitty slipped the bridle over the horse's ears. Four boxes away Revelation's groom was already leading the black horse away.

"Take care." Martin felt like a father whose son was having a first ride on a motor bike. "You look after him Kitty. I won't be far away."

"I should hope not. You've got to put the saddle on."

The cameramen, who had been sidetracked by the earlier races, were now speeding about to get good shots of the Gold Cup runners as they were saddled. Horribly tense, Tom lurked in the back of the box, supervising Martin, and not enjoying this forced inactivity. Shane appeared in the entrance.

"Tom?" He peered through the shadows. "How about a quick one?"

"Get lost." Tom didn't move. "If I see another camera, I'll break it."

"Now don't be like that." Shane fortified by whisky and a winner was feeling persistent. "You owe it to your public."

"Rubbish." Tom moved forward. "But as I've nothing better to do right now. Just make it quick."

In the bar Mike Peterson was watching the television. Having left Cynthia to entertain his business colleagues he had escaped to the noisy sanctuary. Tom's familiar face appeared on the screen.

"Sshh!" Someone yelled. "Turn it up!"

A hush fell over the crowded room. Shane was disguising his slurring speech very well.

"He looks magnificent Tom. Are you hoping for good run today?"

"If I wasn't, I wouldn't be here." Tom was deadpan, pale, and tense. there was no heart-breaking smile today, no sparkling eyes. This was a man about to meet his maker.

"The ground is officially good." Shane continued. "But the jockeys have been reporting some soft patches in the back straight. Will this suit him?"

"I could have done without the snow." Tom was speaking rapidly, anxious to get it over with. "It's made the ground a bit on the soft side but that won't worry him. He's a big strong horse."

"And have you spoken to your brother? How does he rate his chances?"

There was a pause that lasted so long the producer began to wave his arms and cue a change of shot. Then came the quiet answer.

"I don't, as I am sure you well know, have too much communication with my brother. But I have no doubt that Jack will have the horse spot on for such a big race."

"So, he's your big fear.?"

"No" Tom shook his head. "My biggest fear is the race itself. If I can take my fellow home tonight safe and sound, I'll be happy."

"That's not bloody good enough!" Mike's explosion shocked the bar. "I came here to bloody well win!"

The crowds that thronged the parade ring, race cards in hand, watched the entrance expectantly. A slim blonde figure leading a big bay horse came into view and a buzz of noise greeted them. Runny, not used to so much fuss before a race, sprang sideways, ears twitching like radars. Kitty, her cheeks growing hot at this unexpected attention, lowered her head. Runny started to spring lightly from hoof to hoof, getting hot beneath his paddock sheet, streaks of sweat darkening his neck, the enormous crowd were winding him up, making him excited. Tom, surrounded by the anxious quartet of owners narrowed his eyes as he watched the horse. He wanted him calm, wanted him to conserve his energy. He found himself murmuring 'easy' and 'steady' under his breath. Over Mike's suede clad shoulder, he could see Lauren and Jack Coltrane watching their horse.

A tall figure was running into the paddock; long leather coat swinging loose on his thin shoulders. Even on this day of wind and pale March sunlight he wore dark glasses. Something twisted in Tom's stomach, making bile rise in his throat. His eyes turned to Kitty, and he saw that she too was watching this man, who was now in deep conversation with his trainer. Colour came and went in her cheeks, then, with a toss of her head, she turned back to the horse, smiling sweetly at the well wishes from the crowd at the rails.

A stir in the crowd announced the arrival of the jockeys. Rick was the last one to come out. As he walked past Dominic, he averted his eyes. He was unusually subdued.

"You fit?" Tom moved away from the other men.

"No. Don't put me through this again." Rick gave a sheepish grin.

Martin pulled off the paddock sheet and at long, long, last Rick was united with his horse. The hype, the attention, the crowds were all getting to him and as he, Martin and Kitty began the parade he wished he could start the race now and get away from the terrible nerves that were attacking him. In silence, the trio walked up the course. Rick had pulled his goggles down already, the tinted lenses hiding his eyes; there was no waving, no smiles for the fans, only a grim face, and a determined set to his strong jaw. Ahead, Arctic Fox was being loosed by his lass. Rick shifted his weight and took up the reins.

"Here we go." He muttered. "See you guys later."

As they watched the bay horse canter away to a burst of applause from the crowd Martin felt overwhelmed by the magical tension of the moment. Laying his hand on Kitty's shoulder he spoke wistfully.

"What was it Andy Warhol said? About every man having fifteen minutes of fame?"

"Something like that." Kitty turned to him. "Why?"

"I have a feeling I'm about to get mine." Martin grinned

wryly. "I'll die if he doesn't win."

"I'll die if he does." Kitty slipped his arm through his. "So at least we won't go together."

The starter climbed slowly up the steps onto his rostrum. Ten horses, six of the best from England, three from Ireland and one from France, fretted as they were drawn into line.

"All right jockeys?" The starter held out his hand. "Come on!"

The tape snapped up and the stands erupted into the famous Cheltenham roar. The Gold Cup was underway.

Throughout the whole race there were really only three horses in it. Arctic Fox, with his usual front running style, forced a strong pace, but soon found himself beaten as he was overhauled within a circuit by two other horses on the hill. Struggling to hold his position he hit one of the 'soft' patches that Shane had mentioned and the off fore tendon, that Greg Westwood had nursed so well all season, finally gave out. Completely broken down he hobbled pitifully off the track and into the horse ambulance.

The crowd, distressed at seeing an old favourite injured, quickly had their attention diverted by the French horse, who, having hunted around at the rear of the pack, began to make up ground with an acceleration that would have done justice to a Paris taxi driver. Joining the two leaders, he raced on the outside as they swept into the turn, opening such a gap that it seemed impossible they could get caught. Stride for stride they negotiated the fences, none of them wanting to make the final, decisive break for the line.

As they raced downhill towards the final turn for home Revelation made the first move. Crouched low over Runny's neck, Rick had no desire to go with him. It was a long, punishing, pull up that hill and he had been beaten by it already at this meeting. Beside him the French horse was travelling with ominous ease. As they reached the second last Revelation had gained a three-length lead, but from his position behind him Rick could see that the hill was already taking its toll. Revelation had to reach for the next obstacle, and the birch cracked as he hit it with his hindlegs. Rick, wanting to save as much energy as possible for that final climb, steadied Runny at the fence and made a cautious leap that lost him a little ground, but took nothing out of the horse.

Unable to bear it any longer Martin was jumping up and down in agitation. Riding every stride with Rick, he couldn't help letting panic take over as Revelation began to draw away.

Rowley Harris shared his fears.

"I hope he's not going to leave it too late."

"He knows what he's doing." Tom's mouth was so dry he could barely speak. "I hope."

Up the home straight came Revelation, chased by the only two horses left with any chance in the race; the speed of these three had left the others strung out, Indian file, around the home turn. Into the last fence, and slowly, but surely Revelation's stride began to falter. He was tiring, and his pursuers were wearing him down. The stands were about to erupt; the course commentator bursting a blood vessel as Revelation took off at the final fence.

"Come on Runny!" Martin was screaming. "You can do it. Come on!"

Behind him, in the owners and trainers stand, Tom held his breath. Unable to watch as Runny rose into the air he turned away.

Rick's mind had become blank. All he could hear was the wind in his ears and the thudding of his own heart. All he could feel was the rhythmic, powerful stride as Runny galloped into the final fence. All he could see was the dark mass of birch in front of him; then passing beneath him, blurring. Through his tunnel vision he saw the long green carpet that lay between himself and the winning post. He sensed, rather than saw the horse fall beside him. Head down, with gritted teeth, he began to ride for the line. In the distance, outside this cocoon he found himself in there was a lot of noise; but here there was only his own breath and the staccato beat of hooves. There was a shadow beside him, a dark form, clinging to him, matching his every move. With an instinctive reaction that his brain barely recognised, he raised his whip. Once, twice, it fell and the dark shadow had disappeared.

The tunnel receded and the deafening noise crowded in. Standing upright in his stirrups he punched the air again and again as the white post flashed by.

He'd done it. They had done it. Olympic Run had done it. The Gold Cup was theirs.

Shaking his head in disbelief he pulled the steaming horse to a walk and collapsed onto the bay neck. The sound of the crowd was almost unbearable. Turning towards it he raised his head and saw people running to greet him.

Martin, tears spilling freely down his cheeks, reached him first. Unable to speak he held out his hand. Rick took it; a smile splitting his face from ear to ear. Hands slapped him on the back as the other jockeys congratulated him. Dave Holloway pulled an exhausted Revelation alongside him and patted Runny's neck in admiration.

"Well done." He panted. "You passed me as if I was standing still. That's not a horse, it's a monster!"

Rick took his eyes off Martin's face and gave another enormous smile.

"We made it a race." Dave tapped him with his whip, disappointment etched on his face. "But we were never going to beat you."

Slowly they made the difficult journey back to the winner's enclosure; difficult because of the hands that reached out to pat the horse, because of the crowds that pressed against the rails and sent Runny skittling sideways and because Kitty, who had been trying to compose herself amongst all this emotion, gave up and walked through the crowds with streaming eyes. Poppy fought her way to their side, and with one hand on Rick's leg she jogged along, smiling up at him in triumph.

Then there was that moment, that one moment that every owner and trainer dreamed of; the pause, the slowing of a pace, the split second before you stepped into that most hallowed of sporting arenas: the winners enclosure at the Cheltenham Festival. Rick's eyes searched for Tom. He was waiting with Rowley Harris, surrounded by people, offering them his good hand. Rick and Martin halted for a second, savouring their moment of glory. Tom turned and looked at the steaming animal in front of him, then lifted his eyes to meet Rick's. A smile of pure relief flooded across his face.

Rick couldn't resist it. Kicking Runny into a walk he stood in his stirrups and gave a whoop of joy, sending Runny shying wildly into Kitty.

"We did it!" He leaped out of the saddle and caught Tom's free arm. "We bloody well did it!"

"You did it." Tom's voice was thick with emotion. "That was the most brilliant piece of timing I have ever seen."

Shane shot into view, camera man in tow.

"Well done!" He gushed. "Rick that was an outstanding ride."

"I'm going to weigh in." Rick was pulling the saddle of the horse. "Or I'll be having an outstanding fine!"

"Wait." A photographer snatched his arm. "Photo first Rick please."

Tom's post-race interview was the exact opposite of the pre-race version. Relieved, happy, he sparkled with wit and charm. The ecstatic crowd roared their approval at his every comment.

"I'll leave you all to it." Shane was wrapping up the interview. "One last thing. What's next for everyone's favourite horse?"

Rowley glowed with pride as he answered.

"The Grand National."

Following the horse out of the winner's enclosure Tom side stepped to let someone pass and looked straight into the haunted eyes of his brother. In all the chaos of the moment he had completely forgotten about him. They both froze, locked in each other's gaze. Dominic was even more pale, gaunter than ever. He broke the silence first.

"Well." He spoke not with enmity, but with the blunt resignation of a man who had gambled and lost. "That's me finished. I suppose I should say congratulations."

"It wouldn't suit you." Tom was aware of eyes on him from every direction and was anxious to avoid a public scene. "That's a very good horse you've got."

"Lauren's." Dominic was squinting at a sudden show of sunshine. "I just wanted to beat you."

"And you didn't."

"No. In the end I just beat myself."

His frankness surprised Tom. Taken aback he searched for something to say, but before he could find the right words Dominic was gone.

"Mr. Chichester." An official was beckoning. "They are ready with the presentation."

The crowds had dispersed by the time Kitty finally led Runny back into the horse box. The press, having had their fill, had disappeared into the bars to load up on scotch and file their copies. Martin was waiting at the foot of the ramp.

"I can't believe it's over. We really did it."

"It's not over yet." Kitty gave Runny another sweet.

"There's a long night ahead of us yet."

"Where's Poppy? Or needn't I ask?"

"She's coming. She's been keeping tabs on Rick; the female autograph hunters were getting a bit close for her liking."

"I could sleep for a week." Martin yawned widely.

"No time sorry. We've got hangovers tomorrow and two runners on Saturday."

"I don't care." Martin pressed his cheek against Runny's silken coat. "I could cope with anything right now. I'm so happy I could burst."

Driving back through the dark lanes, Rick was also very tired. Beside him, the euphoria of the day wearing off, Tom was already half asleep. Turning into the village Rick was startled by a large white banner hanging above him.

"Look!" He shook Tom. "Look at this!"

Tom stirred and squinted up at the banner. 'Well done Runny.' it read, 'Welcome Home.'

"Good Lord." Tom sat up and stared out through the car window in amazement. "The whole village is out!"

Ron's red face appeared in front of him mouthing energetically. Rick lowered his window it so they could hear his words.

"Bloody well done!" A blast of whisky entered the car.

"I can't believe it!" Rick shook his offered hand. "What's going on?"

"Celebration of course. First drinks are on the house." Ron lowered his voice to a whisper. "Yours will be free all night. Can't say that too loud or I'll be bankrupt."

"As if! We won't be too long." Rick pulled forward through the throng of people, laughing out of the window at the drunken celebrators lining the street.

"Do we have to?" Tom rubbed his eyes. "I'm exhausted."

"Of course, we do." Rick had visibly revived at the thought of a party. "Can't let Ronnie down."

The lights of the house were glowing against the hillside. The yard was already in darkness but there was a lot of activity at the cottage. Slowing down as they passed Rick saw Martin running down the path.

"Guv, Rick," He called. "Come and have a drink!"

"Later Martin." Tom gave a weak smile. "We'll be over later."

"I'll save you something then. But the way that lot are going through it it'll be a hard job. The boy's fine, I've strapped his legs up with astringent and he's eaten all his supper. Even shouted for more!"

"Glad to hear it." Tom smiled. "I'll just check him over."

"No need." Martin smiled. "He's all tucked up in bed."

"Okay then." Tom smiled gratefully. "Thank you, Martin."

"Just doing my job." Martin blushed slightly. "Hurry up or Poppy will have finished all the brandy."

Already swaying slightly Martin went back inside.

Pulling up outside the house Rick turned off the engine and ran his hands through his hair, trying to put his thoughts into words.

"Well." He paused. "I want to thank you for today. If you hadn't had faith in me, I would never have made it over here. No way would I have won the Gold Cup. You had enough trust in me to put me up on Runny. I owe it all to you. Thank you."

"Not at all." Tom was touched. "We, both of us, owe today to one horse. Without him, neither of us would have won a Gold Cup."

"Yeah." Rick smiled at the memory of his moment of triumph, the memory that would stay with him for the rest of his life. "He sure is some horse."

CHAPTER TWENTY-TWO

Showered, shampooed, smelling of perfume, Kitty and Poppy walked arm in arm along the verge towards The Plough. Coatless, they were both insulated from the cold by several brandies. A little way behind them the boys were counting the money they had raided from the piggy bank.

"The last time we had a party at Ron's" Poppy steered them around a hole. "You got pissed and the boss had to take you home, and I had my first encounter with Rick."

"Now none of that tonight." Kitty giggled. "This is a staff celebration No men."

"Get lost!" Poppy was walking faster now that she could see the pub. "I know who'll be the first one to forget about that!"

Everyone who lived in, around, or anywhere vaguely near Highford was crammed into the lounge bar of The Plough. A table full of food lined one end of the room. Ron had taped the afternoons racing and was playing it to a cheering crowd.

"I'm saving the best for last." Ron had forgotten his 'first drink free' rule and was handing over pints to anyone who asked. A loud cheer rocked the glasses on the bar as Rick walked in, all smiles, followed by a rather more subdued Tom. Poppy, eyes wide and glowing with love and alcohol, fought her way through the ring of bodies and threw her arms around Rick's neck.

"Hi!" Rick laughed in surprise at her energetic welcome. "How are you?"

Tom moved on and left them alone together. Leaning weakly on the bar he took the large whisky offered him and drained it in one gulp.

"Hello." A tantalisingly soft voice reached his ears. A curtain of blonde hair swung over the bar as Kitty leaned forward into his line of vision.

"Hello." He took in the ruddy cheeks, flushed with more than just heat and alcohol and realised with a pang of guilt just how young she was. Too young for an embittered, middle aged lech like me he thought. Then he shook himself. What was wrong with him tonight? He had just lifted the most coveted prize in jump racing. He should be leading the rowdy celebrations, not brooding into the bottom of a glass.

Ron was about to play his trump card, the recording of the Gold Cup. A hush fell over the room as they watched the parading horses.

"Oh NO!" Poppy wailed. "Fast forward it Ron, PLEASE!"

"Why?" Ron frowned.

"Look at my hair!"

This inane outburst brought a hubbub of noise back into the room. The inebriated crowd cheered every time Runny appeared on the screen; when he passed the winning post, Rick found himself being thrown in the air. Tom, patted so hard on the back that he nearly choked, looked at the image of Kitty leading the horse through the crowd and watching with him, she blushed scarlet at the sight of her red eyes and streaked cheeks. Seeing himself talking to Shane, Tom saw for the first time his own ghostly pallor, and the shadows deep beneath the sunken eyes.

"Wouldn't win any beauty competitions today, would I?"

"Nor would I." Kitty laughed. "We make a good pair."

"Do we?" He raised his eyebrows.

"I think so. But then I am biased." Kitty's colour deepened. "Because I hate to think of you with anyone else."

"That's very bold of you." He smiled.

"Isn't it? Ron's been feeding me Gin, or I would never have said it."

A grimace of pain flickered on Tom's face.

"What's wrong?" She caught his good hand.

"My arm. The painkillers are wearing off. I can't take any more today." He frowned at his Whisky. "I'll just have to drink more of this instead."

There was an air of melancholy about him that Kitty didn't understand. Not knowing what to say to break the silence that fell between them, and afraid of saying anything that may be wrong, she drifted away.

"What's up angel?" Rick caught her waist as she passed and kissed her cheek.

"Nothing." She hugged him back. "Just wandering. Make sure he doesn't drink himself to death." She nodded towards a broad back at the bar.

"What's wrong with him?"

"I don't know. He's in a strange mood. I think he's exhausted but doesn't want to let anyone down. Have you seen Marty?"

"Playing darts. If you can call it that. You leave him to me." He looked at Tom. "I'll sort him out."

Tom was so engrossed in his brooding thoughts that he hadn't even realised Kitty was gone. Rick, taking her place, studied him for a few moments and shook his head. Something was troubling the man deeply, but what? And why today of all days? He took a deep breath before he spoke.

"Good party. Ron will be out of beer soon."

"What? Oh, hello Rick? What was that? I'll get you a beer." Tom was frowning hard, trying to concentrate on what Rick had said.

"I don't want a beer. What's up with you tonight? Come on, let's sit down before you fall down. You look all in."

"No thanks. Too far from the whisky bottle."

"Bring one with you then." Rick waved at Ron and pulled

a roll of notes from his pocket.

"No, no." Ron waved it away. "If that's for you then it's on the house."

"Like everything else!" Rick laughed. "Come on." He turned back to Tom. "This is a party not a wake!"

Tom straightened and shifted his arm in its sling.

"You have to get that sorted out." Rick scolded. "You can't leave it like that."

"You are starting to sound like my mother. Who will run the yard if I'm in hospital?"

"Ryan." Said Rick firmly. "Martin. That's what you pay them. Me if it comes to that. You've got the best staff in the business; they've proved that this week. It's time you trusted them more. Now what's bugging you?"

Tom collapsed back into the chair and took the glass Rick offered him. Rick was watching him intently, the bruising on his cheek faded but not yet completely gone.

"Nothing is 'bugging' me as you put it. I'm just tired. I could quite happily go to bed at this moment."

"So could I." The familiar grin lit up Rick's features. "But not on my own!"

Tom shook his head a faint smile on his lips.

"I wish I was like you." He sighed. "Everything comes so easily to you. In my life everything is a problem."

Rick pointed at Kitty, who was bending over to collect Martin's wayward darts.

"That's no problem. Just relax and enjoy yourself. Whatever else is going on in your life," He added with a flash of insight, "Can take a back seat for tonight."

Tom poured another whisky. Rick was right. He needed to relax; and the key to that relaxation lay in the bottle in front of him.

Anaesthetised by alcohol Tom began to enjoy himself. By the time Ron was throwing people out into the dawn lightened street he had emptied the bottle. His good arm over Kitty's shoulders he was enjoying the sensation of her hair on his skin and the firm contact of her body next to his. Looking into her hazy, unfocussed eyes he had serious doubts about his ability to have sex with her with all this whisky inside him. Rick, on the other hand, had no such self-doubts.

"Time for beddy byes." He was pulling Poppy to her feet. "Sorry Kit but you're banned. I deserve a celebration bonk."

Kitty giggled.

"And where am I going to sleep? In Micky's stable? Nigel's nabbed the sofa!"

"In luxury. Tom can look after you. About time that four poster saw some action!"

Kitty blushed and pushed her nose into Tom's hair.

"I'll sleep on the floor in the living room." She said quietly. "Don't worry."

"You will do no such thing!" Tom got rather unsteadily to his feet. "You come with me."

Ronnie, wiping the bar, watched them tottering out of the door and smiled to himself. In all the years he had known Tom Chichester, he had never seen him look at a girl the way he looked at this one. About time too. Dreading to think how much money the evening had cost him, he consoled himself with the thought of the betting slip tucked away in his pocket. Tomorrow he would give those bookies a right old hammering.

"Trailer for sale or rent," Sang Gareth loudly, "Room to let fifty cents, I'm a man of means by no means..."

"King of the road." Finished Martin. "Oh, hello Guv. You walking?"

"Swaying." Tom grinned into the moonlight. "I couldn't drive even if I had both arms working!"

"Hello Kit." Gareth called. "What are you up to? Here Kitty Kitty!"

"Shut up you stupid boy." Martin took his arm. "And keep walking."

Deliberately slowing down by making a show of losing his key, Martin waited until the couple had passed them and were out of earshot. He laid his hand on Gareth's shoulder.

"Our Kit is going up in the world Taffy boy. No stable boys for her."

"Nor me." Gareth chuckled. "I prefer beer!"

Once out of their range Tom began to talk. At first Kitty half listened humming to herself, enjoying the sobering effects of the damp air. Then she realised with a jolt that he was pouring out his heart to her, tongue freed by alcohol Tom told her of all that ailed him. With a lump in her throat, she heard of his grief at his father's sudden death, his hopes for the future, but most of all his fears of what lay ahead; the constant worry of failing, of letting his father down, of his almost enforced loneliness. Aware that he was displaying a side of his nature he rarely revealed she pulled him off the road and into a gateway.

"Sshh." She put her hand over his mouth. "Wait for the lads to pass us. They shouldn't hear all this."

Tom struggled to focus on the pale circle that he knew was her face, but the only thing he could clearly see were her eyes. Big eyes, dark on this cloudy dawn of mist and rain. He raised a finger and clumsily stroked her cheek.

"You're so beautiful." He whispered.

"Quiet." Kitty pulled him closer to the gate and watched Gareth and Martin pass by, not noticing the couple hidden in the shadows. Taking his hand, she went to move on.

"Stay." He muttered. "I like it here."

"In a gateway full of mud! Come on."

"No." He pulled her back, more roughly than he intended,

and she slipped, falling against him. Cradling her with his good arm he felt the weight of her body against his. Lowering his head so he could see her properly he placed his lips on her cheek.

"I love you." He murmured. "So much."

Kitty looked into the shadowed face and held her breath.

"You don't mean that." Her voice was unsteady.

"Yes, I do." Tom was very drunk, but very sincere. "This may be the most absurd relationship I have ever been in, but I do love you Kitty."

Kitty couldn't reply, she didn't want to break the mood, spoil this wonderful moment. How many times had she gazed into the future and imagined him saying those very words? Kissing his cheek, very gently, she took him by the hand and led him back onto the road. Walking in silence she felt closer to him than ever before. Not only had he told her what she had been so desperate to hear, but she knew more of him, of what made him the man that he was. The man she would go to the ends of the earth for. A smile touching her lips she laid her head on his shoulder and let her stride keep time with his.

Only the hall light in Highford House shone to guide them home. The cottage was already in darkness, barely distinguishable in the grey light.

"Rick doesn't waste any time." Tom laid his arm on her shoulders as they walked up the drive. "I do envy him."

"You? Why?" Kitty was beginning to hang back as they got closer to the door. She had only been to his bedroom once; on a frosty night when his mother was at a bridge party. The thought of actually sleeping in the ancestral family home made her feel a little shaky.

"He's got everything." Tom had halted. "He's handsome, he's brilliant, and he's got the world at his feet and women falling all over him. He doesn't have a care in the world."

"Only whether or not he'll break his neck in the next

race." Said Kitty dryly. "And a family that's halfway around the world. He doesn't have all this."

She waved her hand in the general direction of the estate.

"No, he doesn't. But then neither do I, not really. While my mother lives, which I hope will be for a very long time, this is hers. Then." He paused, swallowing hard. "It becomes ours. Mine and his. This house will never be mine."

"It'll never be his." She squeezed his hand. "He would never be happy here."

"But he can make sure that I can't be. Demand half of it, insist I sell or split the estate." He sighed deeply, beginning to sober. "I still envy Rick. I always wanted to be a jockey, but I was too heavy."

"Rick would love to have lots of the things that you have." Kitty walked on. "Anyone would."

"There is one thing I wouldn't change."

"What's that?"

"You." A smile passed across his face.

"We'll see about that. Get me inside before I turn chicken and run!"

Standing at the window of his bedroom some minutes later Kitty looked out at the misty landscape and shivered.

"Cold?" His hand was undoing her shirt.

"No." She smiled. "Nervous."

"Of what?" His hand slid inside her shirt, stroking her soft skin.

"Of being here. It doesn't feel right."

"Tell me afterwards." Tom kissed her neck. "It'll soon feel wonderful."

Arching her back in pleasure Kitty pulled off her shirt and pushed herself against him.

"Damn thing." Tom pulled at his sling. "I can't even undress you!"

Kitty giggled, undoing her cotton bra.

"What?" Tom smiled.

"What if I refuse to undress you?"

In the empty silence of a service station car park Lauren walked quickly back to her car, a takeout coffee balanced in each hand. Slumped in the passenger seat Dominic took another pull at the vodka bottle in his lap.

"That's enough Dom. Drink this." Lauren sat down carefully.

"I don't want coffee." Despite having consumed three quarters of the bottle Dominic was still perfectly coherent.

"Drink it." Lauren held it in front of him.

"Fuck off." He snarled. "Leave me alone."

Lauren threw the coffee out of the door, wincing as the hot liquid spilled on her legs. From the corner of her eye, she could see his expression, cold, callous, frightening. He was running his hand constantly through his spiky hair.

"Are we staying here all night?" She ventured.

"Why don't you shut up!" Dominic turned his black eyes, full of hate, onto her. Shrinking from him Lauren felt her spine turning cold. In all the time she had known him she had managed to walk a path that was well clear of Dominic's temper. She had heard of his violent mood swings, had even seen him in a full-bodied rage, but had always managed to stay out of his way. Taking a deep breath, she tried to compose her words carefully. She wished that she was already at home. It was cold and miserable here, halfway along the motorway. The thrill of seeing her colours carried so bravely in battle had faded rapidly once she had been alone in the car with Dominic. His mood had been foul from the moment she started the engine, all he had done was drink. Putting as much distance as possible between them as the confined space would allow, she spoke hesitantly.

"Shall we go home now?" Her fingers curled around the steering wheel, her one hand on the key.

"And where exactly is that?" Dominic hurled the bottle out of the window. The crash shattered the silence.

"To the flat?" She asked, softly.

"What flat you bloody silly old bitch! What bloody flat?"

"Your flat?" His words had stung her, but she didn't want to let it show, so she spoke slowly, calmly. "The one I gave you?"

"Yes. You gave it to me didn't you. Another little gift to keep the toy boy happy. Well, it isn't mine anymore."

"What?" Lauren's voice was beginning to rise.

"Belongs to Jack. That horse of yours isn't cheap."

"What!" Lauren was screaming now, forgetting her trepidation as her voice rang around the car.

"Don't you ever shout at me." Dominic's voice was so low in comparison that she could barely hear him. One long fingered, bony hand rested on her shoulder, making her tense.

"What about all my things?" She stammered. "The furniture? The clothes?"

"Spoils of Victory."

"Who to?" She couldn't wriggle free of his grasp.

"I told you. Jack." His fingers were running across her throat. She flinched.

"Get your hands off me." She hissed.

"I beg your pardon?" The fingers closed around her Adam's apple, gripping tightly.

"Don't!" She jerked her head away, wrenching free, tears beginning to slide down her cheeks.

"This isn't like you." He was drawing closer. "You've never turned me away before."

"You bastard." She sobbed. "You've taken everything. My pride, my beautiful flat. What am I going to do?"

"Oh, you've got plenty." Dominic caught her chin and forced her to look at him. "We'll survive. Won't we?"

Lauren shook her head, unable to speak.

"Beautiful eyes." He muttered. "Your eyes are so beautiful when you cry."

In his own eyes she could see the gleam of lust. The undesirable carnal animal was rearing its ugly head.

"No." She pulled back. "Not now."

"Yes." He snarled, taking hold of her hair. "You don't ever say no to me."

"Oh God." Opening the door she made a desperate lurch for freedom, yelping as she tore her hair from his grasp, and sprang away from the car. The lights of the service station beckoned, offering sanctuary. Automatically she began to run towards them.

"Lauren!" Dominic staggered across the bonnet and nearly fell. "Get back in this car!"

"No!" She shouted over her shoulder. "You stay away from me."

"You BITCH" The roar terrified her, and she began to sprint, desperation giving her speed.

She was nearly at the building, nearly safe, when something hit her heavily from behind, sending her sprawling face down onto the concrete. She felt a weight laying on top of her. Struggling to get away she felt him catch her arms and pin them behind her back. Intoxicated as he was, she still could not match his strength.

"I've got you now." He panted, holding her with one hand while the other reached for the waistband of her trousers. "This is new, even for you. And they say I'm a pervert!"

With a jerk he lifted her whole body off the floor and spun her around to face him, hoisting her hands above her head. Lauren sobbed as he pulled and snatched at her clothes; her mouth had been cut in the fall and she tasted blood.

"Leave me alone." She pleaded. "Not like this Dominic, please?"

Her voice rose into a scream.

"Sshh now." His mouth was next to her ear. She could feel him fumbling with his own zip. "Someone might hear you."

Who? Who was there to hear her cries? The place was deserted. But she had to do something, she could not just lie there and be abused. He was pulling at her pants, yanking them down over her hips. Gritting her teeth she pushed her knee upward, hard. He paused briefly, pain flashing across his face, then he raised his arm to strike.

"No!" She clutched at him, desperately trying to hold his arm away from her. "Please, please, don't do this to me Dominic. I loved you, I still love you, please don't hurt me."

She rambled. She knew that she was, jumbled words that made no sense, saying anything to keep him at bay; chaotic sentences escaping between her sobs. Then she felt him become very still, no longer fighting her. His arm relaxed, and he lifted himself off her. As she turned her head, she saw him fall away, his hands over his face. Whimpering, still afraid, she got to her knees, trying to cover her bare skin. He was sitting a few feet away from her, rocking to and fro.

He was crying.

She stared at him: love, hate, revulsion, pity all chasing each other around in her tormented brain. She wanted to run, to hide her shame and her body in some dark place. But, to her own disbelief, she found herself watching his tears through her own.

"Why?" Her voice was barely a whisper.

"I'm sorry." His words were distorted by his strangled sobs. "What am I? An animal? You're all I've got, and I was going to, I tried to. Oh, God, Lauren, what have I become? I hate myself."

Dropping his hands, he looked at her. She was about to flee when she saw the misery on his face.

"Lauren don't leave me." He whispered. "I hate being alone. I won't hurt you, please don't leave me. I can't live without you."

For that moment in time, at least, he knew that what he said was true.

"I don't trust you." She sobbed. "How can I? Oh, Dominic why did you have to this?"

"I love you, Lauren." He mumbled. "More than I've ever loved any woman in my life. When I saw when I realised. God what a vile bastard I am."

"Don't." Something in his voice was frightening her. Cautiously, she got to her feet. "Don't Dommie. Come and sit in the car."

"No." He shook his head. "You'll leave me."

"I won't leave you." Yet, she thought, because right now I have nowhere to go. "We have to find somewhere to stay. I still have a key. We'll see Jack in the morning. He won't throw us out. All I need is a bit of time to give the tenants in my house notice, then we can move. He'll understand."

"Will he?" His eyes were cavernous holes of black in his white face. "He doesn't care about us."

"No. But he cares about Revelation." Lauren was moving slowly away from him. Then a thought struck her. "He is still ours, isn't he?"

"Yes." Tears were dropping from his eyes onto the floor.

"Then we still have something to bargain with."

Like an old man Dominic rose to his feet; stooping and shaking he held out his hand.

"No." She stepped back. "Not now. Let's just get going."

"You hate me." He was shuddering. "You're never going to forgive me."

"Stop feeling sorry for yourself." She was walking quickly to the car. "We'll sort it out. Tomorrow."

She was in the car. Her hand was on the key. He was moving to the door, slowly. With a surge of panic, she pictured his face as he forced her to the ground. She turned the key in the ignition. She could leave, get away from him; if she put her foot down now, she could be miles away in a matter of minutes. Out of his reach. His hand was on the door. It was now, or never. He was in the car, and it was too late. God, she prayed, please let me have done the right thing. As she revved the engine, she glanced across at him.

He was out cold.

Lauren was right about Revelation; Jack Coltrane didn't want to lose him.

"If you go on training him Jack, you have to give me six months, that's the notice I have to give my tenants."

"Six months?"

"Yes." She had tried to sound calm. "That's the terms of the lease, unless they breach contract which they haven't."

"Well. All right, I'll give you your six months. But if your bills are a day overdue, I'm coming in to claim my property. But take my advice Lauren, get well away from that man. He's nothing but trouble."

"I thought you two were friends?"

"Acquaintances. People like Dominic Chichester don't have friends."

No, Lauren thought as she hung up the receiver, and I'm beginning to understand why. Looking at the still comatose form in the bed she shuddered. Jack was right. People either hated Dominic or were blinded by his magnetism. She had been blinded, but not anymore. She thought of Christmas at Highford, of Tom and the jolly happy people she had met at the party. Now that was a life she could settle into. It was the sort of life that she had been living until she had met him; then she had traded it all for his good looks, his promises, the incredible sexual chemistry that existed between them. On the floor was a half-packed suitcase. Her credit cards were still healthy, she could book into a hotel until she found somewhere else. She was standing there, unsure whether to leave, or to stay when he woke. Tiptoeing past the bed, she jumped out of her skin as his hand caught hers.

"Hello." She swallowed. "Would you like coffee?"

Dominic blinked, screwing up his pale face.

"No thank you." His eyes were roaming around the room. "Are you going somewhere?"

His eyes had caught sight of the suitcase.

"I don't know. I wasn't sure how I would feel when you woke up."

"Why?" He was sitting up, slowly. "Did we quarrel?"

"You don't remember?"

"No."

"You." She struggled with her words. "You, attacked me, you tried to..." She paused, struggling with her memory, not wanting to form the only word that could describe the terrible events of previous nights.

"I did what?" His words faded away as his memory came creeping back. "Oh Lord, Lauren, not you."

"Why not me?" She asked quietly. "Have you done this before?"

She bit her lip, dreading the answer that in her heart she already knew. She had heard the tales in the London clubs, the stories of Dominic Chichester's inability to take 'no' for an answer. But she had never believed them to be true. He nodded bleakly, a shudder running across his shoulder. She could see his flesh twitching.

"Who?" She demanded. She had no fear of him in this mood. He was subdued, almost timid. Pale and shaking he was as weak as a kitten; she, on the other hand, having isolated her mind from her emotions during a sleepless night felt surprisingly strong.

"Does it matter?" His eyes met hers, only briefly, and she saw the anguish and humiliation in them.

"Yes." Her heart was pumping. "It does to me."

"I've never, I haven't actually," he hesitated.

"Is 'rape' the word you're looking for?" Her voice was high and unsteady.

"I suppose it is." He wasn't looking at her now, but staring ahead, into the pictures of his memory. "But I never have, believe me."

"What have you done?" The contempt in her voice made him look at her.

"I get carried away." He paused. "As you've found out. It gets a little, well out of hand."

"I know." She said coldly. "Who Dominic?"

"Only one that you might know. One of my brother's stable girls."

"Which one?" Lauren's stomach was churning.

"Kitty. The blonde one."

"Jesus!" Lauren was horrified. "Poor little thing. She's no more than a child."

"Old enough." Dominic was staring at his hands. "Old enough to lead someone on."

"That's always the excuse, isn't it?" She yelled. "You're pathetic!"

"I know." He stared at her.

"And the rest?" There had to be more.

"One of my brother's ex-girlfriends. I didn't really fancy

her, not really, I just wanted to get at Tom."

"As always." She interrupted.

"Yes, as always. It all went wrong, she tried to run out on me, I was rough. She got pregnant; I think she must have had an abortion."

"Oh God." Lauren was heaving on the point of being physically sick. "You utter bastard."

"She was just one of many." He lifted his heavy eyes to hers. "There have been so many women Lauren. But not one of them like you."

"Not fools you mean?" She was shaking, unable to stop the tremors that were racking her body.

"When I was fourteen, that's when it started." He was in a trance, unaware that she had even spoken. "A girl accused me of raping her. I didn't. I thought it was what she wanted; it *was* what she wanted at first. Then she got scared. I didn't believe her when she said no, and I wouldn't stop. Then I realised what I was doing, and I panicked and ran away. The next thing I knew the police came to the house and told my father I had been accused of raping her. It was awful, and it wasn't true. How could she have lied like that? No one would believe me, no one, not even my own father. No that's not true. My mother believed me. But only her. Then the truth came out and it all got swept aside. But by God it hurt. Women." He paused, and when he continued there was a cold edge to his voice. "How I hated them. All of them. But then I found out just how easily I could use them to get what I wanted, and how badly I could treat them and get away with it. I even grew to like it. Revenge; getting my own back."

He paused and looked at her. Repulsed, she wanted to claw his black eyes from their sockets and beat at his anorexic body until it turned blue beneath her fists. Every inch of her flesh crawled with revulsion at the memory of his hands on her flesh and inside her body. She retched and turned away. Dominic saw her emotions in her eyes, saw her standing sickened in the doorway and deep down inside him something hurt.

"What have I done?" He buried his face in the quilt. "I love you so much."

"And I loved you." She was crying too. "You were the most beautiful man I had ever met. Now I despise you, you're sick, you need help. You twisted, pathetic bastard. How could I have been so stupid?"

Shaking his head, pleading for forgiveness, Dominic got out of bed. Standing in front of her, tall, lean, and naked, he brought back to her all the reasons why she had fallen so deeply in love with him. This was not an affair of the heart; it was an affair of the flesh. His body was so beautiful, and his dark, haunted eyes. She had longed to ease the pain in them, to take the torment from his troubled heart. For a second her heart softened. Then she remembered the fear of an empty car park.

"No. I can't forgive you." She shook her head. "What if you did it again? No, Dominic, it's over, it has to be."

"Lauren." He reached for her hand. "Haven't I always given you everything you ever wanted?"

"Given me!" She snatched her hand away. "You've taken from me, and I gave it all willingly because I was so desperate to keep you. But not anymore. I've been a fool for long enough!"

"Lauren." He snatched at her arm, holding it tight. "Don't go. I need you!"

"It's too late. You've ruined everything. Now let me go!"

Rigid with fear and anger she looked into his eyes. For the first time she saw compassion in them, almost love. There was fear there too, real fear. His lips, always so pale, were flushed an angry red; his eyes swollen from his crying. Dark stubble lined his chin. He looked so beaten, so helpless that without fully realising what she was doing she kissed him, very gently, on the lips. As he pressed his mouth back onto hers, she forget everything except the overwhelming need her body had for his. It was stronger than her, this desire, stronger than her morals and her beliefs, it took over her; and venting her emotions in the most primitive act known to man she made love to him.

When it was over, and her pulsing body had calmed itself she remembered. Running to the bathroom she only just reached it before she was violently sick; staring at her own reflection she heaved again. But it was too late. It was done. Her mental anger could do nothing to prevent his allure; she had fallen straight back into his trap.

CHAPTER TWENTY-THREE

The nurse had ginger hair and a kind, freckled face. Placing the tray on the table that sat across the bed she smiled.

"There you go Mr. Chichester." She had a sweet, lilting Welsh accent. "Now can you manage?"

"Of course, I can manage." Tom sat up straight and picked up a fork. "What is it today? Potted pussycat?"

"It's beef you cheeky boy!" She tutted.

"Boy indeed." He smiled. "I'm probably the same age as your father!"

"Is that so?" She sat on the edge of the bed and turned on the television. "I'm a lot older than that pretty little blonde girl who visited you last night. And there was nothing fatherly about *that*."

Tom tried to kick her with his foot.

"Don't be naughty. I'll tell matron."

"Huh." She was changing channels with vigour. "That old battelaxe."

Chewing on the beef, which had all the texture of an old riding boot, Tom admired her profile. Snub nosed, with a thick head of wavy hair she was no beauty; but there was something welcoming about her, homely, satisfying.

"Oh! What a handsome man!" She turned up the volume. "Must be a film star. Oh yes, has to be, look at his girlfriend."

Tom leaned forward, his fork falling onto the tray with a clatter.

"Turn it up again." He demanded. "Quick!"

Giving him a puzzled glance, she increased the volume. The cameras were outside a courthouse, filming the man and his companion as they were escorted out of a black car.

"Oh, I know who it is!" Her voice rose. "It's that big drug

case, isn't it? He's one of the leaders. What's his name? Darren something, no it's more upper class than that...I know, Dominic, Dominic Chichester. Oh." She stopped abruptly. "Oh."

The picture had switched to one of the channel's newscasters who was talking rapidly to the cameras.

"The trial began today of Dominic Chichester, reputed head of one of the biggest drug smuggling operations seen in Great Britain. One notable absentee from the witness list and also the public gallery was his brother Tom, trainer of this year's Cheltenham Gold Cup winner."

The little nurse had gone scarlet.

"I'm sorry." She babbled. "Me and my big mouth!"

"You weren't to know." Tom had lost his appetite.

"I'll turn it off." She picked up the remote.

"No, don't bother. There'll be some mindless soap opera on in a minute to help me fall asleep."

The nurse stood up and tidied the bed. She enjoyed looking after this man, he was so very attractive and, now that his operation was over and the pain in his arm under control, he had dropped his arrogant attitude and opened up to her. Now she looked forward to coming into his room and had even started making excuses to do so.

"You can take this away." Tom pushed the table at her. "I wouldn't give this to my dog."

"How's the arm today?" She fussed around, plumping up his pillows.

"Okay. When can I go home?"

"Not long now. Doctors coming after lunch."

"Not sticking more needles in me I hope?"

"Not today."

Tom looked out at the neat, regimented hospital gardens which were wearing a heavy mantle of mist.

"It'll be wonderful to go home again." He said softly.

"Is it beautiful, your home?" The nurse was looking at him, not at the garden.

"Very. I think so anyway."

"Lucky you." She backed, reluctantly, out of the doorway. "See you later."

The doctor gave Tom a cursory once over and told him he could go home the next day.

"No good you lying here being waited on hand and foot. You might get used to it."

Rick parked his Porsche in a space that said 'surgeons only' and bounced into the hospital.

"Hi." He hung over the reception desk, smelling of a strange combination of horses and Eternity for Men. "I've come to collect Mr. Chichester."

"I beg your pardon?" The white-haired receptionist looked over her bi-focals and eyed him with suspicion. "Are you the taxi driver?"

"Something like that!" Rick laughed. "Can you let him know that I'm here please?"

"I will." The receptionist picked up the 'phone. "It's Mary here at reception. I've got a boy here who says he's to pick up Mr. Chichester."

Boy? Thought Rick, Boy? With a wicked smile he went to take a seat, kicking his feet up onto the coffee table. A few minutes later a familiar figure emerged from the lift carrying a leather overnight bag.

"Well, hello big boss!" Rick crossed his legs and saluted. "How are you doing?"

"I'll be doing a lot better when you take this damn bag off me!"

"Why? You're not an invalid." Rick lounged in the chair.

"There's plenty of work waiting for you at home."

"Move it." Grinned Tom. "Unless you want to spend the rest of the season in here yourself!"

The fresh air was the best medicine that Tom could have been prescribed. With the window wound right down he took in great gulps of clean Cotswold morning.

"That's better. I hate hospitals. They stink."

"Me too." Rick was speeding around the narrow lanes. "Every time I'm inside one a part of me hurts!"

"How is everything at the yard?"

"You should know!" Laughed Rick. "I've never answered so many 'phone calls in my life! Everything's great, no problems. No that's not strictly true; there was a nasty morning when the cooker in the Coach House packed up. Gareth was refusing to work without food!"

"Sounds about right." Tom smiled. "What happened?"

"Mr. Benson changed the fuse. Cars I can handle, horses, maybe even women, but electrics are a nonstarter."

"Join the club. How's Runny?"

"Magnificent." Rick's voice mellowed as he moved onto one of his favourite subjects. "Awesome. He's jumping out of his skin. Those couple of days holiday have put him right back on the rails. You'd think he'd never even run in the Gold Cup."

"Good." Tom was closing his eyes. "The mare?"

"I've told you all this before." Rick winced as he missed a gear. "She's fine. They are all fine!"

"I'm like an old mother hen." Tom reclined the seat. "Clucking over her chicks."

Rick smiled.

"There is one thing. Timepiece has gone."

"Gone!" Tom sat upright again.

"Home. Don't panic! His owners picked him up this

morning. Mike says he'll need a few months to recover fully from that back problem, so they took him home."

"Well financially that's a blow." Tom frowned. "But Gareth will rest at night now."

"So will I.," Laughed Rick. "I was glad to see the back of the old rogue."

The gates of Highford loomed ahead of them, and to Tom they had never looked so beckoning. The drive took them upwards through the valley to the house, which was basking in the only piece of sunshine for miles. Eleanor, who had been watching out for them, came down the steps accompanied by the two dogs, both barking and wagging tails. Squeaking in delight Spock put his little paws on Tom's knee as he opened the door.

"Kettle's on." His mother smiled. "Come on you dogs. Behave yourselves."

The house was warm but pleasantly airy after the stuffy atmosphere of the hospital. After putting his bag in his room Tom headed for the kitchen where voices were only just audible above the noise of crockery being laid on the table. He stopped as the sight of Ned Benson met his eyes.

"Hello Ned." He moved to the Aga, savouring its homely warmth. "I didn't expect to see you."

"I'm sure you didn't. The court is in recess. The prosecutions key witness has changed his story. Without him their whole case weakens, so their lawyers are frantically searching for new evidence."

"Does it make a difference?" Tom took a cup of coffee. "I mean caught red handed is caught red handed, isn't it?"

"Your brother wasn't exactly 'caught' as you put it. He was named, along with four others, by the pushers that worked for them. He was picked up on his way to the next delivery. I believe these tacky American law shows call it 'the drop'."

"That's what we used to call hanging." Said Tom dryly.

"But surely it's the same thing? You don't mean he may get off?"

"Aren't you supposed to sound pleased?" Ned narrowed his eyes. "Not exactly, no. But he would be looking at a much more lenient penalty. This witness is the only real link between him and the orders from abroad. If he changes his story, it all becomes circumstantial. No one can prove that the delivery was on its way to him."

"Innocent until proven guilty." Tom looked out of the window. "Although with Dominic it should always be the other way around."

"Tom." His mother frowned. "Don't say that. He needs us to be on his side, not against him. He's on remand while they chase up this evidence. Ned says that he's in a bad way." Her voice broke slightly. "Don't you Ned?"

"Mentally yes." Ned helped himself to another biscuit. "He's under a lot of strain. Physically he's always been a wreck, hasn't he? But I think this has really got to him. Prison is not a pleasant place for someone of Dominic's temperament."

"Time something got to him." Tom wasn't to be moved.

"That's being pretty hard on the guy." Rick, home from home now, was putting his sock clad feet onto the Aga. "I was at Warwick yesterday. Brian told me the rumour is that Jack Coltrane is keeping Revelation in training purely because he has the deeds to both Dominic's flats. Lauren has persuaded Jack to let them stay at the one she gave him until she gets her house back. Basically she," He looked at Eleanor. "And of course, you, are all Dominic has got left. He lost the lot."

"Oh, don't expect me to feel sorry for him!" Tom snapped. "He's ruined more lives than I care to remember, and he very nearly finished this place. I'm going to the yard; I hope that my horses haven't lost their senses."

The group of people that remained in the kitchen were silent for some time after he had left.

"Have you mentioned it to him Eleanor?" Ned cleared his throat. "About Dominic coming here if I do get him out?"

"No. Eleanor collected the cups, avoiding Rick's eye. "That's one bridge I'll cross when I come to it."

The yard was in its usual state of post lunch slumber. Only Streak, with her insatiable curiosity was looking out to greet him. Swinging her nose from side to side she gave a deep whicker of greeting.

"Hello you." He pulled her ears gently. "Still on the lookout?"

On the opposite side of the yard Runny was in the middle of his siesta. Flat out on his bed, head resting against his manger, nose upwards, he was snoring loudly, lips flapping loose as he breathed. With his ears hanging sideways he looked like a mule, not a champion racehorse.

"No greeting from you then?" Tom leaned on the door and watched him sleep. A cough behind him made him turn around. Martin, alert has ever, had spotted him from the cottage.

"Hello Guv. Welcome home."

"Thanks Martin. It's good to be home. What's wrong with you?"

"'Flu." Martin moved to the door. "Lazy old pig." He said fondly.

Tom was looking around, taking in the immaculate yard. No one had been slack in his absence. Two stables were locked up, a sign that they were no longer needed. A third stood with both half doors wide open.

"Where's Enigma?" Tom frowned.

"At the old farm with Micky. I thought she might rest better away from all the activity."

"Good idea. How is she?"

"She thinks that there's nothing wrong with her! Jumping around like a two-year-old, silly mare, make it ten times worse if she was left to her own devices!" Martin looked at black cloud sitting on the hills. "Here it comes. In for a storm, they say".

Voices were coming down the cottage path. Tom's heart lurched at the sight of a familiar blonde head appearing over the gate. Poppy spotted him first and hesitated.

"You go on Kit. I've forgotten something."

"What?" Kitty was already halfway over the gate. "Oh."

"Go on!" Poppy was retreating, smiling broadly. "Give him a kiss!"

"Oh, shut up." Kitty dropped off the gate and straightened her ponytail.

"Hello." Her legs felt a little unsteady as she walked up to him.

"Hello." Tom's eyes roved over her figure. "How are you?"

"About the same as I was two days ago."

"Good." Tom gave her a peck on the cheek.

"Arm feeling better?" She muttered, embarrassed by this show of affection.

"Yes, well no. It feels strange. Heavy. I hope that you haven't picked up this 'flu Martin's suffering from."

"No." She shook her head.

"Glad to hear it. In that case you'll be well enough to come out for dinner tonight?"

"Yes please." She looked him in the eye for the first time and felt the usual heat growing in her belly.

Putting his arm around her he kissed her properly for the first time.

"You haven't said you missed me." He lifted her face to his.

"I didn't." Her eyes twinkled. "It's been quiet around here for a change."

"Cheek!" He laughed. "I'll pick you up at eight and give

you a good spanking for insubordination!"

The house was in darkness when he let them into the kitchen much later that evening. Kitty was still very wary of encroaching on this personal domain; even more so now that Rick was temporarily installed in one of the bedrooms. Spock bounded out of his basket to meet them, little claws clattering on the polished floor as he scampered around Tom's legs.

"I won't stay." Kitty wrestled with the little dog. "Just a coffee please."

"Why not?" Tom sat on the edge of the table and lifted her hand to his lips. "Would you really deny me what I've looked forward to most these past few days?"

"Yes." She grinned. "You're supposed to be recuperating."

"Getting my strength back." Tom leaned forward and began to slide his hand up her skirt.

Spock, intrigued by all this hand activity, jumped up and nipped Tom's wrist.

"Seems I'm outnumbered!" He laughed. "Spock is defending your honour! Coffee it is then. Then home to bed. Alone."

Ned was anxious. The crown's witness was sticking like glue to his revised version of events. Whoever had got to him had done a good job; but as the recess lengthened the strain on Dominic grew. He was visibly deteriorating. Facing Ned across the table his whole frame shook with nerves, his one hand constantly plucking the skin of the other until it turned blue.

"How much longer is this all going to take?" Dominic had bitten his lips, and his mouth was stained with blood.

"I can't say. Not too much longer."

"Can't stick this place much longer. If I have to stay in here, I'll top myself."

"Now don't be silly." Ned tried to sound calm, but there was something about the hunted expression in Dominic's eyes, an honesty in his voice, that frightened him.

"You have no idea what it's like in here." A particularly vicious tug had drawn blood. "I can't stay here. Locked up like an animal, no privacy, no room to breathe."

"Hold tight a bit longer Dommie." Ned reached out and stilled the damaging hand. "You'll soon be home."

"Home. Now that is a joke."

"Listen Dom, I've told you," Ned stopped when he realised that his words were falling on deaf ears. Dominic had switched off, staring into space, locked in a tormented world of his own. Ned nodded to the officer at the door and got to his feet.

"I have to go Dominic. I'll see you tomorrow."

There was no response.

On his way-out Ned stopped beside the Prison officer on guard.

"Keep an eye on him, will you? I really think he might do something stupid."

Watching the stooping figure being led away Ned had a feeling that he was in this on his own. No one else could help him get Dominic out of here, least of all Dominic himself.

The message on his answerphone told him that the court would resume its hearing at ten a.m. the following morning. He pondered this information for a moment, staring at the city skyline through his window. He had no idea what line the prosecution was going to take; had their witness decided to stand by his original testimony? Or was whatever had prompted his change of heart still driving him? Whichever it may be Ned could not rely on it. Dominic was right, he would not stand up to a term in prison; he was almost over the mental edge of stability now. If he ever had been stable. The thought struck Ned and lit up his path as clearly as if someone had turned on a light. Diminished responsibility. The living proof would be sitting right there in the dock.

Flicking through his diary, Ned found the name he was looking for. An old medical friend whose opinions were invaluable at times like this. Perhaps Dominic could help himself after all; perhaps his own precarious mental state would provide the key to his own freedom.

Eleanor finished her fourth whisky and paced another circuit of the study. Outside it was growing dark. Tom, close to the dwindling fire watched her progress in silence, knowing that his opinions were not welcome here. The 'phone rang. They both stared at one another, neither moving.

"Answer it, Tom." Eleanor caught hold of a chair and leaned heavily on it. "I can't."

Reluctantly Tom picked up the receiver. Eleanor stared at the floor, heart pounding, unable to breath. Eventually the soft click of the handset being replaced made her look up.

"Well?" She gasped.

"I don't believe it." Tom was shaking his head. "I don't bloody well believe it."

"What? What's happened?"

"You've got your wish mother. My little brother is going home."

"Thank God!" Eleanor collapsed into the chair. "I knew he hadn't done all those dreadful things!"

"You don't understand." Tom could not keep the bitterness from his voice. "They didn't find him not guilty. Ned's even more talented than I thought. He provided medical evidence that Dominic is unstable. I don't know how the wheels of legality work, but whatever sentence they impose will definitely be suspended because of his health. Apparently, he collapsed in the court, adding plenty of fuel to Ned's fire."

"Oh my God!" Eleanor's hands flew to her mouth. "At least he'll be here where I can look after him."

"What?" Tom turned, very slowly, to face her. "What did you say?"

Eleanor struggled to find the right words.

"He has to come here Tom. He's ill, isn't he? And he has nowhere else to go."

"While Jack has that horse, he's got a roof over his head."

"And who would look after him?"

"Lauren. If looking after people is her style, which I doubt. But I'm sure he'd cope."

"I'm his mother!" The whisky glass flew from Eleanor's hand and smashed into the hearth. "As long as I'm alive Tom Chichester this is my house. If I want my *son* here with me, the son *I* gave birth to, then you can't stop me. If you don't like it then you know what you can do!"

He stared at her with total incomprehension. It had been such a long time since she had lost her temper that he had forgotten how quickly she could react. There was no point in saying anything to her now. Picking up the fragments of broken glass he put them in the wastepaper bin.

"Very well then. Have it your way. But don't expect any help from me."

Without looking at her, failing to see how much it had hurt her to say those things to him, he walked out of the room.

Ned drove Dominic to Highford the next morning; all the while suppressing the dreadful sensation that he had somehow been made a fool of. Once outside the claustrophobia of London's streets Dominic had begun to change, visibly. Stretching out in the luxury of Ned's

Mercedes he had pulled off his dark tie and let it fly out of the window onto the hard shoulder. Kicking his shoes from his feet he scratched his heel, then rested it on the dashboard. With the seat reclined, he lay back and took deep breaths of the cool air that flowed through the window. Colour began to return to his cheeks.

"Dominic?" Ned studied him sideways as he drove. "Are you feeling okay?"

"Fine." Dominic grinned. "Any chance of stopping for a drink?"

"Pardon?" Ned pulled into the middle lane, suddenly finding it difficult to fully concentrate on his driving.

"A drink. You know, alcohol?"

"Do you think that's wise?" Ned shook his head.

"Shouldn't it be?" Dominic laughed. "I just thought that I would like to say thank you."

"That's nice of you but there's no need. Your mother will be waiting for you. She's worried sick about you. I think we should just get there as soon as possible, don't you?"

"What for?" Dominic yawned. "Here."

Ned looked at the piece of paper being thrust in front of him.

"What's this?"

"Address in Gloucester. Take me there, an old mate is going to put me up for a bit. I didn't think it too clever to go straight back to Lauren's. Not yet. Look too normal."

Without checking his mirror Ned cut in front of a Transit van and screeched to a halt on the hard shoulder.

"You set me up!" He roared.

"I thought it would make a change." Dominic grinned again.

"Now look here." Ned spluttered. "This just isn't bloody well on! You must have pulled a phenomenal piece of acting to get Phil Knight to sign that medical report. You even had him fooled! I don't know, don't want to know, how you did it; but your poor mother is falling apart in that house! She really thinks you've cracked up! If you tell her that this was another one of your scams it will break her heart. Like it or not Dominic, I'm taking you there. Now. What happens then is entirely up to you."

"Carry on." Dominic stared at him coldly. "And don't worry about my mother. She understands me, she's the only one who ever has. But don't go getting any ideas about going back to the court. You're in this as much as I am."

Ned glared at him for a second then crashed the car into gear. Why hadn't he listened to Tom? Because now this obnoxious bastard sitting next to him had him hung out over a barrel.

Tom watched Dominic's return from the safety of his bedroom window. He wanted to cause his mother as little stress as possible, but he couldn't stop the waves of loathing that beat at him as he watched his brother getting out of the car. Squinting, he peered through the glass, studying the emaciated, red eyed caricature that emerged. Shocked, he stepped back. Surely that could never be his conceited, arrogant, spiteful brother? Amazed, horrified he watched the stooping figure walking to the house, leaning on their mother's arm. Ned was getting back into his car. From his expression Tom could see that something was wrong. Curiosity overcoming him, putting Ned's anxiety down to what he had just seen himself, he crept downstairs to the kitchen; hovering outside he listened to the voices that came through the door.

"You must eat something darling."

"No thank you. Just a drink. Then I'll go to bed. I'm tired." Even the voice had changed. But warning bells kept ringing in Tom's head. Don't trust him. Don't believe him. Remember this is your brother. Tom shook himself. Even Dominic couldn't be capable of what he was thinking.

Taking a deep breath, he went to go in and join them. Then he hesitated as his mother started speaking.

"Now don't worry about Tom. I'll see to him." Her voice was high pitched and emotional. "I just want you here where I can keep an eye on you and get you better. Tom just still thinks of you as a naughty child that's all. He's so different from you and I; he's just like his father. While there are horses Tom will never need people. He'll never need anyone to take care of him."

Listening to her words Tom leaned weakly against the wall. Even after all this time his mother didn't really understand him. He did need people. Far more than she realised. Far more than he had ever realised; he just didn't know how to let it show.

The food on the table remained uneaten. Tom had fed himself whisky and Dominic hadn't moved from his room. Eleanor, having no great appetite of her own, scraped the meat into the dog's bowl and wished that Rick had left Bozo with her. She was not the only one who missed his cheering stupidity; Spock was sitting at the kitchen door, waiting patiently for his friend's return. Tom got to his feet and headed for the door.

"Bed already dear?" Eleanor looked up, desperate for someone to talk to.

"No. Just out for a while."

Tom went to the front door and hesitated. He knew that his mother needed his company; but he felt hurt and betrayed. He needed space, away from the house and everything in it. But he had no idea where to go, even less how to get there. To fall into Kitty's ever welcoming arms was too easy; he would find no comfort in them tonight. The solitary animal in him wanted to brood alone. Picking up the keys of his car he went and let himself into the driver's seat. He could just, if he was very careful, balance the steering wheel with his fingers as he changed gear. It hurt, but he could no longer stand the feeling of invalidity. Turning on the engine he drove slowly, and awkwardly,

357

down to the drive and into the lanes.

"Where's he off too at this hour?" Poppy watched the BMW creeping along from the bedroom window. "And without you as well!"

"Who knows?" Kitty was fighting Bozo for her bed. "Will you please get this dog off my pillow?"

Poppy caught Bozo's collar and yanked him to the floor.

"Where do you think it will all end? You and him I mean, me and Rick?"

"In tears Martin says." Kitty wriggled under the duvet. "And he's probably right."

In his room Dominic lay on his bed and stared at the ceiling.

He heard Tom go out, and, much later, heard his mother climb the stairs to bed. When all was quiet, he crept to her bedroom door and peered in. She was fast asleep. Easing the door back onto the catch he moved, light footed as a cat, along the hall and down the stairs. Sitting on the floor, hidden by the shadows, eyes fixed on the front door, he pulled the 'phone onto his lap. Huddled over the receiver he waited impatiently for a reply, kicking at the hall stand with his bare foot.

"Lauren?" He whispered. "It's me. No, I'm at my mother's house. What? No, I'm fine, really. Don't you worry about me. Look, this will only be for a little while; but can you send some of my things? My credit cards? Those papers too, you know where they are." He paused, listening to the voice at the other end.

"Yes." He hissed. "I am going through with it. I need that money to get away from here. To get both of us away. Just do as I ask, okay?"

He listened for a while longer and then interrupted.

"I have to go Lauren. Send me those papers, quickly. Yes." Another pause. "Yes, I do still love you. You just have to trust me."

Replacing the receiver he stood upright, catching sight of his reflection as he did. Staring at himself, he frowned, and then a broad smile of satisfaction spread across his face. Creeping back to his room he stifled a laugh, as, opening the wardrobe door, he found the well-hidden bottle of vodka.

The next morning Martin was finishing his routine check of the yard when he heard the sound of an engine on the drive. Curious, wary of early morning press invasions, he went to the yard gate. The BMW was purring along the gravel; its dishevelled, distinctly hungover driver puling at his hair and rubbing his stubbled cheeks. Martin raised his eyebrows. It had been a long time since he had seen his employer in this state. He had believed that Tom's newfound contentment with Kitty had put a stop to these all-night sessions. He must have been wrong. Turning, he found Ryan behind him watching the same thing.

"Back to his old self, is he?" Ryan echoed Martin's thoughts. "I thought he couldn't drive yet. Got to hand it to him, his timing couldn't be better!"

"Kitty won't think so." Martin went back to his rounds. "Best to say nothing."

Kitty, however, badly smitten, needed no words to inform her of her man's change of attitude. One look at Tom's face as he entered the yard much later that morning told her the full story. Biting her lip, she let Martin leg her up into Prince's saddle and avoided Poppy's inquiring eyes.

"Slap me if I'm wrong." Poppy muttered. "But I thought you slept in your own bed last night?"

"I did." There was a tremor in Kitty's voice. "But I can

show you someone who didn't."

"Don't worry." Poppy leaned out of Streak's saddle and patted her friend's arm. "Don't read too much into it. He's bound to react badly when he's got the brother from hell in residence. Talk to him before you judge him."

"Wise words." Kitty smiled sheepishly. "Which I know you wouldn't follow if the rules were reversed."

"Half day today. Poppy brightened. "Nothing like spending your salary to cheer you up!"

"It might take more than that." Kitty turned Prince out of the yard. "But I'll give it a try."

Tom watched the conversation from a distance. His reckless attempt at driving had left him in a lot of pain, which his painkillers weren't touching. But far worse, far more distressing to his tired brain was the memory, vague as it was, of the night before. He couldn't remember her name, or even where he had found her; but it had been good, very good. Until now. Now, when he saw the hurt and bewilderment in Kitty's blue eyes it was rapidly becoming a nightmare. His already ebbing spirits sinking even lower, he went to join Martin in the Land Rover.

CHAPTER TWENTY-FOUR

Poppy heaved her bulging mass of carrier bags onto the seat beside her and blew out her lips.

"Phew." She puffed. "That was hard work. Good old retail therapy. I'm just about spent out; I think I've enough for a glass of lager and a ham roll."

"I'm skint too." Kitty surveyed her empty purse. "At least you still have someone to take you out and spend money on you. I haven't. Not anymore."

"Oh rubbish!" Poppy hung her denim jacket on the back of her chair. "Minor hiccup that's all. Haven't been in this pub for months, have we? I'm sure the curtains used to be green and not blue?"

"Blue suits me." Kitty got to her feet. "Stella? Or are you too poor?"

"Not quite. Ham salad roll please." Poppy's face changed. "Oh, hang on Kit. Don't go yet."

"Why?" Kitty looked at the bar. "It's not busy."

As she spoke her eyes fell on a long lean figure opposite them. Sitting alone he was staring into an empty glass. As she watched him, frozen to the spot, throat tightening, he looked up. The blank stare barely registered their presence before it returned to the glass.

"Come on." Poppy took her hand. "Let's go somewhere else."

"No." Replied Kitty firmly, astounded at her own bravery. "I can't spend the rest of my life dancing around the bloody Chichester's. I came in here for a drink and I'm going to have one!"

Poppy watched the small, slender figure as it weaved through the tables to the bar and felt her heart going out to her. Kitty was going through hell, she knew she was, but it seemed to have set off some new spark of resolution in her character that had been absent before. Looking at Kitty's flushed face as she stood at the bar Poppy saw a new glint of determination in her eyes. Perhaps Kitty wasn't the soft, love-struck character that they had all thought she was. Or perhaps the events of the past few months had just started a change in her. Shaking her head, she looked across the room at Dominic, who feeling her resentful eyes on him, looked up and returned her stare. Scarlet, Poppy turned quickly away. She hated to admit it, even to herself, but she still found him attractive. A roll appeared on the table in front of her.

"You, okay?" Kitty frowned.

"Yeah." Poppy shook herself. "Just thinking. You?"

"Oh, I'm fine." Kitty sat down, facing Dominic, and opened her crisps. "Didn't expect to see him in a pub. I thought he'd had a nervous breakdown?"

"So, they said." Poppy's mouth was full of roll. "Personally, I don't think he's capable. Only people with feelings have breakdowns. He hasn't got any."

"Oh, I expect he has." Kitty replied. "But they're probably all focused on himself. Like his brother."

"Hell!" Poppy sat up straight and stiffened. "He's coming over!"

The sensation of Deja vu was so strong that Kitty thought she would faint. She watched Dominic pull up a chair, sit down, look first at Poppy and then at herself. She waited for the cold wash of panic and revulsion that his presence normally instigated and was surprised to find it absent. Dominic's black eyes turned down to the table.

"I owe a lot of people apologies." He began meekly. "But you most of all."

"We don't want to know!" Poppy snapped. "Come on Kit let's go!"

"No wait." The new, bold Kitty, free of terror and intimidation narrowed her eyes. "I think I'd quite like to hear this."

Dominic looked up, startled. There was an edge to Kitty's voice that he hadn't anticipated.

"Well come on then." She was leaning back in her chair, eyes never wavering as she stared at him "I'm waiting."

"I'm sorry for what I did to you." He mumbled. "And for everything else. I'm not proud of myself. I wish I could turn the clock back but can't. I know there's no way you can ever understand, or to forgive me."

"Too bloody right!" Poppy interrupted, jumping to her feet, her hackles rising. "Do you think our memories are that short? Do you think we can forget what you did to her? Or Runny and the King George? You and that scheming bitch!"

"She had nothing to do with it." Dominic's eyes flicked up slowly. "It was all me."

"Probably." Kitty spoke slowly. "I feel sorry for her. I know what it's like to be controlled by a Chichester."

"Do you?" Dominic lowered his eyes again. "You should have met my father. He was the master of the art."

"Oh, I'm not staying to listen to this crap anymore! You pretending to be sorry! You are just wallowing in self-pity you bastard" Poppy snapped. "Are you coming Kitty? Kit? KITTY!"

"In a moment." Kitty reached for her bag. "Have you finished?"

She spoke to Dominic.

"There's nothing else I can say, is there?"

"No." Kitty put on her jacket. "There isn't."

Stepping past him she bent to pick up her shopping, brushing against him as she did so and catching the familiar smell of leather and aftershave. Jerking upright she stood, trembling, as memories battered at her brain. The taste of him, of his lips, crushing against hers; the feel of his bare skin, the terror. He was watching her, waiting, studying her reactions. She could feel her pulse quickening as she looked at him.

Dominic saw the colour in her cheeks, saw the emotions flickering in her eyes and reached out. Gently he closed his hand around her wrist.

"I really am sorry." He spoke too quietly for Poppy to hear him. "Believe me."

"So, you said." The feeling of his fingers in her wrist was like a ring of fire burning her skin.

"I wish I could make it up to you."

"You can't." She gently removed her wrist, relieved to feel his grip loosen so easily.

"Don't waste yourself on my brother." Dominic got to his feet, towering over her. "You deserve better than him. He's too selfish. He'll never satisfy you."

Kitty looked at him, straight into the fierce black eyes. His words made her think of Tom, and what she had to face in the morning.

"You're right." She said quietly. "He won't."

"If." Dominic hesitated, lowering his voice even more. "If I had been kinder to you, used a different approach, could the result have been different? Would you have ever been interested in me and not him?"

"Maybe." Kitty couldn't look at him, shocked at the words that were coming out of her own mouth. Was that her speaking or someone else, some scheming stranger? "Probably."

"What about now?" Dominic's stare intensified as he saw the pulse in her neck quickening.

"Who knows." Kitty turned away.

Dominic watched her go and smiled to himself. So far so good. But he had to be very careful not to give himself away.

Outside, Poppy was open mouthed with disbelief.

"I don't believe what I just saw!" She gasped. "You were giving him the come on! After what he did! Now he'll think that you fancy him after all!"

"So!" Kitty snapped. "Tell me that you don't?"

Poppy didn't answer but began walking along the street. She had a feeling that Kitty had just put the ball into play in a very dangerous game. But she had to admit, if getting back at Tom was what Kitty wanted; there could be no better way of doing it.

Tom paced the office floor and stared at the clock. They should have been back by now. He had given up all pretence of working long ago and was watching the cottage like a hawk.

He had to speak to Kitty. He had to try and talk his way out of this, try to explain to her what he didn't understand himself. At first, he had tried to make himself believe that he didn't care if his actions had ruined their relationship; but now he knew that wasn't true. And that he would do anything he could to save it.

The dusk was closing in on the yard when they finally returned. Shadows filled the unlit room he stood in, the lights from the loose boxes glowing orange on the misty air. He watched the two figures walking to the cottage. Holding his breath, he waited until the kitchen light came on and then followed them.

Kitty answered the door herself.

"Oh." She said coldly. "Can I help you Mr. Chichester?"

Tom caught her arm and pulled her out of the doorway.

"I have to talk to you Kitty." He whispered. "Come over to the office?"

Kitty didn't move.

"Kitty." Tom sighed. "Please?"

"Five minutes." She closed the door behind her and walked mute beside him.

"Look." He turned on the office light and launched into his speech almost before she had entered the room. "I might have made a real mess of this, but I just want to say that I'm sorry."

"Wow!" She interrupted. "Two apologies in one day. I am honoured!"

Tom looked at her, not understanding, and carried on.

"You know how I feel about you Kitty. I don't want to lose you. Please give me another chance?"

"Why? What have you done?" Kitty looked at him, completely calm.

"You know what I've done, don't you?" He said desperately.

"No." She was glaring at him, her eyes belying her words.

"Last night," He paused, unable to bring himself to admit it. "I, last night I went out. I.."

"I want to hear you say it!" She screamed at him. "Go on say it? Or are you too much of a coward?"

"Alright!" He was shouting too. "I slept with someone else!"

Even though she knew it, even though she had forced this confession out of him, it still hurt to hear his confession and tears sprang to her eyes.

"And I am so, so sorry." He caught her hand. "I was drunk. I know it's the most pathetic, over used excuse in the world but it's true. I honestly didn't really understand what I was doing until it was too late. I've regretted it ever since. Please forgive me Kitty. I promise it will never, ever happen again."

The closeness of his body, the warm, familiar smell of him, touched her most basic senses and despite her pride, her injured feelings she collapsed against him, desperate to be close to him. His face was in her hair.

"I'm so sorry darling." He knew that he was repeating himself but didn't know what else to say. "Let me take you out somewhere, let me try and explain it to you?"

Explain? He thought. How could he explain what he didn't understand his actions himself?

Pressing her cheek against his chest, feeling his strength and solidity, Kitty began to feel calmer. He still wanted her, so what else mattered? She had waited so long for this man, was she really going to give up on him that easily? She lifted her head, and his mouth came down onto hers. Then she realised, with a pain that was almost too strong to bear, that last night someone else had felt the same thing; someone else had known the solid warmth of his flesh on theirs, the sensation of his gentle lips, his caressing hands. With a sob that wrenched from deep inside her she jerked away, covering her face with her hands.

"No." She gasped. "Not tonight. I need to have some time I have to think about this."

She looked at him, her eyes filled with tears.

"I can't bear to think of you with someone else."

"Don't." He caught hold of her again. "It was nothing, I swear. It didn't mean anything. It never happened."

"But it did." She sobbed. "And I have to think about it and decide whether or not I can live with it."

Tom stepped back, distressed by the hurt in her voice.

"Tomorrow then." He said softly. "I'll pick you up at eight."

He laid his fingers softly on her lips and stood back to let her pass.

From the office door he watched her walking away with a heavy heart.

Kitty bathed and washed her hair and settled down in the kitchen with a mug of chocolate and the latest copy of Horse and Hound. She was reading the Point-to-Point results, looking, as she always did, for horses that she knew, when she heard something fall through the letter box. Looking out of the door she saw a folded piece of blue paper lying on the mat. Padding barefoot into the hall she picked it up. It had her name on it, written in a bold, black hand. Looking back over her shoulder she took it into the kitchen.

"What was that Kit?" Martin called from the living room.

"For me." She called back. "Nothing important."

Sitting back down at the table she opened the note and stared at the words. "Kitty." It read. "About what I said. I mean it. I hope that you did too. I want to make it all up to you if you're willing. I'll be at the yard gate at nine thirty. Nothing suspicious I promise. A different approach, remember. Trust me if you can."

Kitty looked out of the window into the darkness and trembled. She knew that this was what she had been playing for that afternoon. She knew that then she may have gone through with it. But now? Her memories of that terrible night came flooding back. She couldn't do it.

She was about to drop the note into the bin when in her mind she saw Tom with a faceless female in his arms; and knew that she could.

Only Poppy had the slightest suspicion where Kitty was going when she left the cottage an hour later. Shaking her head in disbelief she lay back on the sofa and closed her eyes.

Dominic was waiting in the white E type, the only thing he could still truly claim to be his own. Dressed in a black polo shirt, black jeans, and his leather jacket he had slicked his hair back from his temples and smelt of Obsession for Men.

"I didn't think you'd come." He stared at her.

"Neither did I." She replied, not looking at him. "I don't know why I did."

"I do." Dominic pulled off. "To get at my brother."

She looked at him this time, feeling the old apprehension returning as she saw his face. "Why are you here?"

"To say sorry?" Dominic gave his leering smile. "And for the same reason."

"Good." Kitty took a deep breath. "As long as we know where we stand."

It was strange, and a little unnerving, driving home with him later that evening. He had taken her to a small country Pub some miles outside Tewkesbury, bought everything she had asked for and been polite and courteous all night. No innuendo, no sexual hints, or tensions. A real gentleman. And all the while she had found herself becoming more and more relaxed, more and more at ease in his company, until by the time they left she was completely confused.

"So, tell me." Dominic drove steadily through the narrow, twisting, lanes, one hand resting lightly on the gear stick. "Did I pass?"

"Pass what?" Kitty looked at his profile, pale in the dashboard light.

"The test. Do you think that you hate me a little less now?"

"I don't know." Kitty was still watching him, feeling the same, strange quickening of her pulse that she had experienced earlier. "It's too early to say."

"Does that mean I can take you out again?" He glanced at her.

"Maybe." Kitty quickly averted her gaze and looked out of the window.

But by the time that Dominic turned into Highford's long drive she knew that if he asked her, she would go. Pulling up outside the gate Dominic leaned over to open her door and let his hand rest gently on her leg. Kitty tensed, then relaxed as he made no move to take it any further.

"Good night." He smiled.

"Good night." She hesitated.

"Tomorrow?"

She shook her head.

"No?" He smiled, a different smile; warm, genuine.

"The night after." She rushed. "The same time."

"Good." He put both hands back on the steering wheel. "Don't work too hard."

Kitty got out of the car and watched him drive away. Turning into the cottage she felt frustration creeping over her. She didn't know what she had expected but it certainly hadn't been that. Tension? Arguments? She had at least expected him to try and kiss her. But his polite and considerate actions had completely thrown her. Feeling no satisfaction at all in her twisted attempt of revenge, she went inside.

CHAPTER TWENTY-FIVE

For the next five days Kitty lived a strange triple existence that felt completely wrong and gave her no comfort. The few nights that she spent with Tom were difficult, as she shied away from any physical contact, her imagination constantly taunting her. The nights she spent with Dominic were even more difficult; he had made no moves on her at all, which left her feeling strangely frustrated. Her scheme for revenge wasn't exactly working out as she had planned. There were moments when her memory expanded, and she cringed at her own intentions. But for the biggest part of her time with him the past was temporarily forgotten as Dominic wove his own peculiar web of charm around her, making her own self-imposed task that much easier to bear.

Her third existence, and oddly the one that she had the greatest problem with, was her day-to-day life at the yard. Only Poppy suspected where she went at night but kept her thoughts to herself. Kitty, only feeling totally at ease when with the horses, threw herself into her work, and prayed that she wouldn't give herself away.

Things finally came to a head on the Tuesday evening when, drying herself after her bath, tight with the nervous anticipation that the prospect of a meeting with Dominic always invoked, she heard voices at the door.

"She's in the bath." Poppy was saying. ""I'll tell her that you're here."

Kitty heard the door closing and the sound of footsteps running up the stairs.

"Kit." Poppy's voice was low and urgent. "Tom's downstairs. He wants to see you."

Kitty opened the door, hair hanging wet over her bare shoulders.

"What?" She looked down the stairs. "But I'm not expecting him tonight. What should I do? Can't you get rid of him for me? I'm going out and I'm late already."

"Do your own dirty work." Poppy answered shortly. "I'm off with Rick, in fact I can hear his car. You made this mess Kitty; you can bloody well clean it up."

Kitty saw her steamy reflection in the bathroom mirror and looked into the eyes of a stranger. What was she doing? She felt as though she no longer knew herself. Her hair was dripping water onto her neck, cold and wet on her flushed skin. Had she played this stupid game for long enough? Nothing had been achieved by it; Tom merely thought that he had driven her away, and Dominic believed that she had forgotten what he had tried to do her. Poppy quite simply thought she was an idiot. Was she? Or was she really going to get satisfaction from this new, alien side of her nature. She doubted it. The only mental, or physical satisfaction she ever had was with the man that was waiting for her downstairs. She bent to pick up her clothes.

Then she thought of Dominic. Of the black magnetism that had somehow taken hold of her; she thought of him dressing at that moment, getting ready to pick her up, she thought of the distress that Tom would feel if he knew where she was intending to go. She thought, yet again, of the faceless female who had known the sensation of Tom's body against hers.

One more night. She told herself. One more night and then I'll sort this mess out. Without bothering to dress, knowing full well the effect she would have on him, she went to tell Tom that she was on her way out.

Dominic ran his eyes over the slender body that sat beside him and felt his adrenalin begin to pump. He had been so very restrained with this girl; something that was completely alien to his nature, and his sexual appetite was at its most ravenous limit. Watching her sipping her drink he could see an alcoholic flush colouring her cheeks. Perhaps tonight he could finally move past the first base where he had been stranded.

Kitty, watching him from beneath the safety curtain of her hair, saw the gleam in his eyes and felt her spine grow cold. She had been thinking of how best to resolve this ridiculous situation, without really knowing what she wanted from it. Some perverse, uncharacteristic side of her nature had harboured the idea of a sexual encounter with Dominic, almost encouraged it. But the real Kitty, the one that wasn't being driven by pain and jealousy was terrified of such an ordeal and looking at him now she saw that tonight she was going to have to face it. Sinking the rest of her drink in one large mouthful she pushed the glass towards him.

"Another?" He glanced at the clock. "Or have you had enough?"

"Not yet." She smiled sweetly. "Make it a double."

Dominic got to his feet, eyes never moving off her face.

"Dutch courage?" He lifted an eyebrow.

"What would I want that for?" Kitty smiled. "Hurry up."

Watching him leaning on the bar, long legged, surveying the rest of the room with his usual disdain, she felt her stomach beginning to churn. Aware of her eyes on him he turned, and his dark brows lowered into a frown. His face was ashen tonight; the blue shadows of his eyes standing out vividly above his sharp cheekbones. A ghoul, she thought. But a good looking one. She wondered, not for the first time, about his new, gentlemanly behaviour. Was it due to his breakdown? Or was it all an act? And to what end? He was returning with her drink.

"There you go." he placed in front of her.

"Thank you." She took a large mouthful.

"You're looking very serious." Dominic sat beside her. "What's on your mind?"

"You." She answered truthfully. "I was feeling guilty because I hadn't asked how you were feeling. I mean you seem well enough to me."

"Do I?" Dominic smiled. "I don't think I am. I'm not quite myself at the moment."

No, thought Kitty, I agree with that. The old Dominic would never have taken a girl out three times unless he was having sex with her. Her thoughts turned abruptly back to the situation in hand. Perhaps this last double wasn't such a good idea, she may need her reflexes to stay sharp.

Sometime later, as they cruised through the lanes, feeling more relaxed as they neared home, she was just closing her eyes when she felt the car come to a halt.

"Where are we?" She sat bolt upright, staring into the darkness around her.

"Sorry." Dominic was getting out of the car. "Nature calls."

On his return, he made no attempt to start the engine but turned up the radio and leaned back in his seat, watching her. Kitty stared back; her heart pumping so hard that the soft wool of her jumper flapped against her stomach. Dominic saw it and placed his hand over it, holding the material flat to her skin.

Kitty's spine arched away from his touch.

"You still don't trust me." He spoke quietly.

"No." Kitty's mouth was dry. "I'm not sure I trust myself."

Dominic leaned forward, very slowly, and kissed her pulsing neck. His lips were cool on her hot skin. Startled, she turned her head to him, to speak and found the same cool lips on her mouth. A thousand alarm bells sounded in her head at the taste of him, and, revolted by herself as much as the memory, she turned her head away.

"What am I doing?" She gasped.

Dominic caught her chin and turned her head gently back to face him.

"I told you I wouldn't hurt you." He said softly, his voice hypnotic. "And I won't. This goes at your pace. I only want to please you."

Kitty turned away again and stared into the blackness outside. She was shaking from head to foot. She couldn't do it. Now, when the stakes were laid on the table, she couldn't do it. Tears stung her eyes. She had played this macabre charade to its limit and couldn't finish the game. Looking back at him; pale faced, silent, she saw him as the attractive companion she had known for the past week, not the fiend of her nightmares. She could smell his skin, feel the heat coming from his body. He had the same smell as his brother. The brother she had loved, still loved; the brother who had taken her adoration and unquestioning faith and betrayed it. The brother she wanted to hurt. He was the reason she was here, and the reason that she couldn't finish what she had started. Even now, he was still in control. Desperation rose and clutched at her heart, throwing her arms around Dominic's neck she kissed him fiercely.

"Jesus!" He muttered. "Who's unstable?"

Her sudden display of passion took him by surprise. Letting her kiss, him, he slowly moved his hand around her body to caress her spine. Cautious, he was delighted to find her flatten against him, pressing her body against his. She was kissing his mouth, his cheeks, his neck, undoing the buttons of his shirt and kissing the smooth boyish skin of his chest. He gave a groan of pleasure as her hands dived inside his shirt exposing his flesh to the night air and her gentle, exploring fingers. Encouraged, he lifted her jumper to bare her flat stomach, his had sliding upwards towards her breast. His heart began to race as his lust took over; this was what he did best.

Kitty, totally absorbed in her own excitement, found herself responding to his every touch, writhing, and squirming beneath his insistent hands. Only when he began to pull at her jeans, sliding them over her hips did she pull away from him. That was too much. She couldn't have sex with him. That was taking it too far. This was enough.

But not for him. Dominic could feel the soft skin of her belly beneath his palm and the sensation made his mind reel. She was so warm and welcoming. All he wanted was to have her. But, for the first time in his life, he needed her to feel the same, to share the desperate urgency.

"What?" His face was buried in her neck.

"Not yet." She pulled at his hand and felt a flood of relief when it moved.

"I told you." Dominic's voice was raw and husky. "I want to please you. Until you want me as much as I want you it doesn't happen."

Kitty straightened her jeans and did up the zip. She felt slightly sick now that the adrenalin rush of her excitement had faded. Dominic had laid his head on her shoulder and was drawing patterns on her stomach. It felt pleasant, and she relaxed. She could almost believe that he genuinely cared about her.

"Two more weeks." He was murmuring, more to himself than to her. "Two more weeks and it will all be over. Then I get my life back. Then I can get away, from *him*."

He lifted his head abruptly, looking at her with burning eyes.

"I want to share it with you." He said softly. "Come away with me."

"What?" Kitty's eyes widened.

"Come away with me. Two weeks, that's all, and then we can get as far away from this place as we like. Then you'll see my brother suffer. You want to see that, don't you?"

Dominic's newfound and alien feelings of care and affection were loosening his tongue. At that moment, curling her long hair around his fingers, he felt completely at ease with her, trusting, safe. It was an unfamiliar emotion. Part of that emotion was a desire to share everything with her, including his plans. He liked the thought of her standing beside him as he struck his final, crushing blow.

"Yes." Kitty answered him warily. His eyes were blank as he brooded on his inner thoughts. "But what are you going to do? What happens in two weeks?"

"You'll see." Dominic ran his finger down her cheek. "Don't you think of backing out of this and leaving me." His voice deepened, became more sinister, becoming the Dominic she feared. "Stay with me and I'll give you everything you ever wanted."

Sitting back in his seat he closed his fingers around the steering wheel.

"So. What's going to happen?" She asked lightly. "Can't you tell me now?"

"No." He said shortly. "It's not finalised yet. But I will. In fact, you could probably help me. I need someone he'll trust."

He looked at her.

"You."

Kitty drew away from him. She had never seen such malice on anyone's face in her life. This was the man that terrified her.

The rest of their journey was completed in silence. Her mind was racing, telling her to stop this now and end this dangerous game. Much as she wanted to hurt Tom, to get back at him for the pain he had caused her, Dominic's methods would be far outside the scope of her simple tit for tat revenge.

Which was why she knew she couldn't stop, not yet; she had to know what it was he planned to do.

"Sunday. Seven thirty." He pulled up outside the gate. "Sweet dreams."

Getting out of the car she stood in the drive and watched

the car disappear with a sinking heart. She had been careless, and stupid. She was caught in his web and, right now, she could see no way out.

Dominic opened the kitchen door to find a tall figure waiting for him on the other side.

"So, you thought you could play me for a fool." Tom spoke quietly. "Pretending to be asleep. Spending all those hours alone in your room. Poor sick Dominic. Poor sick Dominic who wasn't even in the bloody house!" His voice rose into a roar. "How could you lie to our mother like that!"

"I haven't." Dominic threw his leather jacket onto a chair. "I let Ned do all the talking. I just didn't contradict him."

Outraged, Tom grabbed at him, ready to give him the beating of his life. But as his hand closed on the black shirt a familiar smell caught his nostrils and held him back. A light, flowery smell. The smell that clung to him after he had lain in Kitty's arms. The smell of her perfume. Shocked, he stepped back, the colour draining from his face.

"Where have you been?" He whispered.

"Out." Dominic was smiling. "With a friend."

"Who?" Tom's heart was thumping.

"Just a friend." Dominic stepped past him, gave him one last, mocking smile, and went upstairs.

Tom stood in the kitchen and could have sworn that the ground was moving beneath his feet. Breathing in he still caught the faint smell in the air. A million women probably wore that perfume. But here, in this village? Of course, they did, and he didn't know where Dominic had been. He could have been anywhere. But his instinct told him otherwise. He shook himself. Kitty could never do what he suspected her of. It was impossible. But her attitude towards him had changed, she was distant, out of his reach. But that? He had driven her away from him, he accepted that. Just how far would the hurt she felt drive her? How far would she be prepared to go?

Going to his study he poured a large whisky. No, this couldn't be possible. He shook his head violently. The one way to find out was to go to the cottage, now, and face her. But he was too afraid. So, he stayed where he was and drank; and the seed of suggestion, now firmly implanted in his brain, continued to grow.

The atmosphere in the yard was so heavy you could have cut it with a knife. Tom, eyes dark and unforgiving, blasted his way through morning stables. He cornered Martin as he changed Olympic Run's rugs. The horse, in the peak of his fitness, not a gleaming hair out of place, turned to greet him. Even the sight of the noble head, the dark trusting eyes, couldn't touch Tom's troubled heart.

"Not long now boss." Martin saw the tension in the man's face and misread the reasons. "Eleven days from now and we'll be in the winner's enclosure at Aintree."

"Will we?" In his current frame of mind Tom couldn't share his optimism and didn't really care.

"Of course, we will!" Martin looked at him in amazement. "Don't give up on him now boss! As long as he gets there in one piece, and he will because I'll make sure of it, he'll win the double for us."

"You really think that it's as easy as that Martin?" Tom shook his head. "Don't you think others have all thought the same thing? None of them succeeded."

"They didn't have Runny." Nothing could dent Martin's confidence. "He's the best there's ever been."

Tom screwed up his nose and looked glumly at the horse.

"Maybe. Only time will tell. I'll leave you to get on with your work Martin."

Watching him walk away, stern faced, his plastered arm in its sling, martin shook his head.

"What on Earth is wrong with him?" He asked Poppy

as she passed. "This time last year he would have done cartwheels in the nude for a horse like Runny!"

"No idea." Poppy lied. thinking that she knew all too well what the cause of Tom's black mood was.

"Nervous I expect." She bolted Streak's door. "Let's have breakfast."

She collared Kitty in the tack room.

"He knows, doesn't he?" She hissed.

"Knows what?" Kitty turned scarlet.

"About you and the poisonous brother. He must have told him."

"No. He wouldn't." Kitty sat weakly on the rug box. She didn't want to talk about this, to face the situation, or Dominic's sinister hints of revenge on his brother. She had to find out what it was he was planning, then she would know what to do.

"Ha!" Poppy snorted. "How the hell do you know that? I thought that was what you wanted, to get back at Tom."

"It was. To begin with." Kitty chewed her nail. "I was so jealous that I didn't care who it was I used to get back at him. It just happened to be Dominic. He was the first one who came along. And yes, it made me feel good that someone else was interested in me. That it wasn't just Tom who could pick someone up whenever they felt like it. That night when Dominic dropped off the note I just went. All I could think of was what Tom had done. He didn't care about me, did he? I just wanted to stab him back. But now it's all gone wrong. it's become, well, complicated."

"You can say that again." Poppy sat beside her. Although she thoroughly disapproved of Tom's infidelity, she would never understand what Kitty was doing. "I don't feel I know you anymore. You've changed so much. When I think of that night, I mean how can you do it?"

Kitty got up, tears glowing in her eyes. At that moment she hated both men, wished she had never set eyes on a Chichester. She would do anything in her power to see them both suffer. But she had a feeling that whatever Dominic was planning had something to do with the yard. She couldn't sit back and see him ruin all their hard work. She owed it to herself, to Poppy, to Martin and most of all to the horses to find out what he intended to do. Then she had to try and stop it. She had put her relationship with Tom way beyond the boundaries of repair anyway, so what did it matter if she saw Dominic again. Poppy was watching her, still waiting for an explanation.

"I can't tell you why Pop because I don't know myself. But I have to see him again."

"You don't actually like him, do you?" Poppy narrowed her eyes.

"Sometimes I believe I do." Kitty stared bleakly out of the window. "He's certainly got something about him." She halted as she saw a familiar figure approaching.

"Oh no!" She gasped. "Let's get out of here!"

"Why?" Poppy got to her feet and saw the same thing. She laid her hand on Kitty's arm.

"You have to face him sometime Kit. It may as well be now. I think he wants to have it out with you and the sooner you get it over with the better."

Ducking past the man in the doorway Poppy avoided his eyes. Tom, giving Kitty a look that would have soured cream, shut the door with a bang. Even now, just being alone with him made her feel weak, and she sat back down on the trunk. Tom had locked the door. He stared at her for a long time before he spoke.

"Have you or have you not." He said abruptly. "Screwed my brother?"

"No." She looked up, startled by his directness. "I haven't."

"But you have been seeing him, haven't you?"

"Why do you say that?" Kitty asked. "I think that if you're going to accuse me of something you should explain yourself!"

"Your perfume." The pain Tom felt showed in his face as he spoke. "When he came in last night, he was smelling of your perfume."

"Is that all!" Kitty gasped. The relief was incredible. For a second, she thought of talking her way out of it. But the old, honest Kitty was stronger than the new devious one.

"I have been seeing him." She admitted. "Once or twice."

"Why?" Tom's voice was unsteady.

"Because of what you did!" She sobbed. "You just went out and screwed a stranger. So, I decided to try it. Only the first person to ask me wasn't a stranger. And I couldn't do it. I'm not like you. However, much I wanted to do what you had I couldn't. But I still wanted to hurt you."

"Well you have." He said coldly.

"Well you hurt me!" She screamed. "I worshipped the bloody ground that you walked on. I would have done anything for you, anything, and you threw it back in my face!"

"And I've spent hours and hours apologising ever since." He snapped. "I've never regretted anything more in my life. I thought that we may repair what we had, but you've ruined that."

"Have I?" Panic struck her and she wanted to throw herself into his arms and beg forgiveness, but his eyes, so cold and unforgiving, held her back.

"Yes. You have."

He was turning away from her. He was going to walk away and leave her alone with her breaking heart.

"Tom!" She begged, "Please, don't go!"

When he turned the look in his eyes was so hard that she shrank back.

"Goodbye Kitty." He said calmly and left her.

Revenge was not sweet at all. In fact, it tasted sour. In her attempt to hurt Tom, she had only hurt herself. Far more than she had thought possible.

Rick, tucked up in a human ball beneath the duvet, watched Poppy pacing the room and asked her for the tenth time to get into bed. Unable to tell him the full story, she had filled him in on Kitty's break up with Tom. Although she had confided in him that Kitty had been seeing someone else, she could not bring herself to tell him who.

"Relax." Rick yawned. "They'll get over it."

"Not this time." Poppy sat beside him. "This is the end."

"You forgave me." He pulled her down beside him. "We came through."

"I know." Poppy turned to him and felt her heart swelling with love. "But maybe we are stronger than they are."

CHAPTER TWENTY-SIX

Dominic was asleep. Curled up in the cramped confines of his car, head on her chest, he had given up trying to persuade her to have sex with him and drifted off to sleep. Kitty, who was wishing herself anywhere but here, stared out at the night, tears falling slowly down her cheeks. Stifling a sob, she felt him stir and pulled away as he sat up.

"What's wrong?" he wiped her wet face with the back of his hand.

"Nothing." She lied. "I'm just confused."

"I told you." He stroked her cheek. "Two weeks and everything will be fine. You just have to be patient. Like me." he added sarcastically.

"I wish you'd tell me what was going to happen." She said softly, curling her fingers around his. "I want to know. I'm afraid that you're just going to run out on me."

Oh, the deceit, the duplicity. What kind of woman was she becoming?

Dominic looked at her, his eyes full of mistrust; but the sight of her in the dim light, so wary and gentle, so tempting, melted away all his apprehension. Straightening, he reached up and put on the interior light.

"Okay. Look."

From the glove compartment he pulled a handful of papers and dropped them on her lap. She picked them up, studying each one, her brow furrowing as she did so. One was a bill of sale for Olympic Run, signed by Mike Peterson, the other an equine insurance certificate for five hundred thousand pounds. The insured horse was Runny; and the policy holder was Mr. D. Chichester.

"I don't understand?" Kitty looked at him. "You own half of Olympic Run?"

"Not quite." There was a satisfied smirk on Dominic's

face that she didn't like. "But that insurance company thinks I do. And there's the receipt to prove it."

Kitty stared from one paper to another, trying to make sense of what he was telling her.

"Mike sold some of his share?"

"No!" Dominic laughed. "Don't be ridiculous! What do I want the bloody animal for? I told Mike the paper was to endorse payment of a vet's fee. The stupid bastard will sign anything!"

"Jesus!" Kitty stared at him, her mind racing, trying to stay one step ahead. "So, if anything happened to Runny, you'd get five hundred thousand?"

"Not if." he gave a sarcastic laugh. "When. You are a little slow aren't you sweetheart? Not like Lauren. She was onto this before I'd finished talking to her. Not if, my precious girl. When."

Kitty swallowed hard, as the terrible meaning of his words sank in. When she spoke, it was in a whisper, although there was no one to hear her.

"Dominic." She paused, afraid to hear the answer. "What are you going to do?"

"I personally am going to nothing." Dominic caught hold of her chin. "But I have some friends who will make sure that horse doesn't get to that race, or any other race. And you." he saw the horror on her face and smiled. "You, are going to keep my brother out of the way."

"No!" She pushed his hand away. "I won't have any part of this Dominic!"

Dominic looked at her, perfectly still, eyes narrowing as he studied her reaction. Kitty's brain went into overdrive; she had to think, quickly. If she protested too much, he may be afraid of her telling Tom his plan, and what would he do to her then? She was alone with him in an isolated place. For her own safety, she reasoned, as well as for Runny's, she had to make him believe that she was still on his side.

"I can't help you." She muttered. "But I won't stand in your way. Not if you promise to get me as far away from here as possible when it's all over."

"Oh, you can rely on that." There was an edge to Dominic's voice that made her skin cold. "But why won't you help me?"

"Because of Runny." Her own voice was breaking. "I don't care what this will do to Tom, but I love that horse, we all do, and I can't stand the thought of him being hurt."

"So how do I know." Dominic was moving closer; she could feel his breath on her cheek. "That you won't turn on me to save him?"

"I wouldn't!" Kitty had backed away as far as she could. "You have to believe me."

"Prove it." He said quietly.

She understood him perfectly. The only way that she could convince him, the only method she could use that Dominic would understand was sex. A week ago, she may have been tempted by him, convinced that it was what she really wanted, blinded by the excitement of her tawdry little affair. But now, after all the nights when she had believed that she was the one in control, she saw that he had in fact been playing with her, making sure of her so that he could use her as a pawn in his game. She could not let him hurt Runny; she knew that; but somehow, she had to keep his trust without submitting to his desire. To let him think that she was giving in, just once, would be too dangerous. Once she lowered her guard there would be no turning back. Once she gave him what he wanted she would never be free of him, ever.

She raised a finger and stroked his cheek, hoping that he would take her trembling for something other than nerves.

"Oh Dom." She said softly. "Not like this. It would spoil it."

"Would it?" Dominic was tense, and it showed in his face.

He wanted this girl as badly as he had ever wanted anyone in his life, and he had thought that at last he had found a route to his satisfaction.

"You know it would." She lowered her eyes, withdrawing her hand. "After what you've just told me I'd feel used."

"Why?" Dominic didn't care how she would feel; he just knew that he had to have her, and soon.

"What you want me to do." She looked at him again. "Keep Tom out of the way. I'd feel that you only wanted me to make love to you to show you I was on your side."

Dominic narrowed his eyes and looked past her, out of the window. His whole body was throbbing with excitement. He was desperate to have her, but something of what she said made sense to his hormone charged brain. If she felt used, then wasn't she more likely to turn on him and foil his plan? Better perhaps to keep her sweet a little longer, to comply with her wishes. After all this was Kitty; loyal, trusting, broken hearted Kitty, who his brother had hurt so badly. Now he was offering her a new life, healing the wounds. He liked the idea. Another point scored in his lifelong battle against Tom.

"Kiss me." He caught hold of her wrists, seeing fear flickering in her eyes as he did so. "You're still afraid of me, aren't you? When are you going to believe that I don't want to hurt you?"

"Dominic." Kitty tensed, trying to free herself from his grasp. "Please?"

"You're right princess." He was moving closer. "This is the wrong place, and the wrong time. I trust you. My brother had you in the palm of his hand, so he thought, but you want to hurt him as badly as I do. You're with me now, on my side, so I can wait. Because believe me, it is going to be worth waiting for."

Kitty felt her pulse slowing and pecked him on the cheek.

"Call that a kiss?" He still had her wrists and pulled her tightly against him. "I know I said I'd wait, but I have to have something to keep me going."

More confident now, Kitty kissed him properly. It was not that unpleasant a thing really, being in his arms, and she had to play along with him, for now. Until she knew that Runny was safe.

Poppy could hear Kitty throwing up from the kitchen.

"Kit!" She banged on the door. "Are you okay in there?"

Kitty opened the door and staggered out her eyes full of tears.

"I'm fine." She mumbled, "Too much to drink."

"You liar!" Poppy caught hold of Kitty's arm and steered her to the bedroom. "You had sex with him, didn't you? How could you?"

Kitty yanked Poppy into the bedroom and shut the door.

"I have not!" She sobbed. "Please believe me Pop. You were right all along, he's no different, just the same as before. No, he's worse than before, he's going to do something to Runny, something awful."

Poppy narrowed her eyes, looking at Kitty's flushed face, her cheeks and neck rubbed raw by a man's stubble.

"Then where the hell did all that come from? How could you Kitty? How could you let him anywhere near you?"

"Because I had to let him think that I was on his side." Kitty looked at her with pleading eyes. "He told me what he was going to do, the only way I could help Runny was to play along with him. But I didn't have sex with him. I swear I didn't."

Poppy studied her friends distressed face with wide eyes.

"What are you going to do?"

"Tell Tom of course. If he'll listen to me. But I can't tell him until tomorrow night. Dominic thinks that I'm going to be keeping him out of the way. If I tell him before then and he confronts Dominic. Oh God, Poppy, what would he do to me?"

Poppy sat on the edge of the bed and stared at the ceiling.

"Tell Martin." She said slowly, biting her lip. "So that he can keep an eye on Runny in case Tom won't listen to you. How are you going to tell him Kit? How are you even going to get him to talk to you?"

"I don't know." Kitty shook her head. "But I have to try."

"Was it awful?" Poppy asked softly. "Letting him touch you, after you knew?"

Kitty hesitated.

"What was worse." She spoke slowly. "Is that it wasn't. Although I knew what he was going to do, although I knew then how much I hated him, always had, the thought of hurting Tom made it all bearable. Knowing that what I was doing would make him crawl inside; in the same way as I've been crawling inside. That's why I feel so bad. because of him, I've let myself down. I wish I had never got involved, then none of this would ever have happened."

"Yes, it would have." Poppy stroked the tangled blonde hair. "Those two have been scheming and plotting against each other for far longer than you and I have been on the scene. You haven't let yourself down Kit. You are only human."

"Yes." Kitty looked at her with empty eyes. "I just hope I can make him listen to me before it's too late."

"When it's all over." Poppy hugged her. "We can put it all behind us and get back to normal."

"Can we?" Kitty's voice was shaking. "I don't think my life will ever me normal again."

"It will." Poppy put her face in her hands, tears of her own trickling through her fingers. "I hope. I want the real Kitty back. I'm not sure I like the other one."

"Nor am I." Kitty laid her head on Poppy's shoulder. "In fact, I hate her."

Tom would far rather have faced his maker than the small blonde figure that confronted him the following evening.

"What?" He stood in the doorway, blocking her entrance.

"I came to return this." She held out her hand. The blue sapphire twinkled in the light from the hall.

"Don't be silly." Tom pushed her hand away. "It's yours."

"I don't deserve it." She looked at her feet. "Please take it back."

"No."

He stared into the night, unable to look at her any longer. Dominic had left the house hours ago so at least she wasn't with him, which was some small consolation. As if reading his thoughts, he saw her looking up at him.

"I won't be seeing him again." She was relieved that it was finally true.

"That doesn't change anything" His voice was stone cold. "You do realise that."

"Doesn't it?" She gazed up at him with such love in her eyes that he felt himself weakening. "Please Tom. Can we talk?"

She had to get him away. Dominic would be watching. She couldn't tell him here; it wouldn't be safe.

"There's nothing to talk about." He went to close the door.

"Please!" She grabbed his good hand, desperate. "One hour, that's all?"

"I can't drive." He looked at her, well aware that she had seen him doing just that.

"We'll walk." She ignored the comment. "To The Plough? Please?"

Tom rubbed his face and looked, briefly, like the

exhausted man that he was. He had no strength, even this minor confrontation had drained him.

"One hour." He said slowly. "That's all."

Dominic watched them walking down the drive and picked up his mobile 'phone.

"Coast is clear." His voice was triumphant. "Do it."

From the kitchen window Poppy saw the couple pass the yard and bolted to yard. In Runny's box, where Martin, baseball bat in hand was waiting a phone vibrated. Martin picked it up. A message flashed on the screen.

"They've gone. For God's sake be careful!"

In the Plough Tom was very aware of Kitty constantly looking at her watch. It was beginning to irritate him.

"Are you sure you want to be here?" he snapped.

"Yes." She looked at him. His eyes were heavy, his skin dark and stubbled. She wanted to talk about them; about this ball of lead in her throat that made it impossible for her to eat or drink, about the twisting knife in her stomach that kept her awake at night. Of the fact that she quite simply couldn't face her life without him in it. But there wasn't time. If what she was about to tell him could heal the great rift in their relationship, then it would. But she would just have to wait and find out.

"Look." She leaned forward and lowered her voice. "There isn't much time. You have to call the police and then get back to the yard, now. Dominic is going to do something to Runny. I don't know what exactly, but he's got some plan to hurt him and stop him getting to Aintree. He's got an insurance policy so that he can claim on him. Martin's waiting to try and hold whoever it is off until the police get there. I don't know when this is going to happen, I just know it's tonight. You have to be ready."

"Is this a joke?" Tom had gone pale.

"No." She shook her head. "I wish it was. But it's real. I couldn't tell you before tonight because he would have known. I was scared."

Tom got to his feet, a look of panic coming to his eyes.

"How do you know that he isn't lying?"

"I've seen the papers. And," She paused. "He trusts me."

Tom froze.

"Why?"

Kitty looked at him, hoping that no one else in the room could see her shaking.

"He thinks I'm going to leave with him as soon as it's over. He believes that I care more about hurting you than anything else."

"And do you?" His eyes were very pale.

She lowered her head.

"No. I care about Runny. He means everything, to all of us, especially you."

Tom was silent. He stared at her.

"I know that you'll never forgive me for going out with him in the first place." She sobbed. "I don't think I'll ever forgive myself. But I wanted to hurt you, or so I thought. Then when I found out he was planning something I had to find out what it was, and when I knew..."

She looked up, searching for understanding in his face. But he was gone.

Martin was never sure who moved first. Himself, Bozo, or the large man with the ugly hairy arms that carried the heavy metal bar. The bolt had slid back, the lower catch had clicked open; there had been an eerie moment of silence as the door swung open, then there had been chaos. Martin had lunged forward, catching hold of the metal bar as it was raised to strike, only to be seized from behind by two more arms, equally strong and hairy, and wrestled to the ground. Bozo, not liking the aggression had leaped into action, snarling and biting, while the bay horse careered around the box, snorting, and plunging in terror, taking defensive pot shots with his hind legs at anything that moved. Martin, his face half buried in the shavings, but still thrashing and kicking, saw through the corner of his eye one man grab the horse by the head and the other raise the metal bar to strike at his legs.

"NO" He Screamed "NO!"

There was a slow-motion moment that seemed to stretch into eternity and suddenly an engine roared, the box was filled with blue light and more arms and legs started scuffling around him. The weight that had been holding him down lifted and gasping for air, mouth filled with blood, Martin rolled over and saw two red faced policemen struggling to contain two of Runny's attackers. The third was sitting on the floor holding his ribs having been kicked full force by the horse himself. Tom, who had been standing outside the door rushed forward to help Martin to his feet.

"Got here quick Guv." Martin panted.

"Yes." Tom was almost as out of breath as the man he was holding. "I was running through the lanes when the officers passed me and picked me up."

He took a moment to steady his own spinning head and looked around him. Having lain in wait at the old farm he and the two young officers had seen a transit van stop halfway along the drive. They had waited, watching three figures creeping through the shadows into the yard. Only then, when there could be little chance of escape, had they pounced. Watching the three men being led into the car Tom felt sick. Feeling Martin sway beside him he turned to him quickly.

"Are you hurt Martin?"

"I think I banged my head." Martin wiped his mouth with his hand. "But I'm okay. So is he thank God."

The sound of hooves rang through the yard and an ashen faced Poppy appeared leading a very puzzled looking Runny. Tom, startled, looked at the sweating horse beside him and laughed. He hadn't even noticed that it was in fact Micky standing in the box with them.

"I couldn't risk him." Martin said quietly, tears in his eyes. "I knew it was a gamble, putting Micky in his box instead, but if they had realised it was empty, and if you hadn't got here in time. Who knows what they would have done."

The sight of the big bay horse had a profound effect on the two men, and as Poppy took Micky back to the sanctuary of his own stable Martin laid his hand on Runny's neck, as if to make sure he was still real.

"They were going to break his legs." Unable to control his emotion any longer Martin sobbed bitterly. "They were going to break his legs with that!"

He pointed to the iron bar on the floor.

"They were going to break his legs and leave him in agony." Martin's breath was coming in heaving sobs. "The bastards. I wish I could get my hands on them!"

"Easy Martin." Tom still had hold of him. "He's safe. Thanks to you."

"No." Martin looked at him, eyes red and streaming. "Not me."

Tom looked at him, understood what he had said, and lowered his eyes.

"She loves you." Martin said quietly. "I know she messed up, but God doesn't saving him make that right?"

Tom didn't answer. He was trying to remember where he had left Kitty.

In The Plough, he had walked out on her before she had finished speaking. He should go back to her, to thank her, tell her what had happened. Then he realised that there had been no sign of Dominic. Fear gripped him and spun to face Martin.

"Martin." He began to move towards his office, pulling Martin with him. "We've got to find her!"

Kitty had sat in the Plough for a long time, turning the sapphire over and over in her hands. Tom had deserted her so quickly that she had no idea what to do next. She did not relish the thought of the long, lonely walk through the lanes. She looked at her watch again. It was ten o'clock. Ron was watching her from the bar.

"You okay there Kit?" He called.

"Fine, thanks Ron." She tried to sound normal.

"Not walking home alone, are you?" Ron frowned. "Shall I call you a taxi?"

Kitty paused for a moment then shook her head. Perhaps the walk would help clear her pounding head. She went to the door and looked out. The village was in complete darkness. About to step out into the dimly lit street she heard, or thought she heard, the sound of a car. A stationary car, its engine ticking over. Waiting. For something, or someone.

She changed her mind.

"I will have that taxi, Ron." She called. "Please."

"Good girl." Ron smiled. "Come on, have a drink on me while you're waiting."

Martin drove through the lanes as quickly as he dared. The Land Rover lights were dim, and he could barely see the road. Beside him Tom was leaning forward, peering ahead.

"Go to The Plough Martin." He clutched the dashboard with his free hand to steady himself as the vehicle lurched around a corner. "With any luck she's still there."

The village was deserted; no lights, no cars, only the dim glow of orange behind the curtains showed that anyone inhabited the jumble of little cottages. Turning into the main street they saw a small group of vehicles still outside The Plough.

"There she is!" Martin pointed to the door. "Getting into that taxi!"

Tom was out of the door before he had finished speaking.

"Kitty!" He shouted. "Wait!"

She watched him running towards her, one hand on the taxi door, her hair blowing across her face.

"Thank you." He bent to speak to the taxi driver. "We'll take her home. What do I owe you?"

"Nothing." The driver grinned. "Just make sure that horse of yours wins the race, eh?"

Tom smiled back and stood up.

"It's because of you." He spoke to Kitty as the car moved off leaving a space between them. "That I still have a horse to win that race."

Kitty looked away. He could see her shivering. Something sparkled in her hands, and he saw the sapphire, still dangling from her fingers.

"Come on." He said gently. "Let's go home."

Sliding into the seat beside Martin, Kitty patted his bloodied lip.

"Hurt Marty?"

"No. I'll live. And so will the boy thanks to you."

"Who's with him?" Kitty looked down at her hands, glanced quickly at Tom, and slid the sapphire into her pocket.

"There's still a police officer at the yard." Martin hugged her. "Don't worry. He's safe now."

Yes, she thought, but am I? She had to ask the question, although she dreaded the answer.

"And Dominic?"

"There's no sign of him." The tone of Tom's voice made her tremble. "But I'll find him, and this time by God, I'll make him pay for what he's done."

"It's time someone did." Martin said grimly. "I take it the breakdown stuff was all a sham?"

"That's right." Tom's stony face stared out of the window into the darkness. "He had us all fooled."

Kitty looked at her nails and realised that for the first time in her life she had bitten them to the quick. Her initial relief that Runny was safe had quickly been overtaken by a bout of the blackest depression. She had saved Runny, and the biggest chance of glory Highford ever had, but at what cost? Her personal life was in ruins, and whatever happened now, her part in it would always taste bitter. Her only hope really was to leave, and get away, to start fresh somewhere else, someone else's yard, someone else's horses. Not wanting to have to talk, she got out of the Land Rover as soon as it stopped in the yard. Heavy hearted, she muttered a hasty goodbye and walked towards the cottage, searching in her bag for her door key. As she inserted it, she heard footsteps on the path behind her.

"You were quick Marty." She said quietly. "Stiff drinks all round I think?"

"Yes." Replied a low voice that wasn't Martin's. "Wouldn't that be nice?"

Kitty spun on her heel and stared in horror. Dominic, pale faced, his expression more haunted than she had ever seen him, stood only feet away from her. His eyes stared, unblinking, into hers. He didn't have to speak. His presence was enough. Kitty fumbled with the catch behind her; she wanted to turn and flee into the safety of the cottage but she dare not turn her back on him.

"So" His voice was barely a whisper. "You came out on his side after all."

Kitty didn't answer. She just stared at him, hypnotized, frozen in terror.

"You let me down Kitty." He still hadn't moved. "I trusted you. I even started to care about you. I thought we could have been something special together. But he got the better of me, as he always does."

"That's not fair." She hesitated. "You do so many things to hurt him and you always get away with it."

"Do I?" Dominic was drawing ever closer. "All my life he's been one step ahead of me. I was always second best."

"That's not his fault." Kitty was backed flat against the door.

"Of course, it is." Dominic's bitter hatred was sounding in his voice. "God, I would do anything to bring him down, anything."

"I couldn't let you kill Runny." She sobbed. "The horses, this place, they mean everything to me. You'll never understand what losing Runny would have done to us."

"Oh, I understand." He was towering over her. "Believe me I do."

"Dominic." She was trying to sound calm. "It's not safe for you to be here. The police are still here, they may find you."

"Oh, don't pretend you care!" He laughed, a hollow meaningless sound. "You tricked me you scheming little bitch."

His voice was changing, becoming more aggressive.

"I had to." She whispered. "You've got to understand that I couldn't let you hurt him."

"All those nights." His face was inches from hers. "All the times I touched you, wanted you; all the times you begged me to take you away from here, you even made me believe that it was right not to have sex with you, but to wait. Wait! I've never waited for anything in my life until now! But I thought that you were different, special; but you're just a common little whore!"

"I am not!" Her voice cracked. "I was scared of you. I've

always been scared of you!"

"So, you should be." His eyes narrowed and he reached out and grabbed her arm. "You're coming with me."

"No!" She screamed, tugging backwards. "Let me go!"

For answer Dominic hauled at her, pulling her to her knees and dragging her behind him. Scrambling to her feet, ripping her jeans, she fought him.

"No!" She gasped. "Where are you taking me?"

"You're the only weapon I've got left." He hissed. "The only thing I can still hurt him with."

"But he hates me too." She shouted, the truth of her words hurting even more than her fear. "He doesn't care about me, not after this."

Dominic wasn't listening. He tugged her to the gate, avoiding her kicking feet and clawing nails. Holding her tightly, one arm twisted behind her back, he fumbled with the catch on the gate.

"Dominic." The voice that came out of the darkness was cool and commanding. "Let her go."

"No." Dominic swung her in front of him, a human shield.

"It's me you want." Tom stepped forward. "I'm the one you want to harm. Let her go."

Dominic stared at him. He could not see his brother's face in the shadows, but he knew how it would look; superior, arrogant, confident of beating him down, again. The wind stirred and blew Kitty's hair in front of him. Soft, silky; its smell reminded him of her warm body, her gentle touch, of tenderness and dark places filled with tingling anticipation that had never been fulfilled. It reminded him that she had taken him on at his own game and won.

Pushing her away from him as if he had been stung, he sent her sprawling to the ground.

"Double crossing little whore." He hissed. "You're not

worth it."

"No." Tom still hadn't moved. "She isn't."

Kitty looked up at him, horrified. He didn't even glance at her. His eyes were fixed on Dominic, never faltering. Only the gate, swinging on its hinges, stood between them.

"Come on." Tom moved first, stepping closer. "It's just you and I now."

Dominic's lip curled back in an ugly sneer. His eyes took in his opponent, one arm still in its sling, the other hanging at his side. His face was heavy with tiredness, his eyes bloodshot. Easy prey. With a snarl he sprang, sending Tom crashing backwards into the fence.

Kitty screamed. For a moment she was helpless, too terrified to move, then, realising that Tom could not beat off Dominic alone, she scrambled to her feet and ran towards the yard, shouting for Martin.

Dominic's fists rained blow after blow onto Tom's body. Tom, caught off guard by the tiger's pounce that had floored him, struggled with his free arm to push Dominic off. Clutching at thin air, he finally found his brother's face and gouged at it with his fingers. Digging deep, drawing blood, he managed to bend Dominic's head back. Swearing, Dominic bit the hand that covered his face, tasting blood and sweat. Tom, winced, but didn't release his grip, straining to sit upright. He was aware of Dominic fumbling in his clothing, squirming as he searched for something. Then, as Tom knew a moment of pure terror, he saw the cold glint of steel in the dim light. Panicking, he fought with renewed vigour, holding Dominic's arm away as he kicked and struggled. Feeling himself tiring, losing his grip, he looked into his brothers' face, intending to plead with him. What he saw turned his blood cold. Never, in his life, had he seen hatred on anyone's face such as that which he saw on the face of his own flesh and blood.

"Why?" He shouted, almost begging. "Why do you hate me so much?"

Dominic didn't answer. The eagle like swoop that Martin made knocked him sideways. Tom, still fighting for breath, crawled across, and helped Martin hold him down.

"Christ, boss!" Martin was sitting on Dominic, holding both hands behind his back. "He didn't hurt you, did he?"

"No." Tom forced a weak smile. "That's the second time tonight you've come to the rescue."

"I know." Martin shook his head. "You'll have to start paying me danger money!"

Kitty came running into view with a policeman at her heels. He had just been getting back into his car when a small blonde with hysterical eyes and dirty cheeks had come racing up to him. Pulling Martin to one side he clipped a pair of handcuffs onto Dominic and hauled him to his feet.

"That's enough of that." He shoved Dominic into the gatepost as he made a lurch for freedom. "You've done enough for one night don't you think? Want to add resisting arrest to the charges? Everyone safe?"

He looked around him

"He had a knife!" Martin gasped. "Look!"

The young man stared at Dominic in disgust.

"There's nothing you wouldn't stoop to is there? I think I need to put you somewhere safe. Where you can't assault anything else!"

Tom followed them to the car. Watching Dominic being thrust, blank eyed, into the back of the car, he laid a hand on the police officer's shoulder.

"Could you let me have a moment please?"

"If you like." The man frowned. "Personally, I can't think why you want to."

Tom nodded his thanks. It was too difficult to explain. Dominic was staring straight ahead, a slight tremor in his cheek the only movement, and for a moment Tom wondered if he even knew he was there.

"Why?" He asked again. "Why do you despise me so much? Is it really that important that you ruin me?"

Dominic turned his gaunt, hollow face towards him. There was no emotion now in the sunken eyes, no expression at all. His gaze lowered until it rested on Tom's plastered arm.

"Do you remember?" He began slowly. "When I sprained my wrist? We were really small. You had to do up my shirts for me, and my school ties."

"That was a long time ago." Tom replied shortly. "Things have changed."

"Haven't they? You're a success, a racing celebrity; and I'm a, well." He paused. "We all know what I am."

Tom looked for the barb, the goad that normally accompanied such comments, but found none. There was a note of resignation in Dominic's voice that struck a chord of sympathy in Tom's heart.

"Why Dominic?" He asked quietly. "Why do you never rest until everyone hates you?"

"I don't know." Dominic shrugged. "Perhaps it's because I hate myself."

"Are you sure it's not just self-pity?" Tom couldn't keep the sarcasm from his voice. "You were always good at that."

"The only thing I am good at." Dominic looked out of the window, his face changing now, hard, bitter. "Unlike you. All the time we were growing up you never did anything wrong. Best school report. Good at games. Excellent grades. You had no reason to feel sorry for yourself. If I sneezed, it was in the wrong direction. I couldn't do anything *right*."

"That's an exaggeration. Mother always bent over backwards for you."

Dominic nodded.

"But not the old man. He only had eyes for you. He hated me. However, much I tried to make him like me I failed. So, I gave up trying. If he wanted me to turn right, I went left. At first it was deliberate, then I couldn't help myself. By the time I realised what was happening it was too late. The black sheep."

"You've played the part very well."

"Too well." Dominic looked at him. "Is there anything in your life you wish you hadn't done?"

"I suppose there must be" Tom lowered himself into the car beside him "There's a hell of a lot more I wish I *had* done. Why?"

"There's so much I wish I hadn't done. So much that it's too late to change. Like not being able to say goodbye to him. I didn't realise that I had loved him at all until he had gone."

"But why carry on punishing yourself, or me, or our mother? She doesn't deserve to have to go through all this. Why didn't you learn from your mistakes and settle down?"

"I couldn't." Dominic said bitterly. "I was caught in my own nets, and I didn't want to. All I could think of was bringing you down, to make you suffer like I had. To make you become nothing, a thing with no worth, a nonentity. Like me."

"Why?" Tom demanded.

"Because you're him." The obsessive hate had returned to Dominic's voice. "The way you talk, how you are with people, talking down your bloody perfect nose at people all the time, to me, to everyone. The way you run your life around those bloody horses, and worst of all the way our mother worships the ground you walk on. You're a living reminder of how unhappy he made me."

Tom shook his head, unable to speak. He had never realised the full extent, or depth of Dominic's feelings. It shocked him. Looking at his thin, almost emaciated brother, he saw past the man that he loathed to the little boy that he had loved. But it was all too late. Perhaps if he had been there for him all those years ago things may have been different.

"Sir." The police officer put his head through the window. "I really must be going."

"Yes." Tom got out of the car, watching his motionless brother. He looked at the young man beside him with sad eyes.

"He's beyond my reach now."

CHAPTER TWENTY-SEVEN

Kitty was waiting for him, sitting on the yard gate, her face pale and nervous. She watched him approach with a sinking heart. Leaning on the gate beside her he averted his eyes. He knew that he owed Olympic Run's life and his whole future to her; he wanted to forgive her, wanted to turn the clock back, but he couldn't. The image of her betrayal was too strong in his mind.

"I don't suppose that you'll ever forgive me." She must have read his thoughts.

"I don't know." He said truthfully. "Whatever happens next week, Runny certainly wouldn't have made it without you. I certainly would have lost this place; who would have trusted a horse into my care after that? So, for that I'm grateful. But I can't forget what you did, how you found out. Is your memory that short?" He looked at her for the first time. "How could you do it?"

She faced him, completely dry eyed. Tears were no use to her now.

"I did it because I knew that was what would hurt you the most. But then I've explained that already. It doesn't matter now. I'll just have to live with it."

"Yes." He had looked away again. "You will."

He turned and began to walk slowly away, his heart laying like lead in his chest. Despite the night's events, despite saving Runny, he had still never felt so low. He heard the gate to the cottage clicking open. The sound made him stop, draw a long, slow breath.

With a vision that was almost too painful to bear he saw into his future. A future without her; and he knew, in that moment, that whatever she had done he couldn't face it.

"Kitty." He turned around slowly, afraid to look, afraid that she may already have disappeared from his life.

Hardly trusting her own ears, Kitty halted.

"Come here." He called, not moving. "Please?"

Too wary to run, she walked cautiously back and stood in front of him.

"Yes?" She whispered.

Tom's eyes scanned her face, taking in the tell tales signs of misery. Lifting his hand to her cheek he touched her soft, warm skin. Shaking his head, tears in his eyes, he caught her in his good arm and held her tight.

"I'm sorry." He muttered, his face in her hair. "This is all my fault. I started this whole bloody mess. You've saved everything I've worked for my whole life. I could have lost it all." He paused, trying to control his breaking voice.

"And I could have lost you." He continued. "That hurts most of all."

She clung to him, unable to speak.

"It's going to take time. But I can't just write this thing off. It means too much to me. *You* mean too much to me. But you'll have to be patient with me if you can?"

"Of course, I can." Her voice was muffled by his sweater." "I'm so, so sorry."

"No." He pulled her away so he could look at her. " Don't be. This is all my making. But I must admit." He forced a smile. "Martin, Ryan, even Rick I could have handled. But him! It was quite a choice."

"Wasn't it." She lowered her eyes. "I'd never realised just how jealous and vindictive I could be."

"Enough." Tom gave her another hug. "Now. I suggest that we bring this night to a close before anything else happens!"

"Good night." She said softly. She wanted to kiss him, to be folded into the comforting warmth of his arms and stay there. But she held back.

"Good night, Kitty." He gave her a smile and turned away.

Watching him walking towards the drive she felt a tiny

glimmer of hope stirring inside her. Looking up into the sky, she saw that the clouds were pulling apart, drawing back the curtains on natures spectacular display. In the cluster of twinkling dots one star burned brighter than the others; staring at it for a second, she closed her eyes and wished with all her heart that whoever had seen fit to give her this man wouldn't take him away.

Rick was stunned. Sitting on the edge of his seat he listened in amazement as Poppy relayed the previous night's events.

"Jesus!" He collapsed back into the chair. "And I missed it all!"

"Just as well." Poppy dipped into the plate of nachos in front of her. "He might have tried to get you as well!"

"That's a thought." Rick grew more sombre. "Good job Kitty came to her senses and spilled the beans. But that's the part I can't believe; her and Dominic! And to think I nearly got my head knocked off defending her before!"

"Did you?" Poppy raised her eyebrows. "When?"

"A long time ago. If I remember correctly it, was you, I did get my head knocked off over."

"So, you should." Poppy giggled. "I've felt like knocking it off myself, more than once!"

Rick put his heels up into his coffee table.

"What a dark horse." He shook his head.

"Stupid horse I'd say." Poppy held out her empty wine glass. "And don't get too comfortable, I need a refill."

Kitty stretched out her limbs in the cool comfort of the cotton sheets and gazed with total adoration at the dark head beside her. Tom was looking at his fingers, protruding grubbily from his plaster.

"They look like the fingers of a ten-year old." He grinned. "All black and grimy."

"You can wash then you know." Kitty poked him in the ribs. "Dirty boy."

"I do." Tom dug her back. "It must have come off you."

Kitty dug him one last time and then laid her head on his dark chest. Things were still constrained between them, but they were improving, slowly.

"I've had an invitation to that new art gallery in Stow on Sunday." Tom was talking to her head. "Enigma's owners. Would you like to come?"

"Me!" Kitty sat up. "I've nothing to wear!"

"Rubbish." Tom pulled her back down. "Talk to Poppy. She'll sort you out. That girl got more clothes than Dorothy Perkins."

On Sundays the yard had become a tourist attraction for the British racing public. First the 'phone would ring, then there would be the inevitable questions, ' We were in the area; could we possibly have a look at Olympic Run?' followed by, 'Oh, thank you, we're just around the corner.' It was totally against Tom's security conscious nature, a state of mind heightened by the last week's events, but the visitors were so overawed by the sight of their equine hero in the flesh that he had come to accept it. The other horses had also grown used to their share of attention, and Martin, who loved nothing better than to talk about his beloved horse, thoroughly enjoyed it. The only problem that ever arose was the after-lunch period when none of the staff wanted to move from the living room to go on parade.

The Sunday immediately before Liverpool was no exception. Full of roast lamb and apple crumble, they were all laying around the cottage watching the afternoon movie when a car pulled into the yard. Ryan, making coffee, heard it first.

"Whose turn is it?" He shouted. "I went last time."

"It's mine." Kitty, who had been half asleep, sat bolt upright. "I didn't think anyone had called!"

"They didn't." Martin was getting to his feet. "Come on, better check it out."

The car was a new, dark green, Japanese saloon. The couple that was emerging from it didn't look like the usual Sunday visitors; and even less like the horse dopers they all feared. The woman, smartly dressed and well heeled, was surveying the yard with obvious distaste.

"Can we help you?" Kitty closed the gate. "Have you come to see... Good God! Mum!"

"Hello Katriona." Her mother wrinkled her nose at her daughter's grubby clothes. "Is that how you greet your mother? In dirty working clothes?"

"I am working Mum, and I didn't know you were coming!"

"Obviously not."

Kitty's father wasn't at all bothered by her dirty clothes, taking his favourite daughter in his arms he hugged until she was gasping for air.

"Could murder a cuppa, Kit." He smiled.

Kitty went scarlet. The cottage was in chaos; Poppy was making a dress and had material all over the kitchen table and the living room looked like a relic of the blitz. Martin, standing behind her found it rather amusing until he remembered his underpants drying in front of the fire. Stepping smartly up he offered the large, grey headed man his hand.

"Hello Mr. Campbell. Nice to meet you. Why don't you come over to the coach house? Mrs. Benson is still there, I'm sure she'll make us some tea. You'll have to excuse us I'm afraid. We're not very organised on Sunday afternoons."

"What's wrong with that cottage?" Kitty's mother set her jaw.

"Poppy's feeling poorly." Martin smiled sweetly. "She's having a nap on the sofa."

"Really?" The woman's eyebrows raised. "How very convenient."

"Oh, for goodness' sake Fiona." He husband remarked, not unkindly. "Does it really matter?"

"Flu." Martin told him, as he led him to the coach house. "We've all had a bout of it. Hello Mrs. B. Couldn't put the kettle on, could you? These are Kitty's parents."

Pulling chairs around the still roaring fire he sat them all down.

"Mrs. B insists on lighting a fire." He smiled. "Although, it's not that cold anymore, is it?"

"There are primroses in the hedge." Mrs. B was piling ham sandwiches onto a plate. "Tiny little yellow faces they have."

Alex Campbell took off his tweed jacket and smiled at his daughter.

"Well Kitty Kat, how are you? You're looking well."

"No, she's not!" His wife snapped. "She's pale, thin and untidy. She could do with a good meal and a hot bath."

"Good meal!" Mrs. Benson laughed. "That one eats like those horses! Her and that Poppy; and don't you worry about her needing a bath. You should see her all dressed up on a Saturday night. They make a fine pair." She warmed to her subject. "There's Poppy with that young rascal Rick eating out of her hand and.."

Kitty opened her eyes wide and mouthed 'no' when the door opened.

"Whose car is that in the yard? Oh Hello. Good afternoon."

"Hello Guv" Kitty jumped up. "These are my parents."

She was scarlet to the roots of her hair.

"Pleased to meet you." Tom held out his hand. The

thought crossed his mind briefly that this man could possibly be his future father-in-law. Immaculate in cream chinos and a blazer he had taken his mother out to lunch, and then spent an hour closeted in the study with Ned.

Turning to greet Kitty's mother he was unnerved by the woman's likeness to her daughter. But this was a strong woman; not one who take too kindly, he imagined, to the knowledge that he was sleeping with her youngest daughter. Kitty was almost comically nervous, rushing to help pour the tea she tipped the milk over the tray. Pausing long enough to admire her rear end for a minute, Tom turned apologetically to the guests.

"I'll have to leave you I'm afraid. It was very nice to meet you."

"Kitty told us about your accident." Alex Campbell was still standing. "Are you healing? I do hope you're going to pull off the double next week."

"Getting better every day thank you. We hope so too." Tom smiled. "We came off very well in the weights. Thank God they handicap before the Gold Cup and not after! We need all the help we can get."

"Could I see him?" Alex coloured slightly. "Olympic Run I mean."

"Certainly." Tom smiled again. "Come with me."

"I'll leave you women to talk." Martin scuttled after them.

"What a handsome man." Fiona Campbell watched Tom going through the door. "It's amazing that he's not married."

"Oh, it'll take a special kind of woman to get him down the aisle." Mrs. Benson sat down with them. "There's many who've tried and failed."

Fiona shrugged and turned back to her daughter.

"What about you? Do you have a boyfriend yet?"

"No." Kitty's cheeks were burning. "I don't want one."

"It's time you did. You can't play with horses all your life, and it seems that Poppy has claimed the only reasonable catch around here."

"I don't want to change yet mother, I like what I'm doing. Please don't nag."

"No." Mrs. Benson muttered as she refilled Kitty's cup. "There's enough of those around here already."

Sometime later Kitty thankfully waved the couple off down the drive.

"Phew." She puffed out her lips and collapsed on the gate in mock exhaustion.

Tom, who had given Alex a thorough guided tour and spent the last half hour in the coach house drinking tea with him, burst out laughing.

"What's wrong with you?" Kitty scowled at him.

"You." Tom chuckled. "I've never seen such a look of panic! When I walked through the door you looked at me as though I'd grown another head!"

Kitty began to giggle.

"Well, just before that, Mrs. B was starting to ramble on, and you know how dangerous that can be!"

He pulled her ponytail playfully.

"What would you have done?"

"I don't know. My mother would have had a fit!"

"That's only because she cares about you." Tom said kindly.

"Maybe." Kitty muttered. "She'd jump into bed with you herself given half a chance."

"Really." Tom raised a wicked eyebrow. "Like mother like daughter then."

"Watch it." She punched him. "Or I'll break you other arm."

For a moment they stood in a companionable silence,

both thinking their own thoughts, and in no hurry to move on.

Kitty was the first to speak. "How did it go with Ned?"

"Difficult." Tom, as if agitated by the topic, walked along the yard towards the office, pausing to pull Streak's ears as he did. "The hardest part was having to watch my mother hear the full story. All these years she's viewed Dominic with rose tinted glasses. Now she had to face him as he really is, warts and all."

"Poor thing." Kitty put her arm through his. "What did Ned have to say about him?"

"Not much really." Tom frowned. "He's in a difficult position himself. Apparently, Dominic paid this Phil Knight off to write that medical report. With Lauren's money of course, as he hasn't any of his own. Then, off the hook yet again, he decided to put into action a plan that he'd dreamed up when he was staying here. All the time I thought I had everything secure from him and he was conning Mike into believing that he was signing a bill for an endoscope! Then he took out the insurance policy and was just sitting on it, waiting. Sad to say that he knows enough unsavoury characters, and had no trouble finding someone to do his dirty work on promise of a hefty pay out.

They were, as Martin correctly guessed, going to break Runny's legs with an iron bar. He would have been destroyed and Dominic would have claimed his money."

Kitty shuddered at the thought.

"Once he had the money of course, he wouldn't have paid anyone. He would have bolted." Tom paused. "I don't think he realised just how long these things can take. There could have been a considerable delay before he got the money, and it's highly unlikely that he would have gotten away with it, really. Insurance companies are more suspicious these days. But his desperate need for money, and this obsession he has with ruining me, made him go ahead. If he'd been thinking clearly, he would have avoided you like the plague. But, as I said, I was his real target, and having you was a massive bonus that he couldn't resist."

Kitty played with Streak's mane.

"It could have gone so wrong." She muttered. "Poor Runny."

"But he's fine thanks to you, and my brother is behind bars once again, hopefully to remain there this time. Anyway." Tom brightened. "Don't forget that exhibition tonight."

"Do I get an early finish?" Kitty grinned.

"Not a chance." Tom moved off. "I've told Martin to make you clean all the tack."

Poppy, as Tom had suspected, provided a variety of outfits for Kitty to choose from.

"Why don't you wear something different? Here, these jeans and my lace top. That would look great."

"I don't know." Kitty frowned. "The top maybe, but jeans? He said it was formal."

"Well, my red dress then." Poppy rummaged in in the back of the wardrobe. "I'll wear the jeans out with Rick."

"That's more like it." Kitty smiled. "Do you remember the last time I wore this?"

"Do I!" Poppy sat on the bed. "If I remember rightly you went on a date with the love of my life!"

"Mm." Kitty stroked the dress. "That was the first time I kissed him."

"Rick?" Poppy's eyes lit up. "No, you mean Tom, don't you? Come on, tell me, I never knew that!"

"Yes. He brought me home remember?"

"Oh yes." Poppy pouted. "After his lordship went for a bonk with Felicity Harries."

"I will wear it please." Kitty hung it back up. "Will you do up my hair?"

"Of course, Cinders. Now come on, we're late."

Long after Tom had collected Kitty in a taxi, Rick came speeding down the drive. Poppy, hanging out of the landing window, squeaked in excitement, and shot down the stairs and into his arms.

"Hello honey." He kissed her with enthusiasm. "That was a real welcome."

"I've just realised how lucky I am to have you." Poppy kissed him again. "Come on, I'm starving."

They ate at a small pub tucked away in the hills. Full and contented Rick drove home slowly, one hand on Poppy's knee.

"Not long now." Poppy was watching the stars. "Off to Liverpool on Wednesday."

"Yup." Rick slowed down to admire the moon lighting up the hills. "I've left myself pretty clear all week until then. Don't want any mishaps before this one. Bloody handicapper, that was my last pig out for nearly a week."

"Why have we stopped?" Poppy sat up.

"I was looking at the moon." Rick smiled at her. "But I'd rather look at you."

She turned to him, eyes sparkling in her pale, moonlit, face. Feeling his blood starting to flow ever faster through his veins he pulled her into him, sliding his hand upward onto her firm breast.

"Rick Cowdrey!" She scolded. "In the car? On the side of the road?"

"Yeah, why not?" He grinned, undoing her jeans. "If it wasn't so cold in this country, I'd lay you on the verge."

"Really?" She was brushing her lips over his neck, slowly, lightly, knowing what his reaction would be. "What if I say no?"

"I'd drag you out of the car." Rick groaned as lips brushed downwards through the groove of his throat. "And tie you to the bumper."

"Really?" Poppy smiled and nipped his skin gently with her teeth. "I'm so glad I'm not going to say no it all sounds a bit too painful for me!"

The lace top had slipped off her shoulders to reveal her bare skin; it gleamed softly in the moonlight. Rick stroked her waist and began to slide the tight jeans off her hips.

"Pop!" He raised his eyebrows. "You're not wearing pants!"

"Of course not." She was undoing his shirt. "I didn't want to waste time."

She loved the feeling of his smooth, warm flesh against hers. With a little sigh of pleasure, she lay back as he reclined the seat.

"What if someone comes?" She murmured.

"That." Rick was sliding his tongue over her stomach. "Is the idea."

The square was empty. Sitting on a bench beside the old stocks Tom and Kitty waited for their car. Leaning on his shoulder she studied the object next to her and tried to imagine what it must have been like to live in a time when people were stoned in public for punishment. Tom, thinking of Liverpool, watched the moon illuminating the bell tower of the old church and fidgeted with his sling.

"I'll be so glad when I can drive." Tom laid his head on hers. "This thing is a nuisance."

"Mm." She slipped her fingers inside his shirt.

"Why are taxis always late?" Tom was getting restless.

"I don't mind." She snuggled closer. "I'm quite happy here."

"I expect you are." He stooped down to kiss her. "That's the dress that you wore the night you went out with Rick."

"The night you first took advantage of me you mean!" Kitty felt a thrill of pleasure at his remembering the evening.

"I did no such thing. That was much later. In Micky's stable."

"Poor Mick." Kitty giggled. "What a sight!"

"He was probably jealous." He laid his hand on her exposed thigh. "I would have been."

"I never believed it would happen, you and I." She said dreamily. "Although I always hoped that it would."

"Well it wasn't something I had planned." He confessed. "But I'm very glad it did."

A car came slowly into the square.

"Here we go." He broke away. "Time to go home."

Kitty hung back a little as he crossed the square. Looking up at the moonlit steeple she said a silent prayer that at long last things would go well. She didn't have the nerve to pray for herself, she didn't deserve it. But the week ahead was the biggest challenge they had ever faced, and a little divine intervention could go a long way.

The two men watched the bay horse cruising up the gallop in mutual satisfaction. On its back, Rick's broad smile spoke louder than a hundred words as he flew past them. Overwhelmed by the feeling of raw power, he leaned forward and ran his hand over the silken neck. Behind him Streak came pounding up in her usual workmanlike fashion, Poppy laughing at her own lack of control. Side by side, they pulled up at the top of the hill and walked back to the Land Rover.

"Well." Tom looked the younger man in the eye. "What do you think?"

Rick jumped off and handed the reins to Martin.

"He's so spot on. I thought that no way would he give

me a better feel than he did before Cheltenham; but I was wrong. He's positively awesome."

"Do you think he'll stay the trip?"

"Sure." Rick pulled off his skull cap and shook his hair loose. "Believe me. It'll be some horse that beats him on Saturday."

"Worried about the fences?" Tom watched with a wry grin as the man's expression changed.

"Now that's something else." Rick had become very subdued. "They won't worry him. But me? Now that's another matter!"

"So, you wouldn't say no to a drink?"

"Just one. I'm fighting the scales remember?"

"You don't have to worry about that." Tom opened the Land Rover door. "Skinny little sod!"

Martin watched them bouncing slowly down the hill. Rick talking non-stop as he steered around the potholes and turned to the big horse beside him.

Three days and it would all be over.

CHAPTER TWENTY-EIGHT

The silence deepened as they walked around the course. The ominous rumbling of thunder and the threatening indigo clouds on the horizon went unnoticed. Standing in front of the vast expanse of greenery that stretched before them, Rick put his hand to his mouth as the churning pit of bile in his stomach threatened to engulf him.

"And this." Tom's voice had gone very quiet. "Is The Chair."

He a wave of sympathy for his pale faced companion. The Aintree fences were intimidating enough to him; but to Rick, who was having his first sight of them in the flesh, they had to be terrifying. Couple this with the fact that he would be riding towards them on the favourite, and it became almost impossible for him to imagine how his jockey must feel.

"The Chair." Rick gritted his teeth. "It should be wired up."

"Don't worry." Tom laid a hand on his shoulder. "Runny will make it look like a hurdle."

"Jesus." Rick couldn't take his eyes off the fence. "Am I insane? Do I really want to do this for a living?"

"Do I?" Tom laughed. "Do any of us? Come on, we don't want to get caught in this storm that's brewing. Let's hope there's not too much of it. This going is perfect."

It was Wednesday evening. In twenty-four hours, this deserted racecourse would be awash with litter and the stragglers of the first day of the meeting. Brassy was already settled into the stable ready for his race; tomorrow night Martin would face the long trek back home to collect both Runny and Streak and bring them back to the racecourse. Every hotel in Liverpool had been taken over by the racing public from all over Britain and beyond.

Practically every room of The Adelphi Hotel housed a jockey. Entering the hotel Rick felt his morale beginning to wane, the hotel's neat, well decorated room left him wanting for nothing, but it had none of the confidence inspiring trappings of home. He had grown accustomed to staying at Highford, or in his own little cottage, and here he felt very much out of place. He was also very much the new boy of the party; watching a group of the younger riders setting out in search of the city's night life, he went up to his room, and began flicking through channels on the television. He was looking for a movie to entertain himself with when his mobile rang.

"It's me!" Poppy wailed. "I hate this poxy hostel. Martin's buggered off down the pub with Westwood's lot and I'm all on my own."

"Come over then." Rick lay back on his bed. "I'd rather have you for company than Julia Roberts."

"Liar." Poppy giggled.

"Possibly." Rick grinned into the receiver. "But you're flesh and blood and she's a moving picture. I'll send a cab for you."

"Are you sure?" Poppy squeaked.

"Quite sure. Get them to call me from reception when you are here. If I step outside, I'll be mugged by someone wanting my inside leg measurement."

As soon as he hung up the 'phone rang again.

"Hi. Ready for dinner?" It was Tom.

"Sorry. Pop just rang, she's on her way over."

"You mean you're leaving me to face Mike and clinging Claudia? Thanks."

"Sorry Tom. The last thing my nerves want right now is an evening with Claudia. I have no wish to be mauled."

"Nor do I." Sighed Tom. "Coward."

"That's the difference." Rick laughed. "You have to put up

with it it's your job. Not mine!"

Tom hung up with a sigh. He had no desire to make small talk with Mike and his idiot wife either. But as Rick had so happily pointed out it was job. His mother had called and absentmindedly wished him luck, but he could tell that her heart wasn't really in it. He shook his head and went to the window. Being alone had never bothered him before but he was becoming increasingly gregarious; that still didn't make him feel better about the prospect of dinner with Mike and Claudia. His next caller was Mike himself.

"All set. There's a chap from The Racing Post wants a word with us. Said we'd meet him in the bar. Cowdrey fit?"

"He won't be joining us." Tom knew that he sounded sharp but couldn't help himself. What right had Mike to set up interviews without asking him first? "He's made other plans. I haven't showered yet, so you'll have to start without me."

Ignoring Mike's protestations, he hung up. Getting undressed, the water already running in the shower he checked the desk for messages and then his mobile. Feeling disappointed he got into the stinging heat of the power shower.

He didn't want to be alone; but there was only one person that he wanted to be with, and she was miles away.

Brassy failed to reproduce his Cheltenham form and trailed home in mid field of the novice 'chase. Rick, although disappointed for his yard, rode his first winner at Aintree for Greg Westwood. Confidence bolstered by his success he took Poppy out to dinner where they drank not only to his success but to Streak, and, of course, to Olympic Run in his bid to make history.

The magnificent bronze of Red Rum gazed out across the course towards the winning post as the runners paraded in front of the crowds. Many of the crowd were here for the weekend and there was a real party atmosphere. Dressed for the wet weather they had suffered the day before, they soon found themselves stripping off as the spring sunshine grew in strength. Poppy, sweating in a polo neck jumper, cursed at the mare as she jogged along the course.

"She's on her toes alright." Martin joined Tom as he watched the runners. "I hope she's not going to boil over."

He got no reply. Tom was watching his mare, white with lather by this stage, and trying to ignore the sense of foreboding that was gripping him. The more he watched her, the more he knew that something was wrong. It was soon obvious to him, and everyone else, that he was right. Streak hit the first fence very hard, and losing ground rapidly, nearly hit the floor at the second.

Rick, who had no intention of letting the winner of the Champion 'chase trail in last next time out, quickly pulled her up.

"Oh oh." Martin began to run of the stands. "Trouble at mill!"

By the time he reached Rick the jockey had dismounted and was walking her slowly back to the enclosures.

"Problems?" Martin took the reins.

"It's her back end. She just isn't taking off. Feels like she has tied up, and bad."

"Oh Lord let it not be an omen." Martin gave the mare a pat. "I'm going to wrap Runny up in cotton wool tonight!"

Rick had to explain his actions away to the stewards who didn't take too kindly to having the second favourite pulled up after two fences. After his grilling Rick's confidence waned further and he failed to get anywhere near the winning post for the rest of the day. Feeling far less optimistic than he had done the previous night, he returned to his hotel alone. Poppy, after several fruitless attempts at contacting him, gave up and joined the others at the pub. Only much later, when Rick was in bed, did he miss her soothing presence and begin to panic.

Tom didn't sleep much that night. He sat in the window of his room and watched the city lights. He thought of Martin, curled up in his sleeping bag in Runny's stable, of Kitty, in the hostel, and his mother alone in that vast, empty house. Emptying a decanter of whisky, he at last began to feel drowsy. He knew that if he made the move to get into bed he would wake up and lose the comforting state of near slumber he was in. So, he stayed where he was, half dozing, until the sky began to turn grey.

The thunder of hooves grew until it was deafening. The wind whipped his face, bringing tears to his eyes. He was in the middle of a jostling, lurching, moving mass of horse flesh. The jump ahead, the most famous steeplechase fence in the world, was waiting, jaws open, to ensnare its prey. All around him the other riders were pulling up. He could see the horror on their mounts faces as they swerved and slid to abrupt halts. The fence began to grow. It gained height until he could see nothing but green bush and sky. Terrified he began to pull on the reins, but he couldn't stop. He opened his mouth to scream, but no sound came. There was only silence as everything slowed down and despite all his attempts to prevent it the horse took off. This time the scream came.

He sat bolt upright in bed, sweat pouring down his back. Someone was knocking at his door.

"Rick, Rick! Are you okay? It's me Tom?"

"Hold on." Rick scrambled out of bed and unlocked the door.

"What on Earth's the matter?" Tom was wearing a dressing gown. "It sounded like someone being murdered!"

"I had a nightmare." Sweat was soaking into Rick's boxer shorts. "Becher's Brook kept growing and growing and I couldn't stop. Shit! What a dream!"

Tom laughed. His hair was hanging over his eyes and his

chin was dark with stubble.

"It's debatable." He pulled his hair of his face. "Which one of us looks worse."

"Mm." Rick peered out of the curtains. "Jesus, it's getting light! Have you slept at all?"

"Not a lot. I did try but I just couldn't. I'm going over to the course to watch Runny canter. Why don't you get on board? Or would you rather leave it to Martin and get some more rest?"

"What rest?" Rick grinned. "I think I'll get on."

Picking up a towel he wiped his wet face.

"No point staying here having the heebie jeebies."

Even at this early hour the racecourse was full of activity. Shadowy figures moved through the mist; ghostlike horses cantering on the hallowed turf, footfalls silenced by the thick moist air. It was a scene that would be transmitted, later, into the households of millions all around the world, and was one the same as those Rick himself had watched every year since he was child. Then he had gazed in awe at giant horses and brave men, heroes to his young eyes, clad in a shroud of mystery. Now he was here; he was one of those brave men, and, walking towards him was his own giant horse. A tingle crept along his spine and grew in strength until the hairs stood upright on the back of his neck.

Tom watched him and knew what he was feeling. The atmosphere of this still, mist silenced morning was unlike anything they would experience anywhere else. This was unique. This was Aintree. This was the morning of the world's greatest horse race; The Grand National.

Runny, as if sharing the sentiment of the occasion, stood like a statue and sniffed the air that carried smells other than those he was used to. With a snort of excitement, he sensed the other horses out on the track and began to sidle around, his ears following the sound of their hoofbeats. Rick stood beside him and looked at the horse's expression.

He laid his hand, for one fleeting second, on the smooth neck and closed his eyes. Then, having said his silent prayer he lifted his leg for Martin to throw him lightly into the saddle.

The ride lifted his spirits. The broad relaxed smile had returned as he emerged out of the mist, Runny's breath like dragon smoke on the air.

"That's better." He sprang out of the saddle. "That's laid the ghosts to rest."

"Ghosts?" Tom smiled.

"Yeah." Rick's eyes twinkled. "All those famous buggers out there who've been here before."

Tom smiled. He knew exactly what Rick meant. You could almost imagine, as the sun broke through the clouds in ethereal rays, that horses from Aintree's past mingled with those of the present.

Martin, laying rugs over Runny's coat to keep him warm, shook his head. They must, he thought, have both been on the whisky.

Walking back to the car Rick took a deep breath of air and looked back one last time, imprinting the scene firmly on his memory forever. He was realising, slowly, exactly what he was riding for that afternoon. Until he had come here, until he had felt this electric atmosphere, he had not quite grasped the enormity of his situation. Today, he was chasing a very special piece of history. Shaking himself he pushed the thought firmly to one side. This was just another race, it had to be, otherwise he'd freak out and be in real trouble.

Tom watched the expressions chasing each other across Rick's face and smiled.

"Breakfast?"

"Nothing like dry toast and grapefruit to bring you down to Earth, eh?" Rick smiled back. "As long as you keep me away from Claudia."

The dining room of the hotel was full of more tense faces than Rick had ever seen. A group of Irishmen, nursing hangovers as well as nerves, were talking at each other at an alarming rate. Mike and Claudia were holding forth to their group, who had arrived the previous night. Only the few jockeys sat silent, reading the morning papers, assessing their rival's chances as well as their own. Rowley Harris was on his own. Seeing Tom, he nodded shyly, too embarrassed to ask them to join him. Mike, however, had no hesitation.

"Tom, Rick. Come and join us."

"No thank you." Rick nodded politely. "I'm on a diet remember."

Mike scowled as Tom and Rick found a quiet table of their own.

"Nerves I expect." Mike's brother was feeling ill after the nights events and was secretly relieved not to have to make small talk. "Want to discuss tactics or something."

"Sullen man." Simpered Claudia. "Very difficult."

"Not surprising." Her sister-in-law lowered her voice. "With his brother being looked after by Her Majesty."

The objects of their conversation didn't stay too long. Unable to eat his meal Tom went to join Rick, who had already gone to his room to watch a recording of previous Grand Nationals. Together they attempted to lay down a plan.

"This will be totally different to any race that you've every ridden." Tom put the film on slow motion. "Not just because of the fences; but because of the place itself. There are parts of this course which can feel miles from anywhere; this stretch before the Canal Turn is one of them. If you're going well, it could be the most relaxing ride of your life; if you're struggling, it's Torquemada. There's no point making tactical plans: stay out of trouble, ride every fence as it comes, avoid the inside at Becher's, and don't go like a bat out of hell, it's a long way around.

Treat the first circuit like a day's hunting, and if you're still there next time round then you're in a race. The most important thing is to enjoy it. You're going to do something today that I can only ever dream about."

Rick had grown more and more pale as Tom's speech had gone on.

"You expect me to enjoy it! I'd rather have all my teeth out with no anaesthetic!"

"Don't be silly." Tom grinned. "Think of all that champagne waiting in the weighing room. That'll get you home if you have to carry him."

The carnival atmosphere was in full swing by the time Kitty led Runny, immaculately turned out, towards the saddling boxes. the crowds stood ten deep on the opposing lawn, all trying to get a glimpse of their pick being saddled. The customary long build up to the proceedings gave everyone a good chance to look at the horses, and there were as many people around the boxes themselves as there were on the lawn. Kitty, growing tired of saying 'Excuse me' and 'Mind your back!' steered Runny through the crowds to the stall where Tom was waiting with Martin.

"How's Rick?" Kitty held the horse straight for Martin to pull back the rugs.

"Believe it or not he's lying down half asleep! The only problem is he's taking up a little too much room. Thirty-six jockeys all trying to change, without all the rest, and valets and stewards; it's a bit chaotic in there." Tom shook his head. "Poppy's gone to join the other anxious wives and girlfriends to wish him luck."

Runny was beginning to shake, staring at the crowds with huge eyes.

"This is where it tells." Tom straightened the number cloth Martin had laid on the horses back. "How well they cope with the preliminaries; how well their nerves stand up."

"Afternoon." The Peterson's had arrived. "How's he doing?"

"Better than me." Tom frowned as a small man with a clipboard looked into the box.

"Any chance of a word Tom?"

"Not off me." Tom nodded at Mike. "This is the horse's owner. I'm sure he'll have a few words for you."

Mike loved only one thing more than being interviewed, and that was being interviewed in the winner's enclosure. With Claudia gushing at his side, he gave Shane a marvellous spiel of his hopes and opinions.

"Finished?" Tom's head popped out of the box. "Good. Then if you'll excuse me, I have to get this horse into the parade ring."

Runny gave a little kick as he left the box. Kitty patted his neck, talking gibberish, trying to keep him calm. Hearing her Tom smiled. In twenty minutes, time he'd be needing some of that himself.

CHAPTER TWENTY-NINE

It was amazing that no one got kicked. Thirty-six horses, their handlers, owners, and trainers left not a lot of space in the parade ring. Add thirty-six jockeys and it became chaotic. There was precious little turf showing beneath the feet as Kitty checked Runny for the umpteenth time to avoid crashing with the horse in front. She had never seen so many people. Her stomach churned faster and faster as she avoided colliding once more with a pair of hind legs.

The jockeys, moving slowly through the crowd to find the right connections, were tense and grim faced. The traditional line up for a photograph had been completed after they had weaved their way through a ranked guard of well-wishers. A few Aintree old hands managed to smile at the crowd but not Ricky, eyes downcast, he grimaced at Tom and waited to be legged up.

"Okay?" Tom looked up as him as he settled in the saddle.

"Sure." Rick grinned. "Just go call my Mom and tell her to put up my life insurance!"

Poppy scampered up to join Martin.

"What I hate most of all." He was biting his nails. "Are these bloody parades."

Together they walked behind the horse on the long walkway out onto the course. Tom headed for the start, wanting to check the horses girths himself, not wanting to take any chances. The horses split into two groups circling around increasingly agitated officials who tried to get them into order. The vast crowd were packing the stands and any other vantage point that would afford them a good view of the course. Rick looked around the expanse of green and shook his head in disbelief; everywhere his eyes went the course was flanked by a sea of spectators, even far out in the country he could see a blur of colour along the rails. He had never, ever, seen anything like this. He could hear cries of ' Good Luck' coming from the rails, but he ignored them, pulling down his goggles to avoid the peering eye of the camera lens, a straight backed, grim faced figure on his calm, dignified bay horse.

They filed along the rails in front of the heaving stands, the horses jogging as they sensed the hour of their greatest test approaching. Kitty, completely overwhelmed by the glamour of the great event, walked at one side of Runny's head, looking about her in awe, nerves temporarily forgotten. Martin, at the other side of the horse, stared at the grass as it passed beneath his feet, not wanting to touch the horse in case his fear travelled through the reins and into the horses own mind.

One by one the horses turned, were set free, and cantered back past the cheering crowds to look at the first fence.

"Well." Martin looked up at Rick briefly. "This is it. Good Luck."

Rick didn't answer. Without looking anywhere bar straight ahead, he gathered his reins and sent Runny into a canter.

"Any misquotes today Marty?" Kitty took Martin's hand. "Minutes of fame and everything?"

"None." Martin's hand, despite the glorious sunshine that shone on the emerald turf, was stone cold. "Not a word."

The runners milled around at the start. Rick felt the sun on his back and still shivered. Brian Hales pulled his amount alongside.

"Cheer up." He looked perfectly relaxed. "You'll enjoy it."

"Will I?" Rick shook his head. "I'm not so sure."

"You will." Brian was pulling his goggles down. "Here we go, they're calling us in."

The crowd was beginning to rumble with expectancy; excitement erupting like a volcano as the horses walked into the tape. Rick's vision was beginning to blur, his pumping heart had migrated into his throat and was threatening to choke him. Pull yourself together man, he told himself, don't blow it.

A cavalry charge held nothing in comparison to thirty-six horses screaming at top speed towards the first flight. There was none of the controlled, tactical pacesetting of other races; this was blood and thunder and not for the faint hearted. A mass of moving horseflesh they spread right across the track as they reached the first. Rick was somewhere in the middle; all he could see and hear was galloping horse. The jockeys were all shouting at each other, jostling for position. The jump loomed ahead; this is it thought Rick, struck by panic, I'm going to die. The wave of horseflesh broke as one over the top of the fence, crashed down, and continued its way.

Rick's senses began to clear. The soaring leap had brought his confidence rushing back; he could hear Tom's words in his head, 'stay out of trouble', and realised that he was in the worst possible position to do that. Stuck in the middle of the pack it was all too easy to get bumped or brought down. Switching to the outside, Tom's warning about Becher's ringing in his head, he found himself more room. It was less chaotic here, and he found himself starting to ride at the fences. At every jump there was the sickening thud of a horse falling mixed with cries of encouragement as jockeys urged their mounts on. There was a lot of other chatter going on as well, and away to his left someone was telling a joke. Rick, half listening himself missed the punchline, but still found himself smiling as the horses galloped alongside a hedge growing on the inside of the course. A hedge that announced the arrival of the most illustrious steeplechase fence in the world. The joke telling stopped, and Rick's heart began to beat faster as the green bush loomed closer. Runny's ears flicked, and Rick felt the surge of power as the horse rose into the air. He seemed to spend a long time suspended in mid-flight, the ground far below him; then he felt Runny stretch, reaching for his landing, there was a slight lurch as the horse regained his balance, then the relentless galloping stride was back in action.

Martin took his hands from his eyes.

"Is he over? Is he alright?"

"Perfect." Poppy was holding his arm. "It was perfect."

As they raced into the canal turn Rick, seeing the acute angle, realised that he had left himself too wide. it was too late to change course without cutting up someone else so instead of swinging left across the fence he had to take it straight on and lost a lot of ground.

"He cocked that up." Mike was straining through his glasses.

"He's still on his feet." Rowley was worried sick; vowing that he would never put himself or his horse through this again. "Be grateful!"

A bunch of horses had broken away from the rest of the pack, travelling quickly on the good ground. As they ran along the embankment, towards the eventual home turn and The Chair, Rick began to enjoy himself. He was not a jockey today; he was a passenger, on the best racing machine in the country. Runny loved the Aintree fences, and took everyone with mechanical precision, never faltering in his enormous stride.

The yawning chasm of The Chair beckoned; waiting like a lurking monster to ensnare a careless hindleg. It was a formidable sight. Rick gritted his teeth and rode into it, pushing the horse into his take off. Runny must have sprouted wings to soar as high as he did, and the sight brought a roar of approval from his supporters in the crowd. The water came quickly after and for a moment Rick's mind flashed back to Raver. Don't be such an idiot, he told himself, don't think back, kick on. The water flashed brightly underneath horse's hooves and with ears pricked he made a magnificent sight as he swung left-handed back out onto the course. The Melling Road flashed darkly across the track, and they had completed one circuit.

Now they were in a horse race.

WINNERS

Suddenly the fences came thick and fast, the carnival atmosphere being replaced by the more normal tactical aggression as jockeys rode for position and began to calculate their chances of finishing the gruelling race. The field thinned out as, fence after fence, horses fell or were pulled up, too tired to continue. Rick never did know whether it was his physical speed that increased or just the pace of his adrenalin charged brain, but suddenly he was riding back into Becher's Brook. Again, he stayed on the outside, again he felt the lurch as the horse landed; and this time thanked God that he wasn't one of the three alongside him who knuckled over and landed in a tangled heap.

There were less horses around him now and he had a perfect view of each fence. He rode the Canal Turn perfectly, swinging across it, losing no ground and with a rush of excitement realised that he was still very much alive in this horse race. Runny was going as well as ever, taking the fences on a long powerful stride, ears pricked with enthusiasm.

They were three fences from home and all around him horses were blowing and struggling as the extra distance of the race took its toll. Scenarios ran through Rick's head of the races he had been watching; of horses fading at the elbow and being overhauled on the long run in. He had to keep his head and not get left in front too soon. His own sudden burst of confidence made him grin and he eased his mount back as they approached the third last. Not yet Runny boy, he murmured, not yet you hold on. Beside him he felt rather than saw a horse range alongside him. Glancing to his right he saw a broad white face on a chestnut head. Side by side the bay and the chestnut came to the second last and rose into the air as one. In front of them the grey that had been leading since Becher's Brook began to falter and they gained on and then passed him.

At the last and again they rose together, the crowd roaring them on. Runny's ears began to flick out sideways, lopping to and fro with every nod of his head, beneath him Ricky began to feel the mighty stride falter, shortening, flanks heaving as he tried to draw more air into his lungs. Rick looked across at the chestnut and saw the same warning signs coming from him; both horses were at the end of their stamina, it would be a matter of who broke first.

"Come on!" He screamed, swiping his whip at the horse's flank "Come on Runny you can do this!"

Head down, reins swinging loose, he threw everything into the punching motion of his hands as he urged the horse forward, kicking, whip swinging, his whole body involved in the desperate drive for the line.

Runny felt his urgings and dug deep into his gallant soul. Onlookers swore afterwards that he looked the chestnut horse in the eye, demoralizing him, before he stretched his neck out to gain the lead.

Ears flat, breath coming in great snorts, tongue lolling from the side of his mouth Runny gathered his tired body for one last supreme effort. His muscles stretched, contracted, and stretched again and with one final stride he galloped off the green turf of Aintree and into the pages of history.

The roar that came rushing into Rick's ears was unlike anything he had ever experienced; it deafened him and brought his horse to a sudden, staggering stop as its tired brain picked up the sound. Rick didn't whoop, or punch the air with delight, he collapsed onto the horse's neck with tears flowing, running down the bay neck to mix with the horses sweat. Runny wobbled slightly beneath him as he tried to regain his breath and get oxygen into his aching muscles. The vets were beside them long before anyone else. Plying the horse with water, catching his reins, and keeping him moving; through his blurred vision Rick saw a blonde head appear through the crowd and reached down to grab her. She too was awash with tears.

"You did it" She sobbed "You did it!"

Rick shook his head and threw his arm around Runny's

neck.

"He did it" He gasped. "Him. This is the greatest horse there has ever been."

"Rick, Rick" Shane was bobbing up and down beside him, cameraman in tow, desperate to get a reaction for the TV viewers. "Rick well done, what a ride; what a race; what a horse!"

Rick looked down at him and opened his mouth to speak. But he couldn't, his emotions were too great. All over the country television viewers reached for their tissues as they watched the jockey sob unashamedly to the camera. Finally, the words came.

"It's been such a privilege to ride this horse. This has nothing to do with me it's all him and the team at home." He reached forward and hugged Kitty again. "They live for this horse you know that?"

"I am sure they do," Shane's delight was obvious, and he kept patting Runny on the neck as he walked alongside him. "He's just made history. The first horse in seventy-six years to do this! Unbelievable!"

The walk back to the winner's enclosure was a difficult one, so many people so many hands reaching out to pat the horse, the jockey, the groom. Then a figure in a suit, fighting his way through the crowds, hands held high, mouth wide open in a whoop of delight. Martin almost pulled Rick from the saddle as he grabbed him. Then someone else, someone with a wild mass of dark curls who threw herself into his arms and as he bent to kiss her broke the hearts of his female fans everywhere.

But in all this there was only one person who mattered; one person who his eyes needed to find. He was stood at the back of the winner's circle talking quietly to a group of journalists. He looked up, saw the steaming horse approaching and broke away. His eyes met Rick's and slowly a smile spread across his face. As the horse halted beside him, he looked up at the big bay head, at the tired eyes, the flaring nostrils and, in a gesture that made the front pages of newspapers all over the world, closed his eyes and laid his face on the horse's nose.

Rick slipped from the saddle and grabbed Tom in a huge embrace.

"I can't believe it" He gasped. "We bloody did it!"

"We did." Tom's eyes were sparkling with his own tears.

The crowd who were chanting and shouting burst into a chorus of "For he's a jolly good fella".

Shane, who had got lost behind the masses of fans trying to fight their way into the winner's enclosure finally made his way to Tom as Rick was ushered off to weigh in.

"Tom" He gasped. "What a day. What a ride. What a horse!"

"Yes," Tom smiled "What a horse. There will be another long wait before there is another one like him."

Rowley Harris, having been smothering the horse, Kitty and even Martin with kisses came to join them.

"I have such a team at home," Tom was saying. "They have worked so hard day and night; Martin has even been sleeping in the stable with the horse to make sure nothing went wrong."

Tom kept the details of the attack on Runny to himself, that was a matter for the courts not the media. He had no doubt it would emerge at some point but now was not the time.

"They have done such a fantastic job" Rowley piped up. "He looked magnificent before the race and has done all season. Tom will never praise himself but of course he has had a massive part to play in this he is a top rate trainer."

"Thank you" Tom grinned. "No rebates!"

"So, Rowley." Shane put his microphone to the little man. "What's next for the nation's favourite horse?"

"Nothing." Rowley said simply. "That's it. He's retired. We

can't ask anymore of him after today!"

Tom raised his eyebrows, that was news to him, and he wasn't sure that Mike Peterson would agree.

"How do you feel about that Tom?" Shane had caught the look of surprise.

"It will be a relief." Tom shook his head ruefully. "Handling a national treasure has its perks, but also its drawbacks."

"And you?" Shane smiled. "What's next for you?"

"Me?" Tom's eyes were on a small blonde figure leading the bay horse away. "I'm getting married."

The racecourse was empty. Silence was slowly taking the place of all the revelry. Camera crews were packing up and leaving, and tired grooms were loading horses onto boxes to start the journey home. Martin, weaving his way back to the stables from the bar found himself alongside the statue of Red Rum. He stared up at it and smiled.

"Thank you." He touched the cold bronze. "You were looking out for him today. This is all because of you, you know that? The reason I am here, why I do what I do? Because of you. I watched you and thought I want to be part of that. I want to feel that thrill, I want to sit on the greatest horse alive. I want to wake every morning and feel that I am involved in something that big that it will last forever. So, thank you for that too."

Smiling to himself Martin turned away and continued his way to the stables. What a life to live, and he was part of it, and he loved every second.

Tomorrow everything would carry on as if today had never happened. But days like this were the reason they all rose every morning; the reason they endured the long cold days of winter; the disappointments, the heartache; and as one dream ends another must start. It was the challenge, the goal that kept them all going.

After all, wasn't that what this life was all about?

Winners.

Epilogue.

Kitty Chichester laid her baby boy into his pram, shaded from the sun by the large oak tree and murmured to him softly as he wriggled himself back to sleep. The sound of car tyres on the gravel drive made her frown. Who could it be on a Sunday afternoon? It was mid-summer and the horses were all out on their break. Tom had long since stopped visitors arriving on a Sunday to visit the yard and Olympic Run. The arrival of baby Charles had impressed on him the need of peace and quiet and time for the family. They still flocked to see the bay horse, they would for years to come, he even had his own social media page. But the page told his fans quite firmly that Sunday was family day at Highford, and the yard was closed to all but staff.

This then had to be someone that they knew. Kitty screwed her eyes up against the sun and looked at the car that pulled up in front of the house. A smile spread across her face, and she began waving frantically. Poppy had already seen her and was racing across the lawn.

"Kit". She enveloped her friend in a giant bear hug. "Oh God it's good to see you. Where is he? Where's my favourite Godson?"

"Only Godson." Kitty smiled. "Here, but don't wake him he's only just gone down. He'll be about soon enough. It's nearly tea-time."

"Oh, he's perfect." Poppy cooed. "He's grown so much!"

"He has." Kitty stopped mid-sentence at the figure standing in front of her. Gone was Rick Cowdrey's tangled blonde mane. Instead, it was cropped short and slicked back from the always tanned forehead. "Rick! What happened?!

"It was me," Poppy laughed. "I'm Delilah!"

"It takes some getting used to." The grin was still the same." But I have to say my skull caps don't smell as they did!".

"Glad to hear it." Tom had wandered up behind them and was enjoying watching the easy friendship that they all still had. "I can't afford a higher retainer to replace smelly hats."

Rick turned and embraced the man who had become one of his closest friends.

"The hair!" Tom smiled. "About time if you ask me."

Rick laughed and noticed the grey appearing at Tom's temples and through his hair. It was easy to forget that they were all getting older. He had been Champion Jockey now for five seasons. He had totted up an impressive tally of wins each year, but nothing had come close to that adrenalin soaring high of Runny's double. Streak had won them another Champion Chase but afterwards her temperament had got the better of her as she became more and more difficult to handle. Rick's dad had always dreamed of breeding a winning horse, so she was currently in Ireland visiting one of the top National Hunt Stallions.

"Where is he?"

"In the stable." Tom smiled. "He's due to go out soon."

"I'll do it." Kitty turned from her baby "If you can watch Charles."

"No." Rick smiled. "Let me. Please."

The big bay horse was standing in the shadows at the back of the same stable he had occupied since he arrived. Every day he came in to lie on his deep straw bed and stay away from the flies. He loved his time of rest in the shade. His deep eyes looked at Rick as he came through the door and an ear cocked forward.

"Hey boy." Rick slipped an arm around the smooth neck. "Remember me?"

Runny lowered his nose and nuzzled in Rick's pockets looking for the ever-present treat.

"I'll take that as a yes." Rick laughed.

Slipping the head collar onto the bay head he took the horse to the field gate where Tom was waiting. Runny sprang off to join the others, a little stiff in his hindlegs now; the toll of so many hard- fought races beginning to tell.

Both men were silent as they watched the animal that had given them their finest hour.

"He is some horse." Rick was the first to speak. "What

could he have done I wonder if he hadn't been retired?"

"We will never know." Tom shrugged. "But my old man always used to say go out at the top boy. No one remembers a loser; but they all remember a winner."

"True." Rick smiled. "So, what's new?"

"Well Mike and Rowley have got themselves another horse. He arrives from France tomorrow. Don't ask me his name, I can't say it, and of course Margie hasn't given up on her dreams. Her new horse is in the top field. Want to see him?"

"Later." Rick smiled. "Right now, as I'm on my holidays I want a piece of your mother's cake. What's he called?"

"The Kingmaker." Tom smiled. "It remains to be seen whether he will be prince or pauper."

They walked back to the house and from against the hedge a chestnut horse watched them go, unaware that he was the subject of their hopes for the future. For now, he was just a horse; dozing in the sun until the shadows moved across the Cotswolds, and they became dark.

THE END.

ABOUT THE AUTHOR

A J Morris

Alison Morris lives in the South Wales Valleys with two rescue dogs, a retired steeplechaser and a retired polo pony. She has one grown up son who is an Actor and Playwright.

Involved in the Welsh Point to Point scene as Public Relations Officer she is a lifelong fan of National Hunt racing and equine sport in general.

She is also a keen traveller and rates Florence as her favourite place closely followed by Cheltenham Racecourse.

Facebook-authorbynature   https://www.facebook.com/

Twitter -https://twitter.com/ajmorrisauthor

Winners

Declan Hyde is the star of the Matros F1 racing team. Talented, temperamental and with all the attitudes of a spoilt child his flamboyance attracts attention both on and off the track. He, along with the teams owner Gerald Matthews, have worked to make the team what it is today; but nothing can stay the same forever. The arrival of a new, younger team mate puts pressure on Declan and causes rifts in the once harmonious Matros compound. This, added with the arrival of a fanatical and obsessive young female fan into the teams workplace pushes Declan to the edge and causes him to drive too dangerously on the track causing a massive accident which nearly ends the life of his closest friend and rival.Through the course of a year in Formula One, First follows Declan and his team mates, his lovers and his rivals. First is the story of Declan's struggle to cope with rivalry, death and love. It follows his fall to his lowest ebb and his struggle to regain respect, trust and confidence in one of the world's most dangerous sports. First is a tale of ambition, desire and obsession set in the high energy world of Formula One.

Travels With A Rescue Dog

One woman One Dog. One Holiday. What can possibly go wrong?
Travels with a Rescue Dog is the true story of my holiday with my rescue dog. It is a non profit book being sold to raise money for The Dogs Trust

Printed in Great Britain
by Amazon